JOHN
WOMAN

Center Point
Large Print

Books are
produced in the
United States
using U.S.-based
materials

Books are printed
using a revolutionary
new process called
THINKtech™ that
lowers energy usage
by 70% and increases
overall quality

Books are
durable and
flexible
because of
Smyth-sewing

Paper is
sourced using
environmentally
responsible
foresting methods
and the
paper is acid-free

Also by Walter Mosley and available from
Center Point Large Print:

Little Green
Rose Gold
And Sometimes I Wonder About You
Charcoal Joe

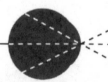

**This Large Print Book carries the
Seal of Approval of N.A.V.H.**

JOHN WOMAN

WALTER MOSLEY

CENTER POINT LARGE PRINT
THORNDIKE, MAINE

This Center Point Large Print edition
is published in the year 2018 by arrangement with
Grove Atlantic Inc.

Copyright © 2018 by Thing Itself, Inc.

All rights reserved.

The text of this Large Print edition is unabridged.
In other aspects, this book may vary
from the original edition.
Printed in the United States of America
on permanent paper.
Set in 16-point Times New Roman type.

ISBN: 978-1-68324-973-3

Library of Congress Cataloging-in-Publication Data

Names: Mosley, Walter, author.
Title: John Woman / Walter Mosley.
Description: Center Point Large Print edition. | Thorndike, Maine :
    Center Point Large Print, 2018.
Identifiers: LCCN 2018035799 | ISBN 9781683249733
    (hardcover : alk. paper)
Subjects: LCSH: Large type books.
Classification: LCC PS3563.O88456 J64 2018b | DDC 813/.54—dc23
LC record available at https://lccn.loc.gov/2018035799

JOHN
WOMAN

Who will believe my verse in time to come,
If it were fill'd with your most high deserts?
Though yet Heaven knows it is but as a tomb
Which hides your life and shows not half your
    parts.
If I could write the beauty of your eyes,
And in fresh numbers number all your graces,
The age to come would say, "This poet lies,
Such heavenly touches ne'er touch'd earthly
    faces."
So should my papers yellow'd with their age,
Be scorn'd like old men of less truth than tongue,
And your true rights be term'd a poet's rage
And stretched metre of an antique song:
But were some child of yours alive that time,
You should live twice—in it and in my rhyme.

William Shakespeare, Sonnet XVII

before the beginning

1

Lucia Napoli's family name had been Tartarelli before her great-grandfather migrated from Naples to the Lower East Side. No one was certain how the name got changed. Lucia's Aunt Maria said it was a drunken Irish customs officer on Ellis Island who mistook their origins for their name. Lucia's great-uncle Christopher said his father, Alesio, introduced himself as Alesio from Napoli so often that the name stuck.

Lucia didn't care where Napoli came from. It sounded better than Tartarelli. There were pastries and breasts and something flip in the sound. She liked the way it brought her lips together. "Like a kiss," she once told her girlfriends after her part-time shift as a filing clerk at Household Insurance Company. The neighborhood girls would go to smoke cigarettes and drink bitter Chinotto sodas at *Uno*, a little coffee shop on the Lower East Side patronized mostly by young students from NYU and old Italians from the mob.

She met Jimmy at *Uno* on a Thursday after-noon, "when it was raining so hard it was like God taking a piss on your head. All Jimmy had on was a T-shirt and some jeans and you could see everything, and I mean everything, that

11

boy had," she said to her twelve-year-old son Cornelius, when he told her that he liked Ginny Winters, the smartest girl in his class.

"You know the first time I seen Jimmy I knew he was the man for me." She lifted a teacup from the coffee table and used a silver spoon to dump sugar in. One, two, three heaping scoops, then stirring . . . "His wet hair was hangin' down on his forehead and he looked at me like I was the only thing in the whole place. You know you can't argue with a feeling like that."

"So what did you do, mama?" Cornelius asked pushing his fingertips against his skinny thighs.

They were sitting at the little table Lucia had set up in the bay window of the living room, looking down on Mott Street just below Grand.

"Do?" she asked. "I didn't do nuthin', CC, just sat there lookin' at him and he was takin' me in too. I waited where I was sittin' with my girlfriends until he walked up to our table and asked me to go take a walk with him."

"In the rain?" Cornelius asked, as he had many times before.

"Yeah," Lucia said, wistfully remembering the wet Jimmy Grimaldi at *Uno*. "I told him that I didn't want to get wet and he said that he'd try his best to keep me dry, but that he couldn't make no promises. My girlfriends told me not to go but I did anyway. He took me down this little

12

passageway at the side of the café and brought me into the alley back there . . ."

"Then what did you do?" Lucia's son asked. He was going to stay at her small apartment for the rest of the week, sleeping on the couch, because his father, Herman Jones, was in for a procedure at Marymount Hospital.

"The same thing you been doin' with that little smart girl in your class. The same thing that all little boys and girls do when they can get away from spying eyes."

Cornelius hadn't done anything with Ginny Winters but he knew not to say so to his mother. She didn't like it when he told her she was wrong. And if she got upset she'd stop telling him about Jimmy Grimaldi and how she came to meet his father.

Cornelius wanted to know what happened and only his mother would be willing to tell him. His father was a good parent but he didn't talk about what men and women did together. Even if Cornelius could get him to talk about sex it would be very technical, like one of the ten thousand books Herman Jones was always reading.

"Did you kiss him, mama?"

"Oh yes I did. Your father has some very nice qualities but I have never met a man who could kiss like Jimmy Grimaldi."

"How come?" Cornelius asked.

"He kissed me like he meant it," Lucia Napoli-Jones said.

13

She was wearing a short black dress and black hose, sitting at the edge of her chair and gazing out the window. Cornelius thought that she was the most beautiful woman in the world. He felt bad that his parents didn't live together. His mother was still young and alive while his father had gotten too old to keep up with her. But, CC thought, maybe his mother could stay with them and still have her girlfriends' night out.

"I love your father, CC," Lucia would tell her gangly brown son, "but I need to be on my own, to come and go when I want to. Herman only wants to stay around the movie house and read his old books."

"I love you, mama," Cornelius would tell her when she complained about his father.

"I love you too, baby," was her standard reply. "And I always will."

"So after that day in the rain was Jimmy Grimaldi your boyfriend?" CC asked.

"Oh yeah," Lucia said with feeling. "You couldn't'a pried me off'a that boy with a yard-long crowbar."

CC felt his heart catch at the passion in his mother's voice.

"I used to climb out my window at night to be with him. There was this apartment building over on Elizabeth Street that had a empty apartment around that time. Jimmy broke off the padlock the landlord had on it and put in his own. Wasn't no electricity but Jimmy had candles and a mattress. Me and him'd drink wine and then he'd curl my toes for hours."

"How did he do that, mama?" CC asked, feeling an empty place in the pit of his stomach.

Lucia stared out of the window remembering things her thug boyfriend used to make her do. Her nostrils flared and a flush came to her face.

"It was how he kissed me, baby," she said.

She sat back in the padded wicker chair, brought her right hand to her throat and sighed.

"That was the best three weeks of my whole life," she said. "Jimmy Grimaldi was something else."

CC leaned over and pressed his fingertips against his hard leather shoes. He wanted his toes to curl and his mother to kiss his cheek.

"How come you broke up, mama?"

"What's that, honey?" Lucia asked.

"How come you didn't stay his girlfriend if he was so nice?"

"It just wasn't meant to be, honey. I mean at the end there he was walkin' me across the floor like I was a lawn mower. He had me eatin' dirt and likin' it." She sighed and looked out of the window again. "But he was just a wannabe TV gangster. Him and his crew would get into fights when we weren't in his secret crib. And then he messed with Timothy Michaels."

"Was he your boyfriend from before Jimmy?"

CC asked, trying to piece together the names his mother had related over the years.

CC mostly lived with his father—who called him Cornelius. The times he got to stay with his mother were magical because they ate out almost every night and she told him about things that made his body tingle.

"No, my old boyfriend was Albert. When I told Jimmy I couldn't go with him because I already had a boyfriend he said that he'd go talk to Albert."

"What did he tell him?"

"I don't know but the next day Albert said that he thought we should see other people."

"Then who was Timothy Michael?"

"Michaels," she corrected. "Timothy was my best friend. He was funny you know."

"Uh-huh. He told jokes like Uncle Christopher."

"No. Funny like he didn't like girls."

"Oh."

"Anyway one day Jimmy told Timothy that he didn't want him to hang out with me and Timothy told him to go fuck himself—excuse my French—then Jimmy and his crew kicked the shit outta Timmy."

Cornelius tried hard to keep up with what his mother was saying. He put the words and ideas into an order in his head. Fuck was originally a French word and Timmy rhymed with Jimmy. Timmy was kicked so hard that he soiled himself, as Herman Jones would have described it. And all this happened because Timmy didn't like girls, which was also funny.

". . . and when I found out about it," Lucia continued, "I told that asshole that he could find some other girl who didn't mind him beatin' up her friends."

"Did he get mad?" CC asked, already knowing the answer from another time.

"Sore as strep," she said. "He kept callin' me and comin' to my window at night. At first he said he was sorry. I made up my mind that he had to say it seven times before I'd even consider goin' back with him. But he only apologized four times before he started gettin' mean."

"Did he hit you?" CC asked, feeling fear for his young mother in the streets of Little Italy.

"No but he said he was gonna. That's why when I was down in the Village and he yelled out my name I ran into the Arbuckle Cinema House over on Second."

"And that's where you met dad," CC said triumphantly.

He sat up in his chair and Lucia leaned over to kiss him.

Whenever she kissed him CC reached out to touch her arm or her knee or some other part of her. And whenever he did that she smiled.

"Not too many people went to the Arbuckle Cinema back then," Lucia said. "I run in the front and up the stairs to the projectionist's door. Your father was sittin' in there with the projector goin', readin' a book under a flashlight that he had wired to the wall.

"I said, 'Help me. A man is chasin' after me.' Herman stood right up, pulled out a bookcase that stood against the wall, and it was a secret door just like in one'a those old movies.'"

CC knew this part of the story word for word but he didn't interrupt. He loved to hear how his mild father became a hero that day, the day he was showing *Grandma's Boy* starring Harold Lloyd and reading *The Third Policeman* by Flan O'Brien.

"A beautiful white girl wearing a floral dress with bare shoulders came running into my projection room," CC's father had said. "She told me that a man was chasing her so I opened my secret doorway and told her to get in."

". . . and then," Lucia said, continuing the narrative going on in CC's mind, "just when the door hit me in the butt I heard Jimmy yellin', 'Where is she, man?'

"'I dunno,' your father says," Lucia remembered, but CC knew that his father would never say *dunno*. Herman Jones spoke only in proper sentences and words. He never used needless contractions and always corrected his son when he misspoke, as Herman called it when *people misused apostrophes, real or imagined, to jam words together.*

"And when Jimmy said that he knew that I was there," Lucia continued. "Your father told him to 'Look around for yourself,' and Jimmy didn't know what to say 'cause the projectionist room was hardly bigger than a janitor's closet.

"Jimmy still threatened Herman but he didn't do nuthin' and finally he left." CC had asked his father what he would have done if Lucia's boyfriend found her in the secret closet, or if he just started beating on him.

"I would have protected her," Mr. Jones said in his proper, acquired accent—a gentle lilt that came from no known country or clime.

"But mama said that Jimmy had big muscles," CC argued.

"Big muscles are not everything, Cornelius. Sometimes," Herman said touching his head, "it takes mind," then touching his chest, "and heart."

This tableau of his proper black father John Woman would hold as one of his fondest memories.

"After that I begged Herman to let me stay with him," Lucia went on. "I was afraid that Jimmy would be runnin' around the neighborhood with his crew lookin' for me. And Herman said that I could wait with him and at the end of the night he'd take me back to my parents' house. I told him that maybe he could just take me over to Penn Station because I wanted to get out of town and go see your Uncle Christopher down in Philly."

"Because grandma and grandpa wouldn'ta liked dad 'cause he was black?" CC asked, knowing that this was indeed the case.

Lucia was looking out the window again. "Herman showed that film four times and read his book and drank tea. He was so shy that he couldn't even look at me, much less talk. But I knew that your father liked me and so I made him marry me."

This was the moment that CC had been waiting for. He wanted to know about Jimmy Grimaldi and kissing but more than that he wanted to hear what his mother did to make Herman marry her. Lucia Napoli was not the kind of woman that CC saw his father marrying. He imagined Herman Jones marrying a plain-looking librarian with thick glasses and sensible shoes. They would sit up late into the night talking about books and politics, newspapers and maybe the difference between humans and other creatures, like mosquitoes and palm trees. The woman his father married would speak proper English and know everything about boring silent films.

Lucia Napoli was a woman of red blood and chocolate cake; she went to live concerts and wore clothes that flashed glimpses of the full length of her legs. CC's mom laughed out loud, left dirty dishes in the sink and sometimes forgot to close the door when she went to the bathroom.

CC didn't know how such a man and woman

could come together, only why they had to fall apart.

"How did you make him marry you?" little, brown Cornelius Jones asked.

Lucia grinned, her dark eyes sparkling with a devious light. The dark mole on her olive throat seemed to bulge. Her right shoulder rose as if one of her boyfriends was rubbing her neck.

"I kissed him," she hissed.

"Like this?" CC raised a dirty knuckle to his lips.

"Welllll . . . yeah, but not really. I kissed the back of his neck when he was readin' that boring book."

"Did that tickle him?"

"He didn't laugh."

"What did he do?"

"Nuthin'," Lucia said, curling her upper lip.

"Nothing?"

"Nuthin'. He froze like a little deer come across the big bad wolf. I pushed the book down in his lap and when he tried to lift it up I kissed his neck again and he dropped it. I told him to lie down on the floor so I could massage his back and he did it. But all I did was kiss his neck again and again."

CC could feel his heart beating. Ginny Winters with her big freckles and ginger bangs came into his mind. He wanted to go to the bathroom but he couldn't get his legs to stand up.

"Did he like that?" CC asked.

"When I moved away he put his hand back and pushed my head against his neck. The film ran out and he had to jump up to switch projectors because people were yellin' down in the theater."

"And then you stopped kissin' him?" CC asked, oddly relieved.

"No, baby. I kissed his neck the whole time he was changin' reels. I kissed it all down the sides."

"And daddy didn't push you away?"

"He couldn't."

"Why not?"

"Because nobody had ever kissed his neck like that and, even though he didn't know it, that was what he always wanted."

"How did you know?"

"I know things about men, honey. I know what they want when I see 'em. I knew what Jimmy Grimaldi was after. I knew what your father wanted and I wanted him."

"Daddy said that after he saved you that you started dating for a long time and then you got engaged."

"Your father took me home when we left the movie house. We went to his bed and made you that night."

Cornelius felt like he was floating above his chair. His mother had told him the truth of his beginnings in the world.

"But why did you want to make me and marry daddy, mama?"

"Because no man had ever saved me before," she said. "No man had ever been so sweet to freeze when I kissed him and so brave to stand up to a bully like Jimmy Grimaldi for a woman he had never met."

"But then why did you have to leave us, mama?" CC asked. He knew he shouldn't have. He tried to keep the words down but failed.

Lucia's warmth drained away in the sunlit front room looking down on Mott. Her smile dried up. Those dark Mediterranean eyes became like twin eclipses, far away and cold.

"I told your father that you would go and see him in the hospital," she said.

"You said we would both go."

"I can't. I have things to do."

Things to do. These words broke Cornelius's heart.

Lucia stood up and went into her bedroom. She closed the door and CC knew that she wouldn't come out again until he was gone from the house.

If only he didn't have to ask her why she'd left. If only he didn't need to know every damn thing. That's what everybody told him—even his father who had read more books than any teacher CC ever had at school.

The boy took his leather satchel from its place behind the sofa. He put the extra T-shirt and notebook in there, then left the apartment being careful not to let the door slam behind him.

2

"Cornelius," Herman Jones said. "Where is your mother?"

He was too weak to raise his head from the pillows on his hospital bed.

"She got sick," Cornelius lied. "Stomachache."

"That is too bad. Tell her I hope she gets better soon," the elder Jones said. "Mr. Cranston, this is my son."

A skeletal, yellowish man, propped up in the bed next to his father's, smiled and said, "Hello, young man. Your father says that you're a great student in school."

Cornelius had the urge to ask, *Where else would I be a student if not in school?* But he knew that his father wouldn't like him being a smart aleck so he said, "Thanks," and bowed his head to keep from looking into the wasted white man's eyes.

Cornelius went to his father's side and touched his shoulder. Herman was dark brown in color. He was thin like his son with large intelligent eyes and the mildest manners. Cornelius rarely disobeyed his father, not from fear of punishment but because he didn't want to hurt him.

Herman Jones wasn't a strong man but that day his voice was so thin his son feared he was dying.

24

"Everything is all right," Herman said, reading his son's eyes. "The doctors say I will be better than ever in a few weeks. It was an obstruction in the small intestine but they yanked it out."

Using a word like *yank* was as close as his father would ever come to cursing. Herman revered the English language.

Language is the pinnacle of human achievement, he would often tell his son. *And English is the most perfect tongue in the history of the world. Ten thousand years from now they'll still be using English the way we use Latin today.*

"So when are you coming home?" Cornelius asked.

"They tell me about a week or eight days. How is it going at your mother's house?"

"Good."

"Are you making her upset or anything like that?"

"No, dad."

"Because you know your mother is delicate. She acts like the toughest man on the block but inside she has the heart of a butterfly."

"I know," Cornelius said. He thought about his mother closing the bedroom door. He knew that if he told his father about it he'd say that was what he meant, that asking her why she couldn't live with them was insensitive.

"Did you want me to read to you, dad?" Cornelius asked.

"Yes. If Mr. Cranston does not mind."

"Not at all," the parchment-skinned white man said. "Probably help me get to sleep."

So Cornelius got *The Life of Greece* by Will Durant from his bag. When he started reading from the first chapter Herman closed his eyes and smiled. Cornelius knew that as long as his father was smiling he was still awake.

Fifteen pages later Mr. Cranston was snoring but Herman beamed.

"Dad?"

"Yes, son?"

"Are you really going to be okay?"

"As okay as any mortal man can claim. The doctors say that I should be able to have regular bowel movements now. Just a little rest is all I need. Tell France that I'll be back on the job three weeks from today."

"Okay," Cornelius said. "I better get back to Mom's. She'll be worried if I'm late for dinner."

"She will if you are," Herman Jones said, correcting both offending contractions.

Cornelius kissed his father's forehead and touched his lean black hand. Between the kiss and the touch Herman fell asleep.

Cornelius didn't go back to Mott Street; his welcome there was over. Instead he went to the Arbuckle theater where France Bickman was collecting money for tickets at the door and running back and forth changing reels on the ancient projectors.

"How's your father, CC?" France asked.

"He's gotta be in the hospital for another three weeks, Mr. Bickman."

"I can't do the projectionist's job for that long. I make too many mistakes, people come in without buying tickets. And if Mr. Lorraine finds out . . . He'd fire Herman if he missed three weeks. You know how much he hates your dad."

"I know," Cornelius said.

Lorraine had inherited the theater from his uncle, Ferro Lansman. The new owner tried to sell the building to a developer but the city made the place a New York City landmark and blocked the sale. Herman was one of the main witnesses for the landmark committee. He knew the complete history of the property. It had been a silent movie theater since April of 1911; before that it was a Jewish theater.

Chapman Lorraine wanted revenge. That's why Herman didn't tell him about the operation; he knew that the theater owner would let him go.

"I can run the projectors," Cornelius said.

"But what if Lorraine finds you?" France asked.

"He never comes in. And dad always keeps the door to the projection room locked since he met mom. I'll just stay inside and it'll be okay."

Tall and willowy France Bickman was well

past seventy. He had worked at the Arbuckle since his retirement from the records department at the New York City Board of Education. France was on duty the afternoon Lucia Napoli ran in to escape Jimmy Grimaldi. When the street thug rushed in after her France had yelled, "Hey you," but he didn't stop, and France didn't call the police because he thought they might interrupt the screening. At the end of the night France drove Herman and Lucia to Herman's apartment in Williamsburg, in Brooklyn.

Lucia had gone in with him and stayed. Herman broke up with his girlfriend of seven years, Kendra Brooks. Lucia's parents boycotted the wedding. Lucia sent them a funeral announcement after the ceremony.

Herman's parents were dead. His sister, Winona, came to the wedding and Lucia's best friend Timothy Michaels gave her away. France was Herman's best man. Lucia was pregnant and Jimmy Grimaldi had been jailed because of an anonymous tip about his involvement in a burglary at the beginning of the year. It seemed that he decided to keep one of the rings he'd lifted from the fat banker who had recently bought a condo just north of Little Italy.

That week was a festival of great Russian silent movies. The first one Cornelius showed was *Battleship Potemkin*—his father's favorite. CC sat in the small booth imagining his mother kissing Herman's neck. With the door closed and locked, under the flickering light of the ancient projector, Cornelius felt somehow safe in the presence of the sacred images of his mother's escape into the arms of his father.

After the fourth film the Arbuckle closed. France went home and Cornelius pulled out the thin mattress Herman kept behind the bookcase door. CC rolled the bed out and curled up under the same suspended flashlight his father had been reading by when Lucia ran in.

Cornelius reread *The Painted Bird*, imagining himself as that boy running in the wilderness, alone and forgotten among the crazy peoples of a lost world.

3

Four weeks later France Bickman and Cornelius helped Herman up the stairs and into bed, where he spent most of the rest of his life. The doctors didn't know why he was so weak but they advised the older Jones to consider retirement.

From then on Cornelius went to school during the day and showed films at night.

Only France knew about the labor deceit and he had no reason to tell Lorraine. Lucia came over on the second Tuesday after Herman returned to make dinner and clean up. When she was ready to leave she stuck her head into Herman's room and said that she'd be back on Friday to cook and clean again.

"Why do you want to come here now that I am sick and confined to my bed?" Herman asked her.

"Because you need my help," she responded sensibly. Her loose summer dress was awash in the colors of the rainbow. Just to look at Lucia made CC smile.

"I needed your help when my legs worked and my lungs had the capacity for laughter," he complained. "Why would I need a wife to see me suffer like this?"

"You're an ungrateful man, Herman Jones," Lucia told Cornelius's father.

"Get the hell out of my house," he replied, shocking both mother and son with his language and rage.

"Why is he so angry with me?" Lucia asked her son the next day. They were having tea at *Uno* in the break between school and when CC had to go to work.

"Because you left him when he was healthy and in love with you then came back when he's sick and sad."

"But isn't that when he needs me most?" she asked innocently. "When he's sick and bed-ridden?"

"I don't think so, mama. When you're sick who cares about how clean the house is or if somebody's in the kitchen making meatballs and pasta? Dad can't even eat your spicy sauce anymore."

Though the boy didn't know it he used language that got through to his mother. She folded in on herself, placing her head on the yellow-and-green Formica tabletop.

After that day Lucia Napoli-Jones worked full-time at Household Insurance. With the extra money she hired Violet Breen as a two day a week housekeeper for Herman and Cornelius.

The heavyset, middle-aged Irish maid and Herman hit it off almost immediately. Among other things Herman had committed to memory thousands of poems, many of them by Irish authors. He recited these to Violet whenever she brought him soup or lingered in his room dusting and tidying.

"He's a treasure, your father," she'd tell Cornelius. "And you are as good a son as any man or woman has ever known."

Cornelius liked Violet. Her short red hair looked like a feather hat and she smelled like soap.

Cornelius's life fell into a routine that he maintained through high school. Mostly it was school and working the projectors at the Arbuckle. He did his homework while the silent movies played. Late at night he'd read to his father from the works of various historians. Among others, Herman enjoyed what he called the *soft historians,* like the Durants and Collingwood, who talked about the idea of history being on a par with actual events.

"Nothing ever happens in the past," Herman was fond of saying, sitting erect among the pillows Cornelius would prop up behind him. "The past is gone and unobtainable. It is more removed from our lives than is God and yet it controls us just as He purports to do."

Cornelius also read long passages from Herodotus and Thucydides, the Christian Bible and Tacitus. He recited obscure Byzantine

32

translations and Chinese and Egyptian records. The only time father and son really talked was after a reading of some book when Herman would ask Cornelius what he thought about it.

Cornelius began to search the library for other historians to read with his father. He discovered Mabillon and John Foxe's *Book of Martyrs*. There was the Italian Muratori and then Gibbon's magnificent *History of the Decline and Fall of the Roman Empire*. There were the historian-philosophers from Vico to Herder and Hegel to Marx; Spengler and Toynbee. The slippery Wittgenstein fit Herman's passion for the lost past—not in his reporting but in his refusal to accept the easy passage of knowledge between cultures, or even individuals.

Much of what Cornelius read he did not understand but Herman would explain now and then. At other times Cornelius would wake up at night suddenly comprehending some quote that he'd read aloud months earlier.

The years passed.

One evening Herman stopped his son in the middle of *The Confessions of Saint Augustine* and said, "This is the power of the world, boy. The memory of an unattainable paradise where everything is predictable and outwardly controllable. It is all that we are: history, memory. It is what happened, or what we decide on believing has happened. It is yesterday and a million years ago. It is today but still we cannot grasp it."

"I don't know what you mean, dad," Cornelius said. He was sixteen that day but his father, for all his interest in history, did not remember the date. Since he was in his bed almost twenty-four hours a day he had no need for a calendar.

"I mean that the person who controls history controls their fate. The man who can tell you what happened, or did not happen, is lord and master of all he surveys."

"But if he claims something that isn't true then he's master of a lie," Cornelius reasoned.

Herman smiled and leaned forward. "But," he said, holding up a lecturing finger, "if everyone believes the lie then he controls a truth that we all assent to. There is no true event, Cornelius, only a series of occurrences open to interpretation."

Though Cornelius did not know it for many years, this was the moment of the birth of John Woman. Herman neither made a cake nor lit a single candle to celebrate his son's birth but he gave Cornelius a great and terrible gift that would deliver him into *a world simultaneously of my own making and unmaking,* as he wrote many years later in a secret journal addressed to the goddess Posterity.

"Are you going to call mom?" Cornelius asked. He'd been waiting for a moment when his father's mood was open and happy.

Up until that evening *no* had been his unchanging reply, but on the night of his son's forgotten birthday, he said, "As you will. Call her. Tell her that she should see the old man before he passes the mantle on to his son."

Cornelius called his mother that night. When she answered he could hear Dean Martin singing *Volare* on the record player in the background.

"Hello?"

"Mama?"

"Hi, baby. How is he?"

"He wants to see you."

"Now?" It was past midnight.

"No," Cornelius said. "Tomorrow at four."

When Lucia came into the Jones apartment she was wearing a low-cut, tight-fitting, short black dress without hose or jewelry. Recently having turned thirty-six she still had the beauty of youth. Cornelius was surprised to see the lack of rings and necklaces because Lucia's new boyfriend, a man named Filo Manetti, had given her many expensive gifts and expected her to wear them. At least that's what she told Cornelius at one of their afternoon meetings at *Uno*. Cornelius hadn't met Manetti. His mother said this was because he was so busy, but Cornelius felt that she was afraid for her boyfriend to see she had a Negro son.

There was only a hint of makeup over her eyes and a touch of blush on her lips. CC's heart went out to her. He hoped she and Herman would get together, that they would be a family again.

"How do I look, CC?" Lucia asked after kissing his cheek.

He reached out, touching her right biceps.

"You're getting so tall," she added.

Cornelius ushered his mother into his father's small bedroom.

Herman was sitting up in bed against three big pillows. He had on a white dress shirt with a collar too large for his small neck. He didn't wear pants because his legs were under a blanket.

"Welcome, Lucia. Have a seat."

Herman nodded at a chair that Cornelius had placed at the foot of the bed. But instead of sitting Lucia went to his side, kissing him twice on the cheek.

"Please sit down," he said, and her confidence drained away. She went to the chair clasping her small handbag.

"Herman—" she uttered.

"Why have you come here, Lucia?" Herman asked.

Cornelius stood by the door feeling that this question was like the first move in a game of chess.

"To see my husband," Lucia replied.

"You have seen me. Now, is there anything else?"

"I'm sorry, Herman," she began. "I know that I

36

haven't been a good wife. But things were never right between us, you know that."

Herman gave a quick nod. His lips were protruding slightly. Cornelius had not seen that particular expression before.

"Do you have a boyfriend, Lucia?"

"I didn't come here to talk about things like that."

"So you just want me to sit here and listen until you are through? I am not only your cuckold but also your minion?"

Cornelius doubted if his mother knew the proper definition of the word *minion* but he was sure that she got the meaning of Herman's words.

"No," she said.

"Then may I not inquire about my wife's fidelity?"

"We've been broken up ten years, Herman. I'm not even forty."

"And I am a Methuselah?"

"No," Lucia said, lowering her head.

Cornelius was witness to his parents' pain. He could not speak. This was their meeting, their problem to solve.

"If I were with another woman would you want to know?" Herman asked. Lucia's head hung down even farther than it had at *Uno*, when Cornelius's unintended accusation cut so deep.

"I love you, Herman."

"And who else do you love?"

37

This question hit Lucia like a slap. Herman's strategy was picking up momentum.

"How dare you ask me that," she spat.

"And why not? Here I am relegated to these four walls. The only reason I am not dead is that my son does my job for me. He pays the bills and takes me for a walk around the apartment every morning and night. He reads to me because my eyes are too weak and my hands are too feeble to hold a book. I am only fifty-one, Lucia, and I may not see my next birthday."

"His name is Filo," Lucia said, her voice devoid of feeling.

"And is he well endowed?"

"What?"

"Can he satisfy you?"

"Herman—"

"Do you do to him what you did to me on the projection room floor? Do you tell him to perform as you told me?"

On this last word Herman's voice faltered, his eyes glistened.

"What do you want from me, Herman?" Lucia asked softly.

"I have not been able to have an erection in years," he answered. "At first I lamented this loss. Then I realized that this was not diminishment but freedom."

"Freedom from what?" Lucia asked, echoing Cornelius's thought.

"From you," Herman said. "Because, you see, I never really loved you, Lucia. It was just that no woman had ever given me such carnal pleasure. I was addicted to my erection inside you, trapped by those cunning kisses you placed on my neck. Those times that you would be gone from my bed then return telling me about how others made love to you. Every word you spoke ignited fire in me. I wanted to kill you but I needed your body more.

"Your whispers about how big they were, how they pressed you against the wall in closed offices at work. I was helpless against my own erection. I could not stop you. I could not stop myself.

"But now that is over. I want to hear about your new lover to see what effect it will have on me. Does he have a big one like that man Mike you bragged about? Does he have a brother as did your Harlem boyfriend? Did he make you *eat dirt?*"

"I'm sorry," Lucia whispered.

Cornelius was sure that they had forgotten about him by then. Their pain was a semiopaque sphere surrounding them. It kept him out while drawing every scintilla of his attention.

"I'm sorry," she said again.

"There is no need, Lucia," Herman said, almost tenderly. "You are no more culpable than the poppy is for opium. You are the drug and I the addict. Now I am immune to your scent. Go on with your tart's dress and your bare legs. Destroy some other man."

After taking a deep breath Lucia stood up and walked from the room, her eyes on the floor. She passed her son without saying a word.

Cornelius stood at the threshold of his father's room. When Herman realized he was there he said, "Go," in a pained tone. At the same instant the front door slammed shut.

"I am alone," CC said to himself, sitting at the kitchen table listening to his father's sobbing and feeling his mother's broken heart.

4

Three weeks later Cornelius was on the mattress in the projection room masturbating while the second reel of Oscar Micheaux's *The Homesteader* played. He had found a magazine called *Dirty Nymphs Crave Big Cocks* in a trash can next to the side entrance of the Arbuckle. On the wadded cotton bedding he examined page after page of skinny young men with large erections in various positions of intercourse with equally skinny, large-breasted women. Cornelius writhed against the mattress imagining those women whispering about what the skinny young men had done. The pain was exquisite and his heart thundered.

He had ejaculated six times already and told himself that was enough. But there he was again, lying on the floor with his pants down around his knees, struggling against the thick softness of the single mattress.

"If you stop I'm leaving for the night," a blond model with two lovers murmured in his imagination.

A moan escaped Cornelius's lips and then came loud pounding on the door.

"Open the goddamn door!" a familiar voice shouted. "Open up right now!"

Cornelius leaped to his feet, pulling up his pants as he kicked the mattress into the secret closet.

"I said open up!"

Cornelius remembered the voice when a key turned the lock. It was Chapman Lorraine, the owner, the man who hated his father.

The door flew open.

Lorraine was the same height as Cornelius but he was three times the tall youth's girth and powerfully built. His hands were thick as winter gloves and his shoulders bulged under a blue velvet shirt. Black hair was everywhere on him, protruding from his ears and the neckline of his shirt, threatening to burst forth from the darkening area of his chin and sprouting in the spaces between the knuckles of his fists.

"Where the fuck is Herman?" Lorraine demanded.

He moved close to Cornelius, grabbing the boy's skinny left wrist.

"S-s-sick."

"Who're you?"

"Cornelius. Herman's son."

"Do you work for me?"

"I took daddy's place," the boy said.

"You go home and tell your father that he's fired," Lorraine said. He breathed into Cornelius's mouth. The breath was rank. The teenager's left hand went numb.

Then time seemed to stop.

42

Lorraine was yelling. Cornelius noticed the reel in the projector coming toward the end. He could still feel the erection even though it had gone limp in his pants. Seemingly of its own accord his right hand clutched the heavy lug-wrench that was used to raise and lower the projectors on their metal stems.

Years later John Woman would blame it all on the magazine.

If he hadn't been in the throes of masturbation when the irate theater owner burst in, CC wouldn't have felt rage along with being scared. He would have feared the threat of losing the job but this would have been a boy's fear, not a man's. Boys submit to the greater power but a sexual man responds with violence, the historian wrote in his private electronic journal.

"You . . . fucking . . . never . . . foot . . ." these errant words made it to Cornelius's ears. He understood their intentions if not their exact context. He knew he and his father would be out in the street if he lost this job. He knew that the street would kill Herman.

But John Woman's historical knowledge could not explain away the crime committed that evening . . . *It came in three phases,* he wrote to Posterity, *each comprised of one blow. The first strike of the lug-wrench was to free my left arm and get the fetid breath from my face. This only stunned the landlord. Lorraine put his hand to his head and then held the fingers before his eyes. When he saw the blood he surged forward. The second blow was to keep the enraged theater owner from attacking. Lorraine fell to his knees after the lug-wrench landed with a sickening thud at the side of his neck. His head hung down, his fists clenched impotently against the floor. If I had stopped there I would have been innocent, having only protected myself from attack. The third, two-handed blow to the top of Lorraine's head was that step over the line. The man was dazed and of no threat. But I hit him with all my might. The bone gave way. It was a clean and powerful exertion. To this day it feels like the most definite act of my life . . .*

The reel came to its end while Cornelius stood there looking upon the corpse at his feet.

"Change the reel!" someone shouted from the auditorium.

Cornelius rushed to turn on the second projector. This done, he closed the projection room door and locked it.

The wall flashlight illuminated the dead man's face. His eyes and mouth were open, the prone body in near-fetal position. Next to him lay *Dirty Nymphs*, a few drops of blood having fallen upon the face of a woman pretending to have an orgasm. The idea of sex made Cornelius sick. He grabbed the magazine and tore it to shreds.

CC stayed locked up with the dead man until

the theater was empty and even France Bickman had gone home. Then he went to the office to call his father.

"Hello?" Cornelius wanted to confess to Herman about Chapman Lorraine but hearing that feeble voice stopped him.

"Dad?"

"Yes, son?"

"I'm doing my geometry homework and it's getting pretty late. I think I'll stay over at Mom's."

"Are you sure she does not mind?"

"No. She said it's fine."

"It is fine," Herman corrected.

"Good night, dad."

Cornelius called Violet Breen asking her to look in on his father the next couple of days. He slept on the stairs in front of the projection room door, his dreams watched over by Lorraine's empty stare.

The next morning, with great strain and difficulty, Cornelius rolled the stiffened corpse into the secret closet where his mother hid from Jimmy Grimaldi. Then he went to school, moving from class to class in a daze.

"Is something on your mind?" Mr. Pearl asked the youth in eleventh-grade English.

"No sir," Cornelius said.

"Then why aren't you leaving?"

Cornelius saw that all the chairs except his were empty. The bell had rung and everyone left him sitting there thinking about Chapman Lorraine, big breasts and bloody orgasms.

At work he averted his eyes from the bookcase. As the evening moved on he began to plan . . .

After the show was over CC went downstairs to find France asleep in a small room behind the popcorn stand.

"Hey, France," the boy said waking the bone-thin septuagenarian. "Did anything happen last night?"

"Not that I know," France replied.

"I thought I saw some people come in after nine," Cornelius ventured. "It looked like they might'a sneaked in."

"Nobody came in. I was at the door till ten at least. You know I only lie down maybe ten minutes before the show's over."

Cornelius knew that France went to sleep after the first reel of the last show but he didn't say anything. He was pretty sure that no one had seen Lorraine come in.

Cornelius slept on the stairs again.

The next morning he went to see his mother. They hadn't talked for some time. She felt bad about the way Herman had spoken to her so hadn't come to *Uno* for their weekly tea.

His mother knew people who had been in prison. Maybe one of them could help him get rid of Lorraine's body.

"Hi, CC," Jeremy Brown, Lucia's upstairs neighbor, said on his way to the front door.

Cornelius had been pushing his mom's buzzer but she wasn't answering.

"Hi, Mr. Brown," Cornelius said. "Have you seen my mother?"

Jeremy, a middle-aged white man with thick dark hair, frowned.

"Didn't you know that she moved?" he asked.

"Moved where?"

"Said she was going out west. Didn't say where exactly."

"When?"

"Two weeks ago," Brown said. "It was very sudden. I thought maybe that gangster boyfriend of hers was in trouble. She seemed upset."

Realizing that he was on his own Cornelius went to the library. A newspaper story he'd once read to his father told about a woman who murdered her husband then hid the body in the basement. The victim was discovered forty-five years later, after the woman had remarried, raised three children and died.

There were five articles on the crime in back issues of various papers.

The first husband, Rhymer Tottenham, had

been a brute by all accounts. Twice he'd put his wife, Alicia, in the hospital. She never brought charges and defended Rhymer to her friends and family, excusing him with explanations of his frustration and rage. Then one day Rhymer was gone. This wasn't unusual. He often left home for days at a time spending Alicia's money on drink and other women. When he didn't return no one put up a fuss. He was no good and no one missed him.

Each of the newspaper pieces partially explained how Alicia Barstow (the name of her late second husband) committed and got away with her crime.

The cause of death was arsenic, probably from rat poison in his food, the coroner reported. Alicia had been a registered nurse and knew that the smell of putrefaction could be covered up by hydrated lime, or calcium hydroxide. She encased the corpse in three successively larger garment bags and hid it in the basement behind stacks of boxes filled with rocks.

Cornelius bought six differing sizes of thick plastic garment bags and a large aluminum suitcase the size of a steamer trunk. He could do this because he controlled his father's bank account. He also bought two fifty-pound bags of hydrated lime powder from a construction supply store in Soho. He had these items delivered the next morning before France Bickman came in.

After the Arbuckle closed Cornelius went to work.

From midnight to six the boy toiled. First he wrapped the hideous fetus in the smallest bag, packing chalky lime all around it. Using the handle of the lug-wrench as a lever he rolled the first bag into the second and the second into the third. When the sixth bag was zipped up CC levered Lorraine into the trunk, then glued that shut with epoxy. It took two hours for him to tumble the body back and forth, then maneuver it into the trunk. Then, for the last time, he closed the bookcase door using twenty-seven nails and more glue to ensure that it would never be opened again.

He made it home by eight in the morning. His father was asleep, ignorant of the fact that there was a murderer under his roof.

5

At night Cornelius dreamed about the corpse walled in the projection room closet. In the mornings he woke up thinking about his mother. Her parents didn't know where she'd gone; neither did Timothy Michaels. Cornelius got Filo Manetti's number from Michaels but it had been disconnected.

"I do not care where she has gone and neither should you," Herman told his son. "She does not care about us."

"But she's my mom," Cornelius said. "I love her."

Herman, who had been looking away, turned to regard his son. His head wobbled a bit because of weakened neck muscles. There was pain behind the ex-sharecropper's eyes. Pain, ten thousand poems and a million years of history.

"I love you too," the boy said.

"You are the greatest event in my life," Herman said. "Greater than my mother's lullabies and my father's homemade bamboo fishing poles. You are the blood of my blood and more."

Cornelius knew this last word held deep meaning. *More* meant hundreds of hours reading history together; it meant their long talks and CC's working at the Arbuckle to pay their bills. This one word was meant to repay him for a

50

childhood of sacrifice. His father loved him, loved his being.

Herman was innocent. It was not his weakness that struck down Lorraine. Cornelius was the killer and he alone.

A few days later there was an article in the *New York Post* about Filo Manetti. He was named on a federal warrant. The government had an informant in the mob who had linked Lucia's boyfriend to a conspiracy to commit murder. The gangster fled before the police could move in.

Fled, Cornelius thought, *with my mother.*

At the end of the first week the police came to the Arbuckle. When asked his name Cornelius told the police he was Herman Jones. They wanted to know if he had seen Chapman Lorraine.

"Not for months, officers," Cornelius said.

Even though he was in the theater office on the lower floor Cornelius thought he caught a whiff of glue from the bookcase-door.

"When was the last time you saw him?" asked the senior detective, Colette Margolis.

"He didn't like the place very much, ma'am," Cornelius said. "He couldn't sell it because it was a landmark building so, you know, he was kinda sour."

"Did he have problems with anyone?" the detective asked.

"I didn't really know him," Cornelius replied.

"What about you?" she asked France Bickman.

"I haven't seen Chapman in four months. The checks come in the mail and he don't like the place too much like Herman here says. I really wish I could help you but we hardly know the man."

The detective had amber eyes. Their beauty struck the teenage killer. Maybe he was staring a little too hard.

"You're a little young aren't you?" she asked and Cornelius wondered what she meant. The question must have shown on his face.

"To be working as a projectionist," she explained.

"Oh. It's after school and I can do my homework right here. You know all I have to do is change reels. It's easy."

She had brown skin like his. Her hair was a wavy brown.

The policewoman smiled. Her partner, a tall Hispanic man, nodded at Cornelius and then touched her shoulder.

"I guess we better be going," she said. "We might come back if there are any other questions."

"Come see one of our movies, Detective," Cornelius offered. "When you watch them it's like you're living a hundred years ago."

"Maybe I will," she said.

Cornelius wished that the woman would return, but without a badge.

"The thesis is a police investigation," Herman said when Cornelius told him about the detectives.

"The antithesis is animal attraction."

Cornelius had decided to tell his father what was going on without telling him about the murder. He worried about the impact this knowledge would have.

"She's a lot older than I am, dad, but I found myself wanting her to come back," the boy said.

"But not in her role as a policewoman," Herman added. "The only question is—what will be the synthesis of the heart's investigation?"

That discussion was a rare moment of lucidity for Herman at that time.

Often Cornelius would come home to find his father in a confused state; the elder Jones sometimes didn't know where he was. Cornelius would try to tell him that he was at home in his bed but that wasn't enough. Herman would have to reenact the journey of his life up to the moment he was there in the room with the young man who called himself his son.

This pilgrimage took many different paths. Herman would, for instance, tell the story of a long and convoluted bus ride from his home in Columbus, Mississippi, through a life of deprivation and joy until the final stop in Brooklyn where he met Kendra Brooks, who later had an operation and became the seductress—Lucia, who made Herman into *her man*. The wordplay would bring a smile to the old man's lips. He'd look up and recognize Cornelius sitting there beside him.

Cornelius continued to read to his father. When he was awake Herman loved the stories but rarely gave incisive interpretations of the uses of history. Late at night he'd wake up yelling for the conductor to stop the train.

"Why do you do it?" Herman asked one morning before Cornelius was off to school.

"What, dad?"

"Why do you make me come back to this?"

"You seem lost," Cornelius explained, "scared."

"But out there I'm having adventure. I got my legs and a big dick. The girls all like it fine."

"You don't want me to remind you that you're here with me, dad?"

"Just be my friend, France. That's all I need. Remember that we have to make sure my son has a pot to piss in when the curtain comes down."

6

Detective Margolis returned to the Arbuckle on a Saturday evening three months after the disappearance of Chapman Lorraine. She came to watch movies. Between films she climbed the slender staircase and knocked on the projector room door.

"Hello, Detective," Cornelius said.

"You remember me?"

"Detective Margolis. You gave France your card."

"You can call me Colette," she said. "I'm not on duty."

She wore jeans and a short-short-sleeve pink blouse. Her thick hair was tied back. Deftly applied makeup made her amber eyes seem enormous. She was a few inches shorter than Cornelius but well-formed and strong.

"You were right about the movies," Colette said. "It's weird how everything in your life seems so far away. You really feel for the characters."

She wasn't forty, maybe not much past thirty, but he could see the hardness in her face when she stood close to him.

"You want to watch the next film from up here with me?" He wondered how the question

55

managed to get out around the lump in his throat.

"That'd be great," she said.

He opened the viewing panel and unfolded a chair for her to sit in. He perched on a stool behind her as she watched *The Sheik*, starring Rudolph Valentino.

The cop leaned forward, lost in long-ago passion. Cornelius's fervor was right there in front of him; there in the room where his mother seduced his father, where he'd squandered his seed turning the pages of *Dirty Nymphs*, where he murdered Chapman Lorraine, where the dead man lay entombed not six feet from them.

After half an hour he put his hands on Colette's shoulders and squeezed as his mother had him do when she had a headache. He contemplated that move from the moment she sat down. When Colette leaned back he took in a breath so deep that it got stuck. His fingers dug deeper because he couldn't exhale. Colette hugged the fingers of his right hand by pressing against them with her jawbone. He let out a loud sigh then. This embarrassed him but he kept on kneading the strong flesh.

When the movie was over Cornelius walked Colette out of the projection room. She held out her hand and said, "Thanks."

After the handclasp she said, "Well . . . I better be going."

Four steps down and Cornelius said, "Can we

have coffee sometime?" She took three more steps, stopped and turned. Her face was very serious.

"Come down here," she said.

Something about the command thrilled CC.

He stopped at her stair. She went a step higher, enabling herself to look him in the eye.

"What do you mean?" she asked.

"Ju-just that I'd, I would like to see you again. Maybe talk about the films." There appeared a hint of a smile on Colette's pursed lips. Cornelius noticed that she had small scar on her right cheek. There was another along the right side of her lower lip.

"Just coffee?"

"Yeah."

A smirk came into Colette's scarred lips, then a smile. "You want my number?"

"If that's okay."

"You know I work very hard," she said. "It took me months just to find time to come here."

"Anytime would be fine," Cornelius said.

"What about school? And what would your parents say about you seeing some woman for coffee who was almost twice your age?"

Almost, Cornelius thought.

"My mother is gone," he said. "My dad is bedridden. I work here to pay our bills. I can do what I want."

Colette took a white card from her red handbag.

Cornelius caught a glimpse of the pistol nestled therein. She scribbled a number on the back.

"The printed side is my work number and the backside is my home," she said. "Call me and we'll see."

The next day he called the home number. When a man's voice answered he hung up. He redialed and the man, now angry, answered again. Cornelius hung up.

For a week the boy fretted.

The man is probably her boyfriend, he thought. *She didn't wear a wedding ring. Maybe it's her brother or her roommate. Lots of mom's relatives sometimes stay with each other.*

He called, the man answered. Cornelius hung up.

The next day he got an answering machine.

"We're not in but you can leave a message," Colette said. "Either Harry or Colette will get back to you later."

Cornelius hung up without a word.

We're not in. The agitated teenager wrote these words down. He thought about her tone of voice and the permanence of the phrase. He called four more times to make sure he heard the message right.

That night he developed a fever. Violet Breen moved in for a few days to care for both father and son.

At night Cornelius could hear the buxom Irishwoman reading Yeats to Herman. He'd drift from the poems into nightmares about the decomposing corpse behind the wall.

France Bickman agreed to do double duty and show the films while the boy recuperated. Cornelius worried that France might remember the secret door and wrench it open with a crowbar. He imagined Chapman's flesh turning to liquid and leaking out from under the door, then Colette coming in her pink blouse to arrest him. He'd start awake with a gasp hearing "A Dialogue of Self and Soul" rendered in Violet's gentle brogue.

On Thursday morning the fever broke and Cornelius went to school. He sat quietly in classes, almost as if he wasn't there. He had no friends among the students and avoided teachers, counselors and coaches with their helping inquiries. He did homework and took exams but Cornelius wasn't interested in school. He knew there was no future; Herman's history lessons had taught him that much.

"We all fade into the tapestry of the past," Herman often said, "becoming like so many tiny knots in the weave of fine Chinese silk. There is nothing to distinguish you, me or even who we might think is a great man. Time passes and we all diminish until the fabric of our age renders unto dust."

School was just another connective knot of thread, a passing moment.

That evening he went to work. It was the week of the annual Charlie Chaplin festival so the theater was crowded. Cornelius opened the viewing panel and watched, while imagining his fingers kneading Colette's strong shoulders.

At the beginning of the second reel he ran down to the corner pay phone and entered the number printed on her card.

"Missing persons," she answered.

"Colette?"

"Who is this?"

"It's me, um, Herman."

"Oh. Hi. I was wondering if you were ever going to call me."

"Yeah," Cornelius said. There was a siren wailing down the street.

"Where are you?"

"On the street. I got a twenty-minute reel playing."

"Did you call my house?"

"No."

"Really? Because somebody's been calling. My boyfriend thinks I have something going on."

Boyfriend.

"I got sick," the boy said. "I had a fever or something."

"Oh. Are you okay?"

"Yeah. Well I guess I better be going."

"Why'd you call if you're just gonna get right off?" There was humor in her tone.

"I just wanted to say hi I guess."

"What about that coffee?"

"Um, wouldn't your boyfriend be mad?"

"You're just a kid, Herman. Why would he be mad?"

"No reason I guess. There's a place I go to on Second. It's called *Uno*."

"I know it."

"What about four tomorrow?"

Colette was waiting for him, sitting across from the booth where Cornelius and his mother usually sat. She had on a rose-colored summer dress with quarter-inch straps and a zigzag stitch pattern across the bodice.

Her light brown skin reminded him of the coffee frosting on his father's favorite doughnuts.

"Hi," she said, smiling. "I didn't order for you because I didn't know what you drink."

"Mocha cappuccino," the boy said.

The waiter, Gino, came to the booth.

"Hey, CC," he greeted. "Long time no see. How's your mother?"

"She moved to Alaska," the boy said, feeling like he was under a light as bright as the sun.

"Hello," Gino greeted Colette.

"Hi," she replied holding out a hand to the mustachioed elder gentleman. "I'm Colette."

When Gino went away to order Cornelius's sweet coffee Colette asked, "Why'd he call you CC?"

"My name isn't Herman," the boy confessed. "That's my father's name. He's been sick so I've been doing his job. It started before I was sixteen and I kept his name so we wouldn't lose the paycheck."

"You work every day?"

"Please don't tell anybody. If I lose that job we'd be broke."

"What about Lorraine?" she asked and Cornelius's fingers went stiff.

"Huh?"

"Won't he get into trouble if he has an underage boy working there?"

"He knows all about it," Cornelius said making sure to use the present tense. "And I'm sixteen now. This way he has somebody in there who he doesn't have to give a raise for at least two years."

"How many days a week?" the policewoman asked.

"Every day."

"You never have a day off?"

"Uh-uh."

"That would put Lorraine in even more trouble."

"Why?"

"He broke the law having you there before you turned sixteen and then he has you on the job every day."

"Please don't tell," Cornelius begged. "I need the job."

"Don't worry." She sat back in her chair and grinned. "I do missing persons not child abuse."

"I'm not a child."

"I know."

They talked about films after that. Cornelius had become an expert in silent films since taking his father's job. He talked to her about great Russian films like *Father Sergius* and *Song About the Merchant Kalashnikov*. They also discussed little-known Asian works such as *The Goddess* and *The Big Road*. From there he started telling her how Europeans always had a better hold on culture because they spoke so many languages and their histories intertwined.

"Americans are so far removed from the actual events in their past," the teenager said. "They don't even know the basic lies that make up our history."

"You sure you're in high school?" Colette asked him.

"Yeah. Why?"

"You sound like you're goin' out for a master's degree in about two or three subjects."

"I read a lot."

"Don't you go dancing or play football or something?"

"Between school and work and my dad I don't have very much time," Cornelius explained.

"But what do you do for fun?"

"Having coffee with you is nice."

Colette was the first friend Cornelius had since taking his father's job. When they got together he would talk for almost the whole two hours before they each went off to work. They went to *Uno* three times before Colette suggested meeting somewhere else. She'd made up her mind not to tell her boyfriend about their friendship because Harry was the jealous type and might try to stop them from meeting. ". . . And I like seeing you," she said.

They met on a Thursday in Alphabet City, at the corner of Avenue D and 2nd Street. Colette was carrying a picnic basket.

She led him past a dark green door, up a winding staircase to the fourth floor.

"Where are we going?" he asked.

"Right here," she said as she worked a key in the lock.

The room smelled musty. There was only a short sofa and an end table. The wood floor was bare except for a small rope rug. A low-watt lamp tilted on the small table. Colette switched the light on after making sure the chain on the door was secure.

"Is this your place?" Cornelius asked.

"No . . . well, kind of . . . It's the precinct's apartment. Anybody can come here if they want to get away."

She reached into the basket and brought out two paper cups of coffee.

"Just like the coffee shop but at half the price," she said. "Sit down."

Cornelius did as she told him. She sat with her back to him and pushed her thick hair aside.

"I've been wanting you to massage my shoulders again ever since that night at the Arbuckle," she said.

Cornelius went right to work.

"Oh yeah," she crooned. "That's what I've been needing. Harry tries but he only does it for a minute and he doesn't know how to grab the muscles like you do."

Cornelius's erection was almost instantaneous.

"Have you heard anything about Mr. Lorraine?" she asked.

Now he was fearful and excited at the same time. This brought back the night of the murder in full force.

"N-no."

"What's wrong, baby? You nervous?"

"Just concentrating on the massage."

Colette leaned back against him and said, "Harder."

He increased the pressure.

"Harder," she said again.

"I don't want to hurt you," Cornelius replied. He was already doing the best he could.

"Do you think that you can hurt me?" she asked.

"Well, I, um."

"Come on," she dared, rising to her feet. "See if you can throw me."

"Uh-uh."

"No really. Try."

"I don't want to."

"You scared?" Her smile was a challenge.

"No," Cornelius said. "Well . . . okay."

He stood up, held his arms wide then lunged at Colette. She ducked under his left arm, rose grabbing the wrist and tripping his left leg, putting him into an armlock facedown on the floor. Colette twisted around until she could wrap her legs viselike around his middle. This pushed all the air out of CC's lungs. He thrashed around in fear of suffocation.

"Give?" she said.

Cornelius nodded.

"Say it."

"I give," he muttered.

Colette let him go, bouncing to her feet.

"You see?" she told him. "You can't hurt me."

"I wasn't ready," the boy complained. "I thought we were just playing."

"You want to try again?"

This time he crouched down managing to grab her around the waist. But Colette twisted to the side, pulling him off-balance. He fell as her scissor-legs wrapped around him. This time she held him for the count of ten before accepting surrender.

"I could get you this time," he said after catching his breath.

"No," she said. "You can't and you wouldn't want to risk losing."

"What do you mean I wouldn't want to risk it?"

"The third win makes me the victor," she said. "I'd own you."

Cornelius leaped through the air intent on using surprise and his weight to bring her down. Colette sidestepped his charge and CC went sprawling. She fell on his back, twisted both of his wrists behind him and locked them together with what he suspected were handcuffs. He tried to get up but she grabbed his hair pressing his face to the floor.

"Stay down!" she commanded and he went still.

She reached around the front of his pants, unzipping them and pulling them down. Then he felt his underpants sliding down. Cool air caressed his backside.

"Stop it!" he cried.

She said nothing but he heard a rustling then he felt her bare skin against his. Suddenly her pelvis thrust forward and she bit his ear.

"You're my boy now aren't you, CC?" she said mid-thrust. "You're my boy aren't you?"

She rolled from side to side on his butt.

"Yes," he said.

"Really, you're my woman right now," she said.

"Yes."

"Say it."

"I'm your woman," he said and she bit into his cheek.

Cornelius started to cry. At first it was just a gentle sobbing because his pride had been hurt.

"That's it, baby. Cry for me," she whispered and he blubbered into the dust-caked floor.

"Harder, baby," she demanded, rhythmically pressing her pelvis against his backside.

Cornelius wept.

There was a dying man back home in bed and the dead man in the closet. His mother was gone and all he wanted was to cry: to holler and yell and kick the floor with his shoes. At one point he bucked Colette off, then went still expecting her, wanting her to mount him again.

"Get up." She had to help him because of his bonds.

"Lie down on your back on the couch," she said.

And he did.

"If it doesn't stay hard I can't fuck you." Her skirt was on the floor already. She pulled off her top.

When she descended he felt something so smooth and so right that he actually gasped out loud.

Then they were both moaning, her nails digging into his right shoulder.

He was looking into her eyes when he came. She smiled and he came again. When it was over she kissed his brow.

Later, when they were both dressed, Colette asked him not to tell anyone.

"No," he managed to say. "I won't tell."

7

Cornelius didn't call Colette again that week or the next. At night he dreamed about her riding him and biting him. He held his breath remembering how he still had a hard-on even though he was afraid that she might kill him.

"Sex," his father had said, explaining the birds and the bees when Cornelius was thirteen, "is the prime mover in social and species discourse. It is brutal and primitive and the one true indicator that human beings are animal and not of divine origin. That is why so-called sophisticated members of society deplore the sexual act, because it takes them away from God, pulling them into the realm of the *primitive* totem."

Herman never got down to genitals in his oratory.

When Cornelius asked what sex felt like his father replied, "You can pick that up in any smut. Your mother can tell you about that. What I tell you here is the understanding of all things human. From architecture to xenial relations sex is the root, the infrastructure, if you will, not only of human activities but of all life. Once you understand that you will have mastered one of the four pillars of historical thinking."

But Cornelius wasn't interested in history

after his first sexual encounter. He couldn't think of anything but the rough-handed Colette. He picked up the phone and dialed her number three or four times a day but hung up before it rang.

He hoped that she would come to the theater and take him out for coffee. He wanted to see her but couldn't call.

Eighteen days passed. Cornelius was sitting next to his father's bed reading from the *Iliad*, a favorite of both father and son.

Homer created fiction that told us more about his era than any historian, Herman was fond of saying. *He is the proof of the fallacy of ninety-nine percent of historians and their lies.*

Somehow sensing his son's distress, Herman returned to his former self and stayed—for a while.

"What's wrong, son?" he asked when Cornelius drifted off from reading.

"There's a girl I like, dad."

"Does she like you?"

"I think so."

"Have you kissed her yet?"

"She bit me."

Cornelius had not seen his father grin for a very long time.

"She did? How did you like that?" Mr. Jones asked.

"It hurt and I was scared."

"Because you are used to television kisses and

radio songs about what love should be," Herman said.

"We don't even have a TV."

"No we do not. But everybody else does. You cannot escape the preoccupation of an entire culture, son. Cultural content, for better or worse, is like a virus. If everybody else has it then you do too.

"But try not to allow these lies to blind you. Try to see why this girl is biting you. Tell her it hurts and maybe she shouldn't bite so hard."

"But that's weird," Cornelius said.

"Better to be a weird dog chop than a mass-produced hamburger."

An hour or so after Herman was asleep the phone rang. Cornelius thought it might be his mother.

"Hello?"

"Is your father asleep?" Colette asked.

"Yes."

"Then come on over to Manhattan, to the place we went last time."

"No."

"If you don't I'll come get you."

Cornelius had no doubt that she knew his address. She had gotten his unlisted phone number.

It was near two a.m. when Cornelius climbed the stairs to the police apartment. Colette stood at the open door, waiting.

"Come on in, CC."

She was wearing a purple dress that went all the way to the floor. But the straps were thin and the neckline was low. He could see her breasts.

"Take off your clothes and lie down on your stomach on the floor."

"No."

"Do you want me to take them off for you?" she asked with not the slightest hint of threat in her tone.

Cornelius took off his clothes but he lay down on the couch.

"I said the floor," Colette said.

"No."

She pulled off her dress then and lay down on top of him. She kissed his neck and he sighed.

"I wanted to apologize," she said. "I didn't mean for that to happen the other day. It's just that you got hard when we were wrestling and that made me excited because you're so damn cute."

All of this she whispered in his ear; her voice raspy, her breath smelling of liquor.

"I won't hurt you again, baby," she said. "Okay?"

Cornelius nodded.

"Will you still be friends with me?"

He nodded again.

"Do you want to cry for me now?"

Cornelius tried to shake his head but a torrent of tears stopped him.

73

"Give it to me, baby," Colette crooned, caressing his legs with hers, kissing the back of his neck. "Give it up. Let it out. Cry for me, honey."

After a while Cornelius turned around wanting to make love to her but she held him off.

She whispered, "After the other day we need some time without it."

"Okay," Cornelius said. "But when can we see each other again?"

"Maybe you should be seeing girls your own age."

"But we could be friends like you said."

"Friends don't have to see each other all the time," Colette argued caressing his fingers.

"I need a friend."

"Call me," she said. "You can sleep here if you want and go home in the morning."

She donned her purple dress and went quickly, leaving Cornelius with a hollow feeling in his chest.

He sat in the dark room, naked and aroused, thinking of how much he was in love with Colette. Her physical warmth, her long nails and teeth, her painful knowledge centered on him.

Herman was right, Cornelius thought, *we are animal.*

He turned off the light but didn't fall asleep.

8

In this way Cornelius entered a new tempestuous period of his life.

The next semester he took four morning classes, forging a permission slip from his father. At noon almost every day he took the train to Manhattan to see Colette. They did things to each other which Cornelius had never read about, heard of, or seen in dirty magazines.

Love, his father had said, when Cornelius pressed him on the subject, *is peculiar. Real lovers' acts of passion are repellent to others, not like the pictures you see in those so-called adult magazines.*

It wasn't much but it was enough to tell Cornelius that he was on the right track with his policewoman girlfriend.

At the end of their afternoons of ardor, and often tears, Cornelius would go to work doing push-ups and sit-ups in the projectionist's booth so that he could outwrestle his powerful lover.

At night he read to his father, though Herman's acumen had become spotty again.

"Who are you?" he would sometimes ask when Cornelius walked into the bedroom.

"It's me, dad."

"Oh. Right. Hello . . . son."

At first Cornelius thought that it was his father's eyesight going. But then Herman began to lose quotes.

"As Hobbes . . . Hobbes once . . . oh. It does not matter really. He was a churl old Hobbes. Anyway philosophy is important only for its understanding of history. History is everything."

He'd strain to recall phrases, which more and more were lost to him. He was nowhere near retirement age but Herman was already an old man.

"All that reading must have burned out my insides, Cornelius," he said on one lucid day. "All the books I have read swirl around like an ocean, with every page a wave. And now I drift in that vastness buoyed up by slippery knowledge, starving from want of anything with sustenance."

One afternoon, while Colette was seeing a doctor in Long Island City, Cornelius came home to find France Bickman sitting at Herman's bedside.

Cornelius fell into the kind of thinking his father had instilled. *When following an idea, event, or person in history, the historian always looks for the anomaly. Therein lie the secret moments of history,* Herman Jones said. *Catching this moment separates the monumental thinker from the mundane.*

"Hi, Mr. Bickman," Cornelius greeted as he did each evening at the Arbuckle.

"Hello there, Cornelius. I just came by to say hello to your pops." He stood up and shook CC's hand.

After Bickman had gone Herman said, "He's a very good man, that France."

"Does he come by very often, dad?"

"Once a week or so."

"Once a week? Why didn't you ever tell me about that?"

"I am still the father, Cornelius. There was no reason to tell you because it is none of your business."

"I guess not."

"What are you doing home this early anyway?"

"I got a headache and couldn't think. I just left."

"You walked out of class?"

"No. I waited for the passing period and came home. I wanted to get some sleep before I had to go to work."

Cornelius knew his father would understand the implication. He was doing everything except for the housekeeping done by Violet Breen . . . Violet Breen . . . the anomaly.

The following Tuesday Cornelius stayed home feigning a sore throat. When Violet came in at ten o'clock, he was waiting at the door.

"Where is my mother, Violet?" he asked without even a hello.

The hefty Irish immigrant looked down at the floor. Cornelius noticed the lovely turn of her face, something he had not registered before.

"I'm sorry, young Cornelius," she said. "But I don't know."

"How does she pay you?"

"Pay me? She doesn't."

"Then why do you still come around?"

Violet looked up into the young historian's eyes as if pleading for him to understand. And he did understand. This woman from across the ocean had fallen in love with the man whose great-grandfather had been a slave on the Russell Plantation in south Mississippi.

"You do it for free?"

"I do it because my father used to read us children poetry every night before bed. No one has read to me since then and no one would if it weren't for your dear father."

Three days later Cornelius came home to find Herman bent and naked, crying on the kitchen floor.

"Dad, what happened?"

"Peanut butter wasn't in the pantry. Bread wasn't in the box like it used to be. Fell when I couldn't find it. Fell."

Cornelius called 9-1-1. In the back of the EMS van CC held Herman's hand while the old man cried out in pain from the jostling of his brittle bones.

The doctor who attended Herman after the emergency hip replacement said that men in his state of poor health didn't usually recover fully.

"He'll have to be put in a home," the doctor told him, "a man his age—"

"He's only fifty-four, Doctor."

"Oh. He seems so much older."

"I have to take him home."

"I'm sorry, young man," the pear-shaped, bald, middle-aged white man said. "He's not well enough to release and not sick enough to take up a hospital bed. We are compelled by state law to put him in a nursing facility."

While they spoke Herman moaned a dirge.

"Herodotus, record me," he sang. "But will you, can you, tell of my forebears?"

"I have to take him home where he knows his surroundings," Cornelius said.

"The paperwork will take ten days at least," the doctor replied. "If he can walk under his own power by then, okay. But I'm sure you'll see he's beyond that."

After the doctor left, Cornelius pulled up a chair to his father's bed, determined to resurrect his mind.

"Dad."

"After the alpha comes the theta," he said. "But not necessarily."

"Dad, it's me, Cornelius."

"It is."

The boy smiled.

"Dad, you have to get up or they're going to send you to a nursing home."

When Herman heard these words his face took on a conspiratorial look.

"I was in the forest pines and spied a man dressed all in black," he said.

"What man?" Cornelius asked hopefully.

"He did not have a name but he was white and there was hair growing under his chin."

"He must have had a name. Everybody has a name."

"No," Herman said sadly. "He had no name or home or even a past. He was standin' in the forest lost to the world and to hisself."

"What happened to him, dad?"

"Who are you?" Herman asked then.

"Cornelius. Your son."

"That ain't a real name," Herman said with a smile. "It's a vegetable wit' some silk hangin' ona end of it."

Herman giggled.

"What about the man in black?"

"The black man," Herman corrected.

"You said that it was a white man dressed in black."

"That's what they want you to think," Herman warned. "They want you to think that they is wolves in sheep's clothin'. But they ain't. They just Negroes. Niggers."

"So it wasn't a white man in the pines that you saw?"

Herman began to cry. His body shook and he grimaced in pain. Tears rolled down his gaunt cheeks.

"Are you scared of the black man in the pines?" Cornelius asked.

Herman could not answer. So Cornelius took out a copy of *The Prince* and began to read aloud. Within minutes his father was asleep.

Cornelius studied the medical charts at the foot of the bed then went off to work.

Next afternoon, in the apartment with Colette, he defeated her in a wrestling match for the first time, handcuffing her wrists to the foot of the sofa.

He pressed down on her, making love slowly while she struggled and moaned.

Afterward they sat on the couch and talked about Herman.

"I went to see him this morning," CC said, "before I came here."

"What about school?"

"Fuck school. They want to put my father in a nursing home."

"Can they do that without permission?"

"If he's out of his head and can't walk. I have to have him on his feet in seven days or they'll move him to a nursing home and I'll never get him out."

"I'll do whatever you need, baby," the detective said. "Just leave it up to me and we'll get your father out of there."

"How?"

"I don't know but we will."

CC took her hand and lowered his head.

"You know I went to the doctor the other day," she said after a while.

"Uh-huh."

"It was a fertility doctor. Harry and I are getting married but he has a low sperm count so I had a treatment that will help—you know?"

"You're getting married?"

"I'm thirty-one, honey. I don't have that much time."

"But you could . . . what about us?"

Colette smiled and caressed his cheek. "You're just a boy, CC. There's a whole life out there for you to live. What would it look like me marrying a seventeen-year-old kid? They'd put me in jail for sure."

A feeling of distance descended on Cornelius. It was as if Colette had been shifted a thousand miles and a thousand years away. He fondly remembered the love they had shared. But she was gone; also his school and job and the corpse he sat next to every evening at work. All in the distance, history.

"I guess," Cornelius said. "Yeah. I got to go, Colette. My father needs me."

She touched his arm and asked, "Do you want me to hold you?"

"Not right now."

"The black man did not see me," Herman said on the fourth day since the story began. "I followed him deep in the woods. He looked sneaky and me and your mother thought he might be a pimp."

"But mom couldn't be in Mississippi, dad," Cornelius argued. "You didn't meet her until she came to your projection room running from Jimmy Grimaldi."

"Oh," Herman said. "Oh yeah, I mean yes. Yes it was not your mother but *my* mother. Yes my mother . . ."

Every day Cornelius discussed and argued about the bearded white man dressed in black, or sometimes the black man, who he was following through the Mississippi pinewoods. He passed the scenes of lynchings and rapes, patches of strawberries and young Abraham Lincoln sitting by a brook. Once he came upon Thucydides. This, Cornelius knew, was a turning point for his father. In the journey through his mind he had come across the historian he loved most. The ancient Greek doctor-general was the signpost of Herman's sanity.

Along the way child-Herman had gone by a bevy of naked white women dancing in a circle. When the black man (he was a Negro at that moment) moved on the women tried to stop Herman, but he shook them off following the trail of breadcrumbs the man had left to find his own way back home.

Herman ate the breadcrumbs. That's how he stayed alive: eating breadcrumbs, trailing the white man in black, the black man.

". . . yes it was my mother there with me. Your mother was not there. My mother said I should go home and I told her, 'Later, mama. I got to find out where this man be goin' to first.'

"And one day, instead of a breadcrumb he tore out a page from a dictionary, leaving that to mark his path. I picked it up and put it in my mouth because I knew paper was made from wood and a man could eat wood if he was hungry enough."

"So you were following the man and eating pages from his dictionary?" Cornelius asked.

"I almost did," Herman said. "I almost did but then, before I chewed, I took the page out from my mouth and looked at it. It was all chicken scratches, black marks on yellow paper. But the more I looked, the more it seemed to make sense. They closed all the black schools down around me. They said black folks would do better in the cotton fields and the fruit farms than they would in no classroom. You couldn't read if you was black. Why read if there was cotton to be pult? Why read when you could slave?"

Herman's eyes opened wide in amazement. He gazed at the ceiling trying to glean an answer from above.

By day six Cornelius had gotten Herman to sit up as he used to do at home. CC had deciphered the doctor's scrawls on the medical charts, changing the morphine prescribed to ibuprofen and removing the Ritalin altogether.

He made these changes after the doctor's rounds.

Every day Cornelius would remind his father where the story had left off. At first Herman claimed not to remember but Cornelius kept asking and after a while he'd have Herman back on the trail of the quarry in black.

". . . the pages was from a dictionary at first but then they was from novels and history books and biographies. I strained so hard to understand. Some people along the way give me hints. There was a white woman on the other side of a river he crossed who told me what a 'Q' was. She told me that there was no 'Q' word that didn't have a 'U' as the second letter. She was wrong but that didn't matter because she was mostly right. . . ."

"Why were you following that man, dad?"

"To find my way back home," he said.

"But you were with your mother. Didn't she know the way home?"

"Not home to Mississippi, ninny. I wanted to come home to you."

"Who am I?"

"My son . . . Cornelius."

And he was back in the world they both inhabited.

"We have to get you out of here, dad. They want to put you into a nursing home."

"What do we do about it, son?"

Wednesday afternoon at three p.m. Herman Jones, using two bamboo canes, walked toward the nurses' desk on the third floor of St. Francis Hospital in Brooklyn. Cornelius was by his side. The elder Jones was wearing blue jeans, a red T-shirt and hospital-supplied paper slippers. The day before they had practiced their trek. It was difficult at first but Herman was resolute and so was his son.

"Where you think you goin'?" a big black nurse with blond hair asked.

She rose up from behind the nurses' station.

"Home," Cornelius said.

"I don't have authorization to discharge this patient. Come on now, Mr. Jones, let me take you back to your room."

"No, Nurse, I am not going back there."

"But Mr.—"

"Please," Herman said. "I do not wish to be transferred to some nursing facility. I can move

86

under my own power and I have the wherewithal to address your inquiries. That accepted, there is no reason for you to hinder my egress from this, this medical prison."

"The doctor has to release you, Mr. Jones."

"What is your name?" Herman asked the nurse.

"Jackie."

"Jackie what?"

"Boughman."

"Well, Ms. Boughman," Herman said. "I take it you are a black woman in spite of your hair."

"Yeah."

"Being of our race you must be aware of the end of slavery in the United States. And so you must understand why I elect to leave these premises under my own power."

Cornelius had never been more proud of his father. He knew how hard it was for him just to stand after being in bed for so long and with a new hip aching in its joint. But Herman was eloquent and dignified.

"I'm sorry, Mr. Jones, but I will have to wait for the doctor's release form."

"Excuse me," a voice said then.

All three heads turned to see a caramel-colored woman who had approached unnoticed.

Only Cornelius recognized Colette Margolis.

"Yes?" Nurse Boughman said.

"I'm a family friend," Colette said, flipping open her wallet to reveal the shiny detective's badge. "I've come to help Mr. Jones home."

"I'm sorry but you'll have to wait for the doctor," the nurse repeated.

"No I don't," Colette asserted. "We're leaving now. If you try to physically hinder me I am authorized to use force."

"Even if you do not remember slavery I wager you understand that," Herman said.

They took the elevator down and walked out to the street. There Colette's lime green Honda was waiting for them. They helped Herman into the front seat.

9

"Who was that woman?" Herman asked Cornelius once he was back in his own bed.

"Just a friend."

Cornelius had walked Colette to the door, where she kissed him then looked into his eyes as if maybe he was someone new.

"Where did you meet her?"

"Um," the boy mumbled, "at the Arbuckle."

"Is she one of the detectives investigating the disappearance of Chapman Lorraine? They suspect he's been murdered."

"How did you know about that?"

"France told me. About a month ago the police called him down to their offices. They told him that the last thing Chapman intended to do before his disappearance was come to the Arbuckle. He was such an awful human being, but still no man deserves to be plucked from his life."

"Yeah," Cornelius said heavily, feeling his father's indictment. "I'm sorry France told you about it."

"Why?"

"I don't want you to worry."

"Worry? Me? You can tell me anything, boy. I am your father not your ward. But answer my question, why would the police help me?"

"The detective questioned me too. She figured out about you and when I told her about your, um, predicament, she just offered to help."

"That was very kind," Herman said, looking his son in the eye.

"Dad?"

"Yes, son?"

"You seem . . . I mean for the past few months, before you fell, you were forgetting things."

"That is true, Cornelius. Ideas had begun to fade. It was hard for me to focus. At first I thought it was our long talks that brought me back to awareness. But there must have been some medicine or nutrient they gave me that rejuvenated my mind." Upon saying this Herman went into a fit of coughing. It was a rolling, raspy, wet cough that went on and on.

"How are you feeling, dad?" Cornelius asked when his father lay back panting from the effort.

"Not too well. My hip aches and it makes me sweat just to lay here. But I have my mind."

Cornelius pulled up a chair and touched his father's hand.

"There is no hiding from it," the elder Jones said. "You saved me from indignity but the grim reaper will not be denied."

Herman's lower eyelids sagged open as if some preternatural gravity was dragging him down.

"Do you want me to read to you, dad?"

"No. You have taken care of me all these years

when it was my job to look out for you. You read to me and prepared thousands of dinners. I have failed you."

"But, dad, you showed me Hannibal and the empire of Kush, the Shang Dynasty and the Inquisition. You taught me how to think."

Herman Jones smiled at his son.

"Your mother and I failed you but you never disappointed us," he said. "You have been a good son."

"I love you, dad. I want you to live."

"I have to sleep for a while, Cornelius. When I wake up *I* will do something for *you*."

He closed his eyes and was immediately asleep.

Cornelius sat there looking at Herman's hands. They were old, intelligent hands that reminded the boy of a da Vinci drawing he had once seen in a book. The phone rang many times over the night. It went unanswered.

The night was cold. The steam heat for the building wasn't yet turned on. The lights were out except for one bulb in the kitchen, two rooms away. This faint radiance filtered through the darkness of CC's mind. It was like a far-off hope. He couldn't tell then if it was fading away or beckoning a new day.

Just after eleven CC realized he hadn't gone to work that night. Maybe the phone calls had been from France Bickman.

Around one a.m. he accepted that his father

would soon die and that Lucia Napoli was gone for good; these thoughts made him shiver so he climbed under the covers with his father.

When he opened his eyes the room was filled with light. His head was nestled against his father's side. Herman was looking down on him. Cornelius held his breath so as not to break the spell.

"Wake up, sleepyhead," Herman said.

Cornelius was a child again with parents who showered love on him every morning.

"Hi, dad. I'm sorry about getting in your bed but it was cold and I didn't want to leave you alone."

"I was not going to die last night," Herman Jones said. "I have a promise to keep."

"What is it?"

"Not really one thing but three. Some knowledge, some advice and then another thing."

"Can I go to the bathroom before you explain?"

"You may."

He remembered that one urination the rest of his years: bare feet on the cracked tiles, corroded copper pipes poking out through the plaster behind the tank, the exultation of release, and the memory of physical closeness with his father. There was salsa music playing somewhere and the sharp smell of tomatoes cooking. A huge fly buzzed in between the screen and the window and there was a rumble in the ground, far away.

The J train Cornelius thought and he laughed to himself, *I've been too busy to notice it.* When he got back to the bedroom Herman was wearing his reading glasses, turning the pages of a book.

"Hello, son," he said in a full, strong voice. "Come sit and talk."

Cornelius pulled up a chair.

"I promised I would do something and I mean to accomplish that end."

"What's that, dad?"

"First I will explain the remaining three pillars of historical inquiry, then I shall give you some personal advice, and sometime later, after I pass on, I will help you along on your journey."

Cornelius was a child again.

"The pillars," Herman explained, "are quite simple. The first, as I told you some time ago, is sex. We need not spend any more time on that subject. The next two mainstays are inextricably intertwined. These are technology and economics, both entities secretly conspiring to inform the relations of humans to their world. Lewis Mumford and Jacques Ellul speak to the phenomenon of technology and its bastard son— technique. Marx is as good an example as any of how economics rears its head in every room in the house of man . . ."

A decade later the boy could recite this lecture word for word.

". . . The fourth pillar is the simplest and by far

the most important. You need not understand sex, money or machines to know history but you must comprehend the shopping list."

"Shopping list?" Cornelius drew his head back like a baby snake.

"There is little verifiable evidence in the courtroom of history," Herman said.

Cornelius noticed beads of sweat standing out on his father's forehead.

". . . You cannot be certain what Lee was thinking when surrendering to Grant or if Napoleon loved his wife. We do not know why primitive Europeans danced about the maypole, not really. Why did Alexander turn his back on India? Was Saint Francis really the deliverer of Ireland? We are given history's stories but they are open to broad interpretation. Human motivation is arbitrary. Most human records are based on lies, misbegotten loyalties and misinterpretation.

"But the shopping list . . . three potatoes, a flint knife, a bag of seed and a jewel of red coral . . . these are things we can believe in. From these items we can extrapolate historical events, stimuli . . . needs. Through lists of larder we can enter the lives of those who have gone before."

A quick rivulet of sweat ran around the dying man's left eye.

"You better lay back and rest, dad."

"No time for resting, Cornelius. I have to finish before the curtain comes down."

"You're not going to die today, dad."

"Maybe not but I will finish the greater part of my gift to you this day. That long journey we took through the Mississippi pinewoods was me looking for the strength to die. Rather than Death stalking me I was after him. I was looking for the courage to meet him face-to-face. That is being a man."

Herman was breathing harder than before. A drop of sweat fell from his chin.

"But that is not what I wanted to tell you, Cornelius. I need you to know something."

"What's that, dad?"

"Most children have it pretty easy. Rich or poor they have a mother, maybe a father, and food to eat. They sleep at night and play in the sunlight. They believe in fantastic things and read books or watch movies about cowboys and nurses. They play at adulthood through fighting and through love. They break the heart of anyone who loves them and never care a whit.

"But not you, Cornelius. You have stood by me and your mother too. You turned your back on childhood and we took your magnificent gifts. I have not thanked you enough. I gave you a good education. I would wager that you are one of the best-educated children your age in the entire world. Who else has read Plato and Aristotle, Vico and Confucius?

"You are well taught but you paid for that

education with your springtime. So now, here today, I release you. Live your life, Cornelius. Go out in the world and love women and drink deeply, pray to God if you so desire or worship the body and the mind, which I believe you will find are basically the same.

"I release you, Cornelius Jones, from the servitude of your childhood. You owe me nothing but to be happy and well. Feel no guilt, for the past does not exist and therefore cannot pass judgment.

"Take my books if you want them. Burn them if they offend you. Go to school or work on an oil rig. I do not care. Not because of a lack of love but because my love for you could never be greater. I confer upon you the greatest gift: freedom from the chains of your blood."

Cornelius was moved by his father's amnesty. He felt that Herman knew about Chapman Lorraine and offered absolution.

Freeing the fledgling from the confines of the nest, John Woman reflected years later. *But still the chick wondered if he could fly.*

10

The next morning Herman was crying in his bed.

"I hurt."

"Where, dad?"

"Everywhere."

Cornelius sat with him until Violet came. He wrote her a check for three hundred dollars asking her to spend a little time each day with Herman.

"You don't have to clean," Cornelius said, "just sit with him and give him water if he gets thirsty."

The doctor who came the next morning was Violet's niece's husband. He was a short, dark-haired Frenchman come to America to live with relatives while he studied heart medicine in Chicago. There he met Stella Breen, a mother's girl who always meant to come home.

"He's very sick," Dr. Artaud said. "But I see no reason to put him in the hospital. They'd only send him off to a nursing home. Keep him comfortable and give him the medicine I prescribe. He won't live very long."

The doctor was sad to see the effect his words had on Cornelius. At that time the boy still believed in the authority of professionals. He thought that there was some injection that might get his father sitting up and talking about the newly released book of slave narratives.

"What's wrong with him?" CC asked.

"It's his heart."

"But why didn't they say that at the hospital?"

"Sometimes," Dr. Artaud said, "American doctors ignore the signs of the poor."

Violet slumped into the stuffed chair and cried at the pronouncement.

They had sixteen thousand dollars in the bank and a few savings bonds in a safe-deposit box that his father kept. The first batch of drugs cost eight hundred and forty-seven dollars. Cornelius handed over the money without hesitation. He gave Violet a thousand dollars to keep coming over the next month, especially to be there in the evenings when he had to go to work.

That was Tuesday.

On Wednesday Herman rallied. He sat up and talked with his son about the history of thought.

"Thought and language are like breathing in and breathing out. They are inseparable and at the same time opposites. Together the two make up the mental image of possibilities in the material world. The closer they come to bringing this reality in line with our experience the more true our expressions of mind."

"So," Cornelius asked, "the advance of the history of thought is more like a science because it gets better all the time?"

"No," Herman said sadly. "Our use of thought and language has deteriorated over millennia. The Greeks saw the world more clearly than do we. The Aborigines of Australia saw themselves as part of a magnificent deified universe of which they were but a small part, while western man sees only a toy-box that was set there for him by some shadow being that has already forgotten humanity."

Every truth the old man sought ended in unconsciousness or death.

The next day Herman called for Cornelius and asked him to please turn on the lights. When Cornelius told him that the lights were already on he said, "Then the darkness is in my eyes."

The next day he began to shout about men crossing the river.

"There's no one there, dad," Cornelius said to him.

"I see them coming. I see them."

His blind eyes were wide with fear, his fingers jabbing the air.

"Over there! Over there!"

By Saturday the autodidact from the Mississippi Delta could only murmur his fears.

"Oh no," he'd cry from time to time, his arms moving about weakly, his flailing hands slowing now and then to fold tissues into tiny squares.

On Sunday Cornelius awoke to the sound of his father's labored breath. He came into the room to see Herman lying on his back, gasping for air. His eyes were wide, his mouth gaping.

Cornelius took the elegant hand and it gripped him like a vise.

With all of his being Cornelius concentrated on his father. The already slender Herman had lost twenty pounds. Cornelius could see the skull under the papery flesh of his father's face. He smelled of dead skin.

Father and son held on to each other until suddenly Herman hiccupped and stopped breathing. It took a few moments for Cornelius to realize what had happened. The room was absolutely silent. There was no salsa music playing, no rumble in the ground.

The young man held his dead father's hand and counted his own heartbeats, each pulse taking him that much farther away from his sire.

He couldn't cry, wasn't really sad. It was just that he could not imagine a world without Herman Jones.

Violet came into the room at four that afternoon.

"Oh my God he's dead," she said from the doorway.

Cornelius looked up at her and said, "Leave us alone please, Miss Breen. I'll make the calls later."

Over the next three days he didn't answer the phone or knocking at the door. He didn't eat or cry. He spent most of his time at his father's side, holding the stiff dead hand.

When the police entered the room, after getting the landlord to let them in, they found Cornelius reading aloud from Herodotus.

"What do you want?" he asked the officers.

"You have to come with us, Mr. Jones," one of them said.

He remembered thinking that this was the first time anyone had called him mister.

He was kept in a holding cell in the precinct where they brought him. Colette came to visit twice a day.

"They have to investigate the death because your father wasn't that old and because you kept the body so long," she'd said. "They're supposed to put you in juvenile detention but I asked for protective custody—this is much better."

"I see," Cornelius said. "Thank you."

"Can I do anything for you?"

"I'd like some books."

"What kind of books?"

"History."

On the day of his release Colette was there.

"What did they say?" Cornelius asked.

"Your father had serious heart disease. That's what killed him. Was he being treated for something like that?"

"Only by Violet's nephew-in-law. But by then it was too late," he said. "Maybe if somebody in the hospital had told us we could have taken him to a heart specialist. We could have given him heart medicine. But I guess it wasn't meant to be. I guess he was always going to die like that."

"I told them that you were gainfully employed and that you supported the household so they're letting you go back home," Colette said.

She drove him in her Honda. When they parked in front of his building she touched his shoulder.

"Harry and I are getting married in the spring," she said. "I'm pregnant with his child."

Again Cornelius's eyes played that trick on him. Colette seemed very far away. He felt that to talk to her he would have to shout and so he didn't say anything. He just nodded and opened the door.

"I still want to see you, CC," she said.

He nodded again, climbed out, then walked into the building without looking back.

11

He spent six thousand of the remaining fourteen thousand dollars on the funeral, which was held at the Baxter Chapel on Flatbush Avenue. The police released the body to Baxter's and Cornelius didn't want to move his father around any more than necessary.

"Bringing a man to his final resting place is a delicate dance," Herman had once said. "The men carry him down but it is the women dancing who make sure his passage is a gentle one."

There were no dancers at Herman's end, no minister because even though Herman believed in a deified universe he had no truck with organized religion. There were obituaries posted in the *Daily News* and the *New York Times*. The coffin was pine for the sake of Herman's Mississippi roots. Collingwood's *Idea of History* was nestled under his right arm. The mourners numbered three: France Bickman, Violet Breen and Cornelius, but four chairs were set out at the younger Jones's request.

The service was set to start at ten. They had fifty minutes to say their last good-byes. The three mourners, all of whom had arrived early, stood by the open coffin and communed with Herman's clay.

Cornelius had decided to dress him in a torn white T-shirt and a pair of faded blue jeans that he'd found in the bottom drawer of Herman's bureau. Both items were very, very old. They were folded into a brown paper bag that had *Greenwood, 1957* scrawled on the side. The mortician's makeup captured the faded character in his face.

The two passions of mankind are the ecstasy of childbirth and the inescapable tragedy of death, Herman had often said. *Without these elements human beings would be no more than automatons wandering blindly through a world of wonders.*

"We should get started, CC," France said.

The two men went to their chairs. Cornelius looked at the empty seat on the far left, then at the door in back of the small chapel. When he turned to look at the coffin Violet was standing there attempting to master her grief.

Short with sturdy legs, wearing a dark blue dress and a black shawl over her shoulders, she wore no makeup. Her hair was wrapped in a dark green fishnet of some sort. Violet's eyes filled with tears as she opened her mouth to speak, then closed it again to swallow. She repeated the attempt seven or eight times. Cornelius thought that this alone was proper tribute to his father.

The cleaning woman stared at Cornelius gathering her strength.

"Herman Jones was a learn-ed man," she said.

"Weak of body but strong in his mind. He had no formal education, which would hinder most people, but Herman loved knowledge, collected it. Even though he was smart and well-read that is not why I will miss him. He was a most generous man. Not like some moneybags who gives his tithe to charity, but like a river that flows through a country village. All you had to do was come on down and he would take you on a journey, clean off the dirt or feed you if you were hungry. There was more life in that little man than in most children."

Cornelius sat forward. He was surprised by the poetry in Violet, who he had known only as a cleaning woman and his father's willing audience.

". . . But his generosity is not why I will miss him either. What he gave he gave freely and so it had nothing to do with debt or sorrow. The reason I'm here is to say that Herman Jones was the only man I truly loved. A black man confined to a bed who never once spoke angry or coarse words in my presence, who recited poetry because we both loved it and who asked each morning about my family and my health." Violet broke down crying and France hurried to help her to her chair.

After helping Violet, Bickman went to stand before the pine box.

He began talking, CC noticed, without ceremony or dramatic tones.

"Herman taught me forgiveness and humility. He showed me through conversation and by example that my college degree was worth less than a Sunday ticket to the Arbuckle. And if I could give up some of my eighty-two years to have him back here today I would do it without a moment's hesitation."

"Oh," Violet said.

His hands clenched into fists, France Bickman returned to his seat.

Cornelius glanced at the empty chair. When France put a hand on his shoulder he stood up and stumbled. The only reason he didn't fall was that France steadied him. He experienced a powerful connection with the old man in the soft gray suit. Then Cornelius took the five steps to his father's coffin.

"When I was in the jailhouse," he began, "I didn't have any books at first, so I followed my father's example and considered the road that brought me to my present location. Dad was always telling me things like that. When I was little I'd get impatient with him but he never seemed to mind. And when I got older I didn't believe that I could ever be as smart as he was, or as kind. He made me the man he could never be and then set me free to be that man.

"I was there in the jailhouse, in Brooklyn, thinking about sitting next to my dad's body. Somewhere in my mind I knew that I should have called somebody, done something. But I couldn't leave his side. My father was dead. The world was going on outside and if I left I would be abandoning him, the only person in the world that mattered to me—except my mother . . . who hasn't made it here today.

"Then the police came and they took me into custody."

Violet started crying again. France lowered his head.

"I owe my father everything. Even when he was on his back, weak as a baby, delirious from the heart disease that the doctors never saw—he was the man I turned to for strength. Good-bye, dad. I will never willingly leave you."

They took a limo to the graveyard and threw clods of dirt onto the lowered coffin. Cornelius wondered if his mother had seen the notices or if someone from her family had seen them and passed the information on. The day was bright and the air cold. He had on a brown sports jacket and black trousers, clothes that had belonged to his father. He was shivering but did not register the cold.

He missed his mother as much as he did his father.

But even then The Plan was hatching in his mind.

When the burial was over the small group

walked back to the limousine. An unfamiliar white man was waiting there. He wore olive work pants and a plaid shirt. He was middle-aged and obviously feeling awkward. When the mourners got to the car he approached them.

Up close Cornelius could see that the man was brawny and broad. He had a bulging stomach and thick brown-and-gray hair.

"Cornelius," Violet said, "this is my husband, John."

A smile came immediately to Cornelius's lips. His shoulders and spirits both rose.

What a wonderful good-bye gift, he wrote to Posterity years later. *My father not only had a woman who loved him but he stole her away from a big strong Irishman.*

"Pleased to meet you, Mr. Breen."

"O'Connel," Violet said. "That's my married name."

Cornelius's smile turned into a grin. "You have an exceptional wife, sir," he said. "She made my father's last days tolerable."

Cornelius's friendliness put the dour man further off balance. He nodded, mumbling his thanks, then shaking the teenager's hand.

"Sorry for your loss," he said.

"Thank you. Thank you very much."

The limo dropped Cornelius and France off at the Arbuckle. There was a handwritten note on the front door saying that it would be closed in deference to the death of the projectionist.

France took Cornelius to the office behind the tiny concession stand. There he kept supplies for popcorn sales and the accounting ledgers.

"Sit," France Bickman said, "sit, sit, sit."

Cornelius experienced an unexpected feeling of calm. Years later he understood this peacefulness as an easement into freedom.

France sat down on the other side of the walnut dining table used as the desk for the tiny office. There were debit and credit ledgers, silent film catalogs and piles of letters from theater fans stacked up on both ends. France sat back taking Cornelius in with faded gray eyes. Bickman had never looked his age. There were few wrinkles on his spare face and he moved easily without stiffness, hesitations, or trouble bending over to pluck pennies from the floor. He'd always looked younger than Herman.

"I've known you my whole life, Mr. Bickman."

"France," the ticket-taker replied.

Bickman brought out a bottle and two plastic glasses from a wooden cabinet behind him. It was Wild Turkey, about halfway filled. He poured them both shots and Cornelius drank his down. The whiskey clutched at his throat but he kept it from coming up, then he held out his glass for more.

France obliged.

"Your father was a wonderful man, CC."

The boy nodded and chugged down the second drink.

While he was refilling the glass France said, "He wasn't only my friend and mentor . . . he also saved my ass."

"How's that, Mr., um, France?"

"My three girls turned college-age while my wife was dying. Matilda's cancer ate up our savings. When she was gone I had to come to work here because I didn't have enough money to keep up the payments on the loans for tuition. That's when I got the bright idea to skim money off of the ticket sales to help keep me from going down the toilet. I didn't know that part of the checks and balances that the original owners put in place was that the projectionist would count heads every night. It wasn't an exact number but close enough for your dad to tell that I was guilty as hell.

"One night after closing Herman told me he knew I was a thief. He had my butt in a sling; could have sent me and my daughters to hell. But after I explained my predicament he said that he would do the same thing if he had a child that needed to be looked after."

"So he let you get away with it?" Cornelius felt a tingling numbness in his lips as he spoke.

"For all these years. I was over fifty thousand dollars in debt for my wife's medical bills and college was two hundred thousand—more. But what I didn't tell Herman was that, after he let me go, for every dollar I took I set one aside for him."

"You did?" Cornelius said, sipping his whiskey. "Did you ever tell him?"

"When he and your mother broke up I told him. He accepted it because he wanted you to have a good start in the world after he was gone."

"So how much is it, Mr. Bickman?" Cornelius heard himself ask. The whiskey had split him into two distinct people: the one who said things and the other who listened. France swiveled around in his chair and pulled out a small brown leather suitcase that he set on the table between them. He slid the case across the table and gestured for Cornelius to open it up.

There were neat stacks of used bills inside. Mostly tens and twenties in small packs held together by knotted string.

"One hundred and seventy-three thousand dollars," France said. "All of it in three cases like this one. The other two are in the closet there behind you. There's a false door back there. Nobody knows about it but me."

Cornelius's mind went to the dead man in the closet above them. He wondered if every building in New York held as many hidden crimes as did the Arbuckle.

"And it's all mine?" he asked.

"Yes sir. You bet. This is my debt to your father. He risked his own freedom for my daughters' lives. The least I can do is pay it back a little."

"That must have been what he meant by my gift," CC heard himself say. "He said that after he was gone he was going to give me something to help me on my way."

France Bickman nodded.

After they finished the bottle France left. Cornelius told him he'd lock up before going home, but the boy didn't leave the Arbuckle that night.

He walked down the center aisle of the theater looking at the worn leather seats and threadbare carpeting. The nylon screen had been sewn in half a dozen places and was in serious need of a cleaning. The light fixtures above the projection room hadn't been dusted in a dozen years.

Cornelius went to the projection room and queued up a Buster Keaton film that the theater owned, *The General*. Then he went down to the front row to watch. He hadn't sat in the auditorium since before Herman's intestinal operation. When the film was over he played a compilation of Buster Keaton shorts.

Sometime in the middle of the night Cornelius awoke from a dream about somebody crying. He was sprawled out there on the carpet in front of the wide, bright, blank screen.

12

Cornelius couldn't imagine sleeping under the roof where his father died, so instead he moved into a cheap motel called The Starlight. The Arbuckle had a deal there for out-of-town visitors who came in for the few festivals the theater hosted.

CC spent the next week reading death notices from his birth year. The Summers family—mother, father and newborn son Anthony—had died in a car crash outside Philadelphia.

Dead-alive Anthony Summers applied for a social security number at the age of eighteen. He'd attended school in Queens then CCNY for one semester. Tony's essays, forged grades and test scores (taken after graduation) were good enough for a transfer to Yale.

At the end of his junior year Tony had his first name legally changed to John, after Violet's cuckold husband, and his last name to Woman in homage to Detective Margolis making him say, "I am your woman."

He kept using the name Anthony Summers until after entering graduate school at Harvard.

He was a new man in a new world ready to live life freely and without consequence.

Part One

Professor Woman

1

Far out in the high desert, fifty miles or so from Phoenix, stands a very large and circular five-story structure, the walls of which are plated with tile-like strips of white marble and broad panes of dark blue glass; its round, domed, and transparent roof is fashioned from thick, green-tinted, unbreakable polymer. This is Prometheus Hall, the main academic building of the New University of the Southwest.

There are twelve equally spaced double doors around Prometheus; opposite pairs of these doors open onto hallways that cut diagonally across the first floor of the building. Each of these pathways is paved with tiles of one of six colors: the three primary hues and their secondary complements. The tiled paths meet in and cross the Great Rotunda at the center of the huge building. This central chamber is the hollow heart of the desert university: where students, faculty, staff and visitors are welcome to stop and sit on one of eighty-six white marble benches—to read, contemplate or discuss, or merely to rest.

The four upper floors each consist of twelve equally sized pie-shaped classrooms. These forty-eight lecture halls are only eleven feet wide at the entrance but broaden to four times that width at the blue glass windows that look out over the Arizona desert.

Professor John Woman arrived at Prometheus fifteen minutes before one o'clock on the first Tuesday in September. He entered the building through Door Eleven, progressed down North Violet Lane to the periphery of the Great Rotunda where he ascended the zigzagging north stairwell to the fifth floor. He stopped, leaning his back against the triple-barred chrome rail overlooking the rotunda. There he watched as students went through the broad red-rimmed doorway of Lecture Hall Two.

The young associate professor stood exactly six feet tall with thick, curly brown hair; medium-brown skin; and generous, friendly features. Despite his slender build he gave the impression of quiet physical strength.

Professor Woman studied the young people entering his classroom. Some carried briefcases while others lugged big purses, shoulder bags, and backpacks. Three students carried nothing at all, just walked through the door to sit and listen, maybe trying to figure out whether or not to drop John's challenging *INTRODUCTION TO DECONSTRUCTIONIST HISTORICAL DEVICES.* If they weren't history majors, they might switch to a pottery class or Felton Malreaux's *POETRY*

APPRECIATION. History majors might transfer to Gregory Tracer's *HISTORY OF THE CIVIL WAR* or Annette Eubanks's *FEMINIST OR REVISIONIST HISTORY*?

John checked his father's Timex wristwatch at one minute to one. He took a deep breath and strode toward Lecture Hall Two feeling both excitement and confidence.

He stopped at the doorway, blocked by a willowy young woman with fairly short auburn hair. Motionless at the threshold she seemed to be lost, as if maybe this was the wrong class. Her flimsy gold jacket was more like a shirt with sleeves that didn't quite achieve the wrists. Likewise the legs of her turquoise-colored trousers hovered a few inches above the ankles. She wore straw sandals and the bag slung across her shoulder was white Naugahyde marked by a solitary blue ink spot, a few abrasions and a black skid-mark that ran along the bottom.

The young woman was tall but John was taller. Over her shoulder he could see the twenty or so students who had staked out the first three rows of the classroom that could have easily seated two hundred.

"Excuse me," John said.

The young woman gasped and turned. While not pretty, she was, at least to his eye, handsome in the extreme. With butterscotch skin, a strong jaw and tawny eyes the crystalline hue of topaz marbles; she had the long fingers of a pianist. The eyes slanted up just a bit. Her thick hair was crinkled.

"Sorry," she said taking half a step to the side. "You trying to get in?"

"Yes I am," John said with a smile.

"You're taking this class too?"

He shrugged, tilting his head to the side. It was no surprise the undergraduate hadn't identified him as a professor. He was only a few years past thirty. His Asian-cut, soft-milled black cotton jacket and loose coal gray trousers were not professorial—neither was his slightly faded scarlet T-shirt.

"I heard it was hard," the young woman said, anxiety eeling its way across her lips.

"New ideas seem hard at first," he said, "but challenge is why we're here."

With that John crossed the red doorsill and went to the semi-transparent emerald green polymer lectern at the front of the class. Any talking that had been going on petered out and, a few seconds later, the uncertain young woman made her way to a seat in the third row.

Professor Woman waited for the last gangly student to be seated before he started talking.

"I am Associate Professor John Woman," he announced, "and this class is Introduction to Deconstructionist Historical Devices."

A hand went up in the second row.

"You will be able to ask questions in a few minutes," he said and the hand went down. "But first I'd like to explain what will happen, what you might learn and what you cannot learn, in this seminar.

"It is my position that history is an unquestionable certainty, the absolute outcome of an incontrovertible string of ontological events. It, history, reaches all the way back to the origin of the race and beyond through the chaotic unfolding of existence. In our history, our one indisputable history, are contained assassinations, inspiration, instinctual urges, friendships, conflicts, the multiplicities of gravity and material, black holes and supernovas. Our bodies are formed from the fabric of the universe and so consequently there is a touch of the divine in each of us. You and I are part and parcel of history, slaves of history, playing out our willing and unwilling roles—and so it has been for every living being, every species on earth and, quite possibly, life elsewhere.

"Accepting, for a moment, this position as accurate it is easy to see that the true understanding of history, or any major aspect thereof, requires knowledge that is currently beyond human ken. We are like the blind prophets guessing at the nature of an elephant— only the elephant is in another room, situated on the opposite side of the globe, while we still believe the world is flat."

John stopped for a moment. He had not planned this lecture. He hardly ever worked from notes or predetermined arguments.

Our lives are just one long series of ad hoc debates, Herman Jones used to say. *In the end everybody loses the argument.*

"We cannot comprehend the vastness that is history," the man called Woman continued. "Our capacity for knowledge is mortal even if our bodies are deified. We are incapable of knowing with certainty what has happened while at the same time we are unable to stop ourselves from wondering why we are here and from whence we have come. This is the stimulus, the incentive for the study of and the belief in history.

"We, you and I, have been propelled to this moment by nothing less than the conspiracy of eternity. The attempt to understand this scheme is the object of our study like a carrot is the goal of the work-weary mule dragging the plow and imagining something sweet.

"Those of us who crave the carrot of historical knowledge must be aware that we will never achieve this goal but that in our wake we will create something beautiful, fertile and, quite possibly, terrible. We must, as scholars of an impossible study, realize that while history is definite, the human investigation of the past can only be art, the one truly deconstructionist art—because the only way to capture the essence of history is to make it up."

John stopped at that point not so much for dramatic effect as a natural pause in this improvised discourse.

"My first lecture is often brief. Later on we may go overtime. That said, are there any questions so far?"

Five or six hands went up. John studied the faces of his students. They seemed engaged.

"When you speak," he said, "I'd like you to give us your name and any other information you deem pertinent. In this way I'll get to know you and you will further identify yourself with your query.

"Yes," he said, pointing. "The woman in the red blouse."

"Star Limner," said a twentysomething white woman whose black hair was heavy and damp from a recent shower. She sat in the second row on John's right. "Second-year poli-sci major."

"What's your question, Ms. Limner?"

"Excuse me, Professor Woman, but it sounds like you're saying that nothing has ever happened in the past and that we can't believe anything we study."

"Yeah," a brutish young man from the third row chimed in.

"And your name is?" John asked the heavy-muscled student who was clad in overalls and a black-and-white-check T-shirt.

"Pete."

"Pete what?"

"Tackie."

Pete Tackie was also white with straight brown hair that came down to his ears. He wasn't fat but rather beefy with small eyes and a frown that John imagined never relaxed, even in sleep.

"And what would you like us to know about you, Mr. Tackie?"

"I wasn't askin' a question," the dour young man complained.

"I asked," John said, "for anyone speaking to give us their name and anything else we should know."

Pete Tackie rubbed his face with broad, strong fingers.

"I play rugby," he said. "I came here from Dearborn."

"Michigan?"

"Yeah."

Smiling, the young associate professor held Pete Tackie's gaze for a few seconds. He had learned how to keep order by sticking to the promises and requests he made.

"No to the first part of your question, Ms. Limner," John said, still looking at the rugby player. Then he turned to her. "Quite the opposite—everything has happened. This much is apparent. So you're right, I'm saying you cannot believe anything you study because it is, necessarily, incomplete speculation . . . albeit, sometimes quite convincing speculation."

"But how can that be?" another young woman asked. When John turned toward her she shrugged and said, "Beth Weiner from Santa Monica, California. I haven't declared a major yet but it'll probably be business or maybe economics."

"You were saying, Ms. Weiner?" John asked.

"We know that there was a Civil War, that all those people died."

"Excuse me, but why was that war fought?"

"Over slavery," a student in the front row said. This was the only male student who was formally dressed. He wore a blue blazer, tan slacks and a white dress shirt. The only thing missing, John thought, was a tie. His hair was black and his eyes might have been green.

The young man smiled and said, "Jack Burns. I'm from right up the highway in Phoenix."

"So, Mr. Burns," John said. "You don't subscribe to the notion that the war was waged over a dis-agreement concerning economic questions and the southern states' sovereign right of secession?"

"Well," a sweatshirted black student said. "Micah Short, here. Maybe the war had other causes, but they seceded because Lincoln was going to free the slaves."

"But he said that he wouldn't demand freedom

for the slaves," the professor argued, "only that new states could not be slaveholders."

"But they thought he would."

"I see," the professor said doubtfully; "they thought . . . Let me ask you this. Was there a Holocaust in which six million Jews were exterminated?"

Voices sprouted among the class without identification and maybe, John thought, without volition.

"Yes."

"Of course."

"Sure there was."

"Well maybe not all that many," one dark-haired girl said.

"And who are you?" John asked gently.

"Tamala Marman. I want to be a history major."

"What do you mean?" a girl in the second row challenged. She was Asian, possibly Japanese. "We know the number. The records have been counted."

John thought of asking her name but didn't want to slow the interaction.

"It was a big war," Tamala Marman argued. "A lot of people got away. And people overreact when they see horrible things. Somebody could say that they saw a thousand bodies when really there were only a couple of hundred."

"Only a couple of hundred?" Pete Tackie shouted. "What are you? A Nazi?"

"I'm just talking about the numbers. Maybe

there were only three million dead. It's possible. That's all I'm saying."

"No," said a male student with a deep commanding voice. "There were more than six million killed. They have the names and Nazi records. The families have remembered them."

Following this claim silence filled the room.

"And you are?" John asked the handsome young man in the center seat of the first row.

"Justin Brown." He had a tanned complexion and steady gray eyes. "I'm a chem major, senior. This is an elective course for me."

"And so," Professor John Woman said after an appreciative silence, "we have learned from Justin Brown that the Holocaust really did occur and that the number, approximately six million, is an accurate count."

One or two heads nodded. Every eye in the room was on John.

"What proof has he put forth?"

"The proof is in—" Justin Brown began.

"Please, Mr. Brown, allow some of the other students to reply."

"Sandra Levy," a walnut-haired woman chimed in, "transfer from BU. We believe him because he said it with conviction and passion."

"That is correct," John allowed.

"But what I say is true," the chem major complained.

"Of course it is, Justin. Of course. It's true

on many levels. You know because of your reading of books, Allied reports, and the trials at Nuremburg. You know because of the state of Israel and its commitment to Jewish peoples around the world. But . . .” John Woman paused and gazed around the classroom. Through the bank of tinted windows that made the outer wall he could see the desert under cloudless skies. “But does that make it a true history or simply something that many of us believe? I say this to you not because I want to negate your beliefs. Really the opposite is true. I’m teaching this course because history is being rewritten, reenvisioned and reedited every day, every hour of every day. There are people out there who would like to tell you that there was no Holocaust whatsoever. They write books, give speeches, make arguments that sway especially those who have no passion for the subject. Deconstructionist history is not a spurious branch of study. It is what every enemy of everything you believe practices day and night. Who killed the two million Cambodians and the Argentine Aborigines? Who was responsible for the slaughter of the Hutu and Tutsi, Congolese and Somali? Who profited from the slave routes to the Caribbean, North and South America?”

“Those are things we don’t know,” Justin Brown said with disgust in his voice. “It’s not the same as Nazi Germany.”

A few mutterings agreed.

"I know the names of the men who assassinated Julius Caesar but I cannot know the companies, extant today, that profited from four centuries of slavery?"

The class went silent again. Even Justin Brown seemed a little daunted.

"The sugar companies," Woman said. "The rum distillers, shipping lines and banks that underwrote thousands of slaving expeditions; the plantation masters, many of whose children today are wealthy landowners.

"You can't have it both ways, Mr. Brown. You can't pick and choose your way through history taking what you want to believe and relegating the rest to the limbo of ignorance. You must take a stand, commit yourself to the truth, while understanding that the ground beneath your feet is nothing more than shifting sand.

"One day America may be vilified in the annals of history. We may be seen as an aggressive imperialist nation bent upon the subjugation and domination of the rest of the globe. Our capitalism may be as reviled as Hitler's anarchy. And who are we to say which version will make it into the history books, into futuristic vid-classes and, most dangerous of all, into the language we speak?

"Who remembers that the Vandals were a people before they became an evil noun?"

"So you don't believe that there was a Civil War or a Holocaust?" Justin Brown asked.

"Belief, my friend, is the right word," John Woman said. "History is only, is always little more than an innuendo, a suggestion that we decide to believe, or not. Of course you are right about the list of the dead read aloud day and night in Jerusalem. But in positing one thing you call another into question. Where is the list for the millions of Armenians slaughtered, the Cambodians, Nicaraguans or Vietnamese? If their names are not registered then did they really suffer and die? These questions are the ones we shall address in this class. Questions, I might add, that have no answers, no complete and certainly no permanent answers. We shall fail because history is that unsteady ground I spoke of. It is not a rigid truth but an ever-changing reality. If it were an ironclad actuality then we would be able to learn from it. But all we can do is learn about its edges, insinuations and negative spaces."

Some of the better students wrote down this last quote.

"But, Professor," the young woman he met at the door said.

"Yes?"

"Carlinda Elmsford," she said. "I'm a second-year student and this is my third school."

"Yes, Miss Elmsford." John, for some reason, didn't use the term *Ms.* for her.

"The name of the class refers to historical devices," Carlinda said. "That would indicate you believe there are tools we could use to unlock the secrets of history."

The question put the professor off balance. He was surprised, not only by the sophistication and insight of the query, but also by the gracelessly elegant student who, he now realized, he'd been wrong about. Because of her indecision at the doorway he assumed that she was unfocused, flighty. He dismissed her potential and now had to fight down the desire to start a completely new lecture on the rigor that any investigators have to go through to rid their minds of prejudices and cultural assumptions.

With Winch and Wittgenstein on the tip of his tongue he said, "You are correct. But the devices we shall use are not mechanical or theoretical. *We* will be the tools. Our minds and hearts, keen and necessarily faulty insights will, in this seminar, deconstruct the presumptions of historical thinking and, so doing, will partially free us from the knee-jerk, rote expectations that litter the field."

"How?" Carlinda Elmsford asked.

"That's the question I'll be asking at every class and office hour," John said. "It will be the inquiry you make of each other and of the mirror in the morning when you are brushing your teeth."

John wanted to go on, to tell his students

that the certainty of mortality and true creative thinking were one and the same. He would have continued but noticed a movement to his right. Glancing toward the door he saw Theron James, dean of the social sciences department.

"But," he said, addressing the class, "we will have more than enough time for that. Right now I'd like you to check out two books that I have reserved for you in the library—*The Idea of a Social Science and Its Relation to Philosophy*, by Peter Winch, and *Culture and Value*, culled from Wittgenstein and translated by Winch."

John waited while the students wrote down the information or entered it on their electronic devices.

"That's all for today," he said. "I'll see you Thursday when we start in earnest."

The students filed out through the red-rimmed doorway passing between the smiling dean and the history professor.

Pete Tackie, Star Limner, John said to himself. This was his technique for remembering names quickly. *Justin Brown, Beth Weiner*.

Carlinda Elmsford stopped at the door again, this time wondering, John surmised, if she should leave. She had more questions for him; he could see that in her strained expression. She almost lurched toward him but then moved through the doorway, maladroitly brushing against the jamb with her shoulder.

She was, it seemed, the last student to leave.

John wondered why her question had stirred him. He allowed a few seconds to consider his odd response, then looked up at Dean James.

"Theron."

Instead of replying the dean made a gesture with his head. John looked behind and saw the young student, waiting for him to notice her.

"Yes? Tamala isn't it?"

"I didn't mean that I thought that there was no Holocaust, Professor Woman," Tamala said without preamble. "I was only trying to show how I understood your lecture."

She wore a lemon yellow sundress that contrasted perfectly with her light brown skin. Her eyes were a darker shade of brown and her features both delicate and classic—*almost Persian,* John thought, *but probably not from Iran.*

"Absolutely, Ms. Marman. You were trying to get at the heart of the argument. I appreciate that—very much."

"It just seemed like people were mad at me," she went on, "that they thought I was being anti-Semitic . . ."

"When," the professor said, helping her sentence along, "you were actually underscoring the point I was trying to make."

She smiled and breathed in deeply.

"You're from Turkey?" John asked.

"How did you know?" She was surprised. "Yes, I mean, my father's from there. But I was born and raised in Maryland."

"You're going to be a valuable asset in our class, Ms. Marman. You will help me show the class, over the next semester, how history is our intellectual culture. It passes through us, creating and abandoning us at the same time."

John noticed the swelling of her chest and a slight shift of her hips as he spoke.

"But I have to go," he added. "If you want to talk more about it come to my office any Tuesday or Thursday, four to six. That is, except today. I like my lectures to simmer after the first class."

"Thank you, Professor," Tamala said, looking down shyly; then she moved quickly past the dean and out the door.

Theron approached the lectern smiling.

"That was magnificent," he said.

They clasped hands and held each other's gaze a moment.

Dean James was the shorter by an inch or so but his shoulders were broad; his demeanor was more that of a car salesman than a scholar. His gray suit was of a business cut. There was a scar under the left eye making John suspect that Theron had a rough life before entering the halls of academe.

But, John advised himself, *it might just be a trophy from a tough game of rugby at Oxford.*

"Thank you, Theron."

"You know they argued against us hiring you," the dean said. "I was warned that you weren't old enough, didn't have the experience. Professors across the line tried to convince me that your brand of study would undermine the history department. But I knew you would engage the students in a way that no other professor could."

"I do love it," Woman said. "Students are ready for deeper thinking than they know. My job is to tease it out of them."

"Teaching them," Theron added, "that they will be the ones making history rather than just becoming aggrandized, half-blind scribes."

As always John was impressed by the dean's keen perceptions. He thought of an essay he'd never write—"The Subtlety of Car Salesmen."

"You just passing by handing out compliments, Theron?"

That familiar huckster smile crossed the shepherd scholar's lips.

"You haven't published since coming here," he said. "It's only been two years but two can turn into ten before you know it."

"Recently I've come up with an idea about academia and car salesmen," John said. "Maybe that will be my first."

"The history department review committee will

be meeting soon," Dean James posited, his smile gone.

"And I'm at the head of the list," John said.

"They'll want to hear about the paper you've already proposed."

2

After the dean left John sat in Justin Brown's half-desk chair. Leaning back, gazing at the green lectern, he assessed the lecture, wondering what it was the students had learned.

No one can know what is in another person's heart, Herman Jones said. This was not a memory per se, but was as if John's father was somehow embedded in the emptiness of the classroom, there in spirit as a hopeless optimist might opine.

John put this thought aside because of Theron James's warnings: *you haven't published* and *the history department review committee will be meeting.*

Then there was Carlinda Elmsford. She was . . . unexpected. A student who easily engaged with ideas, so intent that the class felt threatening to her . . .

. . . *to her soul,* phantom Herman Jones said, completing the thought.

John sighed in his chair. He reacted similarly to the beginning of every semester. The first class was where he was the most lucid, certain and self-confident; but directly afterward he felt fragmented, unable to keep his mind on any one subject for long. He usually conjured his father at these times, though not so much as to actually hear a voice . . . And he'd reexperience delivering the third blow to Chapman Lorraine's skull. That solitary act defied John's deconstructionist prowess. Once again he was Cornelius Jones. Once again he was vulnerable, culpable . . . identifiable.

The exultation of life in the university was stalked by guilt, a dogged predator snapping at the heels of a noble elk—and John stood between the two . . .

You were a boy, Herman said without sound or substance. *He was a man and should have shown restraint.*

Twenty minutes later he stood up from the half-desk, walked toward the red outline and blundered out of the empty room into the sheltered hall, where students, and a professor or two, walked with purpose in the long passageway that circumnavigated the open inner wall.

He was thinking about Herman, about how his father should have been there instead. In that hermeneutical instant he felt his father's smile.

What you have done is good, the elder said, momentarily free from the grave, *but not yet (at the level of) Thucydides—not yet a man of his age documenting the world while participating in its unfolding.*

John stopped there at the railing, in the middle of the great architectural achievement of NUSW. The ghost of his father had never spoken to him before. Herman Jones was a mild man who would not, even as a spirit, haunt anyone. He was too gentle and considerate to bring fear, pain or disorientation to the soul of another.

"I'm exhorting him," John whispered. "No, I am calling on him because there is a danger somewhere."

He looked down from the high floor of the hollow structure. Green light filtered through the roof, tinting the rotunda and the people laughing, eating and reading on the alabaster benches below. He could hear voices but an acoustic trick garbled the words, making them turn in on themselves so that although they still contained humanity, the meaning was stripped away.

And so language, sweet language, Herman had said years before, *stays alive. All the so-called dead tongues survive in the words extant today. That is just another example of how you cannot know history but at the same time you will not escape it.*

John wasn't resisting his father's presence now. He was exhausted from the desert heat, the self-imposed challenge of teaching without notes and the threat contained in the words of Theron James . . .

"Professor Woman?"

"Yes?" he said, turning.

It was a young woman in a dark red dress that was formfitting at the bodice but which flared out on its way down to her knees. It was an old-fashioned outfit reminiscent of the fifties TV shows John sometimes watched on late night.

She was a bright brown girl with almond-shaped dark eyes. The young professor did not know her.

"I looked up your class schedule and it said that Decon met in Hall Thirty-Six," she said, her tone imparting an apology. "I was waiting outside but when the class was over it wasn't yours at all."

"I taught Decon, as you call it, in Thirty-Six my first two years," John said.

"I guess they didn't enter the new number in the semester schedule," she said. And then, "I'm Tyne, Tyne Oliver."

"And why were you looking for me, Ms. Oliver?"

"Oh," she replied lifting her shoulders to express the recognition of her oversight, "sorry. President Luckfeld."

John raised his eyebrows and turned his left palm up. He was enjoying the dysfunction of the conversation: her speaking in fragments and his resorting to sign language.

"He wants to see you," she added.

"President Luckfeld does?"

"Yes."

"When?"

"Right after your class," Tyne replied. "I got there five minutes before it was supposed to be through but then it wasn't you. Dean James saw me and asked why I looked so confused."

"And he sent you to room two."

Tyne Oliver smiled and nodded.

Herman Jones receded into the ether. John was aware of him as he was of the tinted sunlight and the television shows that were brought to mind by the cut of Tyne Oliver's dress.

Walking in the desert sun Tyne talked and talked.

She was from Montclair, New Jersey, but hated the winter and came out west for school. That was two years ago. She hadn't been back home since. Her father died in the first week of her freshman year and though she thought she should go to the funeral she didn't.

". . . He wasn't my real father," she explained. "I didn't know my biological dad and Harold, my stepfather, never adopted me or my brother, and it was my first week at school. Harold didn't have life insurance and all my mom owned was the house so she couldn't pay for me flying out. My grandfather left a college fund for me and Toby, my brother, and mom said that I'd have to use some of that to come back home. But it was way expensive and Harold wasn't my father and anyway it was only the first week of school and I'd miss so much that I finally didn't come but sent flowers instead."

John listened closely thinking about the

concept of jabber: trillions of words squandered in air containing the emotional, organizational and social backgrounds of any and all eras.

"Here we are," Tyne said.

The administrative offices of NUSW were opposite in many ways to the blue-and-white classroom building. The dun-colored bungalows were herded together in a compound surrounded by high adobe walls painted salmon pink. The office complex was accessible by only one gate, which was watched over by round-the-clock security guards. "Hi, Mr. Gustav," Tyne said through a microphone mounted on the outside of the gate.

The guard, John knew, sat in a small air-conditioned booth watching the entrance through the iron bars of the green gate and on a bank of monitors that gave him a three-hundred-sixty-degree view around the fortress.

"Tyne, Professor Woman," the sixtysomething white-mustachioed guardian said over an electronic speaker.

John imagined Mr. Gustav looking down at his monitors, then, when he was assured that there was no mischief afoot, he hit a button and the electronically controlled gate rolled noisily aside.

Tyne bounded in followed by the young professor. They each nodded at the guardian. John would have stopped to talk with Lawrence Gustav if he were unaccompanied. He liked talking, seeing each person as a historical repository that leaked secrets like so many corroded gas tanks.

The bungalows, laid out like a country village, were uniform single-story structures except for the president's office. This two-story building was reddish brown and most resembled the shape of a naturally formed rectangular desert stone. It seemed to lean to the left and the windows were at an odd angle to the ground. The crenellated plaster walls were uneven with grooves and ridges like actual stone. The doorway was unobstructed whenever John had been there. He wondered if there was a door at all.

There might not be, he thought, knowing that NUSW was founded and run by members of the secretive Platinum Path, a self-described new age religion founded by the guru of *meta-psychic-determinism*—Service Tellman. The Platinum Path subscribed to Tellman's theory that the manifestation of the universal unconscious could be controlled by certain strong-minded individuals working in concert. Only these individuals, Tellman taught, could guide the world to its full potential, that it was the destiny of such men and women to deliver the world from the suicidal *Iron Path* that it had been on ever since the Industrial Revolution.

Service Tellman died seven years before, leaving a group called The Dozen to keep the dream on course. The university president, Colin Luckfeld, was suspected to be a member of this committee; at least that was what John had read in a *Wall Street Journal* exposé. NUSW was Tellman's pet project. Construction was completed eleven years before. And, considering the philosophical proclivities of the Platinum Path, John thought that there might be a wall, an iron gate and an armed guard but still no door barring entry once you'd made it to the inner circle. Such a design would be an apt totem of the elite cult.

"Go right on in, Professor Woman," the chatty, anachronistically clad Tyne Oliver said. "He's upstairs."

"Don't you work here?"

"No, sir, I'm in the bursar's office this semester. President Luckfeld's assistant called me because I'm a floater until my senior year. Floaters always do most of the foot-errands."

John smiled. Tyne took this expression as a dismissal and left, walking down the cobblestone lane laid between the grassy lawns and various flowering bushes that stood out in front of the bungalows. The office facility had its own gardener but John had forgotten, or maybe he'd never known, the groundskeeper's name.

John stood outside the possibly doorless

doorway enjoying the specific language of floaters and foot-errands while feeling the desert sun's heat filter through his dark clothes. He took in three breaths before he was prepared to enter the president's lair.

3

The large room through the open door was a study in blues. The floor had wall-to-wall indigo carpeting. Its six walls were cerulean; upon each wall hung a solitary oil painting depicting some oceangoing sailing ship forging its way across shoreless seas. The eighteen-foot-high ceiling was almost white—like a cloud-filled sky with only hints of a blue beyond.

Straight ahead, maybe twenty feet past the door, was a big metal desk painted crayon blue. Behind the improbable office furniture sat a bronze-colored woman who was easily twice John's age. She wore a dark blue jacket and a bright orange silk blouse. The clothes looked bulky on her lean frame and her smile communicated neither humor nor warmth.

Her hair had already turned white and was now verging on blue, maybe in sympathy, John thought, with the color scheme of her workplace.

"Professor Woman," she said, distaste for the designation on her lips.

"Ms. Whitman."

"Mrs. Whitman," she corrected.

"Mrs. Whitman."

Behind Bernice Whitman were three evenly

spaced entrances to hallways; the outer two at one-hundred-forty-degree angles to the central door. John was always surprised by the magnitude of the president's complex. From outside the building seemed modest despite its extra floor.

"He's waiting for you," Mrs. Whitman said. "You're late."

"You should have somebody enter the right classroom number in the database," John said, unable to ignore the bait in her words. "You're lucky Ms. Oliver found me."

Whitman grunted and John turned to his left where there was a blue-washed wooden ladder that led to the floor above.

"You can take the elevator or the stairs," Mrs. Whitman offered.

But John was already climbing up through the hole in the almost completely white sky.

President Luckfeld's office was not the size of the entire first floor but it was still the largest room that John had ever been in that wasn't a hall, an auditorium or some other public space. The floor was paneled oak, the hall dominated by floor-to-ceiling windows interspersed with white walls sporting oil paintings of modern-day folks in pedestrian poses and garb.

There were open areas in the great chamber that approximated wall-less rooms. To the left were two yellow sofas that faced each other over a bloodred carpet. Behind one of the sofas was a large wooden bookcase. A little farther on, to the right, stood a two-foot-high platform containing an entire kitchen of blond pine and glistening chrome.

On the other side of the chamber, opposite the blue-washed ladder entrance, was a long table behind which sat the president. At his back was a seemingly solid glass wall that led out onto a deck that was twice again the size of the office.

"John!" the president called.

"Yes, sir."

"Come in, come in."

John walked toward Colin Luckfeld counting the steps as he went. By the time he reached the teak table he'd gotten to seventy-two.

The unorthodox desk was a small wonder in the amazing room. It was nineteen feet long and five wide, a single plank cut from the heart of what must have been a magnificent tree.

When John reached the table Luckfeld stood up. He was tall and hale with sun-burnished skin and brown hair that was like a tapered mane. In his fifties, the president had eyes that were olive green, sometimes tending toward brown; his hands were strong with long fingers and perfectly manicured nails. He wore a medium-brown two-piece suit and a black T-shirt.

"Thank you for coming, John," he greeted him.

Everyone said Luckfeld's eyes expressed unspoken knowledge. This was his advantage.

But the gaze held no power over John—he felt safe behind an exhaustive facade that had taken him nearly half a lifetime to create.

"Sorry I'm late, Colin."

"Mrs. Whitman says that the faculty database wasn't properly updated."

John could see the earbud in Luckfeld's left ear. The dour assistant had called while John was counting steps.

"Would you like something to drink?" the president offered.

"Water if you have it."

"Certainly. Why don't you come around and sit here next to me."

Seating in the president's office was one of the many ritualistic elements Luckfeld employed. Most faculty members were directed to sit on hard wooden chairs across the table from the president. He had a seemingly endless number of these chairs which were always set out before his guests arrived.

A few feet behind the big yellowy table sat a camel-colored leather sofa and a matching chair. If Luckfeld asked you to come around and sit on one of these, it was said, he was extremely happy with you and your work.

John counted eleven paces around the table to his host.

"Sit," Colin Luckfeld said, gesturing at the sofa.

John sat at the window end. The president sat opposite him.

John wondered what the superstition would be about Luckfeld sitting next to his guest on the couch rather than across from him on the matching chair.

"There's a wooden chest behind you," the president said. "I'll have one too." Professor Woman lifted up the lid and brought out two label-less plastic containers. He leaned over to hand his boss one of these.

"You're looking well," Luckfeld said. "Nice summer?"

"I stayed in faculty housing and caught up on my reading."

"No vacation?" Colin asked as he cracked the seal of the water bottle.

"Life is a holiday if you enjoy the work."

Luckfeld brought his left thigh onto the cushion and leaned back against the plush bolster arm. This posture made him seem somewhat boyish— very un-presidential. In Professor Woman's mind this was simply another tactic employed by the high official of the worldwide cult.

"You enjoy history that much?" Luckfeld asked.

"More."

Luckfeld brought the pad of his left thumb to press lightly on the indentation under his lower lip and stared with those knowing eyes.

John allowed the gaze to continue at least half a minute before saying, "Those portraits along the walls."

"Yes?"

"I've always wondered about them."

Luckfeld's eyes relaxed. "Great men and women caught in everyday poses. The artist worked from snapshots taken at some point in the subjects' past. You have a captain of industry standing over a barbecue; a woman who is the confidante of monarchs and prime ministers screaming on a roller coaster at Coney Island. My favorite is the one of a man who later in life became the leader of a revolution changing the diapers on his firstborn daughter. I find them humbling and revelatory."

"Revealing what?"

"Humanity," Luckfeld said. "The fragility of who and what we are."

"There's nothing more telling than a man's mismatched buttons and a pretty woman's slight limp," John intoned.

"Where's that from?"

"Something my father once said."

"Sounds like a wise man."

"He was." John took a swig of water and realized that he was quite thirsty.

They sat there in the cool room, under the desert sun, effecting a natural span between niceties and the purpose for the summons.

151

"Annette Eubanks was sitting in a chair across the table from me just this morning," the president said at last.

"And what was Auntie saying?" John used her nickname to show that he wasn't afraid.

"That John Woman is both a Sophist and a charlatan."

"Oh?"

"Is that all you have to say?" Luckfeld seemed a bit nonplussed.

"I don't know in what context she meant. Who knows . . . maybe I'd agree."

"Those are damning complaints against any professor."

"Charlatan alone, maybe," John allowed, "but sophism was an accepted form of education in ancient Greece and later in Rome. Without Sophists you'd have no Socrates or Plato, Aristotle or Cicero. I lecture, I challenge belief systems and I entertain. Nothing wrong with that."

"Professor Eubanks says that you're attempting to undermine the department by teaching that all, or most, history texts are fabrications designed to obscure the past rather than to elucidate it." The president was smiling now.

"You see?" John said. "I do agree with her. I tell my students every semester that written history is an attempt to re-create so-called actual events according to the political, social or religious convictions of the author."

"You make it sound like a conspiracy."

"Conscious conspiracy is the best of it," John said, his fragmented thoughts knitting together as he spoke. "The travesty is that a great many historians actually believe what they're saying. Their motives are unconscious and cultural, based on prejudices and wish fulfillment. They create the ideal father as either a saint or an arch-villain; the mother is most often vilified and then relegated to the nursery. But truth . . . truth is in the distance. It might as well be a mirage because we see it, imagine it, but it's a place we'll never attain."

"You think about these things a lot don't you, John?"

"Day and night since I was a boy."

"It's rare to find an educator nowadays who sees his subject as both the beginning and the end."

The young professor sipped from his water bottle, having nothing to say.

"I saw you on public access TV having a debate with Professor Carmody four months ago," Luckfeld said. "I think it was from an earlier date."

John smiled. "Poor Ira. He's talks about Greek philosophers but he's never taken the time to learn the language, relying instead on translators, most of them long dead. That never looks good."

"You made a powerful enemy showing him up like that."

John remembered sitting in the air-conditioned aluminum hut in the late afternoon at Lehman-Lawrence High School. Carmody, who looked something like Stalin, was so smug when they sat down. No one knew about the younger man's facility with languages. It was one of his many secrets.

Every man is a Pandora's box to someone, Herman Jones said. *You shake someone's hand risking eternal damnation.*

The voice was so clear that John almost turned his head to see if there was someone sitting behind him.

"I didn't expect a debate," he explained. "I thought we were going to discuss simple phrases from Ira's monograph."

Colin Luckfeld took a swig from his bottle and stared.

John was happy that the college president and cult official had not offered him a glass. Then he wondered if maybe there actually was some kind of real insight in those mossy eyes.

"The history department review committee is going to call on you to deliver and defend the paper you proposed last September," Luckfeld said. "What was that title again?"

"Written History," John said: "Reconstruction, Deconstruction or Just Plain Destruction?"

The president smiled again. "Yes, that's it."

"When am I going to be asked to do this?"

"The committee is meeting tomorrow afternoon. They'll set a date at that time."

John gazed out at the deck. The president held parties out there when the weather was mild. The entire social sciences faculty had attended a get-together the previous spring.

"When are you going to settle on a specific subject?" Annette Eubanks, dean of the history department, had asked him. They were standing at the far end of the outside platform. Annette was around fifty with piercing eyes. Unmarried, she was rumored to have had affairs with young male and female students. Her hair was naturally golden shot through with barely perceptible strands of gray.

"My subject is the negation of the negation," John answered.

"Nothing out of nothing," the elder professor retorted.

John knew then he was going to have trouble with her.

"There's something I'd like to ask of you, John," President Luckfeld said.

"Certainly."

"A man, an advisor to the board of directors, named Willie Pepperdine has asked to audit your Introduction to Deconstructionist Historical Devices. Mr. Pepperdine is an important fund-raiser for the school."

155

"How does he even know about the class?"

"He takes his role with the university very seriously. After reading the entire course offering he came to me and asked this favor. I waited to make a formal request because Mr. Pepperdine was out of the country and wasn't certain if he'd be back in time to attend classes."

"I see. Well . . . There's only been one meeting so far. Can he make this Thursday's session?"

"Yes. But he might only be able to attend one class a week. His business has him traveling quite a lot. It's only an audit; you won't have to give him a permanent grade."

"Anything else I should know about him?" John asked, he wasn't sure why.

"He's my age, very intelligent . . . dynamic. He'll make a good addition I'm sure."

"He's an advisor to the board?"

Luckfeld nodded.

"Which board?"

It was an unspoken rule that no one asked Colin, or any other known cult member, about the Platinum Path—that just wasn't done.

"Are you afraid of anything, John?"

"Everything."

"How do you mean that?"

"I work mainly on instinct," John Woman admitted. "My life, my lectures, my inquiries— all of these are reflexes of my body and my heart. I'm afraid of germs, German philosophers and

156

jealous husbands—even when I'm not having affairs with their wives. But being afraid of something does not necessarily make me back off."

"Most college professors I've met tell me that they live a life of the mind."

"At best," John said and then paused to consider; "at best they're lying."

"And at worst?"

"They're fools."

Colin Luckfeld stood up.

John followed his lead.

"It was good talking to you, John. I hope we achieved something here. And about Mr. Pepperdine."

"Yes?"

"He sits on any board he chooses."

"That includes the Platinum Path?" John asked, feeling out of control.

"Those lying historians of yours will one day claim that we conquered the world with little to no violence."

4

Walking to his car John wondered why he'd asked about the Platinum Path. The cult or sect or philosophy, whatever it was, didn't concern him.

"I asked because it makes me feel alive," he said to no one. "Negotiating dangerous grounds is what we human beings are made for—body and mind."

There were times John had to speak out spontaneously. Too much of his life had been conducted in secret—at least he could proclaim random truths in empty spaces now and then.

The words he spoke Herman Jones had once said about *great generals, incurable sociopaths and most of the rest of humanity*. Standing next to his car, on the third level of the parking structure, he thought about self-taught Herman Jones, who was smarter than anyone he'd met at any college or university. After appreciating the idea of his father a moment more, John got into his bright green 1957 Thunderbird convertible and set out for Spark City, some sixty miles off in the seemingly endless desert.

Along the way, John's thoughts turned unexpectedly to a memory of his mother. She wore a little black dress and her favorite greenstone necklace, and she was sitting in the high-backed wicker chair that looked out on Mott from the big bay window of her tiny apartment. He felt a tingle in the heel of his right palm. Smart as he was, Herman Jones had been wrong. The acme of John's life had been Lucia's passion, alongside his father's mind. He had loved her and lost her every day of his life.

He experienced the physical sensation just before tears sprouted but did not cry, because missing his mother kept her alive. Memories of her and his father were all the family he had.

This notion of kinfolk doubled back on Luckfeld's declaration of fealty to the Platinum Path. Though it was no surprise that the Path owned and ran the university, none of its members, to John's knowledge, had ever admitted affiliation. There was one professor who mentioned the organization in an article published in a local paper. That was Dr. Abel Morel, a zoologist from Luxembourg. Six days after the article appeared Morel quit the university and moved back to Europe.

That President Luckfeld entertained John's question might mean that he was considered a useful foil, a dialectic that served them in some way.

Twenty miles from NUSW John said, "Okay, dad, if you're with me then say something."

He waited, half-expecting his father's ghost to be conjured by the offering. But it wasn't; was not.

John wanted to see his father again, to hear him, to sleep in his room at night and wake up to find Herman sitting at the breakfast table in front of a bowl of overcooked oatmeal.

"I like it slippery," he used to say.

"But you're not there are you?" John declared speeding across the vast desert. "It's just me wishing that you'd get off a Greyhound bus and come on back home."

Half an hour later Professor Woman reached the outskirts of the small town, Spark City. There, before the highway turned into Main Street, a quarter mile from the church that was the centerpiece of the town square, two lone structures stood across the highway from one another: Spark City Motel and Spark City Bar.

John pulled into the parking lot of the bar, climbed out through the roof of his car, then sauntered toward the dark maw of a doorway.

It could have been a noir movie set, John thought as he crossed the threshold; it had that perfect balance of malaise, air-conditioning and psychic squalor. The dozen or so weak lights used to illuminate the room were encased in deep green glass. The floor felt gritty through the soles of his shoes. The sour smell of beer was so strong it tasted like a mouthful of ripe buttermilk.

Under a slightly brighter green light at the far end of the longish room stood a pool table where a bearded man played against himself. To John's left, seated at the wall in soggy wood chairs, were a man who looked to be in his forties and a girl no more than sixteen.

". . . and Will and Catherine and Mallory, and, and, and, oh yeah . . . and Darla-Jean were at Mallory's house and his father said that if we were gonna drink we'd better give him a shot too," the girl said and then she laughed and laughed.

The man was smaller than the buxom blond girl, and was wearing the gray uniform of some kind of repair service. Her ample bosom bounced when she laughed. The repairman nodded along.

John went up to the bar and sat on one of the unfinished pine stools, cautious not to get a splinter through the seat of his pants.

"Dr. Woman," the bartender greeted.

"Mr. Lasky."

Lasky was pale, also in his forties, prematurely balding, with eyes that seemed world-weary but resolved to make it through at least one more night.

"I guess I owe you five hundred," the down-market mixologist lamented.

"I told you that Danny-boy would beat Matthysse," John agreed. "The Argentine has the power, sure, but he thought too much of himself and Garcia's from Philly. You never bet against a good boxer from Philly."

Lou Lasky sniffed as if suffering an insult.

"Senta in?" John asked.

After giving this question serious consideration Lou asked. "What you drinkin'?"

"Martell Cordon Bleu."

The bartender frowned as if he'd never heard of that particular poison. Then he went through a door behind the bar, leaving John to listen to pool balls clicking and teenage ramblings.

". . . my mother said that they used to only teach girls how to type and cook when her mother went to school. Back then it was only men who had jobs. I wish I lived back then so I could sit at home and not do nuthin' . . ."

After a while John heard the words as sounds alone like when he stood on the fifth floor of Prometheus. Now and then the man's voice rumbled. It was surprisingly deep for such a small man.

"On the house," Lou Lasky said. He'd set down a snifter with a measured dram of amber liquid and no ice. "Room twenty-six at seven-thirty."

John placed three hundred-dollar bills on the bar.

As Lou gathered the cash he said, "Next time it's the full eight."

"If you don't make any more ill-advised bets."

162

For the next few hours John read *Colonel Chabert*, by Balzac, on an electronic tablet. There wasn't enough light for a real book and John liked e-readers; they seemed somehow secretive to him. He'd read the novel years before but adhered to his father's edict—real reading is rereading.

Herman usually added that *there is more history, more truth in fiction than in most so-called history books. Our dreams and fantasies get it right even when they don't know it.*

While John read the bar filled up. The patrons were white and listless, sometimes loud but more often silent, rarely, if ever, smiling.

One woman, probably in her thirties, came up to where the repairman and the teenager sat. She said, "Lou-Ann, you got no business in here. You should go on home to your mother."

"My mother is across the street, Miss Melbourne," the girl said. "And I'm locked out the house. You wanna take me home with you and Jack Frank?"

Hearing this John finished his third cognac and climbed off the rough pine stool. His left hip ached from sitting too long. Despite the pain he felt as if he was floating.

Outside the sun was set. The stellar desert sky had a magical feel to it. But John didn't stop to appreciate the glittering dome of night. Crossing the transitional highway he took the outside stairs to the second floor of the two-story, turquoise-plastered Spark City Motel. Ambling down the external concrete hall he came to the last door, number twenty-six.

"Who is it?" she said in answer to his knock.

"Me," he replied, uncertainty informing the word.

Forty-four-year-old Senta opened the pale olive door. Tall with a womanly figure, she had white-blond hair.

She had once told John that this was her natural color but she dyed it to get *even blonder*.

"Hi," she said. She wore a pink dress that came down to the middle of powerful thighs. The frock had no shoulders or shoulder straps. Senta's proud chest was enough.

"Hey," John said shyly.

"You gonna come in or just stand there?"

John took a floating step forward.

"I have to go to the bathroom," he said as she closed the door.

"Come on then." She took him by the hand.

The turquoise-and-white toilet was small for two people but Senta didn't leave him. She pulled down his zipper and rummaged around until her cold fingers found his penis. She pulled it out and said, "Okay, you can go now."

After relieving himself John said, "I don't want to move too fast tonight."

"Of course not," Senta agreed, shaking the last drops at the commode. "Lou says we have all night. Do you want to be tied down to the bed or the chair?"

When Senta was on top of John she climaxed at unpredictable moments. He wasn't sure if these were real or feigned orgasms. He'd told her she didn't have to pretend.

"You don't believe that a whore can come?" she'd answered. "Don't you know I really like you, Johnny?"

"You do?"

"I do."

"Why?"

"Because you talk real nice and you're always a gentleman. Most guys don't know it but good manners will make a mature woman come way more than all them gyrations they do in porn."

There were things they did every time; Senta, for instance, would tie John down with leather restraints. She was inventive and sensually perceptive. That evening she decided to spend a good deal of time kissing her twice-monthly client. Her kisses were soft but definite; up and down his arms, legs and torso . . .

She kissed him for nearly a quarter hour before mounting his straining erection.

John started bucking under her and when

Senta told him, "Calm down, baby. We ain't goin' nowhere . . ." he came so violently that she was thrown from the bed; after that he lost consciousness for a while.

When he came to Senta had loosened the restraints.

"Wow," she said. "That was wild."

She lit a cigarette and poured herself a shot of sour mash. There was a fifth of the whiskey sitting on the nightstand next to her side of the bed.

She inhaled some smoke, took a swig of whiskey and exhaled the cool misty breath over his chest.

"I was scared that you had a heart attack for a minute there," she said.

"Not me," he assured her.

"You don't know. Sometimes a young man can have what they call a irregularity in the heart and all of a sudden outta nowhere he falls down dead. I went to high school with a football quarterback who died like that."

John put a hand behind his head and groaned contentedly.

"You don't mind if I smoke?" she asked.

"I mind."

"Then why don't you ask me to put it out?"

"You need to smoke and I need you."

"You could ask Lou for a girl who doesn't smoke."

"She wouldn't be you."

Senta stretched out next to John, laying her fair hand across his brown chest.

"What's your real name?" she asked.

"John."

"I mean your last name."

"I'm John Woman, no middle initial."

"I never heard of the last name Woman."

"What's your last name, Senta?"

She froze and he smiled.

"That's okay," he said. "I need you, not your name."

"You don't need me."

"Oh yes I do. If I didn't know you were out here I'd have gone crazy two years ago. You are the glue that holds me together."

"I'm just a whore."

"That word doesn't mean a thing to me. You are Senta, no last name, and I come here because I need something only you can give."

"What's that?"

"Intimacy."

They didn't speak again until Senta was finished with her cigarette.

"Why don't you ever ask me on a date?" she said stubbing out the butt in a pink tin ashtray that she brought to their assignations.

"Isn't this a date?"

"You know what I mean," she complained. "A real date with dinner reservations and flowers . . . and clothes."

"Could you pour me a drink?" he asked, sitting up. "Do your other clients ask you out?"

"Most of my regulars do at one time or other," she replied, delivering the whiskey glass into his hand. "They want me to go to the movies or company barbecues. This one guy asked me if I'd go with him on vacation to Hawaii."

"And what do you say to them?"

"No."

"So," John said with a grin, "you want me to ask you but you don't want to go."

"Maybe not," she said. "Maybe I'd say yes."

John frowned and Senta put a hand on his shoulder.

"Don't, baby, don't," she said.

"What?"

"I'm just tryin' to let you know that I like you. It's not marriage or some kinda boyfriend-girlfriend thing."

"What is it then?"

"Why do you come all the way out here to spend the night with me?"

John almost said something and then didn't. He took a sip, then another, got up and went to the turquoise-and-white toilet. When he returned she'd refilled his glass.

"For this," he said.

"What?"

"So we can talk."

"Yeah," she said. "That's why it's a date . . .

because you want to tell me what you're thinkin' and, and you listen to what I got to say too. It's the listenin' part that makes it a real date."

The young professor put his hand on Senta's thigh and sighed, understanding that what he said was true.

"What do you want to talk about tonight, baby?" Senta asked.

"It's about my job."

The conversation took them to the bottom of the whiskey bottle. Sitting cross-legged on opposite sides of the bed they were both tipsy and serious.

"Why can't you just write that paper?" Senta asked. "I mean all you do is read and write about history, right? You should be able to do somethin' like that, no problem."

"I guess."

"What's so hard?"

"I, um . . . it's like . . ." he said.

"You don't know?"

"It's like a pismire steeped in sap."

"A what in what?"

"You ever see a piece of amber with bugs in it?"

"Sure."

"Like that."

"Oooooh," Senta said, gazing somewhere past John's left shoulder. "You're stuck like when I wanted to go to college but never filled out the application form."

"What did you want to study?"

"Bookkeeping and literature classes."

"Did you ever go?"

"Something . . . something happened and I just couldn't think about it anymore, like with your paper."

"It daunts me," John said.

"Haunts you like a ghost?"

John giggled and said, "I'd kiss you but I'm too drunk to crawl over there."

"I like being kissed."

This reminded CC of his mother explaining why the name Napoli was superior to Tartarelli.

At seven minutes past two John got out of bed. He pulled on his soft gray cotton trousers and lurched toward the door, kicking the night table along the way.

"Where you goin', baby?" Senta said reaching out.

"Out on the walkway."

A half-moon hovered above the stony landscape. Spark City Bar was closed. John breathed in Senta's jasmine scent, rising from his skin.

"What's wrong, John?" she asked from the doorway.

"I had a dream."

" 'Bout what?" She put her arms around him pressing her nose against his shoulder.

"My father."

"What'd he say?"

"That . . ." John saw a falling star, then he became aware of the sky full of stars.

"What?"

"He told me that I wasn't writing my paper because I resented having to prove myself. He's always saying things like that."

"I thought he died."

"Yeah."

"Oh . . . Was he right?"

John turned to kiss her. Gazing into his eyes she returned the kiss.

"Yes," he said, "dad's right. He's always right. I've never had one decent thought that didn't come from him. He created me."

"So what are you going to do?"

"Write the paper."

"You can do it now?"

"Because of you," John said. "You and the goddess of history."

"Who's that?"

"The Greeks thought that it was Clio, one of the Muses, but I prefer to call her Posterity."

"You wanna come fuck again to work off some'a that whiskey?"

At 3:56 a.m. John was fully dressed. Senta walked him across the highway to the bar parking lot. He climbed over the side of his topless T-bird.

"You want a ride?" he asked.

"My car's right across the street."

"I'll wait for you to get in and drive off."

"Ray," she said.

"What?"

"My last name, it's Ray, Senta Ray."

5

The speedometer hovered around ninety. John didn't feel the cold—only speed and wind. Ten miles from faculty-housing a shiny-eyed coyote darted into the road. It lowered itself on its haunches, yellow eyes glaring at the sports car's headlights.

Without thinking John jerked the steering wheel to the left. The car skidded out into the desert, spinning uncontrollably as it went, knocking down several ocotillo trees. Finally the car raised up on its right side, almost rolled over, crashed down on its wheels, then juddered for long seconds while the metallic frame strained and creaked.

The radio came on. James Brown was singing, *say it loud, I'm black and I'm proud,* on an oldies station.

The right headlight winked out.

The stars, John thought, must be laughing at the crazy dance of the classic car. He also wondered about the meaning of the song. Though he'd learned his profession from Herman, his mother's superstitions still held sway over his heart in much the same way that the hovering half-moon controlled faraway tides.

Twenty or so feet from the car the topaz-bright

eyes of the coyote blinked. The creature, John imagined, had run away but then returned thinking that maybe there was some spilled food or, better, blood to lap up at the scene of the accident.

Gazing at each other over the desert span, both man and canine were motionless. John considered honking the horn to frighten away the sometimes deadly desert jester. But instead he climbed out over the side and stood there.

Illuminated by the single headlight the black-and-brown streaked beast sniffed the air. Maybe John had been wounded, the scent of his blood in the air.

The coyote yipped; hopped; and then, in the middle of a turn, disappeared.

John leaned back against the warm hood. There was a chill in the air. His mother would have said that this was all a single sign; he should see either a priest or a fortune-teller to decipher the meaning.

But he was afraid of seers and holy men, worried that their powers might be based on something real, that they'd find him out if he got too close. So he climbed back into the one-eyed green T-bird and drove the ten miles back home.

The faculty complex was protected by twelve-foot-high matte adobe walls. The wrought iron gate across the driveway was locked at night, attended by a uniformed guard. But the late-night sentry was not at his post.

John stopped at the barred entrance, sat back in the driver's seat and fell immediately asleep.

He was sitting in a dark room. Fanciful pulsing light came through large industrial-like windows; the neon pulse was from a blinking sign somewhere outside. This light was blue and red; these colors refused to combine. Each time the sign flashed John saw something different.

The first burst revealed a bookcase filled with tomes, some of which were hundreds of years old while others were modern-day publications with gaudy book jackets promising things unworthy of the written word.

The second flare of blue and red illuminated a high wall where some mad painter had fashioned a huge ogre made mostly of thick black and brown brushstrokes, with hints of scum green here and there.

The third blaze slammed down on Chapman Lorraine's corpse, a deep and bloody cleft in his temple. The dead man was seated awkwardly on a tarnished brass throne festooned with huge cool-colored man-made jewels that were both opaque and brilliantly striated with platinum radiance.

The light faded but John could see the after-image of Lorraine quite clearly. There seemed to be some kind of intention in his unfocused eyes, in the crooked grasping of his powerful fingers.

He's trying to hold on to life through me, Dreamer John thought.

The neon pulsed again. John was afraid that the new brilliance would bring Lorraine fully alive; that those dead hands might drag him back to pay for his crime.

But instead the light seemed to trap the dead man in its cloying glow. Chapman was stuck to his blackened throne. Dreamer John took in a deep breath that came out as a relieved sigh.

After two or three of these exhalations he noticed a sound, a gentle tapping.

The light went down and the tapping stopped. When blue and red filled the room once more, it started up again. John found himself walking down a long, dusty hall guarded by dogs sleeping beneath hanging candelabras. The candlelight flickered, forming and re-forming the walls into hallucinatory images; these possible/impossible subjects ranged from hummingbirds frozen in mid-flight to huge Soviet farm tractors that appeared to be breathing.

His father was there wearing a scuffed-up suit of armor, seated upon a brass-plated horse. John wore a shapeless straw hat and carried a rude rucksack fashioned out of simple calico cloth.

A column of tiny spiders marched in the opposite direction along the edge of the wall. Looking closer John saw that the spiders were actually little severed hands, their fingertips frantically stamping on the wood floor.

The tapping came again. John looked up. He was standing at a plain wood door.

"Who is it?"

"Me of course," a woman said. She sounded older if not elderly.

It was a familiar voice but he couldn't place it; like the first notes of a song on the radio—you know the tune but cannot name it.

He hesitated. After a few seconds he felt something wet and warm against his hand. He flinched then saw it was one of the guard dogs now awake and come to greet him. John smiled at the friendly gesture and pulled the door open.

The woman standing there was short, in her early fifties, thin but not skinny, with dark brown skin like chocolate fudge. Her full-length dress was made from natural canvas-like material printed with five or six rude images of blue and red roses. She wore a cotton hat that was round with a ridge along the brim. Half a dozen daisies grew out of the top as if from soil.

Her glasses had delicate pewter frames, surrounding large brown eyes that watched him closely.

There was a half smile on the woman's lips. This smile tweaked his memory . . .

"You're . . . a . . . a fairy godmother," he stuttered.

Her smile deepened.

"You're *my* fairy godmother," he said, shocked.

"How are you, Cornelius?"

"Not too good," he said. "I mean . . . nothing's all that bad but it's cold in here and my homework is so boring and I can't get the man I killed out of my head. He's back there in the living room. I don't remember his name but . . ."

"Yes, yes, yes," the children's goddess said. She patted his shoulder and walked past him down the candlelit hall of dust, drowsing dogs and impossible images. "All that's over now."

When he turned to follow John felt burgeoning elation in his chest. After one step he was grinning, another and he began to laugh. Instead of a third stride he hopped, landed, then swung from the waist like doing the hokey-pokey dance when he was in kindergarten.

He stopped there watching the brown goddess traipse toward the flashing neon at the end of the passageway. He wanted to go after her but was suddenly afraid of the passion rising in him . . .

"What's your name?" he shouted.

"Posterity," she said not turning.

"Professor. Professor."

Someone was shaking his shoulder; there was an intense light shining. John's head hurt so badly that he wanted to tear out his brain.

"Professor!"

"Stop shakin' me, Jasper," John complained. "My head feels like it's gonna bust."

The big Hopi had a set expression that revealed nothing; not joy or glee, anger or love. He called himself Jasper because he liked the stone. Jasper Hutman was the name the university put on his paycheck but John knew his given name was Hototo.

Hototo believed that his tribesmen were put on earth to bring peace and harmony everywhere they went.

"Does that mean the Hopi people are here to save the world?" John asked Hototo early one Tuesday morning when he'd just returned from Senta's motel room.

"No," the big, brick red man replied. "There are too few of us and too many of everyone else. All we do is to carry a little peace here and there casting it on the waters and hoping for the best."

Jasper shook John's shoulder again and the history professor sat up straight.

"You shouldn't sleep out here in your car, Professor, there's all kinds of bad characters up and down this road. And you know they won't think twice about people like you and me."

The memory of a fairy godmother came into John's mind.

"I was waiting for you and fell asleep," he said.

179

"You were smiling," Hototo remarked.

"I think I had a revelation."

Jasper "Hototo" Hutman went through an iron doorway to open the larger driveway gate. John drove through but found the uniformed Hopi standing in the middle of the lane holding up a fancy beaded belt. The guard approached, handing the bright strap to John. The yellow, red, and blue beads might have been the scales of a fanciful viper. The silver buckle was quite large.

"For you," Hototo said firmly.

"It's very handsome," John said.

The eight-inch buckle had a turquoise bird set at one side. The bird had a red eye and one greenstone feather.

"If you press the bird's eye it releases a silver knife and handle," Hototo informed him. "My father gave it to me but I'll never use it."

"What makes you think I would?" John asked.

"You're a wild man, John Woman. I see it in your eyes late at night when you come from Spark City. A man like you needs a weapon."

Having no reply John put the belt on the seat next to him then drove on feeling as if some kind of unwanted destiny had been foisted upon him.

I have seen you in a dream, he pecked on the virtual keyboard of his smart phone. *This image my father would call a hermeneutic construct*

. . . an element of my mind that has become a separate entity. That's what I would say if a potential employer asked me to explain but really you are Posterity, the goddess who embodies a future that will one day only dimly remember my foggy existence.

John was sitting in the window ledge of the second floor of his apartment, Cottage 16, upper level. Each structure of faculty housing was a four-story faux adobe building encompassing two two-story apartments with one big room per floor. The first level had a stove and refrigerator along the wall. John kept a table and desk on the kitchen level with only a low-riding Japanese platform bed against the north wall of the upper chamber. Through the large window of either room a red rock plateau could be seen in the distance. There was enough room in the recessed window to sit comfortably and write while the desert loomed beyond.

History is the world we live in, he wrote. *It's not a thing of the past, neither, in human terms, is it separate from the person witnessing it. History is not an external object that can be weighed or quantified by any extant measurements. Indeed, the study of history is much like the contradictory study of the human brain: a gooey mass that contains incongruous images which are affected*

181

by tides of emotions, instincts, indecipherable reminders and faulty memories, all of these elements being continually changed by time, trauma, interpretation, and, ultimately, by death.

I will always remember, Goddess Posterity, the moment of our meeting but I will most likely forget the day of the week, your face, the guard dog's warm nose on my fingers. I'll forget the exact words you spoke, what I replied. If I tell someone else about you they will misremember what I have told them. And when, and if, we ever speak of you at some future date (which will also be forgotten) our conversation will make you over yet again.

So history for human beings, rather than one undeniable unfolding of existence, is instead millions, billions, trillions of warped and faded images that morph into self-contradictions, false promises and unlikely convictions . . .

John wrote for hours that morning. When the battery icon turned into a red outline he plugged the cell phone charger into a wall socket. The wire being too short to reach the window, he had to sit on the blond bamboo floor with his back against the east wall; there he continued the one-way conversation with his private god.

He was reminded of his long-suffering father sitting in much the same pose in his deathbed. This memory contained the story he would tell

Posterity, intended for the history professors' tribunal to overhear.

The faculty at NUSW, he wrote in a footnote to Posterity, *is asking for me to prove myself in concrete terms. This expectation is pandemic in the impossible study of what has gone before. To prove myself is like asking for proof of existence. I think therefore I cannot know. I can discuss with you because I know that you are the embodiment of that which transcends me. This is the only way for me to make certain that I am trying my best to come as close as possible to truth and not making up complex arguments for my faculty-tribesmen to be impressed by.*

Just as he had finished this last sentence the doorbell rang.

John bounded down the stairs to his front door. There he stopped and smiled—welcoming the unknown.

"Who's there?"

6

"It's Carlinda Elmsford, Professor Woman."

The door was yellow with a ceramic green knob. John saw the colors quite clearly wondering if would he would have been able to describe them before this moment. His digital thesis, desert accident and dream—all combined with the gangling girl thinker's voice making his awareness more focused, present.

"Come on up," he said, pressing the release for the downstairs entrance.

In the outer hall he listened as the double transfer student came up the first flight of stairs, then rounded the corner.

She wore a long blue dress that varied in hues, blending from light to dark. Her straw sandals had been replaced by black fabric dancer's shoes. Her handsome features were permanent like those of a marble sculpture but her expression was flighty, almost frightened, liable to change at any moment.

"Miss Elmsford," John said.

"I read the syllabus and course outline on the university website," she said blinking as if he were a bright light.

"The entire document?"

"Yes."

"That's more than half the class will ever do."

The sophomore tried to smile but only managed a halfhearted frown.

"I wanted to talk to you about it," she said.

"My office hours are on the top of each section of the outline and syllabus. Tuesdays and Thursdays, four to six."

He wasn't sure why he was keeping her at the threshold. Maybe there was something about her and doorways . . . them and doorways.

"I know," she said. "I would have waited but I might have to drop the course and the deadline is this Thursday, before the class meets."

"Why would you have to drop?"

"The personal history assignments."

"I see," John said and then paused a moment. "Do you ever stop and wonder about the point in time you're in right that moment?"

"Yeah."

"What do you think?"

"That whatever I'm doing will go echoing down the ages and maybe make a serial killer or help find a cure for cancer. Whatever I'm doing has to be important otherwise it just wouldn't be."

Hearing these words John stepped back, gesturing for her to enter.

She considered a moment then stepped through.

"Let's sit at the table," John offered.

Carlinda went to the table, pulled out a chair

and sat with much more grace than she had previously exhibited.

"Would you like something to drink?"

"Water, please. This is a nice place. Are all the faculty apartments the same?"

"If they have a family with more than four members they get the whole building," he said. "I think that's right. It might be three but I'm pretty sure it's four. My upstairs is one big room but they have prefabricated partitions to subdivide."

He took a twelve-ounce bottle of Nouvelle spring water from his refrigerator, thought of getting his guest a glass then decided against the nicety.

He sat on the chair that abutted Carlinda's side of the table. Her crystalline eyes opened wide for a moment, then squinted as she studied him.

"What's your problem?" he asked.

"What do you mean?"

"With the personal history requirement for Decon." John liked the word the floater had used to describe his course.

"Oh," she said. "It's too much . . . I mean even when I just think about it I get a headache."

The first assignment in IDHD, Decon, was to take five steps toward creating a preliminary draft of the personal history document. He'd see what assignments arose from the work the students had done at the halfway mark, but the final personal history document (FPHD) would count for at least half of the student's grade. The FPHD requested that:

> . . . *each student create a series of personal histories.*

1. The first assignment is to write your personal history as a series of events and so-called facts using no more than a paragraph to describe, explain and/or excuse each. This list will include at least half of the following topics: birthplace, income bracket (class), education, relatives, race, religion, gender, major achievements, sexual experiences, fantasies, enemies, loves, hatreds, likes, dislikes, skills, ineptitudes, and opinions held of you by your friends and those who don't like you, your teachers, your favorite color if you have one, your pets, taste in clothes. And then you must delve deeper, giving an inventory of your disgusting habits, your unsavory secret desires, the crimes and wrongdoings you have committed. Examples? Smelling your own feces, eating the hardened mucus from your nose, killing the neighbor's dog, rape, murder or the most serious crime in America, theft.

2. Write a similar document on someone you know without that person being aware of the project.
3. Write another personal history on someone you don't know well.
4. Blend the histories into someone you like best. Create a new man or woman out of your research. Discover the ideal being and bring that history into class, sharing as much of it as you dare.
5. Throughout this assignment we will study methods, techniques, research systems, and various other arcane approaches to accomplish these ends.

"Maybe your headache is an indication that the work required is work you need to do," John Woman suggested.

"No," Carlinda said. "It's intrusive and disturbing."

"Certainly."

"You admit it?"

"Of course," John said with aplomb. "The study of history is not like going to the movies. It's not even like a film critic giving her needless opinions. The very study of history is intrusive, invasive and ruthless . . ."

Carlinda gulped and John smiled.

"Most of my fellow faculty members would have you believe that historical analysis must be an objective exercise, something gleaned from old papers, letters and books. They discuss murder, sex and madness without the slightest idea of what state or states of mind are required. They are virgins giving advice about sex; pampered aristocrats striving to understand the starving poor.

"If you want to be a historian you have to know what it's like to put as much of the truth as you can bear out in the light of day. You have to shatter your illusions, be willing to suffer revelation."

John stopped because he felt a full-blown lecture coming on and that was not where he wanted this visit to go.

He noticed that there was a line of sweat across the ridge of the sophomore's upper lip.

"But, Professor," she said, "once you tell people the things you asked for they will look at you differently. Suppose I'm the only one to take the assignment seriously?"

"Then you would be the only student in the class who has a prayer of success."

"Do you have to go through something like that just to write or teach?" she asked.

"Just?" John asked. "Have you ever been raped, Miss Elmsford?"

"No . . . and that's the truth."

"If you were to write a paper on the political use of rape throughout history, from the abduction of the Sabine women down to present-day conflicts in Africa, could you give me an accurate rendition by reading historical and official reports and interviews with the rapists and their victims?"

"I, I . . . don't know."

"If you were one of the women experiencing this crime would you have a deeper understanding of what was happening?"

"Possibly," she said. "But . . . maybe that would put me too close to it."

"Exactly so. Without proper training a victim of any crime or tragedy wouldn't be able to have . . . perspective. But a researcher in a university library might not have the visceral experience to fully embrace the subject either. The paper I'm asking for will underscore this dichotomy. It will give you the ability to identify with the historical characters you wish to imbue with life. Without this simple self-exploration the contemporary historian may not have the awareness to understand the immensity of her or his study. Thucydides was a physician who contracted and survived the bubonic plague. Therefore he was able to render the experience with accuracy and acuity."

"It wouldn't be worth it to infect myself with the Ebola virus in order to understand it," she said with abject certainty.

"What are you, Miss Elmsford?"

"I don't know what you mean. A woman? An American?"

"Let's start with race."

"That's kind of confusing," she said.

"Confuse me then."

"My, my mother's father, Joel Pena, is Mexican, a descendent of the Aztecs he says. Mom's mom is third-generation American Japanese. My father's father is a black man from Ghana and my grandmother on that side is Danish."

"So what are you?"

"A little bit of everything, I guess."

"Where does the name Elmsford come from?"

"It used to be Prempeh but my father's father changed it when he migrated with my grand-mother to the U.S."

"And so your name is a lie of sorts," John said kindly. "A bit of deconstructionist history, if you will."

"Okay," Carlinda agreed. "I could say our real family name. I guess that would be interesting. But what if I robbed a bank and wrote it down? Then somebody might call the FBI and have me arrested."

"Of course," John said.

"It's not worth destroying your whole life for a class paper."

"You have to write down everything you know," he said sternly, "every act and sin; every omission and mistake; every dark thought and belief . . . But you don't have to share everything with the class."

A sudden light emanated from the worried student's eyes. John stifled an urge.

"You will be graded," he continued, "on the quality and fearlessness of your work. It will be one of the few times in your experience of higher education that you will be rated on courage."

Carlinda leaned forward, listing toward the young lecturer. He wiped the sweat from her upper lip with his thumb and then kissed her. She moved easily from her chair into his lap. There was no hesitation or clashing of teeth. Carlinda's kisses were soft and somehow enduring. He leaned back in the hard chair. She caressed the side of his neck with both hands.

In the middle of the night, John was sitting up considering the sleeping Carlinda. The sex had been, as he expected, awkward, punctuated with hesitations and surprise. Her first orgasm brought tears to her eyes. When he asked her if she wanted to stop she shook her head, binding him in an embrace of extraordinary strength.

"Have you done this with other students?" she asked.

"No," he answered truthfully.

They'd said a lot more but John couldn't remember it.

How could that be? He remembered everything said or read in his presence, every word: obscure passages in Latin and Greek, the lectures of his father and the passionate revelations of his mother. John could recite word for word the sermon given by Pastor Lionel Rehnquist at Wanderers' Baptist Church. He'd gone there by himself when he was a child of eight.

Young Cornelius asked his father what they talked about in church and Herman said, "It is your assignment to go there next Sunday and find out, an infiltrator in the house of their god."

He could recite Rehnquist's entire homily but the words he'd shared with Carlinda were lost.

He got up from the bed, took the smartphone from his pants on the floor and went to the deep windowsill to lounge under the desert moon.

If I am to teach history, he wrote to Posterity, *then I must be history. If I am to know something I must live it.* He stopped for a while to consider these words. After a few minutes he continued, *Otherwise life would be like TV, like bread and circuses to the ancient Romans. Human life is a tactile experience. The mind, after all, is a physical thing no different from tomato cans or alley cats. We do not transcend physical experience; it surpasses us. Realizing this we understand that knowledge is secondary to the hunger for knowledge . . .*

The soft sensation of her hand on the back of his neck held no surprise. She'd moved soundlessly across the room and reached out . . .

"What you doin'?" she asked.

She came around and sat across from him, naked and spread-legged so that he could make out the contours of her sex in the moonlight.

"I have to write a paper for the history department," he said.

"Like personal history?"

"Just the opposite."

"I have a boyfriend."

"He's a lucky guy."

After a few moments she said, "You must have had a lot of experience."

"Why do you say that?"

"The things you did."

"You liked it?"

"I want to feel something," she replied, not looking at him. "I want to be out of control, at least a little bit. I want to have to try to get away but not be able to . . ."

There was surety in the silences he experienced with Carlinda. He realized, with mild surprise, that he was aroused by their talk.

"I've never had a girlfriend," he admitted.

"What do you mean?"

"If I were to write a personal history paper," he replied, "one of the admissions I'd make would be that I never had a real girlfriend. Mostly I've just paid for what I needed."

"But why?" she asked, turning her eyes to him. "You're cute and funny and smart . . ."

"There's not much room on my little island," he said meeting her gaze.

"I'm not going to fall in love with you," Carlinda warned.

"Okay," he said, amused.

"This was just a physical thing," she continued, "something I needed like a massage or a cold glass of water."

John thought about his words to Posterity: his claim that the physical world was preeminent in human awareness.

"Me too," John said.

"So you're not going to try and be my boyfriend, my lover?"

"Things will be what they are."

"You don't want to get in my life and mess up things with me and Arnold?"

"You've already defeated me, Miss Elmsford."

She reached over touching his erection lightly. "And what if I got on this right now?"

"We could sit face-to-face and continue our talk," he said. "And in the morning I won't even ask for your phone number."

7

When John woke up the next morning Carlinda was gone. His phone read nine forty-seven. The desert outside was overcast. Downstairs he made coffee in a French press. Standing naked next to the ultramodern smooth-top stove John wondered about alienation intrinsic to technology and the immediacy of sex.

While watching the water in the clear Pyrex pot he felt a sudden chill at the back of his neck. He tried to ignore the sensation—as he should have ignored the sweat forming on Carlinda's upper lip.

History is just as much superstition as it is study, Herman Jones once said when Cornelius was young and did not yet fully appreciate the complexity of abstract thought. *As much as religion the study of the past takes a monumental leap of faith.*

Savoring the strong coffee John picked up the smartphone to continue the dialogue with Posterity. He was about to engage the word processor app when he noticed the icon of an envelope at the bottom left of the screen. It was a message from his online news alert service.

He touched the little image with a baby finger.

This called up a list of related topics that had recently been in the news.

Desiccated Corpse Found in Wall of Silent Screen Movie House was the lead headline from a New York newspaper. *Dead Man Murdered and Sealed in a Wall for Over 15 Years*, the *Wayne Report Online* declared.

There were seventeen news reports on the discovery of Chapman Lorraine's remains. The Arbuckle Cinema House was undergoing internal renovations initiated by new owners. When the construction crew tore down a wall in the projection room they discovered a desiccated male corpse wrapped in garment bags and stored in a big aluminum trunk. In a public statement homicide officer Lieutenant Colette Van Dyne said that there was a suspect that the NYPD was actively seeking.

John supposed that Colette had taken her boyfriend's name; that she had indeed married him. He was certain that the NYPD was looking for Cornelius "CC" Jones. France Bickman had to be dead after so long and there was no other possible suspect.

John went upstairs to don pants, shirt and shoes. Clothes were necessities for a man on the run. There was money in a safe-deposit box in Reno, Nevada. He'd created yet another identity—Reflex Minton. All necessary documents for Reflex were salted away in a safe-deposit box in LA.

Why hadn't he called himself Robert or Bruce or even Omar? Did he want to be captured?

The clouds outside were lifting. Watching them part John thought about the chill he'd felt even before he knew what happened. The accuracy of premonition had a calming effect. He was probably safe. No one had his fingerprints. Even when he was taken by the police after the death of his father Colette made sure that he was in protective custody and not under arrest; that way they didn't book him. The only photographs that possibly existed were from childhood, and those snapshots had most likely been lost. Lucia's family didn't claim him and Herman's sister only met Lucia when she was pregnant.

His alienation from culture and community cocooned or camouflaged John in nonentity. He breathed in deeply and returned to the kitchen. There he sat, not writing or even thinking much. Now and again he'd run the tip of an index finger over the smooth finish of the cherrywood table. The sensation was almost imperceptible.

A solitary beam of muted sunlight struck the far end of the tabletop. John was thinking that light had mass, that there was weight even to that faint illumination on a plank of wood.

At 12:47 p.m. he was once again walking down North Violet Lane toward the Great Rotunda. The past two days were jumbled but not lost to him.

There were touchstones of thought: Carlinda, Senta, Chapman Lorraine, the dark-skinned fairy godmother and his first lover, Colette Margolis—now his nemesis.

His misdeeds would be touted online and in tabloids for the next few days.

He took the stairs two at a time to the fifth floor of the gigantic canister of education. At 1:01 the entire class was in attendance, plus two more.

There was a serious-looking black male student sitting in the front row wearing a black T-shirt, army fatigue pants and five or six thick silver bracelets on his left wrist. At the far left in the otherwise unpopulated fifth row sat an older man in a gray suit. He had on a dress shirt but wore no tie, sporting silver, not gray, hair. His face was economical and somehow sculpted. This, John knew, was the professional board member Willie Pepperdine.

The young professor glanced around the class but when his eyes met Carlinda's she looked down. This was no surprise. He wondered if she had confessed her infidelity to a girlfriend or maybe even to Arnold. It wasn't a good time for that kind of notoriety.

"Good afternoon," he said. "I know I had you reading Winch and Wittgenstein but we're going to put off discussing them for the time being. Instead I'd like to talk about the implications of

199

the theory of a finite universe and the impact this might have on the study of history."

With these words John Woman started his spur-of-the-moment lecture.

"Some physicists believe the universe to be finite, that this limited existence's absolute god is gravity. Gravity explodes with love creating existence, then recoils in horror at what it has made. It draws back into the primal atom; then, forgetting revulsion, it explodes again . . ."

For the next fifty minutes or so he spoke of the ancient Hindu belief in reincarnation and Nietzsche's dictum of eternal recurrence not only of life but of the entire physical world.

"Within this philosophy," he lectured, "science is subsumed. History in its most absolute and unknowable form locks itself into a pattern of repetition and our ability to know it becomes an act of faith."

"But Professor," a young man with olive-brown skin said.

"Yes?"

"Claude Hernandez," the student said, "from New Orleans, second-year student, majoring in American history."

"Yes, Mr. Hernandez."

"What use is this kind of thinking? I mean, if we can't know history and are condemned to repeat it then what's to study?"

John hadn't considered why he'd decided on

this lecture; it was one of many tools he used to break up rote thinking. But with this question he understood that his tenure as a professor was just an extension of the lessons his father had taught him; that his entire life, even the murder of Chapman Lorraine, was merely assignment.

"*Amor fati*," he said to Claude Hernandez.

The student from Louisiana frowned and cocked his head to the side.

John looked around the room. The man he assumed to be Willie Pepperdine was grinning.

"*Amor fati*," the professor repeated.

Carlinda made a sound.

"Yes, Miss Elmsford?"

"Love fate. It's, it's Latin."

"And what does this Latin phrase mean to you?"

They could have been fucking on his window ledge under the protective lunar glow.

"It," she said and paused. "It means that one has to accept fate but more than that, it means that you can, you should love what is meant to be."

Carlinda exhaled as if she had been holding a breath.

"Exactly," John agreed. "The elephant I spoke of Tuesday has now become the universe. Our limited ability to study this behemoth is informed not by knowledge but by our attitude toward the study."

• • •

There were many questions after that. John bantered and argued, learned names and felt more and more relaxed. They quarreled over free will and entropy, the apparently obvious unfolding of the past into the future and the loss of faith that many feared they would have if they accepted the concept of *amor fati*.

In response to these fears he said, "My job has two main objectives. The first is to teach you how to think about history. The second is to dissuade you from following that path of study."

"To *per*suade us, Professor?" Tamala Marman asked.

John smiled. "No, Ms. Marman—*dis*suade. It is my experience that the profession of history is a harsh taskmaster; that anyone embarking on that road should be aware of the tribulations they will encounter."

"Shouldn't we make those decisions ourselves?"

"Of course you should. But your resolve must be based on something. The lectures, class assignments and private meetings with every professor at this school will influence your decisions. It is my position that if you take your chosen vocation to heart you may, as many do today, experience the threat of heartbreak."

Soon after John dismissed the class. They filed through the red-rimmed doorway looking somber.

Carlinda faltered at the threshold, then passed through.

Soon the only students left were Willie Pepperdine and the young black man in silver bracelets and quasi-military dress.

The younger man approached John first.

"Do you have a minute, Professor Woman?" he asked.

"Office hours are from four to six at number eighteen Southeast Green Garden Path."

The young man's brow furrowed ever so slightly. He would have been good looking but somewhere along the way his confidence had transformed into anger and the delicate features of his dark face did not hold anger well.

"I was hoping we could talk," the student said.

"What's your name?"

"Johann Malik."

"Pick any time between four and six, Johann. That will be your time."

"What are you doing right now?"

"Or you could just drop by and take your chances. The first few weeks are usually pretty slow."

"We could grab a coffee in the rotunda," the glowering student offered.

"Between four and six."

Johann Malik looked over at the elder white man in the fifth row, grunted, then stalked out of the classroom, silver bracelets clanking like manacles.

"Masterful," the man in the fifth row said. His tone was strong and rich; *baritone tessitura*, John said to himself.

"Mr. Pepperdine?"

"You got me."

John went to the fourth tier and sat.

"What can I do for you, sir?"

"Willie."

The Platinum Path board member, maybe even one of The Dozen, was handsome in a fabricated way. The face was perfectly balanced but his steel gray eyes spoke of the scars and indulgences of a mercenary or pirate.

"Willie," John repeated.

"I want to learn from you."

"Excuse me if I'm a little mystified, Willie, but I can't imagine a professor in an obscure branch of study could in any way edify a worldly individual like yourself."

"I don't know. I learned something today."

"And what is that?"

"Everything I believe instinctively has a basis as old as ancient India and Egypt; that an upstart nation like Rome had scholars who knew what I'd be thinking nearly two thousand years before I was born."

John nodded while wondering about the man he faced. He could *read* most people simply by engaging with them for a few minutes, no more. But every now and then he ran across someone who defied his intuitive abilities.

"President Luckfeld says that you want to audit the class."

"It would be an honor," Pepperdine said. His skin had a platinum patina, not the drab worn color of gray age but a deep vibrancy that matched his bright smile.

"Have you studied history before?"

"Only as an elective in the school of hard knocks."

"What's your profession, Willie?"

"Distilling money into meaning."

"Whoa," the young professor declared. "I've never heard that particular phrase before. What does it mean?"

"I try to get people to see the world for what it is, not what they expect it to be. Once they know where they stand, what they can and cannot do, their choices often . . . shift."

Pepperdine looked to be fifty so he was probably sixty. Both brutality and subtlety radiated from him. John wanted to ask if he'd ever killed someone but this, he knew, came from his own desire to share the guilt for Chapman Lorraine.

Two wrongs, he thought.

"You're welcome in my class at any time, Willie Pepperdine."

"The class description says that your students are expected to create a personal history," the auditor offered.

"Yes."

"I might not have the time for that. I can do the reading though. I read on long flights."

"You travel often?"

Pepperdine nodded and stood up.

"I've taken up enough of your time, Professor. There must be a new class coming soon."

"No. I, um, I always get a classroom that doesn't have anything scheduled for at least an hour and a half after. My lectures often exceed the allotted time."

"I should be going anyway, have to be in Ho Chi Minh City in thirty-six hours." Pepperdine wasn't a tall man, five eight at most. His shoes were made from red-brown leather and probably cost at least a week's salary of any professor on the campus. He moved at a leisurely pace with no limp or hesitation.

John remained in his fourth-row desk-chair for long minutes wondering why a man like Pepperdine would pay such close attention to him and his class.

These thoughts led naturally to a life crafted to be undetectable. If he was a ghost then maybe Willie was a ghost hunter like they had on reality TV.

The idea of ghost hunters further distracted John. He thought that the sham television shows were little different from history classes. The history department was the ghost hunter of the university. Actually most researchers were in pursuit of knowledge even more unlikely than poltergeists.

"John?" She was standing at the doorway wearing a gray dress-suit that complemented her short gray hairdo. John found it impossible to imagine Annette Eubanks as either young or old. She seemed like the image, even the icon, of some human trait that had been minted on an ancient silver coin.

"Ms. Eubanks," he said. "Are you lost?"

"I saw that your class was scheduled from one to five. I was just going to look in and wave but then there was no class."

"It's a seventy-five-minute Tuesday Thursday period but I try to find a time slot that allows me to go over."

"You can't organize your lectures to fit into the time allowed?"

Allowed.

"There is no such thing as equality or perfection," John replied trying to sound as if the words were from a quote, "except in the theoretical disciplines of math and sometimes physics."

"Some of us enjoy the illusion of order," she said walking toward the rows of desks.

"What can I do for you, Annette?" John asked when she'd reached the first tier.

"You received the departmental summons," she stated.

"Like a parking ticket?"

Annette Eubanks curled up her lip, maybe unconsciously.

"You shouldn't make light of department procedure, Professor Woman."

"I've never heard of a departmental summons, Ms. Eubanks."

"We expect you to deliver your paper to the review board at some point this semester."

"Written History; Reconstruction, Deconstruction or Just Plain Destruction?"

Eubanks's lip curled again.

"That's not much time," John said.

"You've had a year."

"Whitman worked on *Leaves of Grass* for years," John offered, "and then spent the rest of his life rewriting."

"You compare yourself to America's premier poet?"

"Why not?"

Looking into the unfiltered hatred of her eyes John thought, not for the first time, that his character was not designed for the life he'd embarked upon. He should be making this professor like him, ingratiating himself with the faculty.

"We would also like you to present a preliminary talk about your paper at the next departmental brown-bag lunch."

"Really? That's tomorrow isn't it?"

"You can't pretend you didn't know. These requests were put in your box."

"My box?"

"Faculty mail."

"Oh. I never pay any attention to that. I figure if anything is important enough somebody'll tell me face-to-face."

"Consider yourself told."

He was standing in the doorway of 18 Southeast Green Garden Path when John arrived at 3:48.

"Mr. Malik."

"Professor," Johann Malik said.

"Nice to see you."

John took out his electronic key-card and held it against the black ceramic pad under the doorknob. He heard the click, pulled open the gold-green door and ushered the sour-faced student in.

The room was small, the size of two broom closets, with a ceiling that was sixteen feet high. John kept no books, papers or knickknacks in his office. There was one metal filing cabinet painted drab green, a walnut desk with a reclining office chair and three hardback chairs for visitors. A green metal trash can sat in a far corner.

John went around the desk and sat in the fabric-padded black office chair.

"How can I help you, Mr. Malik?"

"I need to talk to you about your class."

"What about it?"

"Why you want to lock us in a box like that? Like some prison warden."

"Us? Box?"

"Black people, man. Here you gonna say that slavery was fate, then tell me to love it."

John enjoyed this interpretation. The political activist angle was always a monkey wrench in the delicate gears of historical investigation.

"I merely provided one of many physical analyses of the past and future world. Would you have me tell you to walk into a room with men who hate you, men who could obliterate your soul, without a warning and at least some means to defend yourself?"

"You the one giving ammunition to them," Malik argued. "You're telling them that they're not guilty by saying that destiny made us what we are."

"That's one way of looking at it."

"That's the only way."

"Then let me ask you a question."

"What?" The solitary word bristled with violence.

"Imagine yourself on the edge of a high cliff. A group of your enemies happen by and throw you off the side. Then you're falling, falling for what seems like forever. Instinctively all you can think of is how to back away from that moment in time, back to the hour before you arrived at the edge. But this is not a child's game. You can't

210

take it back. The only hope you have is that you survive the fall. And, even if you live, you will never be able to go back."

"That's just some talk," Malik said, disgusted.

"This is a university," John said lightly. "That's what we do here. We talk. Through discussion, debate and disagreement we come up with answers that, if we're lucky, can be used as tools in the fabrication of our temporary survival."

"There's a world outside the university, Professor."

"Don't I know it."

John's tone had more effect than his words. Malik's angry expression turned suddenly speculative.

"Where you from?" he asked.

"A very dark place, Mr. Malik," John lamented. "A place from where you can't take back a thing."

"We didn't deserve what happened to us," Johann said, sensing a potential comrade in John.

"And if a young, white woman's three-year-old daughter is kidnapped, raped, murdered . . . interred in an unmarked grave," John replied, "if all that, did either mother or child deserve their fate?"

"That's just two people. I'm talking about a whole race."

"As am I," John said. "Every human being

211

faces tragedy. It's coded into our blood. There's no escape except through acceptance."

"So I'm supposed to accept five hundred years of slavery?"

Nodding John said, "Then pick yourself up and battle for the future, not the past. The past is a battle you cannot win."

"They stole our history," Malik complained. "I'm just trying to get it back."

"Not stole, Mr. Malik, but utterly destroyed. Where our people came from was ripped from the minds of our ancestors. We can rebuild but never retrieve. And there's an even larger catastrophe intrinsic to that crime."

"What's that?"

John almost smiled then. The words passing between them were more or less meaningless. Malik was there to learn from him because of the common past that their skin implied. The student would trust his professor even if they never agreed on one thing.

"That in destroying our history," John said, "they asphyxiated their own."

Malik tried to come up with a rebuke but instead he shuddered. The hatred in his eyes could have easily been love.

"Are you German?" John asked.

"No." It was a victim's rote reply to the torturer's question no matter what that question was.

"So your parents probably named you after

Bach, one of the great geniuses of music. Your last name is Aramaic for king; the Genius King."

"So what?"

"Those words propel you into the world."

"Can you see any reason I shouldn't drop your class, Professor Woman?"

"Because you are a sword and I a whetstone?"

Johann's lip curled as Annette Eubanks's had. He stood shaking his head.

"I'm outta here," he said.

As he went through the doorway John called out, "If you want a permission slip to drop I'll be unhappy but I'll sign it."

Johann Malik was the only student to visit him that day. John had hoped Carlinda would drop by. They'd reconnected talking about loving fate. It would have been nice to close the door and kiss her cheek.

But he didn't need that kiss. Today there was a triumvirate that judged him: Pepperdine, Eubanks and Malik. He didn't have to worry about the NYPD. His fate was laid out in front of him like a fall.

He'd fallen asleep early for the first time in years, lying there naked on top of the blankets with a window open to let the desert air in. His dreams were centered in a large room where people appeared in no particular order or context. His mother and father were on the periphery. Colette was there with France Bickman, Carlinda and President Luckfeld.

Strolling around John came upon a waitress who asked him, "Would you like to see my breasts?"

His erection was immediate and insistent but it wasn't until he felt his sex enveloped by moist warmth that he opened his eyes.

Fully dressed, Carlinda straddled him, slowly rising and lowering on his erection.

"How did you get in?" he asked.

She smiled and shimmied.

"How?" he asked again.

"There's some overgrown yuccas at the back wall. I climbed behind them. I turned the lock before leaving this morning. I figured you wouldn't check it."

"You wouldn't even look at me when class started today."

"That was before you said *amor fati*."

8

John woke up alone, nestled among the rumpled bedclothes. The scent of Carlinda's lavender perfume rose from the sheets. She hadn't worn perfume the first night they were together.

He sat up feeling that there was something he should be concerned about, something important. After drinking from the bathroom sink spigot and splashing a little water on his face he remembered Chapman Lorraine's body behind the secret door. But Lorraine was dead, gone . . . history. The police were looking for Cornelius Jones, also a thing of the past. No . . . he had to do some kind of presentation on a paper that only had a title. He had to defend himself without the help of a heavy lug-wrench.

Downstairs he took out a pad of flimsy airmail paper, a brand-new yellow number two pencil and a penknife—all from the drawer in his table. He made coffee, closed the window, used the blue-and-silver penknife to shave the wood away from a quarter inch of lead and started writing.

When he was finished John picked out a deep ocher two-piece suit and a spring green T-shirt. He decided on white tennis shoes with no socks.

. . .

The history department was located in the president's compound. John approached the gate at 12:52.

"Professor Woman," Lawrence Gustav greeted him from behind the metal bars.

"Sir," John rejoined.

"They're waiting for you."

"The meeting isn't scheduled until one," John said as the gate rolled open.

"The bigwigs had a powwow at noon."

Walking down a cobblestone path that snaked between the lodge-like buildings John came upon the compound's gardener.

An inch shorter than John the elderly man moved spryly. He had a full mane of salt-and-pepper hair, sun-squinted brown eyes and skin deeply tanned by years of working outside. He wore dark green gardener's pants, a shirt that was an oddly clashing blue, and walnut brown, cracked leather shoes. He was trimming one of eight dark-leaved rosebushes growing in front of the Psych Bungalow.

John stopped and said, "Hello."

"Hi," the elder replied with some surprise in his voice.

"You're the one who takes care of all these bushes and cacti?"

"I certainly am." He took off his gardener's gloves and reached out.

As they shook John said, "I'm John Woman. I teach here."

"Ron Underhill," the man said, maybe grinning a little at the professor's name. "I've worked on these plants since before the school even opened."

"So I guess you've always been a gardener."

"No. Before I came here I was a businessman."

"What kind of business?"

"Doesn't really matter," Ron said. "Most everything people do in business is just a waste of time. Now I tend to the plants that need it and every other month water those that don't."

"The flowers are beautiful."

"Thank you, sir."

"John."

"John."

"It must be a very different experience to be outside all day working under the sun and against it at the same time," John observed.

"Like I said, some plants need a lot of care," the landscape gardener agreed. "But often your delicate breeds bring forth the most exquisite blossoms."

There was wonder in the older man's voice. As if he discovered this truth every time he knelt down to work.

"I'd like to talk to you about that sometime," John said. "But right now I have to be raked over the coals."

"Education's a business too I guess." The gardener was now peering directly into the professor's eyes.

John was struck by the obvious and yet oblique truth of this notion. He wanted to say something but realized he couldn't enhance the older man's assertion.

In contrast to the president's building the history department bungalow had a door. It was pale pink with a blue knob and no bell.

John opened the door and walked in.

Kerry Brightknowles, a senior majoring in Eastern European history, sat behind the reception desk.

"Hi, Professor," she greeted him, smiling.

Kerry was big. She had a large frame and plenty of flesh but only someone in the fashion industry would have thought her fat. Striated blond hair and freckles accented her fair face and arms. She was well formed and carried herself as lightly as a ballet dancer moving across a stage.

"How's it going, Ms. Brightknowles?"

"Graduating this May."

"Happy to be getting out of here?"

"Happy to be getting on with my career," she said. "I'm going to graduate school at Harvard but even if I studied for a hundred years I don't think I'd ever know as much as you do."

"How much you know is of little consequence

in our field. It is mastering the techniques of discovery that makes any researcher rise above the herd."

Hearing this Kerry smiled . . . but that soon turned into a grimace.

"I'm sorry about what they're doing to you, Professor. I tried to explain to Dr. Tracer how great you are in the classroom. He said, 'I see you drank the Kool-Aid too.'" Her quote sounded like Tracer's gravelly voice and John laughed. He liked Kerry.

"I guess you should go on in," she said. "It's in the conference room."

There were eight offices, four on either side of the hallway that led to the glass-walled conference room. Secretaries and assistants behind the open doors glanced at John but looked away before he could greet them.

As he approached John could see the other professors through the glass: jurors facing each other across the long white table. Annette Eubanks had taken the head position. She was looking straight ahead as if she had no idea of his approach. Her dress-suit was shamrock green. Gregory Tracer in a faded blue suit sat to her right. He was in his late thirties. It was said that he'd been Annette's protégé since he was her student and secret lover at the University of Chicago.

There were five other professors from the

department, Theron James and Willie Pepperdine in attendance. Willie was seated not at the table but against the far wall. John went through the open door then stopped one pace into the meeting room.

"Hello, everyone," he said cheerfully.

Willie Pepperdine saluted then leaned back in his metal-and-plastic chair until it was propped against the wall behind him.

"Professor Woman," Annette Eubanks said. She was certainly the one in charge. "Have a seat."

She motioned toward the foot of the judgment table where a solitary chair sat turned out slightly like an unwanted invitation.

John saw another chair placed in a corner behind the department head. He went to the empty chair, grabbed it by a slot in the red plastic back and dragged it over to Willie. He lowered into the seat and sighed, a man taking pleasure in a moment of rest.

"Why don't you come to the table, Professor?" Eubanks directed.

"I thought this was a brown-bag lunch?" John replied.

"It is."

"Brown-bag lunches," John said, "are informal gatherings. Not even in the royal houses of classical China did informal gatherings involve seating charts . . . except, that is, for the emperor and his queen."

John counted out Eubanks's silence in four-four time. He made it through a few bars of this silent melody before she spoke.

"Again I must complain, Dr. James," Eubanks said turning her attention to the dean. "It is irregular for a meeting of this sort, informal or not, to be attended by someone from outside the department."

"Like I told you, Dr. Eubanks," Theron said. "President Luckfeld wanted to be here but had other duties. He sent Mr. Pepperdine as his representative."

"What are his qualifications?"

"I am advisor to the president of the board of directors of the university," Willie said using every iota of authority in his deep voice.

Dean James smiled and gave a sideways apologetic nod to concur.

Annette Eubanks went through all the possible replies she might make, came up with nothing satisfactory and then turned to John Woman.

"Do you have something to share with us, John?"

The young killer from back east sat up straight trying to recall the posture that made him a good student in school before his father got sick. He looked around the table, took a deep breath through his nostrils and began to speak.

"I only found out yesterday that I was expected to speak at this monthly get-together," he said.

221

"So I'm glad that this is just a casual gathering among peers.

"I wasn't able to create formal arguments about my paper which, I'm told, I am to present to the history review committee this semester. I couldn't fabricate an argument but I did manage to write a letter."

John tapped his right hand against the left breast of his yellow jacket.

"I have it right here but I don't think I'll read. Instead I'll summarize the content."

This introduction brought frowns to a few faces. Already the unofficially accused professor had abandoned protocol. At every other brown-bag lunch session the speaker started by introducing an argument about a little-known personage or event that influenced or elucidated what was already known.

John had such a story in his repertoire.

The summer before he came to NUSW he spent nine weeks reading about Lincoln in the Smithsonian archives. There he discovered a name—Elisa Borgone, an alleged prostitute who had been sent a letter by the president. The letter itself had been lost but it was mentioned in a journal entry of Lincoln's White House butler, Peter Brown. Later in life Borgone became a fiery minister of an unaffiliated Baptist church in Baltimore. She had a tall and brooding son named Abraham but there was no father documented.

John could have made quite a career for himself following that possible liaison. He would have had the added satisfaction of eclipsing the resident expert on the Civil War—Gregory Tracer.

But John didn't want to play the game of departmental one-upmanship. He didn't care about presidential trysts or an illegitimate child who might have joined a circus but instead flew into a rage and killed a man named Booth in a St. Louis restaurant.

"The letter is addressed to someone named P," he said. "P is, for lack of a better term, a hermeneutic device; but instead of me taking on her qualities I used her implied existence to confess my sin of knowledge. P is not an expert in our arcane field of study so I had to translate pretentious jargon such as hermeneutics, ontology and epistemology into more pedestrian terms like: *pretend you are, the world* and *what people think is true*. I believe that my slightly inaccurate language enhances the crux of historical analysis rather than minimizing its power."

John stopped there a moment and smiled brightly.

"Dear P," the professor intoned entering a fugue state. "I want to tell you the story of a man named HJ—a black man come to awareness somewhere in the earlier half of the twentieth century. He was raised in the Mississippi Delta but HJ was different from you and me because he was a man without history. I don't mean to say that he had amnesia or that he didn't have family or friends. HJ's people lived inside the dream of another race. We'll call this other group the meta-culture. HJ knew the meta-culture's heroes, religions, languages and moral codes. He knew everything they did including the fact that he and his people were inferior to them in every way that was moral, sophisticated or intelligent.

"HJ couldn't read and there was no school for him or his little black friends. He picked cotton for ten cents a day from the age of nine. Not only was HJ a child with no past; he, and his people, also had no voice. Don't get me wrong; they could speak and yell, cry out and sing but the way the world unfolded around them fell upon their backs and there was no ballot box to express their dissatisfaction with the crushing weight of the meta-culture's progress.

"HJ had no history but he believed that he could steal the meta-culture's past, claiming it as his own. He suspected that books held the secret of becoming the meta-culture.

"In a deceitful move HJ convinced a local minister that he wished to read the word of God, that he wanted to serve the meta-culture's deity so that he could better praise the world that was not his.

"He excelled at reading and was seen as the possible successor to the aging minister—a Negro named August Acres.

"But as soon as he could properly read the first few books of the Old Testament, barefoot HJ embarked on a long trek north, along the western bank of the Mississippi River. His destination was Chicago. Once there he got a job in a factory that took Mississippi cotton and wove it into fabric for poor people to make into work-clothes for factory workers and migrant farmers alike.

"Every week he took three books from the library and read them late at night by the light of a kerosene lantern in a room he shared with three other boys. It was there, in that stuffy attic room, that HJ slowly came to understand that the meta-culture's history was a lie. By leaving his people's history out of their records they had perverted the memory of their own past.

"As he grew older and learned more HJ understood that the crime committed against him and the people who oppressed him was enacted again and again throughout what might be called history. He understood that the only way to claim true knowledge of the past was to live outside its rubric. . . . When I say rubric, P, I mean rulebook. HJ came to understand that the only way to own the past was to live outside the rulebook of history in whatever form that structure took. He realized that he was not inferior to the oppressors, because they themselves were the victims of their own crimes.

"Armed with this rare form of anti-knowledge HJ began a lifelong study of the half-truths and lies that formed a world at once ignorant and arrogant about that ignorance. And though HJ was, admittedly, no one from nowhere, he took solace in the fact that he was that rare individual who knew his place in history.

"If this is not deconstructionist historicity in practice," John said breaking out of his trance and addressing the men and women in the glass room, "I don't know what is. HJ learned to read and later learned that all he read was lies—this made him a man outside history; a position that every historian must attain before she, or he, can lay claim to the past. HJ and his people had their story demolished by people who had no idea that they were committing cultural suicide by excluding members of their own society."

John took a deep breath as if his talk had come out of one great inhalation. He felt a little dizzy, somewhat satisfied and curious as to what his peers would think of his mostly accurate rendition of Herman Jones's journey.

For a few moments the room was silent.

Theron James's face was blank but mild. His thoughts, John decided, were about the impact of the brief talk rather than its content. Willie Pepperdine smiled and nodded as if he were replaying the words in his head; Annette Eubanks's head and neck juddered now and then, for probably the same reason.

"Is that it?" Abel George, the resident Middle Eastern expert asked. "I mean what are we supposed to acquire from this, um, this short story?"

George was hardly older than John; he was in his mid-thirties with black hair, and his skin was the color of pale straw. Tall and loose-limbed, George often reminded John of the scarecrow in the *Wizard of Oz* if that fabulous being had become a somewhat less interesting mortal man.

"It is fiction certainly," John replied. "HJ is an amalgam of people I've known and read about representing an entire so-called race whose past had been annihilated and who are simultaneously excluded from the scholarly awareness of the people that murdered their souls."

"HJ was not murdered in your fable," Lucy Orcell, the department's Europeanist francophone, pointed out.

Lucy was fifty-one with mild features except for her large hands. Her skin was olive hued. She was from St. Louis—a graduate of Oxford.

John shrugged and gazed into the older woman's light brown eyes.

"It is my stance," he said, "that if you take away a human being's anchor to the unfolding of his past then you effectively remove that

227

person from society. And, as we all know, there can be no me without you and me. This crime is tantamount to murder, wouldn't you agree?"

Orcell frowned, possibly realizing her assumption that history was always equally present in every human experience might need some . . . retooling.

"The question is," John added, "if a person inside a culture has no knowledge of his place in the unfolding of that culture, or in the history of any other people, and if no one else among either the oppressors or the oppressed has that knowledge, can that person be said to be alive? Indeed on what plane could he possibly exist except as chattel whether he is a slave or not?"

"But you said that the minister could read," Oscar Pine said.

Oscar was the senior professor of the two-member ancient history department. He was in his seventies, unusually tall, six five, and playful. He was the only other professor in the social studies department who could converse in both ancient Greek and Latin. Annette Eubanks did not intimidate him. He liked to banter with John.

"Yes he could," John said. "I see this . . . this irregularity as a solitary beam of sunlight that somehow has found its way into a dark dungeon."

Pine nodded his long head. His still mostly

brown hair was tied back into a ponytail. His much younger Chinese wife, Su Yen, had once told John that she used the thick braid as her reins when she rode him around the bedroom.

"So," Oscar said, "this light, if it encounters a seed in that dark environment, might engender enough growth to break down the walls from the inside."

"This is prattle," Ira Carmody exclaimed. "There is no basis for the argument. Actually there's no argument at all."

John liked Ira even though the political historian hated him. The little man with the thatch mustache was an expert on the Soviet satellites prior to the lifting of the Iron Curtain but he liked to dabble in ancient thought. He wrote tight scholarly monographs, usually with more footnotes than content, and gave lectures on obscure internal events that he claimed became a part of history whether they ever happened or not.

"You're wasting our time," Carmody added.

"If your time is at such a premium, Ira," Willie Pepperdine said, "then maybe you should leave us and make better use of it someplace else."

"Who the hell do you think you are to speak to me like that?" Ira dared Willie.

Oscar Pine's eyebrows went up.

John smiled, softly appreciating that the focus of his lecture had been commandeered.

Willie let the front legs of his chair come down to the floor and then he stood.

"Come over here and ask me that," the perpetual board member dared Ira.

"What?"

"I got two or three inches on you," Willie said. "You have at least a decade and half on me. Let's see if you can bully your way out of a ass beating."

John expected Dean James to interrupt but he didn't.

"Ira," Annette Eubanks said.

"What?" The last thing in the world he expected was to be physically challenged.

"This meeting is over," the department head said.

Willie was staring at Carmody. John had no doubt that the wealthy board member was ready to fight. But for what?

"Professor," Annette Eubanks called out as John was walking down the concrete path toward the southern end of campus.

John stopped and turned. With heavy steps she walked a straight line. Just as she reached him automatic water spigots came on for the daily drenching of the lawn.

"Do you know that thug?" she asked.

"President Luckfeld asked me to let him audit my class."

"Which one?"

"I only have one this semester. Last year I did double duty for Cynthia Grey when she had to go down to Florida to help her mom after the stroke."

"This isn't over," Eubanks said. John had to admire her brevity in all things.

"That's not quite right," he replied.

"What do you mean by that?"

"I mean *it* hasn't yet begun."

"This isn't a game, John."

It was a game, he thought, a game that she was forcing him to play. He didn't care about tenure. But there he was listening to her deny, and believe in the denial of, her own actions. It was like listening to an accident victim talk about her car insurance while blood flowed from an open wound in her chest.

At the far southern end of the campus sat Deck Recreation Center: a huge white-paneled, black-ribbed geodesic dome covering a deep crater. Deck contained restaurants, the student cafeteria, four auditoriums, recreation rooms and meeting halls.

John was just about to go through the double doors when he felt a hand on his shoulder.

"Professor."

Willie Pepperdine stood there smiling beneficently as a steady stream of students flowed around them.

"I thought you were headed for Ho Chi Minh City, Willie."

"I was. But then I heard about the inquisition that Carmody and Eubanks had engineered."

"Why would you be concerned with that?"

"Same reason I'm taking your class," Willie said. "I'm interested in how you perform inside your chosen environment."

"But isn't your vocation the transformation of currency into significance?"

Willie smiled at all the big words and John felt a little embarrassed.

"I'm a rich man, Professor. I can afford to do what I want, when I want."

"Would you have really come to blows with Ira?"

"I'd'a stomped his prissy ass into the linoleum. Can't stand bullies."

"You're the bigger man," John reminded him.

"But," Willie said with a grin, "Ira has a second-level black belt in Tae Kwon Do. He can bench-press one hundred eighty-seven pounds."

"How would you know that?"

"Did you know that there's an enormous underground lake below this campus?" Willie asked instead of answering the question.

"No."

"There is. It's populated by a wholly unique breed of large, blind, freshwater sturgeon, some of which weigh upwards of two hundred pounds."

232

"Really?"

"I've seen them with my own eyes," Willie assured John.

"How?"

"When the board of directors bought this property the lake was discovered. A team of private and state investigators had to study it to test for the environmental impact of the buildings we planned to erect. I went along on the dive."

"What does that have to do with your knowledge of Ira's strength?"

"I saw those blind fish, crayfish and albino water worms in their natural environment. The only way you could know those fish and other creatures was by getting down there with them. As you said in your very interesting lecture, Professor—in order to know a man you need to understand his environment."

"And I'm the man?"

Pepperdine smiled and tilted his head to the side.

"Almost sounds like you're stalking me, Willie."

"So this fellow, this HJ," Willie said. "What you were saying was that he alone knew the history of his world because he could see the lies that the people who thought they owned history were telling themselves."

"Yes."

"And that only a man in HJ's situation can even hope to understand what has happened."

"Absolutely," John said.

"Not stalking, Professor, but learning. I'm learning how to articulate an argument as rare as those fish hundreds of meters below our feet."

"Why, Willie?" John asked. He was captivated by the billionaire's motives.

"Like you said, Professor, there is no me without you and me."

9

When John got home he expected Carlinda to be there but instead there was a camel-brown envelope on the kitchen-level table.

He pulled out a chair and sat in front of the letter, not touching it at first. There was no writing, no stain, crease or irregularity in the rectangular fold. It lay at an odd angle. *Just dropped there,* John thought; *exactly what Carlinda would do.*

What Carlinda would do? Did he believe that he knew this young woman? How had she gotten so deep into him after only two nights and two classes?

He picked up the brown envelope and tore it open. He read it then read it again—a dozen times over.

Dear Cornelius,

You probably believe that you are safe here in the middle of the desert while they search for you in New York. You think because they don't have your fingerprints or DNA that they won't be able to find you. But if this note has found you then anyone, given the proper motivation, might also. You have done an excellent job of hiding and making something of yourself after that craven act. It will be interesting to see where you go from here.

An Interested Party

P.S. No one escapes without leaving at least one footprint behind.

The writing was educated; the hand unfamiliar. It posed no immediate threat but still there was the definite knowledge of his, John's, guilt.

France Bickman? Maybe he was still alive. Or possibly the investigation turned up semen residue on the bedclothes beneath the trunk/ casket. That didn't make sense. No one could have located him within the last forty-eight hours. John's mind felt like a mackerel flopping hopelessly on a pier. Maybe someone already knew who he was and somehow heard his name in connection with the murder investigation. But why not just turn him over to the police? Maybe someone had. Maybe Phoenix PD was coming to arrest and extradite him.

What most interested John about this letter was his response to it; he was confused by the implications but not worried, not even perturbed. *Truth,* he had often lectured, *is never a threat. It*

is sometimes dangerous but all of life is danger.
Only in death are we delivered from peril.

The interested party had transmitted truth.

He was still thinking about the letter, now in his pocket, when the hand touched his shoulder.

"I was expecting you to be here when I got home," he said.

"I went to the Korean bathhouse in town," Carlinda said, "to get a mineral oil enema."

"Why?"

"For you." Her fingers lifted from his shoulder to caress his ear. They had yet to face each other.

"I didn't ask for that."

"No. Arnold is always asking me. This morning we were fooling around and he asked me again. That's when I decided to come do it with you."

"Why?"

"Because you make me feel like I'm in charge."

"It feels all greasy," she said later that evening. They were lying naked on top of the blankets, a slight breeze wafting in from the window.

"You want to take a shower?"

"No. I like how it feels. It reminds me of you."

"But I'm right here."

"Yeah." She reached out running her fingers across his right nipple. "You are here with me, here in my mind, and between my thighs. It's like you're everywhere and I am too."

For a brief instant John caught a whiff of Senta's after-sex cigarette. She was there too, he thought.

"What you thinkin'?" Carlinda asked.

"About you saying you won't love me."

"What about it?"

"If that's so why are you here giving me what your boyfriend wants?"

Carlinda sat up, then sighed. She leaned over and kissed John's forehead.

"Because I need a man," she said. "A man that needs me."

"Doesn't Arnold need you?"

"You remember his name."

"You talk, I listen."

Carlinda leaned back on her elbows. "Arnold wants me. He wants me all the time. He wants my company, my ass, my attention. He was my boyfriend in high school in Trenton, and then when I applied to U Pitt he did too. I didn't like Pittsburgh, transferred to NYU and he followed."

"Does that bother you?"

"Not really. He always asked if he could come. He's very sweet and I love him."

"But you don't need him because he doesn't see you."

"You're very smart, Professor. You say things I know but can't say."

"That doesn't explain why you think I need you."

"I'm not talking about you. I'm in love with Arnold."

"But you need me because, you say, I need you."

"Yes." She strummed his penis and he was immediately erect.

"And what is it that I need?"

"Not this," she said. "You don't think about my body except when we're having sex."

"Making love?"

"Whatever. You give me physical love but then let it go. I like that very much."

"You're mature for a second-year student."

"I have two younger sisters, one younger brother, an older brother who's a loser, a father gone away somewhere forever, and a mother who has serious prescription drug issues. I don't remember ever being a kid."

"And what about me?" John asked. "How do I fit in all that?"

"Kerry Brightknowles," she said to the ceiling.

"What about her?"

"She's my dorm advisor."

"And she told you about the meeting today?"

"What meeting?"

"In the history department."

"Uh-uh. I haven't talked to her since the night after orientation."

"Then what could she have said that makes you think I need you?" John's professional interest was now aroused also.

"Administrators and professors that have admin positions come to work two weeks before the semester begins," she said. "Kerry had to be there because they needed someone to print their reports and get them coffee. She heard Annette Eubanks and Ira Carmody talking about how they were going to get you fired."

"When did she tell you this?"

"Really she was telling my roommate Tamala Marman and I was there."

"But you didn't know me."

"Not until class. I really was worried about that personal history paper but I could see how great you were and I just got mad about them trying to fire you. Then, when you wiped the sweat from my lip I knew we had to be . . . not in love but lovers."

"It doesn't really make a lot of sense," John said.

"I need you. Does that make sense?"

"But I could never have you."

Carlinda smiled and he was aroused again.

At four in the morning they were both wide awake and sated.

"What do I need you for?" John asked.

"What?"

"Yes . . . what."

The young woman twisted her skinny, naked body and groaned, stretching like a satisfied house cat. She sat up in half-lotus and gave her professor a meaningful look.

"Natasha Bien."

"Who?"

"My best friend in high school. Her boyfriend, this mechanic called Stitch, was banging her mother when Tasha was at school. One day she came home early and saw them on her father's workshop cot out back. She saw 'em through a window. They were going at it like porn stars."

"And?"

"She was crazy mad yelling about Stitch and then her mom betraying both her and her dad. She wanted to hurt them but didn't know how.

"I told her that we could ditch school and sneak around to the window again and record them on my phone. After that all we had to do was release it on the school website."

"You did that?" John asked.

"It took us a couple of weeks to catch 'em again. But when we did, it really fucked up Tasha's mom and the asshole Stitch. Both of them left town."

"Together?"

"Uh-uh. Stitch joined the Marines and her mom went to live with her sister. So I thought I could do the same thing for you—instead of my personal history paper."

"You're saying that I need you to do home-work?"

"You need me to stop them from getting rid of you."

"Even President Luckfeld can't stop them from refusing me tenure," John said. "What can you do?"

"What I did to Tasha's mom. Me and Tamala and maybe Kerry could find out things about Eubanks and Carmody and then put it out around the school. They'd be too upset to mess with you and then I could jump the fence whenever I needed somebody to be with without them being in love."

"Without *you* being in love."

"You too," Carlinda chided. "You don't love me either."

John experienced an unfamiliar urge.

"What?" she asked in response to his blank stare.

I murdered a man and put him in the wall of a silent cinema, that's what he wanted to say, to break the silence he'd held since childhood. But swallowing the truth had become second nature; he couldn't admit guilt even though he wanted to.

"What?" Carlinda asked again.

Cornelius was thinking about his days at Yale as the newly minted John Woman. That was when he started seeing prostitutes. They didn't care about a name or the history attached to that name. He had very few school acquaintances and not one of them knew one true thing about him.

"John."

"What?"

"What are you thinking?"

"That I like your proposal to do a personal history outing of my enemies."

"Enemies?"

"Yes. But I don't want you to do it. I don't want you fighting my battle for me."

"Okay," she said reluctantly.

"But if you were to take on such a project, and I definitely don't want you to, but if you took on this project you couldn't just target Annette and Ira," John said. "That would be too obvious."

"What then?"

"You'd do six or seven professors in various departments. Find their hidden truths and then attribute them to another person. For instance if professor number one was a convicted sex offender and professor six was an embezzler then you would switch their crimes giving just enough information that the real malefactor would recognize him or herself."

"It'd be so close; like a tooth feeling the sing of pain waiting for the full-on toothache," Carlinda said. "That's really devious. And, and, and Eubanks and Carmody would just be another two."

"But I don't want you to do it."

"Of course not. I was just saying it because I

want you to know that I really like you even if I don't, you know, love you."

"It would be fun though," John admitted. "They'd be too afraid to blame me for putting out the information even though it'd be obvious."

"I think that I need some more ass-fucking, Professor Woman."

"I don't want to hurt you."

"Don't worry, you can't."

10

Later that morning John awoke, alone as usual. It was Saturday. John's custom on Saturdays was to walk around the campus, especially near the dorms and through Deck Rec, to be among the students observing how they interacted. He liked to note their clothes and slight changes in language.

But that Saturday he was inclined to go into the little town annexed to the university—Parsonsville.

Before NUSW opened its doors, Parsonsville was populated by lettuce farmers who numbered fewer than two hundred families. The main street used to sport a general store, a diner, and Leonard's Hardware Store, which sold tools, work clothes and tractor parts. The original residents were now relics in their own town. Since the influx of disposable cash Parsonsville had ballooned to a population of nine thousand permanent residents and half again that many students, faculty, and staff when school was in session. There were fancy restaurants and coffee shops, a modern movie theater with four screens, clothing stores and even a hotel—the Stafford Arms. Lettuce farms surrounded the school and town—like old castles on the outskirts of so many modern European cities. It was hot that morning so John wore a blue-and-red Hawaiian shirt and white trousers. The university crowd was still asleep so John found himself among farmers driving their pickups and walking into and out of the twenty-four-hour drugstore that sold everything from aspirin to cigarettes, fresh produce to bicycles.

At the corner of Prospect and Main he saw a small leather notebook that had been tossed into a bright orange public trash can. The black-bound journal had maybe fifty or so sheets of unlined paper, each of which had been scrawled over in mostly blue ink forged into letters that reminded John of tiny, frantic dancers making their way across the pages. Each sheet was written upon top to bottom, edge to edge, back and front. There were no paragraph breaks, dates or even spaces between sections of thought.

. . . she's at it again. Had her lawyer call me to say that I had stole her family's airlooms and killed her dog. Damned dog. It bit me four times before I put it down. And Shelly gave me that damn watch and paintin of old Colonel Blue. Lawyer said that if I don't make recompents (that's the word she used) for the hound and return her clients property that she would have me in court. Damn bitch lawyer and fuckin fool Shelly. I should do to them what I did to that damned dog Milo. A man has to protect himself. A man has to stand up for what he knows is right. I aint afraid. I been in jail before. I fixed Shellys front steps and painted her garage. I aint askin for any of that back. Dogs dead and the watch and paintin are mine. Shelly gave them to me. Me . . .

John sat on the university bus stop bench, reading, wondering how the diary found its way into the trash. It looked pretty old. The pages had been white but the edges were turning yellow beneath armies of bright blue and blue-black letters. It was mostly a litany of complaints— people who had crossed the diarist and situations that betrayed him (John was sure the memoirist was male).

The writer had taken his compulsive obsessions out on the pages of this book. Now someone had thrown it away. Maybe he did it himself as a kind of exorcism.

. . . nigers spicks and chinks all over the place nowadays. Schools full of them. Town too. It makes me mad when I see them dressin and talkin like us. Goin to our schools and breathin our air like it was natural. Nigers spicks and chinks all up behind stupid white girls with their asses and tits hangin out. I saw this one niger in a 3 piece blue suit at Darlene's Cafe outside town. He was just sittin there eatin meat loaf actin like he was readin a book. I went up to his table and asked him if he was a butler. He looked at me with his mouth open and his eyes all googly like a big black fish. I had my 38 in my pocket. If he had said somethin I would have shot him right there in front of Darlene and everybody. I wasn't afraid of him . . .

John thought that the man in the suit was probably Earl Vashon, the resident poet in the creative writing department. Earl always wore suits and usually had his nose in a book. He'd won a Pulitzer decades ago. Earl was from Mississippi like Herman and also like Herman he spoke in a cultured accent that didn't exist anywhere but in him.

My brother George died last March in Indiana. Luce his wife said that it was a heart attack but you never really know. Terry my other brother buried George outside Phoenix. I'm goin to go up to see him now that he's dead and buried and all the excitement have died down. George and me did not speak. I forget now what the last fight was about but it doesnt matter because we were always fightin me and him. It seamed like all we had to do was look at each other and we wanted to come to blows. Luce been writin me but I never answer. I know she wants somethin and I'm not a bank or a head doctor either. I don't want her cryin to me. I did not kill George and he never liked me . . .

A big turquoise-colored bus trundled up to the stop and opened its door.

"You gettin' in?" the old white bus driver said after five seconds had passed.

John looked up from the journal and shook his head.

"Bastard!" the driver shouted.

The door closed and the bus rolled off.

John walked across the street to the air-conditioned coffee shop, ordered a medium latte with two extra shots of espresso, sat down at a window table and continued to read.

He christened the diarist *Brother of George* (BOG) studying every word, phrase, idea and grievance BOG had to offer. Imagining he lived millennia in the future, John scrutinized his subject as if it was the memoir from a representative of an extinct ancestral branch of what humans had evolved into. From his lofty point of view John imagined that BOG was culturally insane but through that insanity might be uncovered intellectual and linguistic precursors of his highly advanced species.

For the next week John spent every spare moment reading, notating, and considering BOG's journal. He wrote to Prosperity about his thoughts but shared them with no one else. He lectured, maintained office hours, made love (that was not love) to Carlinda, and effectively ignored the camel-colored letter, the discovery of Chapman Lorraine's body and the paper he needed to deliver to the history department review committee.

On the morning of the following Saturday John awoke with the understanding of what his paper was to be. At the corner of Prospect and Main in Parsonsville he sifted through the orange trash can finding a set of white plastic dinnerware utensils, wrapped in a white paper napkin, a broken set of fancy headphones, and a list of some sort. These treasures he took over to the coffee shop for study.

The list was jotted down on a small sheet of lined notepaper, written in fountain pen blue-black ink that blobbed up now and then. Iron Man, Mandarin, Unicorn, Jack Frost, Sunturion and Stratosfire, the Stark . . . There were sixty-three entries on the paper front and back. It took

John a while to realize that this was a list of comic book characters. It wasn't until three days later he figured out that all these names were fictionally related to the first name on the list—Iron Man.

There were ecological and economic issues bound up with the slightly stained napkin wrapped around the plastic fork, knife and spoon. The broken set of headphones (made in China) presented a more advanced interpretation of the same issues.

Monday afternoon after the second Saturday at the trash bin, John drove to Spark City, not to see Senta but to buy an old traveling trunk at the used furniture store on the opposite side of town from the motel and bar.

That evening John placed BOG's diary in a corner of the trunk. By Friday the comic book characters list, disposable dinnerware set and headphones were nestled next to what he called the First Find.

Every Saturday for the next few months John made his way in the early hours of the morning to the orange *real-time capsule* where he uncovered a trove of data-laden material which would become the reconfigured history of today.

He wrote to Prosperity that his discoveries *were both exotic and pedestrian, the two main requirements for reconstituted history, like dinosaur footprints in stone-hardened mud or some obscure measuring tool from an ancient Egyptian architect.*

There were nineteen installments in the Containment Report, the name which John ascribed to the traveling trunk. There was a cake, still inside its pink baker's box, that read HAPPY BIRTHDAY SADIE in hardened pink sugar letters. The cake was frosted in thick white icing. No candles but there was a red sugary drawing of a clown hovering above the pink words. One corner of the cake had been slightly crushed in but other than that it was in perfect condition. There was a monogrammed light blue handkerchief stiffened with a goodly quantity of dried blood; the monogram was AKI and the blood still damp when John retrieved it. An envelope that had been mailed, read and discarded, all in Parsonsville, contained a letter from a lover who could not keep up the lie any longer. The letter was written to someone named JD and was signed Lynn. There were three shopping lists, one balled-up photograph from a pornographic magazine, a broken cell phone, a used condom, a wallet that at first seemed empty but, upon closer examination, had a secret compartment containing a snapshot of a face contorted by fright. There was a receipt from the twenty-four-hour drugstore that listed twenty-one items purchased by a shopper at a register manned by Andrew H and a nearly full pack of Camel cigarettes.

Finally there was a small black velvet sack containing a jury-rigged syringe made from a rubber-bulbed eyedropper and a hypodermic needle, a small plastic bag of white powder, a real silver spoon, four cotton balls and a box of wooden matches.

Every night, when he was alone, John studied his finds. He had a student in the IT department copy the contents of the journal and letter into a program that separated out the words as symbols and numbered them. There were one hundred sixty-three thousand two hundred forty-one words crammed into BOG's diary.

Over the next four months John studied the materials and annotated his finds with sparing use of public records or the Internet. He interpreted the data and gave it meaning primarily by using the skills that any historians or anthropologists would have at their disposal.

"I want to tell you some things," Carlinda said to John on the Monday after his final foray into the downtown public trash receptacle.

Drinking port at his downstairs table, they had not yet kissed or even touched.

"Talk," John said

"Not like this."

"Like what then?"

"Naked in the bed," she said, "with me on top of you and you inside me."

"Why?"

"I'll tell you upstairs."

It was difficult at first but they were finally able to achieve the position Carlinda required. She was breathing deeply and he felt distracted—the Containment Report was sitting on the window ledge with two padlocks keeping it secure.

"Arnold only knows how to make love one way," she said.

John could feel his heart beating.

"You're getting harder," she told him.

"Uh," John replied.

"He can only do missionary or he goes limp and if I talk while we're doing it he loses concentration. He's got a big one but it doesn't get hard like yours is right now."

"I don't know what to say," John muttered.

"The reason I like you is that your dick talks for you. I never knew it before but I like that in a man."

"I thought you had other lovers."

"I never went all the way with them because Arnold would find out and come back into my life.

"Last Wednesday I told him that if he wanted sex he'd have to let me chain him down to the bed. I used handcuffs from the new sex shop in town to shackle his wrists and ankles to the metal frame under his mattress."

"What did you do then?" John asked shifting his position slightly.

"Stay still, Professor. I just want to feel it without you moving around."

"What did you do then?" he asked again.

"I tortured him with pleasure until he could do it the way I wanted. He complained that the cuffs were too tight so I made them tighter. He said he couldn't do it but when I got on top of him he could . . ." At that moment Carlinda began to shudder and moan. When John moved with her she slapped him. He stopped moving and she continued with her orgasm.

When she was finished she said, "I told him that any other night we could do what he wanted but on Wednesdays he had to let me have my way."

"And what did he say?"

"Nothing."

In the morning, alone again, John took digital photographs of the contents of his Containment Report trunk. These he e-mailed to Talia Friendly, his IT specialist. She would create the slide shows he wanted.

That afternoon he drove out to the Spark City Bar, nursed a club soda until 7:45 then went over to see Senta.

When she opened the door he walked past her into the room and sat on the bed.

"Do you have to go to the toilet?" she asked.

"No. I went in the bar before I came over."

"Do you want to take off your clothes?"

"Not now, maybe later."

Senta dragged a pine chair from the table over to the bed and sat down facing her john, John.

"What's wrong, baby?"

"Nothing," he said, gazing at the floor.

The dirty pink carpet was wall-to-wall and had probably been red at one time. He hadn't remembered the rug. This simple fact disturbed him. He was an observer. He should know everything about every place he'd been.

Reaching over, Senta extricated his left hand from the right.

"What's going on?" she asked.

He shook his head.

She smiled and asked, "Are you breaking up with me?"

In unison they brought all four of their hands together.

"I have sex with you because I want to," he said.

"Well duh."

"No, Senta, you don't understand. I have sex with you because I want to but I come here because I need, I need you."

"You need to have sex."

"No," John said.

"You're hurting me."

"I'm sorry," he said, letting go.

"What are you telling me, John?"

"I get pretty drunk with you sometimes right?"

"Yeah. We both drink too much. But I like it with you because you talk about things I never thought of before."

"And I like you because you're always here in this room when I come calling." Senta smiled and then grinned.

"What?" John asked.

"When I was a little girl me and my sister would stay with my grandmother for the summers. She had a cabin on Lake Spofford up in New Hampshire. There was a picture of granddad on the mantel above the fireplace. He died before we were born so grandma'd tell us stories about him. She used to say about when he'd *come calling*. That's what they called dating back then. Do you think you're dating me?"

"I love you, Senta."

She frowned and he took her hands again.

"I'm powerless," he said. "I can't ask you for anything but this room. It's the only place where I don't feel like I'm manipulating the world around me: here and when I'm doing my work."

"Are you drunk?" Senta asked.

"No. I haven't had a drink in a month or more."

"Why are you saying all this to me?"

"Wednesday after next I'm supposed to deliver a paper for my department. My future at the university depends on how they respond to it."

"You're ready though, right?"

"I am. But they won't understand."

"Why not give them what they will understand?"

"It's just not in my nature," John said, recognizing the truth in his words.

"Will you lose your job?"

"I've already lost it."

"And what does that have to do with me?"

"You are the only person I can tell," he said, "the only one I know who I feel will be there. The rest of my life is like a bottomless pit that everything is dumped into but it never fills up."

"That's how I feel," Senta said, "like one'a those ants we studied in science class, the one that hangs from the top of a tunnel while the other ants pour honey down her throat. Her bottom blows up to twelve times normal size filled with honey. Then in the winter the other ants touch a place on her throat and she vomits up food for them."

"Yeah," John agreed. "We studied those ants in school back in Brooklyn."

"You could write a paper about us, John. The Professor and the Prostitute."

"Why don't you light up a cigarette?" John suggested.

"We haven't had sex yet."

"I know."

Senta poured them both drinks while balancing a cigarette between her lips. They sat quietly, him at the edge of the bed, Senta on the hard chair.

"What will you do if you lose your job?" she asked at last.

"I don't know."

"Is there any way you can save it?"

"Maybe. The president likes me. Maybe I could get him to do something."

"Ask him then."

"The whole thing is a game anyway, like in Vegas, you know? There have to be stakes. If you lose, you lose. If you don't feel the loss then you never took a chance."

"You don't care if they fire you?"

"I care. But there are many more important things on my mind."

"Like what?"

"I did something . . . something wrong."

"Against the law?"

He nodded.

"Are they after you?" she asked.

"Like Monday up Tuesday's butt." It was something his mother used to say.

"Could you go to jail?"

"Definitely."

"So why do you even care about this paper?"

"Because you have to take a risk. You have to take the steps laid out in front of you because that is your destiny."

Senta blinked and frowned.

"Will you spend the night here with me?" she asked.

"I will."

"We don't have to have sex if you don't want."

"Yeah. I know."

11

Eight days later, at 11:49 on Wednesday morning, John Woman and Talia Friendly were setting up for the presentation in the main hall of Deck Rec. She had given him a Bluetooth earbud to hear her questions from up in the control room.

"You can either nod or shake your head or you can just call out to me over the house mike. I mean this is still a little informal."

The stage was set so that there were three screen-like walls opened up behind an old oak lectern and a high table, upon which sat the Containment Report trunk.

The mostly empty auditorium was fitted to seat 999 souls.

"Remember that the upper part of the center screen should be running as they come in," John said. "Then you just follow the cues we talked about, the lower part and the other two."

"You got it, Professor," Talia agreed. She was a blocky young woman with crew-cut black hair. "All you have to do is point at a screen and it'll go. I got it all programmed perfect."

At a quarter past twelve John was standing in front of the table facing the hall, his hands behind his back, a pose he'd adopted as a boy from a painting of Napoleon in exile. He believed that the deposed dictator struck this pose to overcome humiliation and fear so used it whenever he wanted to master his own anxieties.

The audience trickled in. Dean James came down the main aisle accompanied by President Luckfeld. They both wore dark suits and ties, hard leather shoes and short-brimmed Panama straw hats. They marched to the front of the middle section and sat together.

John was considering going down to say hello when a noisy group of students entered the auditorium. It was his class, almost all of them. Maybe, he thought, they wanted to see how his crazy ideas held up under the scrutiny of the other professors.

But then he saw Carlinda. He knew that she wouldn't be part of any kind of hazing. On her right was Tamala Marman wearing bright red. To Carlinda's left was a solid-looking young white man with wiry black hair and dark-framed glasses. He was holding her hand but when she saw John she pulled the hand free to scratch her nose. This move convinced John that he was looking at Arnold Ott, the young man for whom Carlinda professed love but not passion.

"Now, Professor?" Talia Friendly asked in his ear.

He nodded and then turned to look at the top half of the center screen. There the words **She's**

at it appeared—black letters against a yellowy background. John counted to ten and the words **again**. **Had her** replaced the first three words.

"You cue the puzzle too," he said aloud.

In an upright rectangle of light, below the slow progression of words, tiny pieces of a huge jigsaw puzzle flitted on and off at different places in the frame. Now and again, every ten seconds or so, a random piece would stick.

The screen reminded John of the silent films shown at the Arbuckle Cinema House.

There is no sound, Herman Jones often said. *It is like trying to glean meaning from a partial experience, through faulty memory. Like those books you read me, son—not everything, but enough if you can suspend disbelief.*

When John turned back to the auditorium more than a hundred people had entered. Eubanks and Carmody were there and most of the rest of the faculty from the history department. In the far left corner of the last aisle sat the gardener Ron Underhill.

The auditorium was filling up quickly.

John wondered why Ron would come to such an event, indeed, how had he found out about it? Meanwhile dozens more sauntered in. There were greetings and kisses, smiles and quite a few serious, even worried, looks.

John was elated. Behind him Brother of George's journal was being parceled out three

263

words at a time. Below that an as yet indefinable picture was taking form. *There are moments in life,* Herman Jones once said from his long-tenanted deathbed, *when we can see clearly that every day, every second before now has brought us to a moment of grace. I feel it sometimes when you are reading to me, Cornelius. I hear your voice and know that we are together on this road.*

Thinking about Herman's lessons John felt his father standing next to him in front of nearly a thousand people waiting to see him rise or fall like a gaudy paper kite in an autumn wind.

John took seven long, slow breaths then spoke out loud and clear, his voice magnified by the tiny microphone attached to his shirt.

"The words appearing on the screen behind me were retrieved from a trash can. Some man, I call him Brother of George, wrote down a big piece of his life and then threw it away, or maybe he lost it. It could have dropped out of his pocket and a street sweeper gathered it up and tossed it—there for me to find and now for you to witness, three words at a time.

"The frame of light below the words is using specialized software that is a self-solving ten-thousand-piece jigsaw puzzle of a photograph that will be revealed in time. The trunk on the table is my Containment Report, the receptacle binding the data I've gathered for this Deconstructionist Historical Event.

"I was asked to present a paper detailing the approach to a branch of historical study that includes itself while excluding the potential of, the possibility of, absolute truth. It came to me one Saturday morning some months ago that asking for a paper in this day and age is tantamount to asking Charles Dickens to chisel a novel on stone. Language, in the form of a written paper, is the transmutation of the material into the speculative. And though this method is still in use the technological and cultural zeitgeist has evolved far beyond its limitations.

"The transmutation of the material into the speculative," John repeated. "History is, first and foremost, a material thing or, from another point of view, a concatenation of material events that are interpreted through the human fallacy of time. And therefore, in order to present a cogent argument, I find that I must include the material bases of my so-called paper."

John felt a cold drop of sweat trickle down his back. He took off his black jacket and placed it on the table. Then, slowly and deliberately, he used his keys on the padlocks and threw open the lid. He looked out at the packed house noting that there were people standing at the back of the hall. Everyone was looking at him as if he were a magician about to conjure a white tiger out of an old traveling case.

"I spent sixteen Saturdays visiting a real-time

time capsule, what you would call a public trash can, and retrieved the base materials from which a glimmer of the notion of history might be garnered.

"There was Brother of George's lost memoir and the magazine photograph which is being re-membered on the screen below." He took the leather-bound journal and a balled-up magazine page from the chest, held them out for verification and then placed them on the table. "But this is only the beginning of our history-rich material discoveries . . ."

John then produced the comic book character list. When he gestured at the screen to his right the names (starting with Iron Man) began appearing one at a time at six-second intervals— slowly reconstructing the list.

". . . This neo-mythology," John said of the list, "may one day be used to study the people of this age by creating a window into this time as Gilgamesh, Hercules and Jesus allow us to understand the races and events of history— superheroes of a bygone era."

He showed them the plastic cutlery set discussing briefly petroleum, derived from prehistoric plant matter, the napkin made from contemporary plants.

Indicating the broken headphones he talked about mass fabrication and how this process of *making things* in return creates the people as they practice the repetitive act of fabrication.

"Human history is the labor of men," he said, "and women."

After this pronouncement John turned to look at the progress of BOG's diary. The words **Nigers spicks and** were on the screen. John smiled at the synchronicity and waited for **chinks all over** to appear before he continued.

He gestured at the other screen, and the short letter from Lynn to JD appeared in totality. John waited for the audience to read the beautifully rendered handwriting while BOG spewed overhead.

"They're fucking," an audience member said somewhat above a whisper.

The jigsaw puzzle was now allowing images from the pornographic magazine to become evident.

"Yes," John agreed. "While Lynn talks to JD about lost or impossible love the recovered photograph represents desire."

He presented the birthday cake, drugstore receipt and blood-crusted handkerchief as *proofs of event* . . . "without explanation or understanding." The images of these items disrupted the comic book list for a few moments and then let the listing continue.

The talk continued and John produced items that, one after the other, appeared on the screen to his left.

". . . was this nearly full package of Camels the

attempt of some poor soul to stop that dangerous habit or was it a mistake? Maybe someone controlled their smoking by buying a pack, smoking one or two, and then throwing the rest away . . ."

John had been speaking nearly an hour. That put BOG's diary at about word ten thousand. Below BOG's rant the partially formed image was of a woman in a nun's black habit. The floor-length hem had been raised above her buttocks; she was praying to a priest while a man penetrated her rectum from behind and others waited in line for their turn.

John raised the broken cell phone up and the auditorium's speakers began to replay a recording of a man's voice, *Hey, Mo-man, I hope everything's goin' good with you and Felicia. I'm working on that project and I need electronic pictures of you, Felicia, the kids and grandkids. Hopefully Regine and I can see you guys in Seattle next month. The city is wonderful in the summer. Do you have state-issued ID? If so we can go up to British Columbia in Canada. It's about two hours from Seattle. Talk to you soon . . .*

"Using the tools available to me in faculty housing," John said. "I was able to fix this broken, discarded cell phone. The data was more or less destroyed but I managed to cull this snippet from voice mail.

"A voice from out of the well of time speaking

to us as though we coexisted. We're given a few names and a nickname, a city and the possibility of travel to another. We know that they dealt in electronic data and felt some kinship over a distance that curtailed physical intimacy.

"This is history at its best. It's not Abraham Lincoln's brain suffering the indignity of John Booth's bullet. It's not Attila the Hun raping ten thousand subjugated women. This is the fragmentary grist of life; what we are all made of and at the same time indicative of the vast ocean of knowledge that is mostly unavailable, or only partially so. We pretend to know the story of humanity because we have agreed upon the information and people that are most important. But we cannot, with any degree of accuracy, define a single day in the life of a comatose quadriplegic in an isolation ward under twenty-four-hour audio and visual surveillance. There are just too many variables. The symphony of a single trash can gives us more than any computer could contain."

John gazed out over the hall and was gratified to see that very few had left. The spectators were reading the angry laments of BOG, watching to see what new elements of the photograph would be exposed.

"The last two elements of my presentation bring a new wrinkle into the scope of our studies and ourselves," he said. "Here we have a simple brown leather wallet that was discarded. It is empty. No money, credit cards, receipts or family photographs. Maybe it's the castoff of some pickpocket or mugger. Maybe the previous owner bought a new wallet from the twenty-four-hour drugstore and moved the contents from the old to the new. Maybe . . . But on closer examination I found that there was a flap on the mass-produced wallet sewn shut by hand, not machine. When I cut the thread this photograph was revealed."

John held up a tiny snapshot and instantly the blown-up image was displayed on the screen to his left. It was the portrait of a young man. He was grimacing through a bloody lip and a missing tooth. The subject was so frightened that the photograph evoked the depravity of the photographer.

One woman in the audience gasped. Murmuring could be heard among the spectators.

"An odd keepsake," John noted. "And a find for any historian."

The murmuring continued.

"Then we have this," John said taking the black velvet sack from his Containment Report trunk. As he held up the little bag a photograph of its contents appeared on the screen to his right.

"All you would need," John said, "for a night of opioid debauchery. A junkie's fix thrown away. Maybe some concerned friend took it from him, or her. Maybe the police were closing in. Or possibly, as we speculated about the cigarettes, this was a last-ditch attempt to kick the habit and go cold turkey.

"But we don't know any of that," he said. "It's not you and me here in this auditorium in December two thousand thirteen. No. We are another species evolved from humanity by technologic and biological means fifty thousand years in the future. We have ocelot genes in our eyes and elephant folds in our brains. Our socialized souls have been colonized by bee and termite DNA and our emotional hearts have been conditioned by the best fiction ever written. Every one of us has the same last name and the stars have replaced our monetary system. A poor man owns only a few suns while the wealthy count their hoards in galaxies. We don't even know what a turkey was. Drugs are manufactured by synthetic, surgically implanted organs. Our condition has surpassed the archaic definition of life with physical hearts replaced by plasma cells and micro-robots, instead of blood, replenishing and evolving us.

"And when we look back on these items—shopping receipts, traces of blood and memoirs—we find that they are priceless touchstones to our onetime humanity. Abraham Lincoln is of no more importance than Andrew H the checkout clerk at the twenty-four-hour drugstore. They, Abraham and Andrew, were just two apes who used primitive sounds to communicate rather than the subtle manipulation of the ten thousand strands of gravity."

John stopped there. He'd taken the sense of history beyond its accepted border. Six months later he would look back on this talk as intellectual flummery.

The faces in the auditorium were angry, rejuvenated and bemused.

A man who makes his stand, Herman had said of heroes past, *is a man ready to dig his own grave.*

"Questions?" John said in an upbeat tone.

He luxuriated as the seconds passed.

Then:

"Shouldn't you have turned the drugs and photograph and maybe even the bloody bandanna over to the police?" The questioner was Arnold Ott.

"I'm a scholar not a policeman," John said. "I don't know what this white powder is. Blood alone does not indict and photographs without a pedigree mean nothing. I am simply a conduit for the partial knowledge allowed mortal human beings. In other words—a historian."

"But," a female voice chimed in, "isn't it dangerous to get that close to your subject?"

"Exactly!" Professor Woman ejaculated. "The most important lesson to learn is that we are dealing with life in all of its beauty and peril.

Our history is material but it is also subjective, experiential. It can be as dangerous as a blow to the head."

"You're saying that Abraham Lincoln, the greatest U.S. president, is no more important than a late-night checkout clerk in a small-town drugstore?" Gregory Tracer asked.

"Yes," John answered.

"That's ridiculous," the Civil War professor said. He then intoned, "Great men made this world."

"No," John replied. "Unknowable historical fate created us."

"That's crazy!" Ira Carmody shouted. "The world would have been a vastly different place without Socrates, Aristotle and Plato."

"And they themselves would have been different without mothers, fathers and lovers. What about the ancient Greeks? Where would they have been without their tongue? Beyond that where would they have been without their Egyptian forebears?"

The shouting match continued for long minutes. John had one or two allies in the crowd but most of his peers thought him a fraud and a fool. His scholarship was dismissed, his renunciation of the written word ridiculed; his comparison of the great works of history to a public trash can caused the greatest insult.

"That is what you want to do to our lifework,"

Annette Eubanks said, "discard it in the garbage with maggots and refuse."

John smiled at his tormentors, returning time after time to his theme of the impossibility of the project on which they had all embarked.

"History is the primary edifice of the universe," he said in an attempt at a summation. "We are bit players in events that surpass the religions, sciences and philosophies of the world. There is nothing too small or insignificant to have a place in this tapestry. There is nothing that can exist without the collaboration of everyone and everything else. It is ecstasy beyond our imagination and truth exceeding our ability to comprehend or express."

Soon after that Dean James ascended the stage and dismissed the audience. He wouldn't allow any more questions or anyone to approach John, who now sat on the table between his jacket and the Containment Report trunk.

He was exhausted and exhilarated by the presentation, feeling that he'd actually accomplished something. He sat on the table looking at the polished pine stage unaware that the room had been emptied and the doors locked.

John went over the words spoken and questions asked. He was aware that he'd soon be fired, that maybe he'd be arrested and dragged off to prison, but none of that mattered. He stood his ground before bellowing barbarians ready to end him. That was worth a reversal or two.

"That was a pretty good talk," a man said.

John raised his head. Ron Underhill was the last person he expected to see.

"You liked it?" the professor asked the gardener.

"Very much. It made me think about things. You know most people believe that they understand their world but really it's not true. I mean, we know things that we do with our hands pretty much. But what happened in some other country or century or even behind a closed door while we slept, well, it's all just speculation now isn't it?"

"Have you always been a gardener, Mr. Underhill?"

"I told you before," he said gently. "I used to work in an office. I started out shuffling papers and then it was computer files. One day my position became what they called redundant and I was unemployed. But that was okay because gardening was always my first love."

"For me it's history," John said. "It's like some mythological beast that preys on the souls as well as the flesh of men. I follow it through the battlefields of our defeats knowing that one day it will turn on me."

There was concern in the older man's mild

features. In ways Ron Underhill reminded John of France Bickman.

"I only had one question, Professor," Ron said. "I didn't ask because I'm only just a gardener and this seemed like some kind of official thing."

"What's that, Ron?"

"Why do you bother trying to educate these people?"

"What do you mean?"

The gardener hopped up on the table next to the teacher. John looked up and out at the empty hall.

"You been studying this idea of yours for a very long time haven't you?"

"Nearly my entire life."

"But the people out there." Ron gestured at the empty pews. "They haven't spent two hours thinking about any of it. They came here to advance their careers not get down on their knees in the dirt and smell the droppings they grew from. They don't want to hear about blood and hatred, about the junkyard that's their history."

"You *did* listen," John said.

"Talk like that takes a whole lifetime to understand, Professor. These people here are apprentices, tyros who can't imagine what the war they're marching to will be."

"You're well read, Ron."

"I only got one room and no TV or radio. Once a year I go to a family reunion but other than that my nose is either in the earth or a book."

"I don't know why I feel like I have to say something," John said answering the gardener's question. "I guess it's my duty."

"Duty is any creature's greatest virtue," Ron said. "Most people have no idea what it means. They think they do. For them it's badgering children to get good grades or making piles of money, making sure some dead religious leader's ideas are made sacrosanct or simply that the world doesn't change."

"Maybe you should teach here, Ron."

"I do, but hardly anybody ever listens."

12

"I think Arnold knows about us," Carlinda said later that night.

She'd climbed over the back fence but had to ring the bell because John locked the door.

She was ecstatic over his presentation and told him that she had to make love to him so as not to fall in love.

"What makes you think he knows?" John asked.

"It was the way I was looking at you during the talk. That's why he asked you that question. And later on, at the cafeteria, he said that we could do whatever I wanted in bed. I forgot it was Wednesday. All I wanted to do was get away so I could see you."

"And he got suspicious?"

"He came to my room one night last week when Tamala was in Phoenix with her parents. He knew I wasn't there and when he asked me where I spent the night I just didn't answer. I don't want to lie to him."

"Huh," John grunted. "Well if he wants me he'll have to get on line."

"I should probably stop seeing you."

"Probably."

"But I don't want to."

"Why not? You say you love Arnold."

"But I need you . . . right now anyway."

Carlinda was gone when John woke up. That was 9:47 by the digital clock on the wall shelf next to his bed. He lay there feeling a little hungover but he hadn't had a drink. The previous day's talk was the best he could do and it certainly wasn't enough. The history department would never accept his ideas.

It was time to move on.

There was another camel-colored envelope carelessly tossed on the kitchen table.

Dear Cornelius,

Your talk yesterday was impressive. Quite a few students recorded it and maybe it will go viral. People all over the country will see the crazy history professor who looks for his lessons inside a trash can. Do you think anyone will recognize you? Will this be your red flag?

You know you can't run forever, hide indefinitely. The question is—how will you stand up to your fate? This is the only question that a man has to answer in the otherwise pointless ditherings of his existence.

An Interested Party

John read the letter twice. He was struck by the notion that there might be just one important moment in any human's life. This concept was somehow reassuring.

"Yes, Ms. Marman?" John said calling on Tamala at the Thursday afternoon seminar.

"Do you actually believe that a president and, let's say . . . a carpenter have the same level of importance in history?"

"The Christians certainly do," John replied. "But really . . . how can any historic figure stand up under the weight and the scrutiny of centuries? Once this individual becomes a legend what possibility do we have to truly understand him?"

"Or her," Star Limner corrected.

"Or her," John agreed. "We're like crows attracted to shiny objects strewn in the desert. We collect these baubles and stand guard over them. One day we die and the trove is lost, possibly to be found again, totally transformed in the eyes of a new being."

Seventy-five minutes passed with John answering and not answering students' questions.

Finally he said, "What you must understand is that the most important history is your own. Right now, here in this pie-shaped classroom, you are building yourselves, tearing down walls and adding halls, digging into the firmament seeking foundation. And at any moment you may pack up and move on."

After class John went to the back row of seats and turned one of the desk chairs to face the blue-tinted desert. He felt that he had reached a barrier and was about to pass through. It was time to leave the university, to escape the not-love of multiracial Carlinda, and the persona of John Woman. He wondered if the brown envelopes would find him in LA.

"Professor?"

It was Johann Malik.

"Mr. Malik. Office hours are from—"

"Four to six," the dark-skinned, military-clad student said with a forced smile. "I know. I just came to see if you were okay. I mean, I was waiting for you at the door but you didn't come out."

"Yeah," John said. "I have a lot on my mind."

"I finally get it," Johann said.

"What?"

"This deconstructing stuff. You're takin' away their claim to history and putting it back in the hands of the people. You're tellin' them that Lincoln was no better, no more important than a Chinese ditchdigger. They want to put their face on everything that ever happened but you stick a pin in that. That's revolutionary shit."

The young Race Man's compliments, John

281

realized, were probably true. His attempt at the demolition of the sanctity of historical interpretation would surely disrupt the hierarchy imposed by bankers, so-called scholars and political parties. It wasn't John's intention to politicize his teachings but, just as history cannot be known in its totality, neither can any individuals fully define their roles.

"Thank you, Mr. Malik. That means a lot."

"You wanna go grab a beer?" Johann offered.

"Another time, my friend. Right now I have a few things to think about."

Malik held out a hand and John shook it. Then the young activist walked away, leaving the phantom professor to plan his escape.

Departing Prometheus Hall, maybe for the last time, John wandered around the desert campus following a path of habit rather than intention. He ended up at the real-time time capsule at the main intersection in Parsonsville. The trash can had been emptied. The streets were crowded with university people and others.

John leaned against a lamppost at the corner, considering his escape. He needed a mode of transportation that could not be traced and the alternative identity papers stored away. What kind of work could he do now that he'd lost his name and education?

Maybe he'd become a gardener.

Gazing without focusing through the window of the upscale coffee shop across the street John wondered how many people around him were living hidden lives. They could be murderers or thieves, terrorists or the homosexual husbands of suburban trophy wives, Christians without faith or racists working for public welfare . . .

There was a copper-haired woman wearing black, standing at the delivery counter inside the coffee shop. Even though she was turned away she moved her head in a way that caught John's attention. He dismissed the image and thought about bigamists and so-called illegals, of women who slept with their best friends' sons and husbands—maybe with their daughters too.

Maybe keeping secrets is our most human quality, John mused.

The woman with the copper hair moved again, this time taking her paper cup to the condiment shelf. She dumped sugar in her coffee from a glass container: one, two, three shakes, then she stirred.

One, two, three.

Secrets abound.

One, two, three.

Shocked to awareness John focused on the woman. He could see only her profile but . . . it could have been.

Just then the woman started moving quickly toward the back of the coffee shop. John took a step into the street and a loud car horn made him jump. Cars were coming fast from up and down the four-lane artery. He braved the traffic while horns honked and brakes screeched.

"Asshole!" a man shouted.

"What's wrong with you?" a woman yelled.

By then he was going through the glass door of the coffee shop.

He didn't see the metallic-tinted hair. Toward the back there were two restrooms—one for men, another for women.

A young, milk-chocolate-brown woman with a halo of curly, naturally red-brown hair stood at the women's door. She was large but not fat, young but not a child. She noticed John looking.

"What?" she asked.

"Um, uh, nothing," he said.

"Then why you lookin'?"

"My friend's in there. I'm, um, waiting for her."

The woman squinted and pushed her face forward.

"You're that professor right?" she asked. "The one that used garbage to make a history lecture?"

"Yeah."

"That's cool."

When the door to the toilet came open two tall and skinny blond girls came out.

John moved past them into the toilet and saw that it was empty.

"Hey, man, that's the woman's restroom," the young black woman said.

John went past the men's room through a door that opened onto the coffee shop's parking lot.

There were seven cars parked out there.

"Mom?" John shouted. "Mom, it's me, CC!"

But Lucia Napoli-Jones was nowhere to be seen.

At 7:57 that evening John approached room twenty-six of the Spark City Motel. She opened the door before he could knock.

"What's wrong?" Senta Ray asked. She wore a simple and markedly unsexy maroon cotton dress that buttoned up the front and came down below her knees.

"Can I come in?"

"What is it, John?" she asked as he slumped into the chair at the little utility table. "Lou called me at my other job."

"What other job?"

"I'm a sorter at the big Post Office facility outside Delby."

"You work for the Post Office?"

She nodded.

"Why?"

"Health insurance."

Grinning, John sat up straight.

"Join me," he said, gesturing at the other chair.

"If I do are you going to talk to me?"

"That's why I'm here."

Senta smirked and sat down.

"You're a piece of work aren't you, John Woman?"

"How many days a week do you work at the Post Office?"

"I do three twelve-hour shifts a week," she said. "You told Lou it was an emergency."

"I told him that it was important," John corrected her.

"But he said there was a crazy look in your eye. He didn't want me to come."

"He thought I was going to hurt you?"

"I'm supposed to call him ten minutes after you get here or he's gonna bust in with Big Ben."

"Who's that?"

"You don't wanna know."

"Then you better call."

Senta entered digits on her bright red cell phone while John watched. She reminded him of one of those few screen actresses who were pretty when they were young but beautiful in middle age. Her posture was easy, provocative and wholly unconscious.

"Lou?" she said. "Yeah. Yeah. No he's okay. Something happened and he feels like I'm the only one he can talk to. No, baby, it's just a onetime thing. Okay. I'll call you tomorrow."

286

She disengaged the phone, put it into a blue purse on the bed then looked expectantly at her john.

"You and Lou have a thing?" he asked.

"Would that make you jealous?"

"I think I saw my mother today."

"So?" Senta asked.

"My mother abandoned me and my father when I was a kid. She left town with this gangster guy when he got in trouble."

"Where did you see her?"

"In Parsonsville."

"What did she say?"

"There was traffic," John explained. "I was across the street and by the time I got there she was gone."

"Didn't she see you?"

"Her head was turned away."

Senta smiled.

"What?" John said.

"You're still having the same troubles you did the last time you were here?"

"It was her. I know it was."

"Okay," Senta said, relenting only slightly. "Let's say it was her. That sounds like a good thing. If she lives in the area you'll probably see her again and you could look her up too."

"My history talk didn't go well," John said looking down. "And, like I said before, I got bigger problems."

287

"Legal problems?"

"Felony issues."

"Then you need to get away from Arizona. You want me to give you a ride?"

"No thanks," John said. "I would have already been gone if I hadn't seen her head move and the way she put sugar in her coffee."

"It could have been anybody," Senta reasoned. "Maybe you just needed to see your mother right then."

These words galvanized John. Suddenly he was certain. He looked up at Senta. Her eyes were hazel and she wore more makeup for the Post Office than she did as a prostitute.

"Your hair is different," he said.

"I braid it when I'm at work."

"Do you really have orgasms with me?"

"Sometimes."

"Really?"

She nodded and smiled. "What are you going to do, John?"

"Sometimes . . ." he said. "Sometimes when I think about being with you I remember talking but I can't recall what we said."

"You get pretty drunk," she agreed.

"What do we talk about?"

"You go on and on about what you call the idea of history."

"Collingwood."

"What?"

"Is that all?"

"Mostly." Senta smiled. "Are we going to take off our clothes?"

"Retirement and health insurance, huh?"

"Yeah. A girl's got to look out for her future."

"Boys too."

The next day, instead of taking a Greyhound to Los Angeles, John went to see Colin Luckfeld.

"Do you have an appointment?" tan, rattlesnake-eyed Bernice Whitman asked. That day the president's sentry was wearing a big blue dress that would have looked good on her taller, fatter sister.

"I do not," John stated.

"President Luckfeld is a very busy man."

"Almost all men," the professor opined, "even the busiest ones, fritter away most of their allotted hours."

"Is that the kind of prattle you teach in your classes?"

"Call Colin and tell him I'm here."

Mrs. Whitman flinched. John was sure that if they were at a cocktail party she would have splashed her martini in his face. She depressed a gray button on the phone and John wondered if some kind of security, maybe Mr. Gustav, would come to remove him.

"Yes?" Colin Luckfeld said over a small speaker.

"Professor Woman is here," she said. "He doesn't have an appointment."

"That's all right. Send him up."

Whitman leveled her spiteful eyes at John. She couldn't bring herself to speak.

"Professor," President Luckfeld called from the opposite end of his huge office. He was on his feet, headed John's way. "Wait there. We can meet in my little library."

John went to sit on one of the facing yellow sofas. A minute later the president lowered onto the opposite couch.

"That was some speech you gave the other day," Luckfeld said. "I mean I've never seen anything like it. Almost everything you said hit home."

"That may be, Colin, but I don't think my peers share the sentiment."

"Oh no they don't," Luckfeld agreed energetically. "Eubanks and Carmody were here fifteen minutes after the talk was over. They say that the department voted telephonically to deny you tenure and request you be suspended from your post."

"Suspended? Why?"

"The main reason they gave was the jigsaw photograph; said that it was irresponsible to show our students pornography. They also pointed out your slipshod scholarship, your contempt for the profession and the deleterious affect you have on students. If I am to believe them only two members of the department did not ask for your immediate ouster."

"Damn. I knew the presentation was strong but not, not overpowering."

"You need a drink?" the president offered. "I have a good whiskey."

"No thanks."

"Dean James was taken with the journal running through the entire session," Luckfeld said. "I think for me it was the photograph hidden in a secret fold of the wallet. Annette was enraged by your dismissal of written papers. She said that comment alone should keep you from teaching at any university ever again."

"How soon do I have to move out of faculty housing?"

The president sat back crossing his left leg over the right. John noticed that he was wearing a navy blue sweat suit. There was a light blue seam running down the outer edges of the arms and legs.

"They can deny tenure but the faculty cannot fire a teacher. They can suggest your removal but the final decision is mine: mine and Willie Pepperdine's."

"Why him?"

"Willie is the man next to the president of the board. Remember?"

"Oh. So . . . I still have my job?"

"Yes. They might be able to remove you from the department," Luckfeld allowed. "I have to ask our lawyers about that. But appointing you a university professor will make departmental affiliation irrelevent."

"Wouldn't that cause a lot of trouble?" John asked. The starting salary for a university professor was more than that of any other member in his department.

"It is a rare thing, John, for a professor of history to end his presentation with postulation on a far-flung future. That's the kind of scholarship we need. If you can make an even playing field between Abraham Lincoln and some counter clerk named Andrew then you're my kind of teacher: the greatest example of an egalitarian."

"So you'd really promote me just like that?"

"It's already been done."

"So I'm not out?"

"Not yet. Eubanks and Carmody can cause a lot of trouble. There may come a point when even Willie Pepperdine will decide to cut our losses."

John smiled, thinking of his plan to disappear only a day before.

"I had an accident a little while ago," John said.

"Car accident?"

"It was late and I was drunk. There was a coyote on the highway and I ran off the road rather than hit it. He, or she I guess, followed the wreck and came looking for a meal."

"Were you hurt?"

"No. I climbed out and faced the prairie wolf."

"What happened?"

"It disappeared."

President Luckfeld considered a moment. He moved his head about like a photographer imagining his next shot.

"The thing about Lincoln and Andrew H . . ." Luckfeld leaned forward clasping his hands together. "Nameless individuals make up this world," he said and then paused, looking into John's eyes. After a moment or two he continued, "I'm going to tell you something, something that if it got out could hurt me and the people I answer to. Is that all right?"

John nodded. He was holding his breath.

"Carl Bova Tillman," Colin Luckfeld intoned. "He owned the property around Prometheus Hall. We offered him six point seven five times the value of his property but he refused to sell; made himself an impediment in the Path. Our founder wanted this university and so we tasked a man to poison Tillman. The causes appeared to be natural and he passed peacefully, without pain or fear.

"There's a wall we have, very far from here, and on that wall there's a list of our heroes. Carl Tillman is among them. He made the ultimate sacrifice whether he knew it or not."

Part Two

The Guerrilla War of History

13

At the beginning of the next semester John was still teaching, a nominal member of the history department. There had been a warrant issued for the arrest of Cornelius Jones in connection with the brutal murder of Chapman Lorraine. Jones was being sought in and around the five boroughs and beyond. Anyone with information was to report to Lieutenant Colette Van Dyne, homicide detective in charge of the investigation.

President Luckfeld had pushed back against Eubanks and her allies saying that pornography was a matter of perspective, that the context of the magazine photo projected was an attempt to validate *new and innovative* research techniques on the part of Professor Woman.

Eubanks was interviewed by the *Parsonsville Investigator*, a paper started by graduates of the NUSW School of Journalism. In the interview she claimed that John Woman *was a charlatan and a fraud.*

John hired a local contract lawyer, Buddy Farr, to sue Eubanks and the history department for defamation of character.

"You do know that I'm a contract lawyer for farmers who live on federal subsidies," Farr told

John. The lawyer was a white octogenarian who was four foot nine and bone thin.

"I don't expect to win the suit," John said. "I only want them to feel what they're doing to me."

John spent his spare moments wandering the streets of Parsonsville hoping to see his mother. On good days he walked around feeling like a fool, on bad ones he worried that he might be losing his mind.

How can the confluence of so many seminal aspects of a life occur at a single nexus? he asked Posterity in one of his daily writing sessions.

Even with these problems, an emotional calm descended upon John Woman. His life, crazy or not, had a purpose and that was enough.

"There are many ways that we can interpret our world's story," he said to the second semester of Introduction to Deconstructionist Historical Devices. "The simpleminded view sees history as a verifiable set of events that occurred, that were somehow recorded and that come to us mostly untarnished and nearly irrefutable.

"Our history, we are often told, is pure objective fact unsullied by the human heart. Richard the Third was a scoundrel and Caligula a man of pure evil. All contemporary historians must do is work out the details by culling from dates, records, contemporaneous events, etcetera. In short, a pig with a good vocabulary and a decent memory could be teaching this seminar."

That got a few snickers from the room of sixty-eight students. Since the Trash Can Lecture John had gotten requests from students across campus to sit in on his lectures. He had said yes to one and all knowing that would enrage Eubanks.

"But, Professor," Justin Brown said.

"Yes, Mr. Brown?"

"How can people know anything if they doubt everything?"

John smiled at the handsome, self-assured chemistry major.

"Doubt is what makes us inquisitive, Justin. Doubt about the world we believe in is what brought the philosopher out of his cave. But truth is a slippery fish, easier to observe than it is to catch."

"But you admit," Pete Tackie said, "that there's a real history just as much as there are laws in science."

"Yes, of course, Mr. Tackie, but you have to remember that even the so-called laws of physics can be overturned. We live by these laws all the while knowing that our understanding is at best partial—and sometimes simply wrong."

"But how can we do work in any field," Doris Heckerling, a frost-headed daughter of Minnesota, asked, "if we are constantly questioning what we know and believe?"

"That, Ms. Heckerling, is the purpose of history. What we know, or what we think we know, is always in the present, here and now. But the future, almost contradictorily, is where the past will change. We might for instance learn that Richard the Third was vilified by the landowners of his time because he wanted to empower the peasants. What was evil for the ruling body then becomes heroic for us today. Because of the natural limits of our perceptions we come to understand that history is always changing. This transforms a static study into a dynamic engine of thought and investigation. It is the process of continual reinvestigation itself that defines and ranks our work."

The students, John thought, were looking into themselves. Willie Pepperdine smiled broadly.

"I think that's enough for today," the young professor said. "Next Tuesday we'll have Justin present a ten-minute talk on how the study of a so-called hard science is at odds with the notion of historical investigation. Read some of Kuhn's *Structure of Scientific Revolutions* to prepare for the discussion."

John was walking down the northern stairwell when he turned a corner and came face-to-face with Carlinda and Tamala. The latter was wearing a formfitting full-length dress composed of bright blue and charcoal squares.

Carlinda wore a pearl gray taffeta dress the hem of which covered the upper half of her knees.

"Professor," Carlinda said.

"Miss Elmsford, Ms. Marman."

"We have to talk to you," Tamala said.

"Here?"

"We could go to the rotunda and take a bench," Carlinda suggested.

Tamala gave Carlinda a hard stare.

"What, Tam?" Carlinda said. "Nobody's gonna listen."

"The rotunda then," Woman agreed. "It will be my pleasure."

They took a marble bench that was partly hidden behind a large potted fern. The professor sat dead center. The young women perched themselves on either side, their knees listing toward John. Restrained excitement exuded from their faces and fidgety hands.

"So?" John asked.

"We don't want you to get upset," Carlinda said. "We haven't really done anything yet."

"Anything about what?"

"Pete Tackie is majoring in computer science," Tamala said. "He's really very smart even if he's kind of a jock."

"Okay."

Carlinda reached into her big white bag coming

301

out with a dun-colored plastic folder. This she handed to her secret boyfriend.

The first page contained a list of eighteen professors down the left side—eight women and ten men. Three of these were from the history department and the rest ran the gamut of the school. On the right side of the page was a list of felonies, criminal investigations and other improprieties attributed to the teachers. There were acts of drug abuse and smuggling, predatory sex acts and even a case of suspected manslaughter. One professor made extra money by selling weapons of questionable pedigree at gun shows across the southwest. The following pages provided further descriptions of the crimes, redacted trial transcripts and other documents.

For the next half hour John read through the sixty-two-page collection of names and accusations.

"Where did you get the police reports?" he asked.

"Most of them were public record," Tamala said. "The rest Pete hacked from computers and police databases over the Christmas break."

"We didn't want to tell you before now," Carlinda said. "We knew you'd tell us to stop."

Carlinda had stayed in the international dorm over the winter break. They saw each other almost every other day. But she'd given no hint of this . . . study.

Gesturing with the folder John asked, "Why?"

"You're the best professor in the school," Tamala said, "and they're trying to run you down just because you don't think like them."

"And how's this supposed to help me?"

"That's what's so great," Carlinda said. Her eyes, John noticed, were glistening. "Kerry Brightknowles's boyfriend is a printmaker in Pine Bluff. He knows how to make these bright yellow posters that have an epoxy base. Once you slap them up on a wall they won't come down and it's almost impossible to mark them."

"So you're going to put this page up on the wall and destroy these people's careers to help me?"

"No, silly," Tamala said. "We're going to say that the killer was a drug dealer and the rapist a thief; then we'll change the place and date of the crimes so that only the perpetrators will know it's them, like you said. Nobody'll be able to prove it has anything to do with you because you'll be out of town the night we put them up."

"But won't the authorities be able to trace the yellow posters?" John asked. "I mean there probably aren't that many made."

"They don't come from the U.S.," Carlinda said with a smirk. "They're fabricated in China and the U.S. can't demand the files."

John stared at his students wondering why he hadn't seen that they could actually enact the theories he espoused.

"I'm sorry I called you silly," Tamala said, misinterpreting his gaze.

"Can we do it, Professor?" Carlinda asked.

"Are you sure everything you have in here is verifiable?" He had no intention of agreeing to the crazy plot but he found the notion . . . interesting.

"Yes," Carlinda averred.

"But even if they aren't all exactly right," Tamala added. "The ones against Eubanks, Orcell and Carmody are incontestable."

"So one of the crimes was committed by Auntie Annette?"

"Yes," Carlinda said. "She was arrested for embezzlement when she was eighteen. The Kansas City prosecutor indicted her but then came up with a deal with her parents and employer. There's a big article about it in a Sunday paper, all about teenage middle-class criminals."

"What if they find you guys out?" John asked, still thinking he should say no. "I mean what if Kerry's boyfriend leaves a print on some computer or Pete develops a conscience?"

"It won't matter," Carlinda said with conviction.

"Why not?"

"Because nobody on this list or from the school would want to have all this come out in public."

John saw the fever in his young lover's eyes. It

was a look his father got when thinking about his beloved books. With that John was drifting again. His father would have called the students' plan an example of *the uses of history*. He would say that *real historians are the ones who edit, embellish and reinvent the details of myths mistaken for facts.*

It was his father, and not the young women, who changed his mind.

"Okay," he said. "Let's do it."

"Really?" Tamala screeched grabbing his biceps.

"Yeah. It's the best student project I've ever seen: taking more or less verifiable facts from the recent past and using them to change or attempt to change the future—where those facts will be judged."

At 4:27 John was sitting at the desk in his Prometheus office trying to remember word for word the Bard's sonnet number seventeen. *Who will believe my verse in time to come?*

It was his father's favorite poem about history and the human heart.

John had quoted the sonnet four times when the tapping came at the door.

"Come in."

Arnold Ott stood five nine but looked shorter because of his box-shaped physique. His thick, black-framed glasses had rectangular lenses and his black hair grew in tight curls. Ott wore a tan jacket, dark green trousers and a button-up shirt the color of natural cream. But it was the student's eyes that arrested John. They were a green that seemed removed from the rest of him, beautiful, passionate—the word that occurred to John was *holy.*

"Can I help you?" John asked.

"My name is Arnold Ott and I'm here to talk to you man-to-man." This curt introduction, John was sure, had been practiced many times.

"Come in, Mr. Ott, have a seat."

With clenched fists and lips compressed Arnold sat down hard, taking his anger out on the chair.

"How can I help you?" John asked. "Um . . . Arnold you said?"

"You know damn well who I am."

"I do?"

"I'm Carlinda's boyfriend."

"Oh? Miss Elmsford mentioned that she had a boyfriend but if she said his name it was only in passing."

"What is it between you two?"

"I'm her professor."

"Is that all?"

"Yes. Why do you ask?"

"Because I thought that maybe you were, um, like her lover."

"There's no love between us," John said confidently. "Physical or otherwise."

A tremor went through Arnold's boxy frame. He brought his fists up then slammed them on his knees.

John wondered if he'd have to kill Arnold as he had Chapman Lorraine. This errant thought started as a mild buzzing, a background noise, but, John knew from experience, it could become a roar.

"What are you doing with Carly?"

"Like I told you, Mr. Ott, I'm her teacher. She's considering me for her senior thesis advisor so we meet and talk about her checkered educational history and her fear of what her studies might bring to the surface. She's a very serious student."

"I know she stayed on campus over the break. Was she seein' somebody?"

"We haven't discussed her love life," John admitted. "But if we had I wouldn't tell anyone."

"Are you lyin' to me?"

"Arnold, you said you want to talk man-to-man but I'm still a professor while you are a student. You asked me if I was your girlfriend's lover and I told you that there is no love, physical or otherwise, between us. I answered your question because you seem distressed but I am not answerable to you. If you suspect her of having some kind of liaison you'll have to ask her."

"I think it's you," Arnold said in a vulnerable, pleading tone.

"Why? Have you seen us together? Has someone told you that we're having an affair?"

"I saw the way she looked at you when you gave that Trash Can Talk."

"And how was that?"

Arnold flinched, lifting his fists again.

"She leaves her dorm room some nights and doesn't come back till the next day. One night I parked out in front'a faculty housing and called her dorm room. She was there at first but then she went out. I stayed in front of where you lived until midnight but she never came. She didn't go home either."

"Doesn't that prove it's not me?" John asked.

"It's not you?" Arnold's holy eyes bothered John. He imagined that a deity in such close proximity could obliterate a mortal soul.

There came a knock at the partially open door.

"Come in," John said.

Willie Pepperdine stuck his head out past the door looking in.

"Should I come back?" he said.

"No. Mr. Ott and I have finished our meeting. Haven't we, Arnold?"

"I, I guess."

"Then if you'll excuse me . . ."

Arnold's steps had a wooden quality as he lurched toward the door. Willie stepped aside allowing the boxy, brooding, beautiful-eyed youth to go past.

When he was gone Willie closed the door and sat without asking.

"That kid looks like an explosion waiting to happen."

"Hormones rage well into the twenties for young men."

"He looks like a jilted lover. That virus can hit man or woman at any age."

"What can I do for you, Willie?"

"It's what I can do for you."

"And that is?"

"I'd like to offer you, on behalf of the board of directors, one million dollars."

John heard the words clearly but they failed to achieve meaning. It was like a familiar phrase in a foreign tongue that he barely knew.

"Come again?"

"It's about the suit Mr. Farr has brought on your behalf."

"And, and . . . and you want me to drop it?"

Willie smiled and nodded.

"It was a good countermove," the self-described philosopher of currency acknowledged. "Eubanks has been begging the school to retain a lawyer for her defense."

"Why not do it? I mean, that would cost a lot less than a million dollars."

"If we won," Willie allowed. "But if we associate ourselves with the case Farr could conceivably expand the suit to include the entire school. Our lawyers believe that he, you could win."

"And so . . ." John stopped to appreciate the progression of the hour since the end of his class. "And so you'll pay me a million dollars to save money?"

"We want the faculty to know we stand behind them. Refusing to retain representation would look bad."

"So this is the path of least resistance."

"Exactly."

"A Platinum Path."

"Precious," Willie said with a smile.

"One million dollars."

"It's not as much as it used to be. A million dollars in today's world is like a, a small nylon pillow on a business class cross-country flight."

"Why'd you decide to audit my class, Mr. Pepperdine?"

"Because you are by far the most interesting lecturer at the school. We knew that years ago when President Luckfeld asked the regents to allow you the position."

"The board okayed me?"

"They were impressed with your credentials. I was excited about your take on history itself. We all know that without a past there is no future but no scholar I knew of has said that by re-forming the past we change the future."

John tried to wrap his mind around the immensity that Willie and Carlinda, Tamala and Arnold Ott had to offer.

"Keep your money, Willie," he said.

"You're going to continue with the suit?"

"I'll call Buddy in the morning and tell him to drop it," John said. "I'd call him right now but he goes to bed in the afternoon and gets to work at three in the morning. Says it's a habit he developed working for farmers."

"You're going to drop a multimillion-dollar lawsuit just like that?"

"Just like that."

"Why?"

"It's those cave fish."

"The blind sturgeon?"

"Sometimes, when I can't get to sleep because my mind is racing, I think about those fish gliding in cold water, knowing things no sighted creature could imagine. Just the thought exhilarates me and then, suddenly, I'm asleep. That was one of the best gifts I've ever been given. And you know I've led a fortunate life."

Willie sat forward, elbows on knees, fingers laced together. Resting his sharp chin on the crest of knuckles he gazed into the young man's eyes, slowly allowing a smile to form.

"You're something else, Professor. I haven't met many men who would turn down that kind of money."

"I got what I need, Willie. I might not want it but I have it just the same."

14

There was no recent reference to Lucia Napoli anywhere on the Internet, neither was she in any local area phone directory. John became a regular at the coffee shop but she never showed. His search was a daily, futile effort. He considered retaining a private detective from Phoenix but the name Napoli would almost certainly be associated with the New York investigation of Cornelius Jones and bring him to the attention of Colette Van Dyne née Margolis.

He found a photograph of his mother in an online photo album that Christopher Anthony Napoli III had put up for family and friends to appreciate and add to. The best photograph was taken with Filo Manetti. They were standing arm in arm, their backs to a guardrail on the deck of a cruise ship somewhere where the water was cobalt blue. Filo smiled into the lens as if projecting his entire essence. John thought he looked familiar but couldn't place the face. Maybe he'd seen him with his mother before she was gone forever.

It was a good likeness of Lucia but the hair was black, not copper as it was at the coffee shop.

Lucia smiled as she always did when posing for the camera, *enough to look happy.* He blew up the photo, asked Kerry Brightknowles to make copies on the history department printer, cropping his mother's smiling face.

He took the picture to every shop in Parsonsville asking people to imagine her with bright metallic hair. But no one recognized her.

Maybe he'd been seeing things like Senta said.

During the same period John was trying to find out who had left those camel-brown letters on his table. He ruled out Carlinda because the handwriting was not hers and he didn't believe she'd take on a confederate to destroy him.

Jasper "Hototo" Hutman, the night watchman, assured him that there had been no break-ins.

"Only that girl who jumps over the fence and goes to your apartment," the severe Hopi said.

"You know about her?"

"Sure. That girl can climb."

"That's all?"

"Now and then a student named Arnold Ott parks across the street looking at the gate."

"Did you question him?"

"No."

"Then how do you know his name?"

"Student vehicles are registered with the administration. I looked up his license on the database."

John decided to expand his search for his anonymous pen pal. Only his mother and

France Bickman came to mind. He failed to find Lucia but, after a week of searches, he located France Bickman, who had moved to Cavaliers Retirement Home in Portland, Oregon. At ninety-seven years old he was the editor of a weekly blog dedicated to spreading knowledge about quirks in the social welfare system. The blog page led to a social network website called The Graying Alliance. This was an Internet site devoted to the dissemination of information for and about the well-being of people who have achieved elder status. France's webpage contained a picture album of him and his daughters (all three of whom were divorced and living in Portland), their children and one great-grandson—Herbert Manville.

On his Facebook page France gave tips on cooking, physical exercise for those over eighty years old, reviews of books he liked and a rambling autobiography that was broken up into chapters identified by month and year.

John spent many hours reading through France Bickman's online memoir. The ex-ticket-taker had served as an ensign in the U.S. Navy during the Korean War and married his wife, Matilda Hadfield, in 1964. He'd done things that he'd regretted all through his years but there were good moments also.

John liked the historical approach to memori-alizing a life. The truth of the document, he thought, was its honest attempt to impose order on memory.

There was an entry especially interesting to John in the section titled 1993.

July 16, 1993. It was on that day in my long life that I was disabused of all the thoughts, ideas and notions I had lived by. That was the day I took the job of ticket-taker at Arbuckle Cinema House in New York's East Village. A soft-spoken black man named Herman Jones took me under his wing. He showed me how to do my job but beyond that taught me that there is no love of self without understanding, that if you didn't know and care about who you are then you'd never be able to love another. For me love was always duty. If you were faithful and paid the bills that was all you had to do. But I was wrong. Herman knew that your history in all of its parts created you. He believed that this history made you who you were but the way he lived said even more. Herman had a son named CC. He loved that boy and respected him in a way that I couldn't have imagined. CC would read to Herman and Herman would then explain to the child what he had read. It was like they were teaching each other, as if Herman was passing the mantle of his manhood on to his son. What he gave that boy was greater than any monetary fortune or set of rules. He taught CC how to love and in doing so he trained me . . .

Cornelius was rereading the entry when the doorbell rang. It was late on a Friday afternoon and he resented the intrusion.

"Who is it?" John said into the intercom.

"Police, Mr. Woman. Can we come in?"

France Bickman and his digital musings vanished. The police were at the front door and there was no back exit, no window he could creep through. Why hadn't he run when he heard about the discovery of the body? Why had he conjured up his mother and used her apparition as an excuse to stay?

"Mr. Woman," the policeman said.

John took his finger from the intercom panel.

His cell phone sounded. The glass panel read, Front Gate.

"Yes?"

"Professor, it's Hototo. The police are coming to your door."

"They're already here."

John disconnected the call and pressed the intercom button again.

"Yes?" he said.

"Is this Mr. John Woman?"

"Professor John Woman."

"I'm Officer Hernandez of the Granville police, sir. Can we come in and ask you a few questions?"

John tried to think of options. What if he said no? Maybe he could keep them off long enough to call Carlinda; she might be able to talk him through jumping over the fence.

"What's this about?" he shouted at the microphone holes.

"Just a few questions, sir."

A few questions. Years of work, mountains of duplicity and now a faceless cop threatened to take it away with some words and punctuation.

"Questions about what?" he asked.

"Can we come in and talk to you, sir?"

John took a step back. He tried to remember what he had been thinking before the doorbell rang but could not.

The bell sounded again—three short rings and then a longer, more insistent tone. Like Beethoven's Fifth in the throat of a small child tonelessly humming.

John smiled at this thought and pressed the lock-release.

He opened his front door listening to them tramping up the stairs. A moment later they were there before him on the third-floor landing. Two men, one tan and the other bronze, both in

317

mostly black uniform and armed with pistols in holsters.

It surprised John when the darker man spoke first.

"Professor Woman?"

"Yes."

"Can we come in?"

John considered making them stand in the hall.

"Okay," he said, stepping back. "Come have a seat."

There were only two chairs but the table was placed next to the deep-set window and so he took his seat on that ledge.

The uniforms looked around the room. The white officer noted the stairs and asked, "Someone upstairs?"

"No. I live alone."

The policemen then sat down looking pleasant enough. John wondered why they weren't reading him his rights, putting him in restraints as they did on TV.

"I'm Officer Hernandez," the bronze cop said. "This is Officer Mulligan."

"Pleased to meet you."

"Do you know why we're here, sir?" Hernandez asked.

John's throat caught before the word could come out. "No."

The young men—they looked to be in their mid-twenties—glanced at each other.

"Did you give a lecture at the main hall of Deck Recreation Center?"

John wondered what had happened at the presentation. Had someone recognized him there? Mulligan, he noted, had had stitches on an old wound at the left corner of his mouth. The small scar was crosshatched where it had been sewn.

"Professor," Hernandez said.

"Yes?"

"Did you speak at the main hall of Deck?"

"Yes. Why?"

"Did you," the Hispanic cop asked, taking out a small notepad, which he read from, "present a bloody rag, the photograph of a possible victim of violence and a small bag of heroin at that presentation?"

John wondered when the questions would get to Chapman Lorraine.

"Professor?"

"Yes?"

"Did you?"

"That was last semester," John said, treading water in an underground lake filled with giant blind-eyed fish.

"Did you present evidence of one or more crimes?"

"I don't, I don't think so."

"Do you have those items here?"

"No. Is that why you're here, because of my talk?"

"Are they at your office?" Hernandez would not be sidetracked.

"No."

"Where then?"

"After the lecture was over I threw the trunk away. Everything was in there. I treated the event in the spirit of the Yoruba mask; that is, it was only alive as the spirit of the talk. After that it was simple detritus."

Hernandez's frown reflected John's.

"You threw the evidence away?"

"I found everything in a trash can," John said. "I just put it back there. Was it Annette Eubanks that informed on me? No . . . no, it would have been Gregory Tracer. He's her creature."

"It's against the law to destroy evidence of a crime, Professor."

"I am aware of no crime, Officer," John said. "I just pulled trash out of a receptacle then postulated on the idea of history."

"The possession of heroin is a crime."

"I don't know that I handled heroin. It could have been powdered sugar. Maybe that's why it was thrown away."

"Why didn't you want to let us in?" Hernandez asked, now unsure of his evidence.

"I've never had the police come to my door," he lied.

"Do you have some reason to be afraid of the police?"

There it was, his chance to confess. *Yes, officer, I murdered a man years ago and the police are after me. That's why I didn't want to let you in.*

"No, Officer, of course not. I'm a university professor but when authority comes calling the everyday citizen has learned to fear the worst."

"Do you have anything to fear, Professor?"

John smiled, then grinned. "Men with guns sitting at my table."

Mulligan had been quiet while Hernandez asked again and again about the disposition of the trunk. Where did he get it? Where did he dispose of it? Who else did he work with? Who told him about the trash can? Before departing Officer Hernandez said they might return after reexamining the video recording of the lecture.

"You're pretty excited tonight," Carlinda said as they lay side by side looking up at the ceiling.

"Your boyfriend came to my office hours the other day."

"He did?" She sat up.

"Uh-huh. He thought we were having an affair because of the way you looked at me at the Trash Can Lecture. He also told me that he's waited outside the gate here to see if you came by."

"What did you say?"

"That there was no love, either physical or emotional, between us."

"You lied to him?"

"Do you love me?"

"Um, no."

"Have you had sex with me because you love me?"

"I guess not."

"Then I didn't lie. I merely interpreted our relationship in such a way as to keep Arnold out of jail for either assault or murder . . . or worse."

"What worse?"

"It occurred to me that I might have hurt him."

"Do you think he could have followed me here tonight?"

"Did you jump the fence?"

"Yes."

"Then no. Arnold strikes me as a front door type of guy."

Carlinda laughed, showing her teeth. "You're funny."

"If you don't lie to him about us he'll do something violent," John warned.

The smile faded. "Yeah."

For a while they were lost in their own thoughts, looking anywhere but at each other.

"I'm going away for a few days next week," he said.

"Where?"

"Up north and down south. I have some people I want to interview."

"For what?"

"I'm going to write a book. If I lose my job I'll need it to prove that I'm a serious scholar."

John closed his eyes and Carlinda said, "Okay."

15

Morning sun through the deep-set window woke him. John showered, shaved, packed and then drove his green T-bird to Phoenix's Sky Harbor International Airport. There he bought a ticket for Portland, Oregon. By two that afternoon he was at the front desk of Cavaliers Retirement Home, a rambling mansion set on a hill across the road from a cemetery that admitted its last tenant more than a century before.

"May I help you?" the broad-faced receptionist asked. She had red, red lips and white powder on her white skin. Her nameplate read Lois Q. Lucerne. John wondered if her middle name was Queenie.

"France Bickman."

A hint of distaste dulled the middle-aged woman's attempt at friendliness.

"You're a reporter?"

"No, ma'am. A friend."

"One of those agitators?" The smile was now completely gone.

"I don't understand," John said.

"Mr. Bickman is always causing trouble," she asserted, "complaining to the press, making the other residents unhappy, telling the attendants how to do their job."

"Oh," John said. "I don't know anything about that. My wife's father was a friend of his and he asked me to stop by and say hello if I was ever in town."

There was a library on the fourth floor of the villa-like rest home. An Asian orderly—a short man with generous tawny features, dressed all in white—walked John to the open doors and left him there. The two occupants of the many-windowed room were an elderly white woman and an even older white man. The woman was sitting in a chrome and green leather wheelchair under a large window. John suspected she sat there out of habit seeking sunlight to illuminate the paperback pages she was reading. But the sky was cloaked with dark clouds allowing precious little solar glow.

The man was France Bickman. He stood before a dictionary lectern thumbing through the pages of a fat, hardback *Webster's*. John walked up to his father's only real friend and stopped there. A minute passed while France searched for his word.

The young professor studied the old man's face. When John was a boy France had looked even older. Now, with France at ninety-seven, they were closer on what Herman Jones once called the mortality scale. France had a full head of hair and his faded eyes were no less inquisitive.

Not satisfied with what he was reading France looked up. Those ancient orbs squinted, the head tilted ever so slightly to the right.

"CC?"

"Hey, France. How are you?"

When France moved from the lectern John could see that he tottered a bit. He staggered toward his young visitor grabbing the biceps of both arms in greeting but also to hold himself upright.

"How are you, son?"

"Fine, fine. Do you want to sit down?"

Holding on to each other the men jostled over to a long mahogany bench.

"I've been thinking a lot about you lately," the impossibly old man confided.

"Oh? What about me?" John asked pleasantly.

"I felt bad that I didn't keep in touch after Herman died. Maybe I could have helped out. You know money alone doesn't do everything."

"I'm fine. Went to college. Got a job. I hear that you're a real rabble-rouser around here. Your blog is wonderful."

John glanced at the woman by the window. She didn't seem to be bothered by their talking. Maybe she couldn't hear them.

"You read it?" France asked.

"Yes, that and the autobiography you posted on your website. I like that you broke it up by yearly chapters and monthly subsections."

"Your father used to say that time and its passage was all we had to take our own measure."

That started the men on a long laudatory talk about Herman Jones and the old days at the Arbuckle. Some of France's memories seemed a little off to John but those days were long ago; the younger man wasn't sure if his own recollections were any more accurate.

At some point the woman in the wheelchair began snoring softly. Soon after the orderly came to wheel her away.

"Has anyone been asking about me, France?" John asked when they were alone.

"What do you mean, CC? Like bill collectors or something? Do you need money?"

"No, no, I'm doing all right. I was just wondering if anybody mentioned me. I've been getting these letters but I can't make out the signature. They seem to know a lot about me. You know the only people I was ever close to as a kid were mom, dad and you. Dad's gone and I haven't heard from my mother in years."

"Anonymous letters?" France winced. "Are they bad? Threatening?"

"No. They're signed but the handwriting is mostly flourish. Postmark is from Arizona. They talk about the old days and I thought it might be someone you know."

"No," France said. "I haven't spoken to anyone

about the old days. I had a girlfriend for a while, Alison Dawson. I did talk to her about you and Herman but she died five years ago and didn't have any friends but me. No, CC, it's probably somebody knows your mother. She always had lots of friends. She liked to talk if I remember right."

"That she did," John said.

"It was probably her."

"Probably so, France," John agreed. "It's not important anyway. I was on my way to Seattle for a job interview. I read about you on the web so I thought I'd drop by."

"What do the letters say?"

"Not much. Just about the Arbuckle and dad. I can't read the signature is the problem. Postmark is from Arizona so I knew it wasn't you but I thought maybe it was someone we both knew."

"No . . . You want to stay for dinner, CC?"

Meat loaf with mashed potatoes made from a powder, broccoli spears and unseasoned apple pie made up the meal. The coffee was decaffeinated and there was no salt shaker in evidence.

France talked about prejudice against the elderly and how when so many people got old they lost heart.

"It'd be better if they offered us suicide alternatives," Bickman said at a table with four of his men friends and John. "We could go out

328

with good liquor, cigarettes and watching movies with naked girls while they pumped a sleeping gas in real slow. Maybe two or three of us could pass on together talking about the old days."

"That sounds grand," Timor Parker, a retired plumber from Redwood City, said. "Maybe we could have music too . . . and dancin'."

Two orderlies on duty watched the table closely. John thought that if he wasn't visiting they might have tried to separate the men.

"If I had my old twenty-two they wouldn't fuck with us," France said when John shared his notion. "Bethy, my youngest, took it out of my suitcase when she put me here. But you know if I had my pistol those apes would show me some respect."

"I have to get going, France," John said, realizing that his presence was exciting the older man to these protestations of violence.

"You go on, son," France said. "And don't you worry about those letters or nuthin'. I got it all covered."

"Covered how, France?"

"Just don't you worry. As long as there's breath in this body I won't let them hurt you."

The next morning John boarded a flight to Miami. The acronym for the airport was MIA. The idea of travel and being missing in action tickled the history professor.

He took a bus into town, found a Cuban diner and ordered a meal that consisted of a pressed ham and cheese sandwich with pickles, Caesar salad, and beer from a local brewery. He asked the waiter if there was a pay phone anywhere around. After a moment of consideration the copper-skinned mustachioed man said, "Down at the library. Not too many booths anymore. But they have them inside the library: the old kind with levered doors, wood seats and everything. Two blocks up and half a block over on your left."

John had gotten two rolls of quarters from a bank in Portland before driving his rental car to Cavaliers. Donning cotton gloves he broke open a roll of quarters and called the operator, directing the woman to dial a Manhattan phone number. She asked for three dollars and he dropped twelve quarters into the old-fashioned pay phone. Each descending coin conjured a gong.

Before the phone could ring a man announced, "Hotline."

"May I speak to Lieutenant Van Dyne."

"She's not here at the moment. Can I help you?"

"Not really. I can only speak to her."

"Then you'll have to leave a message."

"Tell her that Cornelius Jones called."

After a brief pause the man asked, "Who?"

"The man she's looking for."

"Hold on."

Four minutes passed on John's father's Timex when a woman said, "This is Lieutenant Van Dyne."

"I recognize your voice, Lieutenant."

"Who is this?"

"The first time we met was in the basement office of the old Arbuckle. You were Detective Margolis back then." John had designed the sentence to convince his ex-lover of his identity without referring to the intimate nature of their relationship. He thought the call might be recorded and didn't want to cause her trouble.

"Cornelius Jones."

"Yes. I heard that you were looking for me and I remembered how nice you were, how understanding. I thought I'd call and say hi."

"I'd like it if you came in for a talk, Mr. Jones."

"That would be nice but I'm out of state now."

"Where?"

"Minnesota. Been working as a salesman out here for the last few years."

"I could come to you."

"No. That would be way too much."

"We want to talk to you."

"Yes, something to do with Chapman Lorraine I heard."

"He was murdered."

"That's awful."

"Killed in the projectionist's booth of the Arbuckle."

"You don't need to go out of your way, Lieutenant. I don't know anything about Lorraine. That's what I called to tell you."

"We have to meet, Mr. Jones."

"The next time I'm in New York I'll call."

"This is serious."

"I'm sure it is. But as I said, I have nothing to do with it. It's been nice hearing your voice again, Detective Van Dyne. Bye now."

That evening John boarded a flight to Houston. He stayed there in an airport hotel for three days writing a monograph titled *The Inescapable, Unavoidable Democracy of Culture*. On the fourth morning, the handwritten first draft of the sixty-page essay completed, he flew back home, arriving at midnight.

It wasn't until the next morning that he saw the bright yellow broadside pasted up on the external plaster wall of faculty housing.

The lettering was bloodred: VILLAINS IN OUR MIDST! The list of names and crimes, collected by Carlinda and her coconspirators, were laid out like the cast and characters in a movie or play. Someone had tried to rip down and deface the poster but the epoxy sheet resisted most attempts to mute its accusations.

The list consisted of nine professors down the left side of the document including Eubanks and Carmody; opposite each name was a crime that they had, supposedly, committed. There was a wife-beater, an ex-member of a revolutionary cult in Detroit, three fake degrees, an embezzler, a female physical education teacher who was born a man, a convicted felon and a pederast. At the bottom of the poster was the promise that future revelations about the perpetrators of desertion, robbery, theft, hate crimes and assault among others would be made.

On his walk to Prometheus Hall John saw seventeen yellow broadsides pasted up on walls, palm tree trunks and announcement boards. In each instance there had been attempts to rip down, deface, cover up and/or write over the offending document but these attempts had more or less failed.

The damage had already been done. Cell phone cameras had certainly disseminated the image around the school and beyond.

He followed his usual path to the great hall and up the stairs to his Tuesday seminar.

Nearly two hundred students were there to meet him.

16

"The class has grown since last Thursday," John said from behind the semitransparent green plastic lectern.

"We want to know what you have to say about the posters," a young woman called out.

John looked around but could not locate the speaker. He didn't recognize the voice.

"This is a history class," he said, "not a course on current events."

His declaration elicited some groans.

"I just got back," he added. "You guys know more than I do."

"But you've seen them," Beth Weiner said. "Haven't you?"

John frowned and nodded. "When did they go up?"

"Late Saturday night."

"And were there arrests made on Monday?"

"No."

"Have any of the professors mentioned been put on academic suspension?"

"No."

"Then I think that it's a cruel hoax perpetrated by angry and immature minds. That's personal opinion, not professorial authority or knowledge."

"But it does mean you think they were wrong," Star Limner proposed.

"I think," John said, and then he paused, looking around the room for words that momentarily eluded him. "I think . . . this broadside, this salvo, this pretense at a cry for justice is simply an attempt to alarm students, faculty, parents and even the people of the town of Parsonsville . . . this compulsion to destroy is both cowardly and misguided."

"But what if they're right?" Jack Burns said.

"They are not," John replied. "And even if someone is guilty of, or at least culpable for, a crime, do we have a right to murder the person?"

"No one tried to kill anybody," a voice shouted from the back of the room.

"No?" John asked the blue desert beyond the speaker. "What if you had built an entire life dedicated to learning and service? What if any of you had but one love and then the object, the possibility of that love was taken away in a manner so violent and so public that you might never recover? What if you had a pistol in one hand and the long fall before you?

"But it is not simply the callous threat against a few individuals that we're facing. Each of you is suffering from the passions roused, passions that have no anchor and no proofs. You came here to find answers. You want to know that your world socially, intellectually and spiritually is not falling down around your ears.

"Has anyone not in my regular class heard the term *hermeneutics?*"

A young black woman standing at the wall to the left of the lectern raised her hand. John recognized her. She was the woman who had complimented his Trash Can Lecture when he was searching for his mother at the coffee shop.

"Yes?" he said.

"It's like the study of the meaning of scripture," she said, almost as a question.

John smiled and nodded. "In ancient times it was. But in modern philosophy, philology and some branches of history it takes on the meaning of a kind of rigorously applied empathy with the experience of others. In a popular song from the sixties a singer asked his self-avowed enemy to, 'walk a mile in my shoes.' This is what your yellow journalists have left out of their cowardly diatribe. They threaten, condemn and destroy giving no evidence that they understand the human condition."

"What is that, Professor?" the black woman from the coffee shop asked.

"Have you ever done something you wouldn't want others to know about?" The woman hesitated. John noticed she was wearing a butter-colored dress that complemented her dark skin.

"What does that have to do with anything?" she said.

John turned to the rest of the class, looked around a moment and then asked, "Have any of you here committed a crime or misdemeanor that you want kept secret?"

A visible tremor went through the assemblage.

"I have," said a young man in a white T-shirt seated in row seven or eight. "I stole something once. It was a long time ago but I still feel bad about it."

"Me too," said Justin Brown. "It was the last time I ever got drunk."

John allowed seventeen confessions, most without pertinent detail. Theft, violence and silence were the most common offenses. Each admission, John felt, was a brick removed from the walls of their tombs.

"I cheated on my boyfriend," Carlinda Elmsford said. "And I liked it. I liked it a lot."

That's when John took over again. "I suspect that every one of you in this room has done something you consider wrong at one time or another, things you'd never share with anyone. Maybe it's a crime; maybe just your nature."

"So are you saying that these accusations are false?" Carlinda cried out, her voice strained and cracking.

"I am absolutely sure of the professors' innocence," John declared. "But at the same time I don't care about allegations because I live by the rule of law, not rumor."

For some reason this statement cast a hush over the crowded classroom.

John looked around at the faces. He saw a hunger for understanding in most.

"I have an assignment for you," he said. "I want you to get a pad of yellow legal paper and to go to a place where you are completely alone, a place where no one can see what you're doing there, to write down a true statement. Something you've done that would get you fired from your dream job or a crime you committed. In the space that's left you can explain the circumstances or give excuses if you wish. You should not sign the document. Then decide whether or not you would pin this confession on a wall near the yellow broadsides. Would you do to yourselves what the yellow journalists say they have done to others?"

The eyes of many of the students turned inward then.

John recited the Bard's sonnet silently, then said, "Go."

"John," she called as he was going down the south stairs.

He waited for Carlinda to catch up to him.

She was wearing a gray-and-gold full-length dress that might have been a ball gown in some medieval hamlet.

When she reached him she kissed him on the lips then stared him in the eye. It was almost a dare.

"Hi," he said.

A feeling assailed him like a stiff wind; it was the distance he felt when Colette told him that she was marrying her boyfriend. Even though Carlinda was standing before him she was far, far away.

"Did my confession scare you?" she asked.

"No."

"Why not?" she seemed disappointed.

"I asked the question. I can't complain about an answer."

Carlinda searched deeply into John's eyes. Whatever she was looking for—it wasn't there.

"You got to watch out for Pete," she said at last.

"Why?"

"He was real mad at the things you said in the lecture."

"What did he expect?"

"I think he kind of sees himself as a hero," she said with a single shoulder shrug. "He thought you were going to say that the people who put up the broadsides were brave and true historians."

"Damn," John said and then he sucked a tooth.

"What?"

"Nothing. I mean . . . I should have seen that coming."

"Me and Tamala will talk to him but don't go to your office hours and stay out of his way until we tell you it's all right."

"How did you guys finally decide to divvy up the crimes and criminals?" he asked, neither distance nor Pete Tackie being of any concern.

"Um," Carlinda hemmed, "uh, we gave Eubanks's embezzling charge to Randolph Cordell in economics and Carmody's pederast charges and trial to Dov Pomerantz in the art department; like that with all of them."

"You really did it," John said.

"You don't sound very happy about it."

"I guess not. I mean I know how it feels to be vilified, to be aware of your own guilt and there's nothing you can do to change it."

"What's changed in you?" she asked.

"I think I might have lost my mask."

"What does that even mean?"

"I'm not sure, but . . . I have to go."

"Just stay away from your office."

"I will."

17

John noticed Annette Eubanks waiting outside the door as he approached his office at four. She wore a maroon dress. Even from the back he could see that her hair was mussed. She clenched a shiny black purse under her right arm, like a football player about ready to go for the touchdown.

The department chair was looking the opposite way down the hall and so did not see his approach. John wondered if it might be a good idea to retreat before she noticed him. He wasn't bothered by the prospect of facing Pete Tackie's rage but Eubanks might have a nervous breakdown and suddenly pull a pistol out of her bag.

"Hello, Professor," he said, coming up behind her.

She spun around, her shoulders pulled back in surprise. There was a wilted spray of violets pinned over the left breast of her dress.

"Hello, John."

"You here for my office hour?" he joked.

"Yes. Yes I am."

"Come on in then."

When the department head was ensconced in the visitor's chair John said, "This is a terrible business."

Annette's unreadable stare reminded him of the coyote stalking him in the desert. She was, he thought, a woman ripped from her place, torn from the comfort of her fate.

"I've done an awful thing," she said.

John worried that the broadside had broken her will. Fretting thus he realized that he didn't actually dislike the officious educator. Her experience in life was limited and so she fought battles in an imaginary arena called the history department of NUSW.

"What's that?" he asked.

"I sent one of my students into your class today with a camera hidden in his briefcase. Before the class began he put a tiny microphone on your podium."

"You were spying on my class?" he asked, his tone making light of the breach. "Annette, you are always invited to attend with no need for subterfuge."

"I believed that you had sabotaged me," she said not heeding or maybe not hearing his gentle words. "I was sure that you would start to spread poison about me and Ira. I thought that damned poster was your idea. I wanted proof. I wanted to catch you on video trying to destroy us."

Eubanks shuddered and moved her hands around, reaching for words and reasons that did not exist. Her jaw jutted on both sides and then, suddenly, a short burst of tears cascaded down her cheeks.

"Then," she choked. "Then, when I heard what you said, I realized you had no animosity toward us. It was us, always us attacking you. Our fear of you created what we saw when you were simply following your own muse, your own beliefs. We brought those damned yellow broadsides down on ourselves."

"You don't have to worry, Annette," he said. "I'm sure you and everyone else on that list are innocent and I'm just as certain that the university will back you."

"Why don't you hate me?"

"That's a very good question," he said. "It's true that the worst thing you can do to a person is to take away their ability to make a living. Better take a man's wife and children than his job."

"Because he can get a new family?" she asked.

"Because he doesn't need a family but no American can live without a paycheck."

"So?"

"What?"

"I was trying to take your job and blacklist you too."

"Yes."

"Then why not fan the flames of distrust against me?"

"Sometimes it's just easier to tell the truth," he said. "The broadside is a cowardly attack. If any of it was true then the president would have had to put those culpable professors on academic suspension. And, anyway, all of us make mistakes along the way. There's no value in persecuting someone for overcoming their history in an attempt to forge a better future."

Annette Eubanks's roaming hands settled in her lap as Arnold Ott's had done.

"Dean James has provided for a public forum tomorrow at Deck Rec at four," she said. "He's left it up to me to organize the gathering. The entire student body and teaching staff will be urged to attend."

"How will it be structured?"

"I didn't know until I saw your lecture," she said. "But now I believe that you should give the address."

John thought of asking why him but decided that asking the question would only serve to reopen her wounds.

"I'd love to," he said. "That way injury might be turned into something good." Her silent smile was filled with pain. Her hands raised up from her knees and she seemed to expand like an animated character in a Bugs Bunny cartoon—about to explode.

"The department has made a request that you be terminated," she said—her words delivered rapid-fire.

"I know. President Luckfeld offered me a university professorship in recompense."

"Of course he did."

• • •

Eubanks shook John's hand at the door and then walked away. He watched her for a moment then turned. Before he could close the door he was pushed from behind so violently that he stumbled across the room. He didn't try to regain his footing, instead allowing himself to stagger forward until he was close enough to his desk drawer so that he might reach Hototo's knife—the totem intended to keep him safe.

When John turned he saw Pete Tackie slamming the office door with his big left hand. His other fist gripped a baseball bat. Pete then took the bat in both hands and slammed it against John's lone file cabinet.

He hit the metal box again and again, denting the sides and cracking the dark green paint.

John took that moment to sit in his chair. As he drew himself forward he used his left hand to pull open the top drawer from its underside.

"Is there something wrong, Mr. Tackie?"

"Why the fuck you say all that shit about us, man?" Flecks of spittle popped from his lips.

"What did you expect me to say?"

"You called us immature and evil and cruel." Pete slammed his bat against the cabinet to punctuate each claim.

"You called me a coward," he added.

"Yes."

"You admit it?"

"Does anyone other than Carlinda and Tamala know about your part in making those yellow broadsides?"

"Kerry and her boyfriend."

"Do any of them think you a coward?"

"No."

"You did this to help me didn't you, Pete?"

"I guess."

"And if I said that the professors named should be fired and the people who put up the posters should be seen as heroes then I would have been suspected of being part of the posters' origins—no?"

"But you coulda said that we were real historians who knew how to use our studies to change the way things happen."

Pete slammed the bat down on the desktop. With his knee John closed the drawer; the belt-buckle knife was in his left hand.

"So you did this for praise and not the restructuring of social context?"

"We really liked you," Pete said lowering into John's visitor's chair. "We did this so that they wouldn't fire you. And then, and then you called us names and said that we were stupid. We're not stupid."

"No you're not."

John peered into his would-be attacker's eyes.

Pete dropped his bat.

"Then why did you say it?"

"Because my role was to pull everything together after you tore it apart. It has, so far, worked. You and Tamala and Carlinda created an atmosphere that will make a difference."

"But I feel like shit."

"When you play against a really good rugby team," John said, "go into overtime and fight as hard as you can, how do you feel afterward?"

"Sore as hell," Pete said. "Sometimes there's bones broken and all kinds of bruises and shit. Sometimes the girls that hang around wanna take us home but we hurt too bad."

"It's the same thing here. We're doing work that will make a difference. It's hard work and when it's over we're exhausted. You've made a difference and nobody but your friends can know about it."

"Then you don't really think all those things you said?"

"Of course not. I'm merely playing my part. Without you I couldn't do it. And you will gain invaluable experience that will serve you well for the rest of your life."

"I was gonna kill you," Pete admitted. "I was gonna beat you to death with that bat."

Something about the young man's confession was a balm to John's restless mind. He was certain that he would have killed Pete before the rugby thug knew there was a knife. The fact that he came so close to murder brought back a long-dormant memory: moments after killing Chapman Lorraine Cornelius felt completely at peace.

"Go on back to your dorm, Pete," John said. "You did good."

"Maybe I've done it all wrong," John said after Pete had gone.

He was talking to, or at least looking at, the discarded bat in the corner next to the empty chair.

His father's Chapman Lorraine was Jimmy Grimaldi and his Excalibur a heart brave enough to stand unarmed against an unbeatable foe.

John read the same books as Herman, had tried his best to disappear into stories that were both true and indecipherable. But rather than a king in exile he'd become a kind of Tallyrand agitating between the ruling classes, the workers and the revolutionists. Where Herman had been heroic John was just a scarecrow, forgotten in a barren field that had once been flush and fruitful.

Remembering that true self-abnegation was possible only for a man willing to die he replaced the knife and took from the drawer a yellow legal pad and a number two pencil. It took hours to write, erase, write again, reject and finally decide upon the first few words of his second Deck Rec lecture. He didn't trust himself to deliver an impromptu talk this time. His life had been a long series of spontaneous acts—it was time for a change.

We have come here today not to be lectured to or addressed but rather to look into ourselves and see what it is that makes us possible. After writing these words Professor John Woman sat back in his chair and read them over and over until he was satisfied that this was the right beginning for the rest of his life.

18

John spent the night at his Prometheus Hall office, writing. There were so many cross-outs and erasures that at around three in the morning he redrafted the speech. As he rewrote, new ideas formed. What he had written lost its power, so he was compelled to begin again. A few minutes past six he began practicing the speech, making notes and rewording, changing sentence structures and adding asides. By eight he was finished. An hour later he lay down on the hard floor behind his desk and slept. A dream brought him to the secret room in the projectionist's booth. He became Chapman Lorraine sealed away, nearly forgotten. In that stasis there was no guilty conscience or demonic elation. He simply took Lorraine's place for a short while, affording his victim some relief.

When John awoke he felt stiff but exonerated. He'd done penance for the murder and accepted that he and his father were not the same. They loved each other but these loves did not encompass a singularity. They were different men: Herman a teacher and Cornelius an unaffiliated samurai. The elder Jones suffered the curse of physical weakness with superior moral strength in a world that sneered at the first and could not believe the second. John was a trickster, a coyote gratefully licking the bloody wounds of his savior.

On the walk over to Deck Rec John noticed flimsy yellow flags flapping in the breezes around the damning broadsides. It wasn't until he investigated that he remembered the assignment he gave the two hundred or so attendees of the previous day's class.

One sheet read:

> I threw my cat from the roof of my parents' house when I was five and angry that they wouldn't let me ride my bike around the block. The cat, Puddin, didn't die but I knew that I had tried to kill her. I had sex with my mother's best friend, Dora N., when she was taking me to visit a college. My mother was supposed to take me but she had strep throat and Dora stood in. I cheat whenever I can on tests and schoolwork. I need the grades so that I can get student aid.
>
> I have no excuses but at least I know that I am wrong.

The fourth confession was more cogent:

> I did a hit and run when I was drunk one time. The guy didn't die and he got better,

pretty much. I should have turned myself in but I didn't and now it's too late to do anything about it.

The sixteenth revelation made John stop and think:

I steal. Whenever I can get away with it I take things that don't belong to me. It could be a framed picture or change off somebody's desk, an iPod or a pair of shoes. I once took a very expensive vase from the apartment of a house I'd only been to once. I unlocked the back door when I was there in the daytime and came in that night when the guy that lived there was asleep. He was my boyfriend's best friend so I knew him pretty well. I was scared I might get caught. After, I went right home and fucked my boyfriend hard.

I keep the things I take in a chest in a secret place and visit them sometimes. I think I'm wrong but I can't help it. And, anyway, nobody gets hurt that bad.

There were hundreds of sheets tacked, pinned and pasted to the walls and trees, announcement boards and lampposts near the broadsides: many more confessions than there had been people in the class.

John realized that his assignment had started an instant craze among students who were already deeply disturbed by the allegations against their professors.

Very few were out and about on the campus that day. John could hear the whisper of sheets in the breeze calling out to whoever would listen: testaments of young people finally able to admit secrets that were worms in their hearts.

"Professor," Theron James called when John came through the automatic doors of the student recreation center.

"Dean James," said the deconstructionist killer.

"Are you ready?" James asked, taking John by the arm.

"Absolutely."

This was the first time he and the dean had touched except to shake hands. The intimacy was the broad-shouldered academician's way of explaining the importance of the situation.

"The president will be introducing you," James said.

"I thought this was Eubanks's show?"

"It was decided that since she was listed on the broadside her introducing you might taint the way people heard your words," Theron said guiding John by the elbow. "There are monitors set up throughout the center, in the library and in all the offices. Almost everyone on campus will hear you."

"And the Platinum Path?" John asked.

Theron stopped, his fingers clenching John's biceps. The scarred scholar looked his protégé in the eye and said, "Yes . . . that's right."

They continued their walk toward the auditorium.

John noticed that the aisles and halls of the recreation center were crowded with people. Students and faculty, administrators and maintenance staff were standing around talking and watching.

"Aren't you going to ask me what I'm going to say?" John asked Theron as they approached the closed doors of the auditorium.

"Certainly not."

"Why?"

"This is your battle to win or lose, Professor Woman. I wouldn't dare interfere."

Saying this, the dean knocked on the auditorium door. A burly student looked out, then admitted James and his charge. John recognized the big sophomore, he'd taken D-History 101 in John's first semester at NUSW.

"Carlyle," John said, reaching for the name. "Francis Carlyle."

The glowering student suddenly smiled.

"Glad you're doing this, Professor," he said. "People need something to hang on to."

Down toward the stage, on the right side of the center row, sat the college president and

Willie Pepperdine. Luckfeld wore an off-white gabardine suit and Willie a close-fitting midnight blue sports coat and jeans. His yellow shirt was buttoned to the neck but he wore no tie.

When John and Theron approached both men stood.

"Glad you decided to do this, John," Luckfeld said holding out a welcoming hand.

Willie patted John's shoulder. "I'm surprised Eubanks had the smarts to deal you in."

"She didn't have much choice," John said.

"We were thinking that you should wait back-stage until the room fills," Luckfeld suggested. "I'll do the introduction and then you can come out."

"I don't think so," John countered. "I should be up onstage waiting for them and then, when everyone is seated, I'll just get into it."

"That sounds right," Luckfeld agreed after a moment's meditation, "more immediate."

"One thing, Colin," John said to the president.

"What's that?"

"Any truth to these allegations?"

"No," he said, with a grin. "Not a one."

John nodded and moved toward the side-stair that led up to the stage.

This time there was an oak lectern again but no table or Containment Report trunk; no three-screen slide show or slow-moving message from Brother of George.

John took his place behind the lectern and said aloud, "You can let them in," to the four young men who had taken their places at the doors.

As the audience filed down the aisles John thought about the walk across campus, the yellow confession sheets, Chapman Lorraine (of course), his father and how Detective Colette Margolis would wrestle him to the floor in a secret room the police kept for recreation. He wondered how he had maintained sanity in a life that was almost completely separate from the world in which he lived.

People made their way among the aisles and pews. There were students alongside the faculty and others. A few men and women with telephoto cameras stood at the back of the auditorium and a student camera crew was there to film the talk.

When a shadow moved above his head John saw a microphone boom lowering. It was like the final piece of a jigsaw puzzle dropped into place at the end of a rainy afternoon.

The obedient audience went directly to their seats in hushed anticipation.

He looked out upon the thousand and more faces and the hush turned to silence.

"We have come here today not to be lectured to or addressed but rather to look inside ourselves to see what it is that makes us possible," John said without referring to the speech that was still folded in his breast pocket. "That's how I was going to start this address, with words that were smart and vague enough to be a balm for the problems that bring us here, words to deflect the recriminations brought to bear on the walls and halls of this institution. If I could get us to look at our own needs and failings then maybe we could forget.

"But in truth we will not disremember anything or absolve anyone. Human beings hold grudges long past their expiration dates. They wage wars in the names of their great-great-grandfathers and over borders long ago redrawn, yelling out battle cries in languages that are not the tongues of the original combatants.

"We are, all of us, ready to hate and fight back. We despise in free form, casting our gaze from one poor victim to the next. Thieves, child molesters, murderers and liars fill social media platforms and newspapers, TV reports, talk radio and rumor. We remember who murdered Julius Caesar and Archduke Franz Ferdinand. We hate people even after they have died and this spite lives on past our own deaths."

John stopped for a moment to look at his audience.

"We tell ourselves that we are better, that we would stand up against oppression and die for the rights of our fellow citizens. Most of us wouldn't but even if we did who would profit by it? Our fates were written long ago in our stars, our trilling blood. There's no escape, no justice, no respite.

"We have seen on shiny, indestructible yellow posters the accusations against members of our community. If you believe what they say, our university is a den of thieves, especially the professorial class. But how could this be true? Even if you forget that every employee of this school is vetted by the institution, the state, and the departments they serve. Even if you forget that the first rule of law in this United States is innocent until proven guilty. Even if you ignore the fact that you have been given no proof of wrongdoing—still it is unbecoming of you and the perpetrators of this assault to question a fellow traveler who, through no fault of his or her own, is following the same mortal and imperfect path as the rest of us."

The written speech now forgotten, John stopped again to look from side to side. The origin of this talk brought a smile to his lips. He was a killer, a guilty man defending the accused. The contradictions felt right.

"Are the allegations true?" he asked. "Of course not but the issue is not resolved by this answer. The problem is not innocence or guilt but the poison of suspicion. We, the lifeblood of this institution, have been poisoned by faceless, voiceless charges. This is terrible but not a permanent problem because there is a three-pronged cure: cold logic, bright hope and personal truth.

"I slept most of the day on the hard floor behind my desk after a long night of preparing for this address. When I woke up I walked here. The campus was empty because everyone was already here or sitting in front of a screen somewhere. On the way I saw hundreds of confessions penned by students learning humility by revealing their own truths and failings. Rather than leave the indictments to stand alone they put up their own confessions and shortcomings because this juxtaposition is the closest we will ever come to forgiveness.

"We cannot know, understand or, ultimately, judge history. In the same vein we cannot know, understand or judge another human being's soul. We can never be sure of what went before. Certainly we must strive for truth; but that's all we can do—strive. And even though these accusations are baseless we *do know* that we have done things that we're not proud of, that might be seen as wrong. We recognize guilt because we are all guilty. That's what the Bible tells us; the Old Testament that is the foundation for many of the warring religions of today."

John exhaled and didn't take a breath for a few seconds.

"That said," he continued, "this event is a good

thing. We do not naturally seek truth in ourselves. We don't want to be faced with our mortality, limited awareness or inferiority, or God's wrath. We'd much rather inebriate ourselves and condemn, get high on carnal pleasures, hone our fears and guilt into barbs and arrows aimed at our fellows. But every now and then we see our reflections in some glass. At that moment we see that we are the enemy. This is the only truth that abides. Those yellow posters are that glass. These baseless claims echo in our lives.

"Poisoned by suspicion we see ourselves, and if we take the time to work through this convoluted and spiny reaction we might see the hope of building a community of conscience and character.

"We know the charges against us. We know that if the truth came out it would take us along with it. We know about silence. That's what the broadsides are telling us. And so if we wait a moment before condemning others we might find absolution and breathe easier."

John took in a great draft of air. He was ready to continue the oration but found that there were no more words to say. For a moment he was confused by this unexpected dead end.

Finally he nodded slightly and made his way down to the first row of seats.

"Thank you, Professor Woman," Theron James said over the microphone. Somehow he had made it to the stage. "We appreciate your hard work and good words. We will take your talk with us through this difficult time."

There was some applause and then the hushed rustle of people rising and filing out.

A few people shook his hand muttering words he didn't understand. He was thinking about the sudden loss of language and the feeling of release that came with it.

"John," someone said stridently.

Ira Carmody was standing before him, his bearing assertive, even aggressive. John remembered that Ira was a black belt in something. Looking to the left he saw Pepperdine watching closely.

The angry professor's hand jutted out and John took it. They shook, nodded and then released. Before John could say any more Annette Eubanks rushed forward and took him by both hands.

"That was beautiful," she said. "And true."

19

Walking up the stairs to his apartment John wondered if Carlinda would be waiting there. When he came in she was sitting at the small kitchen table.

Feeling a wrenching spasm in his chest John said, "Mom?"

At first she just looked at him with equal measures of mirth, wonder and something triumphant. No longer youthful, Lucia Napoli still maintained an aura of beauty. She wore a brown dress with images of violet ribbons writhing upon it. When she stood her breast expanded with an emotion they shared.

She was barefoot: at home in her son's desert hideout.

Tears flooded her eyes. They came together kissing each other's faces. Then, gently pushing him away, she said, "I have to get a Kleenex."

She lifted a green purse from the kitchen table taking out a tissue and lowered into the chair, dabbing her nose and eyes.

"Sit, CC. Sit."

"Mom?"

"That was the first word you ever said. You were eighteen months and followed me everywhere. If you turned around and couldn't see me you would holler."

"You're really here?" her grown son asked.

"And then one day instead of crying you said, 'Mom,' and then a whole lotta baby talk. Your father called it gabbling."

"I don't understand," John said, thinking of his mother and his father together.

"Sit."

"I saw you in Parsonsville but I knew it wasn't really you. I wanted it to be so bad but, but . . . you have the same red hair."

"Sit, CC."

Overwhelmed by the impossible appearance of Lucia his mind recoiled toward Herman. He tried to imagine what history would say about his mother's magical reentry into his life.

History, he wrote later that day, *is what is left after all living memory is erased . . . A living, breathing datum—like my mother for instance— is outside history: an undigested record, a preformed fact . . .*

"Sit," Lucia said again.

John nodded, moving to the chair opposite her.

"Where have you been?" he asked.

"I can't tell you that. I mean I was staying in Phoenix for a while before coming here. I *was* in town one day."

"You can't tell me because of the gangster?"

"Filo and I got married six years ago. He's really a very wonderful man, CC. He was only in with those terrible men because that was all he knew. But that life is behind him now." With these words she was finished talking about her secret life. "How are you?"

"How am I? I've lived my entire life trying to figure out how I got here."

Lucia took in a deep breath, then she began to speak. "I know it's been hard, baby. I wasn't a good wife or mother. That's why I'm here . . . to try and make up for some of it."

"How did you even know to come here?"

"I been living in Venice Beach, California, with Filo the last eleven years. He doesn't sleep much and watches the TV in the living room pretty late: all these crazy cable-access shows. He says that he likes to see regular people saying things they really believe. I don't know when he ever started talking like that . . . Anyway, one night he sees this show with you and an older man. He said that you were a teacher but with a new name and you made mincemeat outta that other guy."

"He recognized me?"

"I know, right?" Lucia Napoli said. "He only seen you a few times but the minute the camera hit your face Filo knew it was you."

"That was a year ago. When did he see it?"

"About then. I wanted to come right here but Filo said that we had to be careful because the FBI was lookin' for him and if they knew you and I were related then maybe they'd have some kinda eye on you. Not like surveillance or anything but just a look now and then."

"So you're a fugitive?"

"We live a good life. We got friends, go on vacations. It's not like me and Jimmy Grimaldi."

John reached across the table and touched his mother's forearm wanting further proof that she existed. The yellow posters, public address, the defeat of Annette Eubanks and Ira Carmody were long-ago dreams.

"How did you get into my apartment?"

"I went to the front gate and asked the nice Mexican guard if he would let me in."

"Hopi," John said.

"What?"

"Hototo is a Hopi Indian."

"A real Indian? It's a wonder out in the west isn't it? You know me and Filo walk down to the beach every day—every day, even in the rain."

"What happened to you, mom? You disappeared. I went to your house and you were gone."

If he could have seen his face the way his mother saw it CC would have observed the pain embedded in his eyes. If he had seen through her heart he would have felt the hurt it brought her.

Lucia took one of his hands in both of hers and peered deeply into their shared ache.

"I love you, baby," she said. "I might not have been a good mother but I love you, always have."

"But you didn't even know about when dad died."

"I knew, honey. I was there when you buried him."

"No you weren't. I put out a chair but you never came. Violet Breen came, France Bickman came but you weren't there."

"I was."

"No."

"Listen to me, CC. When I heard about Herman I came back to New York. Filo went with me even though he might have been arrested or killed. Your father broke my heart when he kicked me out. I was willing to come take care of both of you. I knew he couldn't work, that you were doing his job. I was proud of you but what could I do? I knew he'd'a never changed his mind. And if I took you away it would have killed him."

"You were saying something about the funeral," John said. Looking at Lucia he felt that she was moving away: that familiar distance.

She must have intuited this feeling because she squeezed his hand very hard. With the pain this distance was quashed.

"I was there but I stayed across the street. I loved Herman, I did, but he was right—I betrayed him. I abandoned you because he needed you more than I did. So when a stool pigeon in Filo's crew fingered him for the cops I decided that at least I could do something for somebody. I ran with him, stuck by his side through reconstructive surgery, got a job at a movie studio as a makeup artist while he reorganized himself. I've tried to be a good woman . . . I have been."

"If you were there why didn't you say anything to me after the funeral?"

"I went to your father's house and waited," she said. "But you never came home. I waited three days then went to see France at the Arbuckle. He said your father left you some money and you had probably gone out to start a new life."

John pulled his hand away but Lucia did not fade.

"Can you forgive me?" she pleaded.

"If I ever said the slightest thing wrong you'd kick me out the house," he said. "I never wanted dad to know so I slept on the floor of the projection room."

"I was wrong. Your father and you were the best things that ever happened to me but my heart had a mind of its own. Red wine and bad men were my downfall."

After long minutes of silence he said, "I can probably get us double-decker apartments and we could live together for a while."

"All right, CC, whatever you say."

"Will your husband get angry at you for not coming home?"

"Filo understands me, baby. He wants me to be happy."

20

The next couple of months were nearly idyllic for young Dr. John Woman. With the help of President Luckfeld and Dean James he and his mother moved into a full family unit in faculty housing. He occupied the top apartment.

Carlinda stopped coming by. He saw her in class but she avoided eye contact and spoke to him only to ask questions about his lectures. Her papers were excellent. She had come up with a powerful theory about the interplay between dialectics, technology and the interpretation of historical events. It was her notion that the present was always struggling with the past because of technology's impact on understanding. *People in the now see the past through an ever-changing, never-repeating kaleidoscope of technological experience,* she wrote. *How can we hope to understand what went before, even in our own nation and language group, if the ability to perceive and empathize has been altered through technology and its attendant technique?*

Attached to one of these papers was a handwritten note which read:

John
I have reconciled with Arnold. The fever is over. It's better this way.

C

The words rang true.

He had stopped going to see Senta. His sexual drive, he came to believe, had been in response to loneliness and isolation. Now that he had coffee with his mother every morning he no longer felt alone.

In the evenings Lucia, whose new name was Rosa Pitkin, made dinner for John and sometimes guests from the school administration and history department.

President Luckfeld and his Panamanian wife, Marte, ate with them four times in as many weeks.

"You are very lucky to have your mother in your life," blue-eyed tawny-skinned Marte said one evening when Lucia had made lasagna filled with linguica and shiitake mushrooms. "Most Americans, I find, run away from their blood and then wonder why they're unhappy."

"He's a perfect son," Lucia agreed. "I don't deserve him."

John found that he spoke less and concentrated even more on his deconstructions of the interpretations of what went before.

The history department vacated his ouster then voted him department chair when Annette Eubanks suddenly decided to step down. Ira Carmody was his opponent receiving only three votes.

On the evening after John was elected chair he took his mother to a restaurant called the Country Road Diner located on the outskirts of Parsonsville. It was an old place patronized mainly by old-time locals. John liked to think that the Brother of George ate there, that maybe they had sat side by side at the counter now and then.

That evening John and his mom sat in a corner booth served by Esther Simmons, whose mother's family had lived in the county for six generations; her father's people had been there even longer.

John ordered chicken-fried steak while his mother had country beef stew cooked in a red wine sauce. Lucia wore a thick silver necklace and rose gold earrings studded with miner's diamonds.

"My son the college man," Lucia said raising her third goblet of wine. "Here I barely made it out of high school, your father never saw the inside of a classroom and you are the boss of a department . . . you could be university president one day."

"Yeah," he intoned, "I'm a real success story."

Ordering her fourth glass of wine she touched the baby finger of her son's left hand.

"You don't think I get the news from home, CC?"

He noticed the concern in her face.

"I read about the old silent theater and the body and who they're looking for," she said.

"So you think I did it?"

"I know it."

"How?"

"Because you were the bravest man I ever knew when you were no more than ten. Because most men need to be stronger or better armed to feel brave but you had your father's courage."

"The bravery that women have in a world dominated by men," John said.

"Just like that," Lucia agreed, slurring her words slightly. "But better because you wouldn't hide behind anybody. And if that Chapman Lorraine came in the projection room and found you, you wouldn't have no choice but to kill him; either that or have you and your father throw'd out on the street. I know that as sure I'm breathing."

"You . . ." John said. "You actually see me sitting here in front of you?"

"You're my son, my blood."

John felt her claim on him. This drunken passion somehow daunted his intelligence.

"My entire life I missed you, mom."

"I only left New York when you were sixteen, baby."

"But even before then you'd be gone in the morning and dad would be so sad that I couldn't make him smile."

"I'm a terrible human being."

"And still I love you more than anything."

"I'm going away for a few days," Lucia told her son seven weeks, three days and thirteen hours after she'd miraculously reappeared in his life. "I need to go see Filo."

"Why doesn't he come here?" John asked, trying to push down the panic in his chest.

"It's that if the FBI is watching thing," Lucia replied. She was dicing onions in his third-floor kitchen.

"How long will you be gone?"

"Three days."

"Could I come?"

"You have that president's lecture."

"Oh . . . right."

"But Filo would like to meet you one day," she said. "He's a very busy man too."

"Busy doing what? I thought he'd retired from being a crook."

"He did . . . he has. Now he works for charities and public groups."

"Isn't that dangerous?" John asked wanting to keep the conversation going.

372

"I told you that he's had plastic surgery and his name was changed. As long as he's no place anybody is looking for him it's okay."

"What is his new name?"

Lucia looked at her son a moment, her eyes filled with tears from the pungent onion.

"I better let him tell you that," she said. "You know just a name could put him away for life, maybe get us both killed."

"Oh . . . okay. I'd really like it if you stayed until after the lecture, mom. Then we could go together."

"Next time."

Heartbreak was a familiar feeling, even older than the guilt over the death of Chapman Lorraine. He remembered clearly when his father was in the hospital and his mother sent him away.

"It's okay, honey," Lucia cooed. "I'm never leaving you again."

"Except to go see Filo."

"Only for a few days."

"When are you leaving?"

"Tomorrow morning."

The next afternoon was the first time he considered calling Carlinda. The apartment felt empty. He could say that he wanted to discuss Carlinda's paper. Instead he turned to the lecture he was supposed to give the next day—History:

The Art of Living with Death. Pencil in hand he sat before a stack of blank paper. He promised himself that if he didn't write anything by seven he'd call Carlinda.

At 6:51 his landline rang.

"Hello?"

"Hello, John."

"Marte?"

"You sound surprised."

"No, no. I just . . . It's nothing. What can I do for you?"

"Colin was called away to Chicago overnight," she said. "And I don't want to eat alone. What are you and Rosa doing?"

"My mother had to go to LA for a few days."

"Oh. Then you're alone too. Why don't we meet at that French restaurant in town?"

"La Reine?"

"That's it. Seven-thirty?"

"So what you're saying is that you have been studying history your entire life," Marte Crespo-Luckfeld said after ordering frogs' legs as an appetizer and mushroom pasta for the main.

Marte was a handsome woman in her late thirties, with delicate russet-color skin, and eyes a shocking crystalline blue. Her face was long and sympathetic while her mouth was set with determination that John had not remembered from their previous meetings.

"I guess," he said, "at least from the time I could read long words."

"But there seems to be something missing."

"What do you mean?"

Marte gazed at him. In her eyes, on her lips there seemed to be lodged a question. "Colin has told you that he . . . we belong to a unique and very confidential organization," she stated.

John became very still.

She smiled and nodded.

"Yes," she said. "You are right not to answer. The Platinum Path is destined for a glorious future but with this ambition come danger and death."

At that moment a waiter came with her frogs' legs and John's onion soup.

When the server was gone she said, "You are on the radar of the senior officials."

"Why?"

"They need young and vital leadership: men and women who are willing to act regardless of law, love or outmoded ethics."

"And they think I'm lawless, loveless and amoral?"

"Be prepared to answer the call."

John sat up that night thinking about people watching him from synthetic shadows.

"Was that a threat?" he asked the walls and then fell fast asleep.

. . .

In the morning John concentrated on the talk he was slated to deliver. Truth, for the historian, was like sand: seemingly whole from a distance but on closer examination it broke down into particles so fine that their forms and natures, not to mention their incalculable number, were beyond human comprehension.

He ascended the stage at Deck Rec auditorium wondering at the previous hour or so: the shower and the dark blue suit over a yellow T, the long walk in strong sun and the hot wind against him. On the way he'd said hello to students and faculty members, strangers and the gardener— Ron Underhill.

"Professor Woman."

"Mr. Underhill."

"How are you today, sir?"

"Going to give a talk about how the architecture of human certainty is built on graveyard soil."

The older man smiled and nodded. "I heard about that," he said.

"You did?"

"They put out a weekly announcement so the staff can avail themselves of what the school has to offer."

"I didn't realize that," John said.

Underhill gave John a big smile. One of his two front teeth was missing.

Looking out over the mostly full auditorium John thought about Underhill. He was a bright man and completely, it seemed, his own.

Carlinda was in the third row in the rightmost tier of pews. Seeing her John decided on the construction of the talk he'd give.

President Luckfeld and Marte were front and center. Colin nodded at John and smiled. Marte was smiling too.

The digital clock on the back wall read 1:58. John felt the sweat from the hot sun turn cold under the air-conditioning. The IT specialist Talia Friendly, wearing khaki overalls, gave him a thumbs-up.

The spectators were still greeting each other when John said aloud, "We don't really learn from history."

People stopped their talking and dropped into seats.

"Take the thumbs-up gesture," he said making the sign with his left hand. "In ancient Rome, at the gladiatorial games in the Colosseum and Circus, that gesture was a death sentence for the loser. It meant to give an upthrust with the sword and end his life. Thumbs-down meant to sheath your sword and let the conquered live. This is as close as we can get to a fact. Thumbs-up is bad, thumbs-down is good. But will you, now that you know the truth, change the way you sign? Of course not. You're not communicating with Latin sign language in twenty-first-century America. You know what the gestures mean today and that's that. We know what is true and will die to defend that truth.

"History is most similar to a feud," he said. "There are sides. One family says that it was started by the murder of an uncle or the theft of some property. The other clan identifies an earlier insult; and so on. Natural law, morality and God himself seem to take sides in the conflict. From this come decades, sometimes centuries, of bloodshed and animosity, misinformation and the steady deterioration of truth.

"The historian has to choose sides. He, or she, makes a choice as to what sequence of events and intentions to highlight. Even while affecting objectivity the historian has secretly, maybe even unconsciously, taken sides. This is the human condition and, whatever else we might achieve, we cannot abandon it."

John kept on talking even though his mind wandered from the lecture. He was thinking of his gone-again mother and Marte's warning. He wondered if Carlinda would see the comparison between technique and nature and if knowledge, like Buddha said and Socrates said, was often the enemy of awareness.

He did not see the three men, led by Officer Hernandez of the Granville police, go around

378

Talia Friendly as they approached the stage.

When they came near, John wondered why. Had they found some proof concerning the Trash Can Lecture?

Maybe this part of the story is over, he thought.

"Cornelius Jones," Hernandez said, "I am arresting you until such time that your case with the state of New York has been resolved. Please turn around, sir."

Part Three
The Trial

21

After photographs and fingerprints John was put into a holding cell in Maricopa County Jail. There he had seven cellmates: two white, the others various shades of brown.

Two of the darker men, a maybe-Mexican and a man the color of John's father, wore fancy but disheveled suits and seemed to be sick. They sat side by side on the floor next to a small cot lolled upon by a very large dark brown man.

A friendly American Indian asked, "What they got you on, brother?"

"Suspicion of murder," John said. "In New York."

"Andrew."

"John."

Andrew looked to be somewhere in his forties with ruddy red-brown skin that had been much in the sun. His dark eyes seemed to be searching for something—on the floor, in John's eyes, outside the cell bars.

"I took three sheep from a dude," he said, "but they called it armed robbery just because I had a knife."

"You had the knife in your hand?"

Andrew smiled and offered John his hand.

Andrew said, "No. It was in a sheath on

my belt. I always carry a knife like that. Not a weapon, it's a tool."

Christopher Minor, one of the white prisoners, was introduced by Andrew to John. Minor was in his twenties with long brown hair that was severely matted. Minor was a known drug smuggler. His crime was that there were traces of marijuana in the trunk of his car; that and one drop of blood.

"Fuckin' cops said that they're gonna test that DNA against ever' open case of assault and murder in Arizona," Christopher said. "I told 'em okay but the first blood they should test is mine."

With that the young white man laughed and laughed as if the best joke ever told had just escaped his lips.

"So you Hopi?" John asked his new friend Andrew.

"Navajo," the nonviolent thief replied. "Largest reservation in the U.S. What you do?"

"I'm a history professor. At least I used to be. I guess after my arrest they'll be letting me go."

"How does a college teacher get mixed up with murder? Was it a woman?"

"Suspicion of murder," John corrected. "It happened seventeen years ago."

"Seventeen? You don't look no more than twenty-five."

"I was sixteen when the crime they say happened."

"'Crime they say,'" Andrew quoted. "You

384

sound more like a jailbird than a teacher, unless you teach law."

"John Woman," a voice from outside the cell called.

"That's me," John said, rising from the floor where he and Andrew leaned against the flattened, crisscrossed bars of the holding cell.

"Come with me."

Three jailhouse guards brought John to a small room where they made him put his hands behind his back. After his wrists were cuffed one of the men led John to a subterranean hallway lined with lime green metal doors. Using a key from a huge ring hanging from his belt the black-uniformed, pimply-faced young white man unlocked a door halfway toward the end of the dead-end corridor.

"Get in."

"What about these manacles?"

"When the door is locked turn your back to it. I'll open the slot to take them off."

The cell was a fraction the size of the one he'd come from. There was a cot, a tiny sink, and an aluminum commode. The ceiling was low and the walls pale gray.

The guard took off the handcuffs and then slammed the slot closed leaving John alone, missing the society of his cellmates.

The cell was virtually soundproof. No phone, computer, TV, radio or sounds through the wall.

There wasn't even paper and pencil to jot or doodle with. John had never imagined a life bereft of pencils and paper or even a knob on the door.

Sitting on the cot John tried to remember what life had been before he came to that cell. His last lecture was interrupted, now lost. His mother was gone—again. There were no lovers, children or friends who would seek him out.

This solitary jail cell, John suddenly realized, was the distilled metaphor of his life, like a living art installation. This was the shell he carried like a hermit crab taking on a discarded tin can for a home.

The first time he'd ever been in a true colony of his kind was in the holding cell. There he could admit his crime if he wanted, say the name Chapman Lorraine. He could be Cornelius Jones, son of Herman and Lucia, heir to hard-bitten mobsters and deep libraries.

He lay down on the cot and masturbated as he used to do in the secret closet of the projectionist's booth. The orgasm was powerful and he cried out behind it. For a moment he was embarrassed but then he remembered that no sound penetrated his shell. He masturbated again, experiencing an even more intense climax. After this he turned on his side and sleep fell like a chain-link blanket.

Sometime later, he had no idea how long, John awoke with the glare of the paneled ceiling light in his eyes. On the floor at the bottom of the metal door was a cardboard tray arranged with a sandwich of white bread and processed American cheese, a flimsy plastic tub of green Jell-O and six wilted leaves of lettuce. No fork or spoon, no napkin. John ate then masturbated then slept.

"Hey . . . you . . . Woman," someone said.

John awoke with the paneled ceiling light in his eyes.

"What?"

"If you want breakfast then pass me your tray."

The cardboard food tray was on the floor beside the cot. He took it to the door where an open square panel revealed the man talking to him.

There was a smaller slot at the floor.

He could see a young black man peering through the square panel.

John tried to push the tray across to him but the face backed away.

"Through the bottom," the guard said. "You have to pass it under the bottom. That's the rules."

John went down on a knee and slid the tray out. Immediately a new tray was passed in. On this cardboard platter there was a slug-like, white-flour burrito.

"Breakfast is the best in here," the guard said. "Scrambled eggs and turkey bacon. Not too dry or nuthin'."

387

"What time is it?"

"A little after eight . . . in the morning."

"Do the lights ever go out?"

"No. Never."

"What are they going to do with me?"

"They want you for extradition to New York."

"How long does that usually take?"

"There was this guy in here one time that fought for nine months before Wyoming got him on manslaughter. If the crime's not too bad sometimes they give up but they want you for murder. On murder they can't give in. Politicians afraid that their voters might hear."

"So I just sit here?"

"At least they took you outta the holdin' cell. Sometimes it can get pretty rough in there. Some niggahs just don't know how to ack."

John had no reply to the guard's wisdom and so instead took a bite out of his burrito.

"My name's Marle Josephson," the guard allowed. "I'm gettin' ready to take the test for Phoenix PD."

"Oh?"

"You a college professor, right?"

"Yes I am, at least I was."

"Maybe you could help me with the test."

"I don't know anything about civil service exams. I mean, all you have to do is memorize the facts they give you and hope that the psych portion doesn't make you seem too crazy."

"How can I fool that?"

"Got me."

"So what good are you?" Marle Josephson asked.

John took the question seriously.

"What's a name like Woman anyway? I never heard'a nobody called that."

"Josephson!" a bodiless voice boomed.

"Yes sir, Captain Anton."

"Stop talking to the prisoner and get back to work."

The upper and lower slats slammed shut and John was left again to his adopted shell.

22

John had been in the cell for seven more meals when Marle Josephson opened the upper slot and said, "John Woman." It wasn't another meal because he'd just finished lunch: an exceptionally dry, overcooked skinless chicken breast and a paper tub of mustard. If he dipped the fowl in the condiment, taking only small bites, it was possible to chew the jerky-like flesh. There was something very satisfying about all that chewing. He felt full and sated.

"Marle," John said.

"Stand at the line with your back to the door and hold your hands toward me."

Marching through the subterranean catacombs of the deceptively large jailhouse John and his guard passed other uniformed men; some in guard-black and others in bright yellow, orange and red prisoner coveralls.

"How come you have me in cuffs, Mr. Josephson? None of the other prisoners are wearing them." John thought that calling Marle mister might get the silent sentinel to speak, but it didn't.

They came to a blue metal door.

"Prisoner for interrogation room nine-A," Marle said to the door as if it were a living sentry.

Various metallic pings, rattles and clanks emanated from the sturdy portal making John postulate the words a sentient door like this might speak.

The door swung inward.

"Go on," Marle said.

John and Marle walked through between two uniformed guards down an aisle of wooden doors with proper knobs. Each portal had an identifying number painted on it, in red. They stopped at 9-A.

Marle knocked three times.

"Come in," a woman said.

Marle had a key for this door too.

The room was as bare as John's cell but the light was warmer. The walls were painted institutional green. The only furniture was a dark brown wooden table attended on opposite sides by folding metal chairs.

A woman was seated in one of these chairs. She rose when John and Marle entered. Wearing a conservative dark green pantsuit she had dyed her hair almost blond, was verging on fifty and had put on ten or twelve pounds. But despite all that John recognized Colette.

"You can take the cuffs off," she said to Marle.

"That's against protocol, ma'am."

"Take them off and leave us."

John was glad to see that he wasn't the only one who could be cowed by the policewoman's authority.

• • •

"Sit down," Colette said after Marle was gone.

John stayed on his feet alternately rubbing his wrists. His fingers felt swollen and on fire with pins and needles.

"Sit," she said and he obeyed.

Lowering into the seat across from him she took a moment to look at the prisoner.

"Do you know why you're here?" she asked.

"Tell me."

"The state of New York has determined that you are the prime suspect in the murder of Chapman Lorraine."

John hunched his shoulders slightly and breathed in through his nostrils the air of relative freedom.

"Being the head investigator on the missing person case," she continued, "I was deposed by the department after the body had been identified. I told them what I remembered and turned over my notes. Last week they tasked me to come here to identify you if I could."

With his eyes alone John asked her the question.

"It is my determination that you are the young man I interviewed."

"I loved you."

Back in his cell for a dozen meals or more John had learned to curb his masturbation regimen.

Too often and the skin of his penis got chafed, the orgasms less satisfying.

He didn't think about the regimen of history. Instead his thoughts were of food and women and too much wine. He longed for the holding cell with its hungover businessmen; tangle-haired Christopher Minor; and especially Andrew, the peace-loving, knife-wielding Navajo.

"John Woman," Marle Josephson announced through the square hole in the door. It had been more than four days since he'd been visited by Colette.

"Hey, brother," the guard said to John as they navigated the underground holding area for the criminal class of Arizona. "I don't mean to be cold or nuthin' but my boss, Captain Anton, been watchin' me like a mothahfuckah so I'm tryin' not to talk too much to the prisoners."

"Okay," John said wondering what Colette would be wearing.

"I been studyin' for that exam like you said."

"How's that going?"

"Not too good."

They passed Andrew just then. He was in a cell with its door open. The Navajo sheep thief was clad in a lemon yellow jumpsuit, squatting in a corner, his hands wrapped around his knees, his eyes searching out beyond the jail.

"How come I don't have a prisoner's uniform?" John asked.

"Only people convicted of stuff get them," Marle said. "You aren't guilty of a crime in Arizona. Are you gonna talk to me about the test?"

"What's the problem?"

"I read the material and I understand it too . . . But just a hour later I don't remember a damn thing."

"That's due to computers," John said.

"I don't even own a computer."

"Even so people are so used to putting something into a screen then calling it back that they think the human brain works the same way."

"What you talkin' 'bout, Woman?"

"Reading is rereading."

"Huh?"

"Read the exam booklet from front to back three times before taking the practice test," Professor Woman advised. "Then you'll find that you know more. Not everything but more. Then, when you see what you got wrong and right, you read it again. That's where the true learning will happen."

"Really? I got to read it four times?"

"Maybe even five or six but that's nothing because you'll be a cop for twenty years."

Marle led John to the same room as before.

The guard knocked again. A woman's voice

said *come in* again. But this time it was a Caucasian with red lips and long brunette ringlets cascading down the sides of her made-up face.

Without her having to ask, Marle unlocked the handcuffs and left the room.

The new woman wore perfume whereas Colette had not worn any. John liked the scent.

"Professor Woman," the brunette said. "Pleased to meet you."

She held out a hand. John shook but couldn't feel it because he was once again numb from too-tight handcuffs.

"My name is Nina Forché," she said. "I'm your lawyer. Please sit down."

Forché was wearing a scarlet dress and a blue sapphire pendant. Her fingernails had been painted peach by a professional and her tan came from long hours on a pleasant beach somewhere. She was past thirty but forty was still some years off.

"I'm here to discuss our strategy at the hearing," she began.

"I don't remember engaging a lawyer."

"I was retained by William Pepperdine."

"Are you on the Path?"

Forché gave John quick smile moving her head and shoulders with a noncommittal shrug.

"How did I get here, Ms. Forché?"

"You mean what brought you to the attention of the NYPD?"

"Yeah."

"An informant told them that Cornelius Jones's mother was living with her son in faculty housing at NUSW."

"Who?"

"Those records are sealed," she said. "We may never know because that testimony would have no bearing on the murder trial, if such a trial were to happen."

"If?" John felt sluggish, like some woodland creature coming awake after a long hibernation.

"If we're smart I don't believe this extradition request will hold."

"Why not?"

"They have no proof that you are this Cornelius Jones."

"None?"

"There are no fingerprints on file," Forché said. "No DNA evidence, no eyewitness, not even anyone who has ever seen you with the victim. There are no childhood photographs except one in an elementary school third grade annual. There aren't even any relatives that could offer a close enough DNA comparison."

"What about France Bickman?" he asked.

"The ticket-taker? He's of no concern to us."

"That detective," John said. "She said that she recognized me."

"First of all she interviewed a teenage boy," the lawyer argued. "Secondly, her records say that the entire interview was less than ten minutes. An eyewitness account of a brief conversation with an adolescent seventeen years ago is not enough for an extradition. They must prove your identity with something more than a detective's say-so."

"What about the woman living in my house?"

"There is no one living in your apartment and the school has refused New York's request to search the premises. When we get in to see the judge he will ask you if you are Cornelius Jones and you will say, 'No, your honor, I am not.'"

"No, your honor, I am not," John parroted. "No, your honor. Yes, I understand."

Nina Forché smiled at her student.

23

In the dream John was standing on a long line behind a large, broad-shouldered man. It felt as if he had been waiting forever. His feet hurt and, for some reason, his fingers were numb. The sun bore down and there was nothing to read. He had an iPod but the battery was low. The woman behind him was chattering on a cell phone. He thought about asking her if he could borrow it to call his mother but when he turned to ask she looked away. He tapped the shoulder of the large man in front of him. Maybe he had a phone.

When the brute turned around John recognized Chapman Lorraine, a bully from the elementary school. He hadn't seen Chapman in many years and the towering giant didn't seem to recognize him so John came up with a plan.

He said, "Your sister passed up word that she's at the end of the line and wants you to come get her."

"My sister?" Chapman said.

"Don't worry," Cornelius assured him, "I'll keep your place in line."

"Thanks," Lorraine said, giving John a big smile and even shaking his hand.

As soon as Chapman was gone the line began to move. At first it was a few slow steps. Then they began to pick up speed. A while later they were trotting like soldiers doing double time in a military review.

Before he knew it John was at the front of the line standing before a huge blue door. He glanced behind. Chapman Lorraine was running, screaming something from far back down the line.

"Open please," John said to the door.

He looked back again; the schoolyard bully was getting closer.

Panicked he turned to the door prepared to pound on it but it was already open. He walked across the threshold and the lofty azure door slammed shut behind him.

Walking down a long corridor on a floor paved with gilded tiles and flanked by bright white walls, John passed many doors, but he knew instinctively that these were not for him.

After some while he came to a bloodred door that glistened as if threatening to revert back into bodily fluid. This was his destination.

"Come in," a man said though John had not knocked.

On the other side of the bloodred door sat Herman Jones—perched on a bench made from glass.

John was delighted to see his father and immediately took a seat at his side.

"Your fairy godmother tasked me to grant you a wish," Herman said.

Cornelius thought of the fudge-colored woman, feeling the elation of her existence in his life.

"Are you really my father?"

"Is the answer to that question your wish?"

Dreamer John nodded.

"Yes and no," Herman said. "I was your father but that was long ago. Since then you have become your own man. Now tell me, why are you here?"

"I was on a line that felt like it went on forever," John said.

"This is the end of the line," Herman said sadly.

"John Woman," Marle Josephson intoned.

John woke up with the paneled ceiling light in his eyes.

"I did what you said," Marle told John as they marched along.

"And how did it go?"

"Great. I finished the practice test and did okay. Then I read the study book again and saw what I needed. How did you know that would happen?"

"My father taught me."

"He must'a been a smart guy."

"Marle?"

"Yeah, John?"

"Where are you taking me?"

"Captain Anton got it in his head that he didn't like you. I think it was because they made him keep you in solitary. It's not like that's any great privilege or anything but he was mad that he couldn't put you where he wanted."

A few moments went by. John looked around for Andrew the Navajo but did not see him.

"What does that have to do with where you're taking me?" John asked.

"Anton been holdin' up your paperwork but then that lawyer, that Nina Forché chick, said you had the right to see the people applied to visit. Anton's madder'n a motherfucker but ain't nuthin' he could do about it."

"So who is it that wants to see me?"

"I don't know. I'm just supposed to bring you to the room and wait. Easy for me."

When the door came open he saw Senta Ray seated in one of the metal folding chairs. She was wearing a fluffy white sweater and tight, faded blue jeans. Her lipstick was redder than what she wore to her Post Office job and when she rose to meet him she stood taller because of her fancy white high heels.

"Hey," she said.

"Hey." John kissed her on the cheek.

Senta smiled at this chaste greeting and asked, "Are they watching us?"

"I don't know."

"You wanna fuck and give 'em somethin' to see?"

"Maybe not right yet."

"Okay." Senta's mood was light and engaging. This was an act of pure kindness, designed to make him feel better.

They settled across the table from each other. Senta leaned forward taking his hands in hers.

"Lou read it in the *Phoenix Herald* that you'd been arrested for some murder that happened when you were a kid," she said. "He told me week before last and I came down the next day but they made me wait until now."

"I don't think the warden likes me." John smiled and squeezed her hands.

"I missed you," she said. "I really did."

"I'm sorry I didn't come by for so long. I just got involved in lots of stuff."

"Don't I know it," Senta said looking around the room. "I missed you but just the little bit we had together changed my life so much that I could never be mad."

"Changed your life how?" John appreciated Senta's smile and touch but what he needed was something to think about, something outside the confines of his imprisonment.

"The things you said."

"What things?"

"The last time I saw you you said that history is a tool like a hammer or a saw."

"I said that?"

"Don't you remember?"

402

"I guess we got pretty drunk most nights."

"Yeah. And you were just talkin'. I mean you probably talked like that all the time at school but what you said was new to me. It stuck. I thought about it for weeks and weeks. It seemed so important but I couldn't tell how. I was going to ask you but you never came back. And that was better because the question stayed in my mind; I couldn't let it go.

"Finally I got it down to one word—history. You had told me that there was the history we read about in books and then our own stories— what we lived through ourselves. I didn't know what that meant exactly but I kept on thinking about it. Thinking and thinking . . . and finally it hit me. I went to the shelf in the hallway closet and took down the old box of photographs. Must'a been a thousand pictures but there was only three of Nesta."

"Who?" John asked.

"My baby girl," Senta said. "Nesta. She was only a week old when I gave her up. I'd just turned fifteen and my parents made me because they were afraid I'd leave my beautiful baby with them.

"When I saw her picture I knew I'd been heartbroken my whole life about Nesta. I remembered what you said: 'The man swings the hammer but it's the hammer that makes the man.' Givin' Nesta away made the rest of my life what it was.

"I hired me a detective and he found my child working in a plastics factory outside Ojai, California.

"I got a lot of money in the bank. Savin' makes me feel safe. This one customer of mine who's a bookkeeper calls me his parsimonious prostitute. I brought Nesta home to me. Her name had been changed to Rachel Dawson but she lets me call her Nesta. We're gonna build a house, a new home that'll be everything we lost. That was because of you, John. You gave me something to think about and the way to think about it. It's kind of like you gave me the bricks to build our house."

"You would have probably decided to look for your daughter one day anyway," John argued mildly.

"I never would have until you made me look in that closet. I came here because I wanted you to know if you asked me out on a date that I would definitely go."

"That's a wonderful gift."

"Do you want me to tell you about our house?"

"Sure."

Senta described the floor plan and the memories that each room would contain. The composition of the building would be what had been missing from their lives.

There was a music room and library; bedrooms on different floors with a spiral ladder that connected them. And for when Nesta decided to go out on her own there was a cottage in the backyard that she could come back to whenever she wanted.

"What does that all sound like?" Senta said when she'd finished.

John lifted her hands to kiss them. A moment later a black-suited guard appeared at a doorway behind her.

"Is it time?" Senta asked the guard.

"Yes," the man said.

"Next time will be about you," she promised.

John kissed her again and she departed.

After Senta left, John expected Marle to come and bring him back to his cell.

But when Marle did not return John understood that there was more company to come; though he couldn't imagine a better visitor than Senta.

When the outer door opened again, the guard ushered in Ron Underhill.

"Thirty-five minutes," the guard told Ron. "Or you can knock."

Ron nodded and the sentry left.

John stood to meet his surprise guest.

The university gardener sported a black suit that fit his slender frame quite well. He wore a white dress shirt with buttoned cuffs that came down half an inch beyond the jacket sleeves, and an orange tie with three blue diamonds stitched down the center. His shoes were black with a dull shine. John thought that Underhill had this ensemble for funerals.

The men shook hands.

"How are you, Professor Woman?" the gardener asked.

"Locked up."

"They treating you okay?" The look on the older man's face seemed to add weight to the question, as if he might do something if the answer was not positive.

"Can't complain. The food's bad but it's the best they can do I'm sure."

"Why don't we have a sit-down?" Ron suggested.

The gardener's body was slight, like that of the coyote that stalked John after the accident. His hands were large and powerful. He was what people call a white man though his skin was a ruddy amber color from day after day under the desert sun.

Not knowing quite what to say John stated simply, "Well . . . here we are."

"Yes indeed. You never know where you'll end up in this life," Underhill opined. "Every day we think we know what's waiting for us but it's always something else."

There came another lull in the conversation.

"I'm a little surprised to see you here, Mr. Underhill," John said at last. "I mean I hardly know you and no one else from the school has come. Mr. Pepperdine paid for my lawyer but that's all the contact I've had with NUSW."

"That Willie's a good poker player."

"You know him?"

"He likes hydrangeas and I cultivate some in the biology department's greenhouse. We play poker there for pennies sometimes. He always walks away with a dollar or more of my money. That's how the rich stay rich, I guess."

"Thank you for coming. I didn't mean to be rude."

"I like the way you talk, Professor Woman. You play with ideas that most people treat with devotion. At first you sound almost sacrilegious but then it's clear as day that you care. I believe that when you wake up in the morning you're wondering where the day will go. So when I heard that they'd put you in jail I decided to come out here and tell you I believe in you and to keep your confidence up."

"But what if I'm guilty?" John smiled.

The gardener returned the grin. "You see? You always twist things around in a light way. Here I am trying to comfort you and there you are making me laugh."

"Thank you, Ron, but you didn't answer my question."

"If you killed a man that doesn't mean you're a murderer. If you murdered a man it doesn't mean you didn't have good reason. I like you, Professor Woman. I came out to Phoenix to look you in the eye and tell you so."

Underhill's smile held both power and conviction. There was certainty in this man. John was reminded of one of his father's frequent admonishments: *the hierarchy of history rarely documents its greatest heroes—they are too busy doing to waste time on legacy.*

"I wish I had some cards," John said, "and some pennies to lose."

"That's all right. I know you got another visitor. She was very kind to insist I went first."

Ron Underhill stood up easily, exhibiting the graceful posture of a much younger man.

"See ya," he said giving a friendly salute. Then he walked to the door and knocked, it opened and the gardener passed through.

In the few minutes while John waited for the next visitor, he thought about the almost magical feeling he experienced considering where the visitors' door led. He'd been locked up for only a short while but he was already feeling keen nostalgia for freedom: unlocked doors and unmonitored locomotion down empty streets; good food on china plates; and a telephone with pencil and paper close at hand.

The door opened once more and Carlinda Elmsford walked through followed by the guard.

"I'll be watching," he warned her.

He'd merely given Ron Underhill a time limit. But the multi-racial student was another matter.

John did not remember climbing out of his chair.

Carlinda's eyes fell upon him registering mild shock.

She approached him but stopped a finger's span beyond reach.

"You haven't shaved," she said. She had on jeans and a frilly pink blouse. Her auburn hair was pulled back and she wore no makeup.

"No razors in here."

John took a step forward and she a step back.

"You don't want me to touch you?" he asked.

"I'd rather you didn't."

"Why's that?"

"Can we sit down?"

John chose a chair. Before sitting Carlinda took something from her right-front pants pocket and placed it on the table. It was a small spiral-bound notepad with a short pencil threaded through the plastic wire coil.

"Thank you," John said. "That was very thoughtful. How'd you know I'd want this?"

"One time my father was arrested for hitting my mom. He had to spend sixty days in the county jail. The only thing he wanted was pencil and paper. He wrote her letters and she took him back."

"You've never talked much about your parents."

Carlinda glowered in response. It was as if she resented his saying anything to suggest they were connected. But there she was, visiting him in jail. Didn't that speak volumes about their relationship?

"I told Arnold about us," she said concentrating on the tabletop.

"Why?"

"One day when we were eating in the cafeteria he told me he'd always loved me, even when I wasn't with him. He said we were soul mates and I realized it was true. Soul mates don't keep secrets from to each other . . ."

"What did he say, I mean, when you told him about us?"

"He was mad that you lied to him."

"Wasn't he angry that you lied?" John asked.

"I never did. I just refused to talk to him about it."

"How did he take it when you did tell him?"

"It drives him crazy I was seeing you both at the same time. He's been studying New York statutes trying to see if there's any chance they'd execute you."

"That's severe."

"He's always asking me about you."

"Asking what?"

"What we did in the bed together. How big your penis is. Whenever we do anything new he wants to know if I learned it from you."

"And what do you say when he asks all that?"

"I tell him the truth."

"But why would you want to hurt him like that?"

"He likes it."

"He likes being hurt?"

"I can tell by the way he makes love to me. He was never so passionate before. He never wanted to experiment at all. But now he's after me all the time. Almost every night I wake up to him kissing me."

There was not much feeling in Carlinda's words but John could glean her passion by the slight sneer on her lips.

"And so you and I are through?"

"Yes."

"What if I told you I loved you, needed you?"

Carlinda sat up straighter. There was actual fear in her eyes.

"Don't worry," he said softly. "We had what we had but that's over. Even if it wasn't what could we do about it?"

She sighed audibly. Her shoulders relaxed.

"Thanks for the notepad," John said. "But tell me, why did you come?"

"Are you going to tell what you know about those broadsides now that . . . you know?"

"If that's what you're worried about why not tell me you love me, that you'll wait for me?"

"Because it wouldn't be right."

"No," John said. "I won't tell. I probably would if it was just you but I don't want to hurt the others. I'd do it if it was only you but I'm faithful to my friends."

Again he suppressed a smile. The delicate wording of his assurance would allow Carlinda to believe she had bested him in their affair while at the same time feeling safe because of John's fealty to others.

"I don't mean to hurt you," she lied. "It's just my connection to Arnold is all."

"I think you should leave now," John told her, though he would have been happy to spend the afternoon playing their game.

24

Carlinda's visit had lightened John's spirit. She was the blue door in his dream. Through her lay a new world where he didn't have to quote Hegel and Doc Ben, Herodotus and the unnamed scribes of ancient China's successive empires.

She was the heart of his rebellious lectures, the revelation of his ridiculous name. She did not love him, was not there for love. Carlinda Elmsford was the perfect woman for the man who had given everything to Lucia Napoli and Herman Jones. She was his pack-mate baying side by side with him at the full moon with fresh blood on their snouts and tongues. She was warmth in the cold, the yipping intelligence as they moved with their gang hunting down prey.

By moonlight he had licked her bloody wounds and now she was gone.

Sitting in the metal chair he wondered why no one had come to retrieve him. Marle should have opened the blue door, chained him and then guided him back to his hole.

The suit that Willie Pepperdine wore was the red-brown color of ancient brick. His shirt was white and his tie scarlet. No guard accompanied him. The door he'd come through merely closed.

John stood to shake the moneyman's out-stretched hand.

"You look very relaxed for someone who's been in solitary confinement the last two weeks," Willie said.

"Gives me time to think," John replied.

"Sit," was Willie's riposte.

"How did you know I was in solitary?"

"The same way I knew you'd probably murdered Chapman Lorraine and that you were born Cornelius Jones."

"The Platinum Path?"

"How do you think Carlinda, Tamala and their friends could dig up so much dirt on your fellow faculty members?" Willie asked.

John waited a moment gazing into the too-perfect face of Pepperdine.

"You're responsible for the notes on my table," John said.

Willie nodded.

"And all the professors you accept you investigate first to make sure that you have something over them," John continued.

"Not all of them," Willie admitted. "All you need is something on about a third of the faculty. But you were a special case, John."

"Special how?"

"At any given moment we have between ten and twenty candidates who might be admissible to the Path. Special testing and certain public and private records bring them to our attention, mostly. One day we might approach them to work for us directly or for one of our subbranches.

"These are, or might one day be, our rank and file. But you, my friend, you we are grooming for a much higher purpose."

"Grooming?"

"Yeah. Those in the upper echelon of the Path see you as material for a senior position. You're a freethinker in a world weighed down by the chains of history. A man like you could be a leader."

"Leading where?"

"To change the course of history," Pepperdine announced. "The human world is on a path toward self-destruction. The leaders are filled with inner conflicts and greed. They pretend to be sophisticated and then tear at each other like rabid dogs. No matter the religion, political theory or lineage—the entire world teeters on the edge of annihilation.

"It is our intention, our destiny, to avert this eventuality. In order to do that we need people like you."

John thought about being an element in the transformation of humanity.

"I'm just living my life, Willie. That has nothing to do with you, no matter what you think."

Saying this John stood. He almost turned away but thought of a question.

"How did you know about Lorraine?"

"We bought the Arbuckle when you joined the university."

"But you waited until now to let people know?"

"There was no rush. He was dead. And you weren't ready to be tested back then."

"What test?"

"The one you're taking right now."

25

I am not now nor have I ever been *Cornelius Jones, your honor,* he scribbled on the pad Carlinda had given him.

No.

No, your honor, that is not my name.

Maybe.

I was born John Woman and I will die the same.

After penning twenty-three possible responses to the query, *Are you the Cornelius Jones named in the state of New York's extradition request?* John decided that he'd wait until the judge had spoken, answering the question when it was freshly worded. Maybe his lawyer would answer for him.

The rest of the night John worked on writing a letter to his mother. He could fit only four or five words to a line on the small sheets. He used his fingernails to bare enough graphite lead to keep on writing. At the end he was manipulating the stub with his fingertips.

He told his mother he loved her, forgave her, and that his father loved her too; she had to do whatever she did because she was an emotional being and what better kind of mother could a son hope for?

He wrote a lot more, careful not to name Filo Manetti in case the judge or Captain Anton made

Marle search his cell for evidence. He told her not to worry about him, and that he finally felt free of troubles he'd brought upon himself.

"John Woman," Marle Josephson said just as John signed *your son* at the end of his eleven-page epistle.

They passed down many corridors, through seven locked doors, up three flights of stairs and then out into an alley where the marshals' van waited.

"Good luck, John," Marle said as he threaded a chain through the prisoner's handcuffs securing him to a stainless steel eye attached to the floor in the backseat of the van. "See you tonight."

The two marshals did not speak. One was white, the other black; both were men. They brought John to a room so small that it could contain only the chair he was chained to.

This was a new restriction. He could not move from the chair and, even if he could, the room was not large enough to take a single step. Tremors ran between the wrists and elbows of both his arms. This jittering frightened him. It felt as if there was some creature trying to claw its way out of his body.

To distract himself from his anxiety John slowly reconstructed Cicero's description of the death of Caesar. His Latin was still strong. Herman had been a good teacher.

His father cried at the recitation of the last moments of the great general and tyrant written by a man who both loved and hated the self-appointed dictator.

"It was a necessary tragedy," Herman told his son, "like every life lived."

An hour later the cell door opened and the black and white marshals returned. John was led into the adjoining courtroom.

The judge was a white man who seemed short even though he was sitting at the high bench. He had a bristly brown-and-white mustache and, of course, black robes. John was brought to a seat at a desk where Nina Forché waited. She was wearing a red jacket. The gallery was packed with sixty or so spectators. Theron James and Colin Luckfeld were there in the row just behind the defendant's bench. Willie Pepperdine sat behind them. Arnold Ott stood at the back of the room, staring at John through the dark rectangles of his glasses.

John looked for Carlinda but didn't see her.

"Please be seated," said a man in a gray suit standing next to the judge's high bench.

When Nina touched John's arm he settled in the hard ash chair provided.

At the plaintiff's bench, across the aisle from John and Nina, sat Colette and a man wearing a maroon suit.

"Professor John Woman," the judge rumbled.

John was trying to catch Colette's eye.

"Professor John Woman."

"Are you speaking to me?" John asked after failing to catch the detective's eye.

The judge said, "This is my courtroom, young man. I ask the questions."

"It might be your courtroom but that's not my name."

"Please stand."

John complied.

"What is your name?" the judge asked.

"Cornelius Jones, son of Herman Jones and Lucia Napoli-Jones."

"The same Cornelius Jones that the state of New York is petitioning to extradite?"

"The very same."

"Do you dispute New York's request to extradite you?"

"No, sir, I do not."

26

John was transferred into the custody of Lieutenant Colette Van Dyne and her partner, Sergeant Leo Abruzzi.

When Marshal Tomas Christo handed over the keys to John's chains the prisoner said, "If you go back to the jail please tell Marle Josephson I'm sorry I didn't make it back there and that I'm confident he'll do well on his exam."

"Why didn't you fight extradition?" Colette asked John after the M80 airbus had taken off from Sky Harbor International Airport. He occupied seat 27a, Colette's was 27b. The aisle seat was vacant.

"Where's your partner?"

"Up toward the middle of the plane, in the exit row," she said. "He's kinda big and that'll be more comfortable for him."

"I thought you two were supposed to flank me," John said. "Isn't that protocol?"

"What do you know about protocol?"

"I read a great deal and my memory is pretty good."

"I asked him to move because I thought I'd do better interrogating you alone."

"Oh."

"Why didn't you fight the extradition?" she asked again. "You had every chance of beating it."

"I was lying to myself."

"What does that mean?"

"It was time for me to come home."

John noticed that they were speaking in the same hushed tones they used in the police pied-à-terre years before.

"How do you feel about me now?" he asked. He would have touched her but his wrists and ankles were chained together preventing him from raising his hands more than a few inches above his lap.

"I don't feel anything about you."

"Then why are you here?"

"I was the senior officer on the Lorraine case."

"That's not it," he said using his most professorial tone. "You could have passed your notes on, let a junior cop come out here."

"Did you waive extradition because of me?"

"Not you sitting here but it was time to come home and you're part of home."

"There's nothing between us," she said.

John smiled at the attempt.

"I think about you," he confessed. "You taught me about physical love. Sex, sure, but love too. A man's first love never leaves him."

"Are you going to talk about that at your trial?"

"No," he said, thinking that this was very much like Carlinda's worry, "never."

"It was just a fling anyway," she said, tossing her hair as she used to do. "I mean I was wrong because you were underage but you were so sweet . . ."

John swiveled his head to see her profile as she talked.

". . . You were doing your father's job and going to school," Colette went on. "You didn't have a mother around to look after you . . ."

She turned to look at him.

". . . I guess I loved you a little."

"Yeah," he said feeling like that sixteen-year-old boy again, the boy who cried because he needed her so much.

"But I knew we couldn't stay together."

"Why not?" young Cornelius Jones asked.

"You were just a boy and I was with Harry . . . we were engaged."

John winced.

"What happened with Lorraine?" she asked.

"I don't want to talk about that."

"The judge and the prosecutor are going to ask. Your defense attorney too."

"The last thing you told me was that you were going to a fertility clinic. Did you have a baby?"

Colette's expression changed from caring to something nervous, vulnerable.

"Yes," she said.

"Boy?"

"Christian." The name called up a smile to her lips. "He's just now seventeen."

"You remember the day we met? You were with your partner. What was his name?"

"Tom Pena."

"Yeah. I was scared and you were beautiful."

"Did I tell you I was pregnant with Chris?"

"Just that you went to the fertility clinic. It was the day you helped me get dad out of the hospital."

"I didn't even think you paid attention to me back then. I mean all you wanted was sex all the time."

"You too."

"Why didn't you fight the extradition? You could have beat it."

"My mother found out where I was and came to live with me. While she was there I was her son and your lover, my father's student and caretaker. It was like I had turned it all off but everything was still there inside me."

She put a hand on his arm, saying, "When they ask you if you killed Lorraine say no."

"I understand," he said.

"I thought I had rid myself of you, CC. I thought when I broke it off that I could be with Harry."

"Don't you love him?"

"Yes. Of course I do. But I never forgot you. There was something so sweet about the way you surrendered but you were, still are, the strongest man I ever met."

"Do you have a picture of Christian?"

Colette gave him a look both contemplative and worried. She took a cell phone from her purse, turned it on and flipped around until she'd found something.

It was the photograph of a teenage boy from the waist up. His caramel-colored face resisting the camera, a space between his front teeth, a skateboard hugged to his chest. He smiled, being forbearing about yet another photograph.

"He looks a lot like my father," John said, "only with our skin."

"His father doesn't know. The doctor told me the test showed that Harry was unable to have kids. He gave me the report to show him but I never did.

"I've never forgotten you, CC. I see you every morning."

27

Thinking about his son John lost track of the rest of the journey. Colette spoke to him in the same hushed tones. He answered her but his mind was orbiting the idea of an heir. Before now, Cornelius and then John had been an only son lamenting the loss of his parents. But now there was a child of his own blood that came from Naples, Italy, and backwoods Mississippi to the Lower East Side via Jimmy Grimaldi.

For the first time the death of Chapman Lorraine took on meaning other than guilt. The landlord's death brought Cornelius and Colette together. His blood consecrated the life of his son Christian.

At Kennedy Airport Colette and Sergeant Christo turned John over to court officers who were tasked with transferring him to Rikers Island.

Colette whispered, "Be strong in there, CC. I'll make sure they look after you."

He was moved from airport to van, van to prison intake. At Rikers he was photographed and fingerprinted, searched for weapons, provided with a dark yellow uniform and then brought to one of the smaller holding cells.

"Lieutenant Van Dyne don't want your hair messed," one guard said. "She says she don't want the judge to feel sorry for your sorry ass."

John's cellmates were three men—one white, another black and a small umber-colored man who looked to be Puerto Rican.

The big black man had a smile that was both friendly and hungry.

Blocking John's view of the other two inmates he asked, "What's your name?"

"John . . . um, Cornelius."

"Hello, John Cornelius. My name is Andre." The big man held out a hand. When John reached out, Andre gripped hard and pulled him close.

"There's a set of rules we live by in here, JC." Andre's breath was hot on the side of the ex-professor's face. "You're gonna be my friend and I will protect you from these other motherfuckers here. And you see over there?" Andre gestured toward an empty corner of the cell.

"That's gonna be our private place," the big man continued. "Whenever we're over there you will do whatever I tell you to do. When we're over there we will be alone, just you and me. Nobody's gonna hear you and ain't nobody gonna come."

John glanced over at the other two men. The white man turned his head away. The shorter, broad-shouldered Puerto Rican watched dispassionately as if Andre and John were two competing creatures in the wild.

Andre took John's chin with powerful fingers applying pressure until the young man's eyes were again on him.

"Don't look at them." He shoved John toward the private corner. "They ain't gonna help you. They cain't. Now lemme see some dick."

John wondered at what moment he would take Andre's life. He might get beaten, even raped before the chance offered itself but the time would come . . . soon.

"I ain't got all day, John Cornelius."

"Hey, Andre," a voice with a Spanish lilt said. "Leave him alone, man. He my homey."

"This ain't none'a your business, Velázquez," Andre complained.

The much shorter Puerto Rican stood up from his cot. "I said leave him alone. I ain't tellin' you again."

"Not till I get me some. You can have him then."

"I will break your head open like a melon."

Andre hesitated a second, two . . . then pushed John away. He went to the cot that the Puerto Rican had vacated and sat down heavily.

"Get your ass up from there," Velázquez told the giant. "That's my bed."

Again Andre hesitated. Again he did as he was told.

"Come on, man," Velázquez said to John. "Let's have a seat."

"They got me in here on murder," the man identifying himself as Jose Velázquez said to John Woman/Cornelius Jones. "The cops say I killed this Cuban who didn't pay his debt but I didn't do it."

The two were sitting side by side on one of three cots provided for the four men. Andre was grumbling to himself trying to come up with the courage to go against Jose. The white man was leaning against the cell wall looking at nothing in particular.

"They have me for a murder that happened when I was sixteen," John said. "I did it."

"Maybe you shouldn't be sayin' that," Jose suggested.

"I don't care. I plan to confess."

John's savior frowned, creating creases radiating from his eyes. He said, "You shouldn't be so serious, John. You got to remember that it's just a game, bro. Just a game. You don't wanna make them think you think they doin' justice. If it was justice they'd be down here tryin' to figure out how a kid ended up doin' a man's job and how that fat fuck got his ass up there to get killed. They don't care. They want you like Andre does, on a dinner plate with your ass up in the air."

"How do you know about my case?" John asked.

"They give us newspapers. You was in the headlines a whole week and then again when you let 'em extradite your ass."

"That's why you were going to fight Andre?"

"I wasn't gonna fight him."

"No?"

"Uh-uh."

Jose gestured at the white man who had a receding brown-and-gray hairline. Propelling himself from the wall with his shoulder blades the lanky white man sauntered the few steps to the Puerto Rican's cot.

"Frank Beam, meet history professor John Woman," Jose said.

John stood and shook Beam's hand.

"Frank here is what they call a living embodiment of death," Jose continued. "He's killed more people than Felix Trinidad have knocked out. Andre knows that Frank got my back. That's why he backed down."

Frank nodded and went back to his personal patch of cell wall.

"It ain't what it seems," Jose said to John. "Here we believe what they taught us in school even though we know it ain't true. Don't you give it up to them, bro. They ain't worth it."

28

Jose told John to take Andre's cot. The big man complained then backed down when Frank Beam said, "Shut your fat yap."

John considered Jose's advice from many different angles. He knew that he was guilty. It was that last blow from the heavy wrench across the top of Chapman Lorraine's skull. He didn't have to kill him but he didn't know how to stop.

The counsel Jose offered caused a resurgence of historical thinking: one had to try and maintain objectivity even though that was impossible— this impossibility was what made life meaningful. Maybe, on some basic human level, he was innocent because he couldn't stop himself.

John dreamt about the desert. He was a coyote that died at twilight; his soul left at that shadowy time to wander the endless wasteland. Heart and body, blood and senses were canine but his mind was still that of a historian. The barren land, even in semidarkness, revealed striations in rock, bones jutting from the ground and out from the walls of great canyons. History was all that remained, measured by discrete moments rendered in stone—each one bearing the same weight, drained of passion, purpose and personality. The coyote, John Woman, with a rolling gait, moved along the edge of eternal dusk, never to see the sunrise and never to sleep.

"Cornelius Jones," a man's voice intoned.

John opened his eyes and sat up. Across from him Andre squatted on the floor staring wide-eyed at nothing. A large gash was open down his left cheek revealing the whitish muscle tissue of flesh under black skin.

"Yeah," John called out.

"Come with me."

He was taken to a conference room that could have been in any corporate office. There were three people sitting at the far end of the walnut conference table: two men and Nina Forché. The men wore business suits, one blue, the other gray. Nina had on a dress-suit in a palette of coral hues ranging from goldenrod to lush raspberry.

Nina stood when John entered.

"Take those restraints off him," she said to his guard.

John's keeper, a tall slender white man who gave the impression of great physical strength, looked at the black man in the blue suit.

"It's okay, Hawkins," Blue Suit said. "Mr. Jones has been granted bail."

"Yes, Underwarden Reese," Hawkins said.

When the restraints were removed John took a

deep breath and realized that he was trembling.

"Mr. Jones," Underwarden Reese said.

"I changed my name to Woman. I'd appreciate you using that."

"You have been granted bail," the prison official said. "This allows you freedom in New York City. You can travel in any of the boroughs but not beyond."

"How much do I have to pay?"

"That's already been taken care of, John," Nina Forché said softly.

"Willie?"

"No."

"Then by whom?"

"An unknown benefactor."

"Oh . . . kay."

"You will be expected to respond promptly if the court or any prison official calls," Reese stated.

"I don't have my phone."

"I have one for you," Nina said. "The number has been distributed among those who might need to call."

"Okay."

"There are some papers for you to sign." Underwarden Reese indicated a chair for John to sit in.

In the backseat of a brand-new Tesla sedan John sat next to his lawyer. He wore a black suit that

Forché had somehow gotten from NUSW faculty housing.

"How much?" he asked.

"One point three million. No bail bondsman would underwrite it so it had to be in cash."

"Who would do that for me?"

"You'll find out, I'm sure."

"Where are you taking me?"

"To the address that the court has been given for you," she said.

"Also provided by my mysterious benefactor?"

"Yes. Now, John, we have to discuss your defense. You surprised me by admitting your identity in Phoenix. I thought we had an agreement."

"I told you I understood what you were saying," John replied, "not that I would go along."

"What will be your plea?"

"Guilty."

"What reason will you give for the killing?"

"I've given that a lot of thought," he said. "The only reason I can give is juvenile depravity."

"And what about the circumstances?"

"What is it that the Platinum Path wants—exactly?"

"Whatever it is you have to offer."

"I don't understand." John was surprised that she engaged with the question.

"Path members, especially in the upper echelon, see the world differently. They are difficult to predict."

"Have you ever killed anybody, Ms. Forché?"

"My training will not allow me to answer that question."

"I have. I crushed a man's skull under the weight of a heavy metal wrench."

Forché gazed at her client but said nothing.

"Thank you for all you've done," he told the lawyer. "It feels really good to be free if only for a few days."

The car came to a stop at the corner of Mott and Grand in what used to be Little Italy.

"What are we doing here?" he asked.

Handing him a key ring that held a worn brass key she said, "I was told that you'd know where you are and where you should go."

"None of this makes any sense," John said aloud, not necessarily to his lawyer.

Climbing up to the third floor of the prewar apartment building John worked the familiar key in the very same door he'd been passing through since he was a child.

When he crossed the threshold, she said, "Hi, baby, I've been waiting for you."

"Mom."

Sitting at the small table in the same window that he'd stared out of as a boy, excited by his mother's stories of love and lust and life, he felt . . . unmoored, as he had in a childhood of wandering between Herman's truth and Lucia's reality.

"Filo kept the place all these years," she said after kissing her son then making him sit. "He kept my old things and had a woman clean once a month. He told me if I ever wanted to leave him my life would be waiting for me just the way I left it. He made your bail."

"I'd like to meet him, to thank him."

"Soon," she said. "He wanted me to tell you that if you needed to run he'd understand."

"And lose a million dollars?"

"You'd be free," Lucia said with pride.

"Thank him for me, mom, but I'm going to trial."

"You've become a real man, CC. I saw that in Arizona. A real man."

"Where did you go?"

"Filo called me. The police were coming to arrest you. He said that if I was there it would cause you more trouble than if I wasn't. So I left."

John tried to call up a feeling about this most recent abandonment but could not.

"Anything else I need to know?" he asked.

"I've done all the shopping and cooking. There's meat lasagna in the icebox. My number is Scotch-taped to the phone and there's also a number for a friend of Filo's if you have any serious trouble."

436

"You aren't going to stay with me?"

"I have to lay low, honey," she said. "The police know Filo ran with me. I'm not wanted for anything but they might try and set me up or something. The name I use in New York is Rita Wentworth but the cops could have a picture."

"You know, mom, I spent my whole adult life trying to imagine that I'm somebody else, that the boy who used to sit in this chair was a dream. But now it feels like I could take the Q to Brooklyn and dad would be there reading *The History of the Decline and Fall of the Roman Empire*."

"I miss him too, baby," she said. "If I could take it all back I would do it in a heartbeat."

"You would?" the child asked.

"Don't you know it."

29

Lucia's black dress hung a bit looser with a longer hem, but it was much like her clothing in the old days of CC's memories. She was carrying a calico bag, standing at the front door.

"Can I do anything else before I go, honey?"

"Are you a member of the Path, mama?" The last word stuck in his throat.

Lucia Napoli-Jones's face took on a serious cast that neither CC nor John had seen before.

"No, baby, no. I know who they are and they know me because they know you."

"What do they want from me? I mean, why set me up to get arrested and tried for murder if they want me to work with them?"

"I don't know. But I believe they see you as a leader, like a second coming."

They stood for a moment in silence, then Lucia turned away and went out the door.

As it had been almost twenty years before, there were no books in his mother's home; just a white leather Bible the spine of which was still unbroken.

After a plate of meatballs and angel-hair pasta John decided to go out walking around Soho, streets he hadn't stepped foot in since the

438

millennium. On Prince a little east of Broadway he found a bookstore.

After an hour or so looking around the fiction aisles he decided on *Chronicle of a Death Foretold*, by Gabriel García Márquez, because they didn't have *The Autumn of the Patriarch*. There had been a fat envelope on the kitchen table containing twenty-five hundred dollars in twenty-dollar bills. He used one of these to purchase the paperback.

"Hi," a young woman said.

He was seated at the window of the large Starbucks next to Cooper Union, reading his book. Her face contained equal parts Occident and Orient (as Herman Jones might have said). Slight and not quite pretty she lowered herself into the chair across from him.

"Hello." John closed the book.

"You want a date?"

John looked her directly in the eye. She cocked her head and gave him half a smile.

"How much?" John asked.

"Seventy-five for hand, a hundred to kiss, and two fifty for it all."

"You know I, I used to be invisible. Nobody saw me coming or going, or if anyone did notice I was already gone."

"I see you," she said. "I like that suit."

John reached into a pocket he knew contained

exactly two hundred dollars. Palming the cash he reached out placing the money in her hand.

"Two hundred," he said. "Maybe if you see me around here sometime again you'll give me another smile."

John got to his feet and left her there at the table.

Back at the Mott Street apartment he went through the bags sent from his Arizona home. He found the beaded belt with its belt-buckle knife and resolved to wear it every day. The young woman might have been just a working girl but he could no longer trust in his anonymity.

The next afternoon John took a taxi downtown to the dstrict attorney's office. Matthew Lars, Assistant DA, sat across a conference table deposing him while Nina Forché sat by his side.

"So, Mr. Woman," said ADA Lars. He was a broad-faced white man with white-blond hair. "In your own words tell me what happened that night."

John almost asked what other than his own words did he have to say anything, but he remembered that he was no longer a professor and ADA Lars was certainly no student.

He described the events of that night, even *Dirty Nymphs* and masturbating on the mattress that had been sealed in the wall with the makeshift coffin.

"And so you're claiming that it was self-defense for the first two blows?" Lars asked.

"I was scared and he was hurting my arm."

"But you didn't have to hit him the third time."

"No. I was still scared but he had fallen down to his knees."

"He was a child," Forché said. "He was afraid. It could very well be that he didn't think that his attacker was helpless until after he had time to consider it later. His feelings of guilt might have made him believe it was murder."

"But he hid the body," Lars replied, "like a professional hit man."

"He was a smart kid," Nina rejoined.

"Why was Lorraine at the projectionist's room?" Lars asked.

"I don't know," John said.

"Did you call him?"

"No."

"Then why would he show up there? Did he do that sometimes?"

"Never."

"And why did you have that heavy wrench close at hand?"

"I used it to move the projectors up and down."

"And you murdered him."

"With the third blow . . . yes."

Tall and wide, possibly forty-five years old, Matthew Lars smoothed his pale hair with big slug-like blunt fingers. He seemed frustrated by John's confession.

John wanted to ask, "What more can I say? I'm

telling you everything." But he did not voice his confusion.

"I can offer second-degree manslaughter," Lars said to Forché. "That's the best I can do. Fifteen to twenty."

"There are extenuating circumstances," she said.

"There's also the concealment of a body and flight."

"He didn't know he was being sought."

"He called Lieutenant Van Dyne from Florida. He taunted her."

"You can't prove that."

"You want to leave it up to the jury? In court it'll be a murder charge."

"Let me speak to my client."

"I'll take whatever he's offering," John told Nina once they were alone.

"We might win this in court," she argued.

"I killed him and I'm guilty," John said. "I will not allow my chance at repentance to become legal sophistry."

"Prison is no picnic, John."

"Neither is a lifetime of guilt."

John accepted Lars's offer.

"We will go in front of a judge tomorrow," the prosecutor told the lawyer and accused.

"That's a record," Nina said.

"Judge Halloran would like to clear his docket.

His daughter is getting married in California next week and with a confession this case is open-and-shut."

"What time should we be there?" Forché asked.

"Early. Eight in the morning. If Professor Woman is lucky he'll be on his way to prison before dinnertime."

30

John started awake early the next morning. Bright blue digits on a clock next to the bed read 3:03. He could recall no dream, just a sudden shock of fear. After a minute or so he remembered the appointment with the judge later that morning. The image of Andre with the side of his face cut open came to mind. This was to be John's future. He would be raped, slashed, beaten and locked away. He'd have to resist becoming either a victim or a predator in the process.

This constant flutter of fear is what woke him: a pulsating moth, the size of a kitten, trying to break free from the cage of ribs.

He'd admitted his guilt to ADA Lars because he wanted to answer for his crime. But now he worried that if he went to prison he might do it all over again, and again. He knew he was a killer when Pete Tackie barged in, when Andre declared John's body and soul his property, like Columbus in the New World or Hitler and his endless annexations. He would, like any true patriot, kill the would-be conqueror trying to colonize him.

Naked, he climbed out of bed and walked down the short hall to the kitchen. Lucia had left him a jar of chunky peanut butter, cherry preserves and cinnamon-swirl raisin bread—his favorites when he was a child. He bit into the sandwich thinking about twenty-four-hour lockdown; the smell of disinfectants; and the gaping, almost bloodless, six-inch wound down the side of Andre's face.

John realized in the early morning, standing naked in his mother's kitchen, that going to prison was tantamount to sealing himself in the wall with Chapman Lorraine. Maybe he should run. There was still time. Filo Manetti told Lucia that he didn't care about the bail money. John had the gangster's friend's number. He could leave the country. He spoke Spanish and French; he'd been to Martinique.

Maybe Cuba.

John went to the red wall phone he'd used as a child to tell his father good night those evenings he stayed with Lucia.

He put his hand on the receiver. That's when the phone rang.

His recoil from the strident sound was so violent that John felt a muscle tear in his right shoulder blade. He gasped and choked—a convict caught in the middle of an ill-considered escape attempt.

The phone kept ringing, wave after wave of clanging alarm. *Danger! Danger!* There was no voice mail service and the caller would not give up.

Before answering John counted seventeen rings but there had been more.

"Hello?"

"John?" a familiar voice asked softly.

"Who is this?"

"Am I speaking with John Woman?"

"Yes. Now who is this?"

"Service Tellman."

John came suddenly to consciousness. The convulsive fear, the retreat to his mother's kitchen, even the making of his favorite childhood sandwich—all this occurred in the stupor at the tag end of a fearful sleep. But now his awareness was crystalline.

"Service Tellman is dead," John said, the option of flight still bright in his mind.

"That's what the world thinks."

"And you're saying he's not?"

"I'm not."

"Playing possum?"

The phantom chuckled in John's ear.

"Only the dead are beyond reproach," he said.

"Oh," the once and future professor mused. "So you're saying that you martyred yourself and yet survived; the cake-and-eat-it-too school of philosophy."

"People need something to aspire to and, as Lear tells us, there is a stench to all things mortal."

"Sainthood?"

"Human potential, as you know, far outstrips human nature," the caller said by way of agreement.

"I've never heard it said quite like that," John replied. "But you're right of course. Parishioners close their eyes and imagine standing side by side with the Deity. But when the prayer is done they find themselves barefoot in pig shit up to their knees."

"You're one of the few professors at NUSW who were truly aware that the acquisition of knowledge, the process of learning, is an end in itself."

"What do you want?"

"I'm calling to offer you membership in the upper echelon of the Platinum Path."

"No."

"You refuse?"

"I don't believe that you are who you say. How can I accept an offer that cannot be made?"

"Why would I lie?"

"Maybe you're an old friend of Chapman Lorraine."

"And Lucia Napoli? Filo Manetti?"

"Your voice is familiar. Do I know you?"

"There's already a question on the table, Mr. Woman. Or would you prefer to be called Professor?"

"You're serious?"

"I am Service Tellman," the voice said, "leader and founder of the Platinum Path, calling to invite you into our ranks."

"I thought you had to be rich and famous or powerful to be considered for that berth."

"Fame has never been a criterion. And you are powerful."

Imagining these last words coming from his father John said, "Thank you."

"Then you accept membership?"

"Even if you were qualified to offer it, I'm going to jail."

"We have members everywhere," the man calling himself Service Tellman said, "even in prison. Jose Velázquez is a foot soldier on the Path."

Before, when he first got up, John was still mostly asleep. Then, when he heard the dead man's name spoken in a voice so tantalizingly familiar, he came to consciousness—a man awake in a world he knew. But when that voice uttered a name that no one outside Rikers should have known, John's mind opened wide. Abruptly a world he couldn't imagine came fully into being, like Athena emerging from Zeus's brow or the atomic bomb exploding over Nagasaki.

"Is this a trick?" Cornelius Jones asked.

"We would like to think that we're the biggest trick ever pulled," the voice said. "We're attempting to rejigger destiny by changing the direction of the soul. We have men and women all over the world. There are professors and billionaires, movie stars and gardeners in our ranks."

"Ron Underhill," John stated.

"Yes."

"You're running a worldwide conspiracy while watering the cacti of the southwest?"

"We have a clear vision of a world that is not tainted by nationalisms, gods or the lies of history."

"History," John repeated the word. "That's me."

"That's you."

"And so all of this has been you? My capture, my lawyer, Jose Velázquez in my cell. Even the letters left on my kitchen table."

"We want you with us, John. If we sit back and leave the world to its own devices—its capitalisms and Holocausts—there won't be a civilization left. As you said in the first lecture at NUSW: there can be no future without a history and there is no history except for what you can imagine and do fear."

"I'm not some savior," John said. "I play with ideas—that's all."

"The play's the thing."

"I appreciate what you claim is your mission, Mr. Tellman, Ron. I mean I often think what's wrong with the world is its honesty about desire. Lies and misdirections might indeed make a better tomorrow except that truth cannot be denied. And the truth is—we're a deeply flawed species."

"Even DNA can be altered," the gardener said.

"We can remake the history of our genes just as well as we can deconstruct our supposed pasts."

"Service," John mused. "Is that the name you were born with?"

"Will you join us, John?"

"No. At least not yet. I'm here in my mother's old apartment saying good-bye to myself."

"You will have to make up your mind sooner or later. One must plan for the future. In some cases, yours for instance, that future is synonymous with the world's."

31

His fears gone, John took Service Tellman's words as a great gift for a man in his profession. The simple idea that a cult leader could make himself into a living martyr embodied everything John taught in his classes. To disappear in plain sight and still remain a force was a trick rarely used in a world of absolute rulers, capitalisms and other megalomanias.

John showered and shaved rather than planning his escape. He made coffee, read an old newspaper, then used the smartphone his lawyer gave him to look up Service Tellman and the Platinum Path on its browser.

There were many photographs of the organization's founder usually in pedestrian poses—as he was coming out of some official door or smiling and turning toward someone at his side. The man in the pictures looked something like Ron Underhill but he had a short beard and a face different enough that one might not recognize him. A razor, a little plastic surgery, tinted contact lenses and the daily blessing of the sun were enough for the chameleon-prophet to continue on his mission unhindered by identity or the stench of his breed.

• • •

It wasn't until John was riding the Number 6 train downtown that he considered running again. The subway car was crowded with well over a hundred passengers.

A young Asian woman in a bright green dress was standing next to him, clinging to the same chrome pole between the center doors of the subway car.

"Nice day," John said. He was wearing the same soft-milled black cotton jacket and loose coal gray trousers he had on when he met Carlinda Elmsford. His T-shirt that day was navy.

"Beautiful," the young woman replied.

"The kind of morning that makes you think maybe you should empty out a credit card and buy a ticket for Rome."

"I like Paris," she said, giving him a conspiratorial smile.

"Too rainy for me."

"You going to work?"

"No," he said, more contemplative than sad.

"You look very familiar. Have we met?"

"I've been in the newspapers on and off lately. They found a dead man in a wall in the East Village. I used to work on the other side of that wall."

The young woman's eyes widened.

"I'm headed down to the court now," he said.

"The judge has to decide whether or not to accept my confession and the sentence suggested by the ADA."

"You did it?"

"Yes."

"And you confessed?"

"Yeah."

"Why?"

"Why did I do it?"

"No. Why confess? I read the articles. There was no witness or physical evidence. There's no proof."

"You're a lawyer?"

"Executive assistant at Resterly and Lowe. I'm going to law school at night."

"Born here?"

"Hong Kong. Why?"

"I think it's the strong green of your dress. It's a little more . . . um, forceful than most American-born women would wear."

"But why confess?" she asked again. "It's been such a long time."

"I've tried for years to leave it behind me. But I couldn't escape the guilt. If I confess and take my punishment I'll have paid my debt and be able to move on."

"You can't change what's done," she said.

In superior courtroom 10a at 7:47, John was standing next to Nina Forché, across the aisle from ADA Lars and a young woman in a gray dress-suit.

I'd like to come visit you in prison, Hong Li had said when they departed the train at the Brooklyn City Hall stop.

"Why?" he asked as she handed him her card.

"My private phone and e-mail are at the bottom," she said. "I'd like to find out if you feel that this was the right move after being locked up for a while."

"All rise for the Honorable Judge Maxwell Halloran," a uniformed guard bellowed.

Tall and grizzled the judge was light-brown like John. He had high shoulders and an unpleasant turn to his lips.

"Be seated," the judge proclaimed as he lowered into his broad-backed chair. John felt as if he could see a shimmering aura of importance between him and the judge.

"John," Nina said. "John, sit down."

She pulled at his sleeve and he relented, still gaping at the magistrate.

Halloran was glowering at a single sheet of paper that he held up to his face. The room behind the defendant's table was filled with people come to see the trial of the murderous child grown up to be a college professor. Reporters had assailed him outside the courthouse but two big men who said that they were with his team shouldered them aside and brought him to the courtroom.

"Mr. Lars," Halloran uttered.

"Yes, your honor," the ADA replied rising from his chair.

"Is this for real?" he asked waving the sheet of paper next to his head.

John was tickled by the dialect-inflected question. He didn't wonder about the paper or its intelligence; only the character of his judge.

"Yes, your honor," ADA Lars apologized.

"The source has been verified and vetted?"

"My assistant took the deposition yesterday afternoon at four p.m., west coast time."

"And before that the defendant confessed and accepted your offer of second-degree manslaughter?"

"Yes, your honor."

The judge looked angry but John couldn't tell if this was his normal expression.

"Cornelius Jones," Halloran cried.

"Stand up, John," Nina said.

He did so.

"Yes, Judge?"

"Did you kill Chapman Lorraine?"

The words, *yes, your honor* were on his tongue but his teeth were clenched shut. Service Tellman was in his mind, Service and Hong Li. He'd followed the rules from Parsonsville to Lower Manhattan; he'd confessed and allowed the courts and police and prison guards and convicts to have their way with his freedom. That was all over. Lorraine was dead, John Woman was alive, and the judge, no matter how magnificent, was no more master over him than the convict Andre had been.

"Mr. Jones," Halloran rumbled.

"Yes, your honor?"

"Did you bludgeon Chapman Lorraine to death?"

"No, your honor."

"No?"

John did not answer this question, because he had already done so. He could feel the guilt rising up and out of his body like morning mist under an unrelenting summer sun.

"Mr. Lars," Halloran said.

"Your honor."

"Do you intend to pursue the state's case against this man?"

"Not at this time."

"You're dropping the charges?"

"We are."

"Mr. Jones."

"Sir," John said to the judge.

"There's something wrong here. Something stinks."

"Is that a question, sir?"

"Don't you get smug with me, young man. This is my courtroom."

John thought that the halls of justice belonged to everyone but he did not voice this opinion.

"I'm going to launch an inquiry into this sudden confession," the judge vowed. "I will see you in my court soon again."

"France Bickman," Nina said to John in a small café around the corner from the courthouse.

"What about him?"

"He confessed to the murder of Chapman Lorraine."

"He just said it was him and they believed it?"

"He had physical knowledge of the murder scene and a motive."

"What motive?"

"He'd been embezzling money from the ticket and the concession stands for many years. When Lorraine confronted him he killed him and hid the body to keep from going to prison."

"But I ran away," John argued. "Isn't that some kind of proof?"

"You left New York years after Lorraine disappeared. That makes a good argument you had no knowledge of the crime."

John was thinking about his early morning conversation with the man calling himself Service Tellman. Somehow the Platinum Path had *rejiggered* the facts in his murder trial.

"Are they going to prosecute France?" John asked Nina.

"No. He's too old and feeble to be removed from the nursing home."

"What about the mattress?"

"The one in the wall?"

"Yes."

"Water damage erased any traces of DNA; also Bickman told the police that you visited him. He said that you told him about the crime being reported over the Internet and he confessed to you. He thought you told the police you committed the murder to protect an old man, the good friend of your father."

"How did the police even know about France?"

"He called Lieutenant Van Dyne."

"And so I'm free?"

"Any defense attorney could get this case overturned under these circumstances. With his knowledge, motive and confession Bickman is a perfectly sensible alternative explanation of the crime. There will always be reasonable doubt."

John called the young law student, Hong Li, but got her answering service.

"Hey," he said into the cell phone. "This is the confessed man-slaughterer you met on the train this morning. I guess we'll never find out what I would think of prison because the judge and the prosecutor proved to themselves that I might not have done it. And who am I to argue with law?"

They were waiting for him in his mother's apartment when he returned later that afternoon. He'd been walking for hours trying to understand how the study of historical deconstruction had come to rule his life. From Herman Jones to Service Tellman he had been reinterpreted until there was no truth possible.

"Hi, honey," Lucia said to her son. She was sitting in her favorite chair looking out the window.

The man sitting next to her stood up and held out a hand.

"Congratulations," Willie Pepperdine said.

"What are you doing here?"

Lucia stood up and said, "This is Filo Manetti, honey—my husband. I told you—we got married six years ago."

There was no more room for shock or surprise in John Woman's heart. Everything made sense and nothing did.

"When did this all start?" John asked Filo/ Willie.

"All what?" Lucia asked.

"Why don't we have a seat in this magnificent window?" Willie suggested.

"I'll go make us some tea," Lucia said. "You boys get to know each other."

When his mother was gone John, CC, returned to the chair where he used to sit for hours entranced by her beauty and words.

"We aren't inhuman," Willie said. "When I met and fell in love with your mother I was mobbed up. I decided to break away because of her. I mean the government was after me but that was par for the course. Pretty soon after we went out west I was approached by Service Tellman. He told me that I'd been on their radar for years. They liked the way I worked with my people and their families. You know I've always been more businessman than thug, so when I broke with my crew the Path offered me a position. Just like they're doing with you now."

"But that's because of you, right?"

"Partially. Your mother asked me to try to find you after your father died and you didn't return home. I was able to trace your father's credit cards. You were Anthony Summers by then, about to enter Yale. I didn't tell your mother, because it seemed like you wanted a new life and we were all safer if that life remained a secret.

"It wasn't until a few years later that I told Service about you. He read the papers you wrote and was very impressed with your knowledge and sophistication. That's when the Path started monitoring you.

"I had convinced your mother that you'd faded into New York somewhere. When you were in your second year at NUSW I told her about the cable TV show and said that we'd figure out how to get you guys together."

"So it was you that had NUSW approach me," John postulated.

"Actually it was Service himself. He was

already dead, and this gave him more time to develop high-level membership. He shepherded you along from the time you were first offered the chance to apply for the position."

"Like I was some kind of lab rat or something."

Willie Pepperdine/Filo Manetti shrugged and gave a half smile.

"The Path is serious business, CC. Our goal is to actually change the course of human events so that people everywhere are on a road to salvation not destruction.

"Every year thousands of geniuses are born but almost all of them fall into poverty, mental illness, criminality, early death and other categories that waste their potential. We take in as many of these advanced beings as possible, giving them a chance to guide their myopic brothers and sisters."

"So you and I are geniuses?"

"You are. If Service has his way you will be one of a triumvirate that will guide us after he's gone."

"He's already gone."

Ignoring these last words Willie said, "We approached France Bickman when our plans for you started, assured him that Oregon would never extradite a man in his nineties residing in a state-certified nursing home. I went to him myself. He truly loved your father. He told me that he owed him his life. I would like to have met the man."

"He was a great man," John said with pleasure. "He would put this whole conspiracy into perspective."

"A conspiracy of freedom," Willie Pepperdine declared.

"I made rose hip tea with scones and clotted cream I got from Dean and Deluca," Lucia said, coming in from the kitchen.

"Freedom," John mused. "The last man to offer me that was my father. Then he died and took all hope with him."

Part Four
The Last Class

32

The first month after the charges were dismissed reporters hounded John whenever he left his Soho apartment.

"Is your name Jones or Woman?" a journalist asked the first day.

He decided to keep the name John Woman because that was the name he'd answered to his entire adult life. He enjoyed the irreverent, unnatural feelings it caused. Much like Lucia preferred Napoli to Tartarelli.

"Did you kill Chapman Lorraine?" a stout woman from the *Post* wanted to know. "How could you have not at least known? He was sealed in a wall next to the projectors."

"Hidden," John said because he was stuck next to her at a DON'T WALK light.

"Didn't you wonder what happened to the closet?" she offered. "Maybe there were smells."

"If someone sealed off the closet what could I do about that? And what odors did you encounter twenty years ago in the middle of the night when you were working a silent film projector, doing homework and worried about your father who was slowly dying?"

"That never happened to me," said the thirty-something reporter. Her face was pudgy and her copper-rimmed glasses magnified impudent eyes.

"And I never knew about the dead man until just this year," John stated when the WALK sign appeared.

John usually ignored the reporters though he didn't mind engaging them. Oddly, the more they asked about the murder the further he felt from the crime.

One older black man calling himself Sharkey Lewis claimed to be a freelance journalist and offered to do an in-depth profile in which John could tell his story the way he wanted to.

"That way you can make sure the public has your side of it," Sharkey claimed.

As a rule Lewis wore a green-and-black herringbone jacket and dark brown slacks. He was short and probably hadn't gained a pound since he was a teenager.

"There's no further story I wish to tell, Mr. Lewis," John said. "I went to school every day, ran a projector most evenings and then read to my father before we both went to sleep. He died and I left those jobs and responsibilities behind me."

One day there were no reporters waiting outside. The restless thirst of the public for news had moved on to a hockey player who had beaten his wife's sister in an out-of-town motel; a troop transport aircraft that was downed by militant jihadists in Iraq; and finally to a billionaire landlord in Cincinnati who had called a group of striking tenants a *bunch of ungrateful niggers.*

John's story got shuffled out of the news deck.

The reporters were gone but there was still hate mail from dozens of sources. Letters with no return addresses came to his mother's mailbox, most of them forwarded from Parsonsville, Arizona. Angry, anonymous citizens condemned him for being a murderer, a liar, pretending he was something he was not. They cursed and threatened him, invoked God's name to sentence him to hell.

Not all of these were unsigned.

Arnold Ott wrote once a week making various complaints. In one rambling condemnation he claimed that John's perfidy (the actual word the cuckolded boyfriend used) caused him to rue his education. In another letter he said that Carlinda wanted to sue John for giving her herpes.

John wondered if his ex-lover had made this complaint because he hadn't exhibited symptoms of the STD.

But even Arnold's vituperations ran their course. One day he received a short note from Carlinda.

Dear Mr. Woman:

You are of course aware of me because of our association in your class at

NUSW. I will not complain about your misrepresentation of yourself in that circumstance because what I learned was valuable and I believe that one must recognize experience for what it is. One concept you taught, *amor fati*, allows me to see my life as a positive experience giving me no reason to regret anything.

I'm writing you, Mr. Woman, to tell you that it has come to my attention that my fiancé, Arnold Ott, has been writing derogatory letters to you, sometimes on my behalf. I became aware of these letters when he asked me to marry him and I asked if he was still bothered by our old friendship. When he told me about his hectoring letters I told him that I would agree to marry him only if he never mentioned you to me or contacted you ever again.

I believe that this should end our relationship and that there will be no further reason for us to be in contact in the future.

Sincerely,
Carlinda Elmsford

John read the letter over and over. He felt a sense of loss inside those overly formal, haplessly passionate words. Though he and Carlinda never loved each other they were, in his estimation, the same breed. They understood the world they lived in with almost pure objectivity. This understanding was like a sturdy fishing boat afloat on a sea of many passions.

Her visit in the Phoenix jail plus this letter effectively ended their connection, making him a dog without a pack. This sense of loss sent him into a depression that lasted for many weeks.

He went to the Strand Bookstore after there was no more he could glean from Carlinda's Dear John letter. He bought for the third time in his life *The Story of Civilization* by Will and Ariel Durant: eleven thousand pages or so of erudition unrestrained by obsessive scholarship—a long, long story of the western world bereft of proof but filled with the truth of culture.

He read the pages out loud, before an empty chair, imagining Herman installed therein. He'd read for hours, feeling loss with every word and re-revelation, to the apparition of his father sitting there, nodding despondently, wondering why Cornelius wouldn't let him go to be one with the phenomenal universe: the true history of everything.

At night he wandered the streets of Soho hoping to see the half-Asian prostitute again. He always wore the belt that Hototo had given him in another lifetime.

One night, when John had walked until his feet ached, a young man came up to him. The stranger had swarthy skin and straight black hair.

He punched John in the chest and then grabbed him by the cloth shoulder of his windbreaker.

"Give me your money or I'll kill you," he said.

Not thinking John unsheathed the belt-buckle knife and slashed the mugger three times: on the wrist, across the chest and then down the center of his face.

The man screamed and blood spurted from the cut that ran from his forehead past the nose to the chin. Something clattered to the sidewalk and the man ran off screaming, calling out for help.

It was after three a.m. and there was no one out on Greene. John watched the mugger run a zigzag path dripping blood, trying to run away from his wounds. On the ground was a sleek blue-black pistol next to a few spatters of fresh blood. John picked it up and walked away.

"Three times," he said to himself. "I cut him three times just like I hit Lorraine." There was no objective insight in this equation. Three blows and someone either lived or died. John was not culpable. He was the crime but not necessarily a criminal.

The next day John no longer felt like looking for the prostitute or reading to his dead father.

He washed the mugger's blood from his hands and clothes, cleaned the belt-buckle knife and examined the pistol he'd won.

It was a .22 caliber revolver with bullets in four of the chambers. John didn't know guns but he looked this one up on his cell phone browser. After unloading it, he made sure that he understood the safety and the resistance of the trigger.

He sat in the window looking down on Mott and feeling nothing in particular.

The phone rang only once on its little table before John answered.

"Hello?"

"Johnny?"

"Who is this?"

"It's Senta, baby. How are you?"

"Uhm, uh, fine. How did you get this number?"

"Nesta works for the phone company. I was so sad about you being in trouble that she set up her computer to get news alerts on you, both names. Then when we found out that you were free she used her access to get your mother's number. You remember . . . you told me your mom's name."

"And this phone is still listed under that?" John said. "Of course—in case she ever wanted to go back to her old life."

"Huh?"

"How are you, Senta? How's Nesta?"

"She's a wonder. Every day I thank God we're

together again. I don't work for Lou anymore. That was just too weird. Taking classes for my real estate license. But I'm calling because I wanted to know if you needed anything."

"This call is the best thing you could give me."

"That's sweet," Senta said. "I'd come out there and tie you down but Nesta and me are working on the house. You could come stay with us for a while if you wanted. We have a room for visitors."

"Um . . . that's really nice, Senta. Actually it's a wonderful offer but I should probably stay put for the time being. How's the house coming along?"

John sat back, closed his eyes and for the next hour listened while Senta told him about her dream house. Every ten minutes or so she'd say, "But what about you, baby?" He'd tell her that it was too soon to talk about it.

When John hung up the doorbell sounded. For a moment he felt that these two events must have been connected.

"Who's there?" John asked through the door.

"Morton Brown," a man said.

"What do you want, Mr. Brown?"

"May I come in, Professor Woman?"

"Maybe after you answer my question; maybe not."

"I'm dean of the social sciences department at Medgar Evers College in Brooklyn."

"City College?"

"It's in that system."

"What do you want with me?"

"To offer you a job."

33

". . . Felton Lewis teaches journalism at Medgar." Morton Brown and John faced each other in the chairs at the bay window.

"He said that he'd talked to you," the dean continued, "and studied online recordings and videos of your lectures at NUSW. He's very impressed with your process, taking on the function of the study of history as well as the meaning of historical forces in everyday life."

"I don't know anyone named Felton."

"He calls himself Sharkey when he's working."

"Oh."

Morton was a tall, fleshy man with gray-brown skin and murky gray eyes. His hair comprised the colors dark copper, dull gold and lusterless gray. John wondered how many races it took to create the academician's features.

"And what kind of job did you have in mind?"

"A visiting lecturer."

"A temporary resident deconstructionist historian?"

"Exactly." Morton Brown smiled revealing a space between his front teeth. "We've already asked the best students in the department. They are very excited."

"I faked my records in the City College system

in order to get into Yale," John said. "I can't imagine that I'd be welcomed with open arms."

"We'll be hiring you as a guest. The central bureaucracy has nothing to say about that."

"But why would you want me, an accused murderer, in the classroom?"

"We believe that you will be a valuable addition to our curriculum," Morton said with emphasis.

"But you don't know me."

"I know Professor Lewis and I've also seen your lectures. I was especially intrigued by the Trash Can Talk."

John thought about the man he had slashed a few hours before. He was bleeding heavily; maybe he'd died. It was clearly self-defense even though John was unaware of the pistol in his attacker's hand. Because of this ignorance he was morally culpable if not legally so.

And now there was a man offering him a job . . .

"Is there a community newspaper that serves the neighborhoods around your school, Professor Brown?"

"Yes. The *Clarion*."

"You know I confessed to the crime of manslaughter?"

"Of course I do," Morton allowed. "You're a kind of hero among us."

"Us?"

"Black college teachers, men and women, who want to, want to actualize the education we're giving our students. I bet even white professors like you. I mean how many teachers since Socrates actually lived what they taught?"

"Socrates wasn't a murderer."

"Neither are you."

"I would have thought I'd become a pariah at places like Medgar Evers."

"No, sir. For many of us you are a herald."

John thought again about the man he'd slashed, about the violence seething in himself. Maybe he needed the protection of a university. There the world might be safe from him.

"I will agree to teach a course I had been thinking about before my troubles out west," he said. "The name of the class is The School of Suspicion."

"What is it about?" Brown asked.

"The subject is suspect."

"Is it how one interrogates their world?"

"More how they fail to understand the world— even as they create it."

"And what does that have to do with the local paper?"

"I will admit thirty students to the class," John said. "Fifteen can come from the student body but the other fifty percent needs to be people from the community who will have to apply directly to me."

"What will be your criteria for acceptance?"

"I won't know until I've read what they have to say."

"You've been thinking about this for some time," Professor Brown concluded.

"Not at all. I do have a question though."

"What's that?"

"Are you acquainted with an organization called the Platinum Path?"

"That rich man's cult?"

"Yes."

"What about it?"

"Are you a member?"

"Do I look like a rich white man?"

"Your race eludes me, Professor Brown, but that's not what I asked you."

"No, I wouldn't even know how to find them."

"Good. It is now July," John said. "I'd like my class to start in the spring term."

By late September John had received two hundred eleven applications from community members wanting to attend the infamous professor's class. The college students would go through the same admission process.

There were one hundred eighty-six student applications but only one of these interested John.

The class was titled The School of Suspicion: The Interpretation of the Formation of the Modern World, Created by Forces Unknown and Undeniable.

The application form consisted of just one

request: *In one page please write, type or word process a thumbnail biographical statement of your life as it pertains to your desire to take this course.*

John spent October alone in his mother's old apartment poring over the applications. Any document over one page was automatically discarded.

Mary Freeman at thirty-one years of age had five children and no husband. She'd been a straight-A student through high school and expected to go to college, there to become some kind of great thinker. Instead she fell in love with a boy named Alonzo. Twelve years, three arrests, one conviction, two addictions (not including love) and one restraining order later she requested admission to John's class in hopes of finding her way back.

William Bluebland was a twenty-one-year old part-time drug dealer. Bluebland was born in Arkansas. He left there for New York because he didn't see anything changing down home. He had little faith it would be different in NYC but *maybe,* he wrote, *what was what down home could be something else in Brooklyn.*

At sixty-three Maya Thoms had lived in Brooklyn since the age of two when her parents emigrated from Jamaica. She said that she now knew everything she'd been taught had in one way or another been a lie, from the newspaper to her job description, from the minister's sermon to politicians' promises, from the television to the words coming out of her own mouth. Because she had read in the newspapers that Professor Woman had made it his life study to understand this world of lies she said that she'd like to study with him to maybe get a hold of what it is *they're lying to hide.*

Talib Mustafa gave his age as *most probably forty-two.* His application claimed that he was a self-rehabilitated criminal. He'd robbed at gunpoint, was arrested, convicted, sentenced and saved—in that order. Now he wanted to sit in the presence of another black man who might have some idea of why nobody seemed to understand his story.

Amber Martins identified herself as an eighteen-year-old high school dropout. Hers was the one photograph application that John read. She printed a full-page image of her face and superimposed the essay over that. Amber's brassy skin had many piercings and tattoos. She'd lived with her grandparents her entire life. She wanted to do well in school but found it hard to concentrate because she didn't care about half of what they were teaching. She wondered why most older black people disapproved of her music, her tattoos and the way she talked. *They remember the civil rights days like they were better than we are today. They get mad because I take things like freedom for granted. It's like they want you to spend your whole life kissing their ass because they marched and protested and got beaten, bitten and hosed.*

Student essays were similar and yet different.

I want to know why I'm here in this world, Martinique González wrote. *I study and fuck and get high every day and none of it really means anything.*

I want to know why I turn right rather than left, Mister Price of Tampa wrote. *I think that there must be a reason, a fate, but I'm beginning to doubt that this has anything to do with the God my mother loves so much.*

I live with my grandmother, Tom Brawn wrote in pencil. *She read about your class in the* Clarion *and told me that your course description sounds like the only thing in the whole school that was about really learning something. She's half blind and in a wheelchair but she told me that if she had just one good leg that she'd use it to get down to you once a week. I want to take the course so my Grandma Mary and I can talk about what you said.*

The shortest application John accepted read: *My name is Christian Van Dyne. I am a first-year student and my mother is Colette Van Dyne, born Margolis.*

34

On January 15 the Brooklyn streets were covered by a thin scrim of snow.

John Woman stood at the front of an empty classroom on the second floor of the main building of Medgar Evers College. He'd been there since 11:38 a.m., eighty-two minutes before the first student arrived—half an hour early. Dark-skinned, short and stout, she carried a walking stick but did not use it.

"Welcome," the professor said to his first class member. "I'm John."

"Maya Thoms, Professor," she replied walking up to the front of the class. "I got a question for you."

"What's that?"

"Are we going to have reading assignments?"

Two young men entered the classroom through the back door.

"All books on the syllabus will be in the library," John said, and then to the men, "Come on in, gentlemen."

"Because you know," Maya said. "I'm not too good at readin'. I mean, I can read words and stuff but if you asked me later on what they meant I might not be too clear on that."

"Not to worry, Ms. Thoms. I will ask you what

was said, the words you read. It will be the object of the class to make those words make sense."

Over the next twenty minutes the classroom filled up. College students and community members sat among each other in the blond chair-desks that furnished the bare linoleum-tiled, neon-lighted room.

John stood behind the nicked and scarred dark-wood lectern provided by Professor Brown's assistant, Dawn Langthorpe. Twenty-three years old, Dawn was a senior with near-black skin and hair dyed platinum blond. She wore bright blue contact lenses and a plastic necklace with a perfect white circle against her dark chest.

"That's an interesting look," John said the first time they met.

"I got it from a novel," she said. "The woman protagonist looked like this before she discovered, or maybe recovered, herself."

"And this is your gesture toward the road to recovery?"

"I'd like to observe your class, Doctor Woman," she said, smiling. "Professor Brown asked me but I wanted to anyway. I applied but you turned me down."

John remembered the first sentence of Dawn's application. It read, "I believe you should accept me in your class because I have studied the uses of history for my entire college career . . ." This alone was enough to make him reject her. Regardless of the fact that she started with a personal pronoun the subject of the piece was her education and not herself. Added to this she minimized the size of the font and pitch of the document condensing three normal pages into one.

Dawn sat at the back of the room as they had agreed the day they met.

The thirty members of the class were there on or before the appointed hour; all but one of them black, otherwise nonwhite, or biracial. Not for the first time John considered the random fortune of being a black historian chosen by his own people to teach. This, he believed, was a fitting beginning of the life he'd run away from. He'd been a fugitive, a murderer and a liar. Now like Nesta, the woman he never met, he'd been retrieved by a twist of fate.

Having these thoughts John smiled at the class.

There was Maurice Middleton, the openly gay architectural student who was working his way through school as a middleweight journeyman opponent for those pugilists trying to make their way to contender status; Lena Oncely, a fortysomething black woman who lived three blocks from campus and worked on Madison Avenue in Manhattan giving hand jobs through a hole in the wall at a massage parlor called the High End.

Seventeen-year-old Christian Van Dyne came

in exactly on time and sat in the third row at the far left, as far as he could sit from John while remaining connected to the class.

With the final member seated John felt the jolt of adrenaline he'd experienced at NUSW when a semester began.

"Welcome to The School of Suspicion," he said. "In this class we will learn what we don't know, what we can't know and how to navigate in a world that the senses, the intellect and the heart deny. I am a history professor by training and this is a class of ideas but I feel qualified to teach it because everything people think and do, say and reel from is in response to the forces of history. From the circumstances of your birth to the primal explosion of the universe there is a story to everything, even those things that most people do not, cannot, will never suspect.

"I have personally chosen each of you for this class. There were hundreds of applications. You are students from the college and members of the community capable of using personal experience to understand the broader world. The only way to comprehend our history is through empathy. How you interpret your environment is more distinctive than a fingerprint. The matter that your body comprises makes you matchless, impermanent and irreplaceable . . ."

A hand went up. John was about to give his usual admonition that questions would be entertained later then decided that he was no longer that man.

"Yes," he said. "And please, everyone, give your name and any other pertinent information the first time you speak."

"Antonio Gargan." He was a long and lanky septuagenarian with red brown skin and a fifty-seven-year membership in the welders' union. He kept his hand in the air as he spoke. "I don't know if this matters, Professor, but I don't understand what you're sayin'."

This got a few laughs from the class. John himself smiled.

"When you're reading a book you often come across passages that don't immediately make sense," John said. "Isn't that right?"

"Like the Bible," Gargan offered.

"Or the Koran, the Bhagavad Gita, the writings of Confucius—even the remembered teachings of the illiterate Buddha. I will, we will say many things in here that might at first seem confusing, even meaningless. That's why we'll have to back up murky assertions with real examples."

"Like what real?" Antonio Gargan asked, finally putting his hand down.

"Recently," John said, "in a plea deal I admitted to the murder, bargained down to manslaughter, of Chapman Lorraine. I confessed to the crime and accepted the fifteen- to twenty-year sentence the district attorney offered. I hadn't shared with him the intimate details of the crime nor did he ask for them. He was convinced that I was the killer and that there was no other viable suspect. But in the courtroom the next day it turned out that there was another man who could have committed the crime. This man had also confessed and provided damning details. He also had a reasonable motive.

"I withdrew my confession and the prosecution found it convenient to abrogate the charges against me. I stand before you an innocent man . . . but is that true?"

"Did you kill him?" a young woman asked. "Marla Robbins. I'm a student here."

"The answer to that, and a thousand questions like it, will be the subject of our class."

John the Professor allowed this last statement to settle in.

"Why did they suspect you?" Christian Van Dyne asked. "Christian. I'm a freshman at CCNY but I'm taking this class."

"Suspicion fell upon me because of the discovery of a corpse and very good, very diligent police work," John said.

"Couldn't be too good if they found you innocent," a young woman noted. There was a perpetual, cynical twist to her lips and unsinkable mirth in her tone. "Um . . . Mary Freeman. I live around here."

"*Bereisheet*," John said, "the Hebrews' word

for the beginning, tells us that there is no such thing as innocence in the human breast. From the judge to the condemned to the executioner we are all complicit in the crimes of humanity. It is one of the objectives of this course to map out an approach that will accurately define these connections."

"But did you do it?" Christian Van Dyne asked.

"A valid question," John allowed, "seeing that I brought up the example. But before we get there I have something else to ask the class—something that will illuminate our purpose here."

Christian frowned, slamming his spine into the backrest of his desk-chair.

John eyed his son a moment and then turned to take in the rest of the class.

"The question I wish to pose is simple," he said. "Who is the most important person in your life? I don't want you to answer immediately. Think about it as we discuss other topics. Ruminate on it."

"What do you mean by important?" another young woman asked. "I'm Cheryl Nord, a senior here at Medgar."

"Good question," John said. "I'm defining importance as need. A person of primary importance in your life must also provide something you need, something you can't live without."

Again John paused.

Morton Brown's eyes and ears in the class,

487

Dawn Langthorpe, was staring at John, smiling broadly.

"The school of suspicion," he said, looking the class monitor in the eye, "in a formal sense can be explained by the works of four great scientists, all of whom lived and died in the last century or just before. These men are representative of the processes that we are trying to understand but their work is not what we are here to learn about. Their methods and their sense of the world are all we need understand.

"These thinkers are Sigmund Freud, Karl Marx, Albert Einstein and Charles Darwin. All of them western thinkers, so-called white men. Scientists who eschewed the obvious in an attempt to address those moments in our lives that were hitherto relegated to the realm of the inexplicable.

"Don't be afraid to take notes," John advised and half the class reached into their backpacks and briefcases, coming out with papers, laptops and tablets. "Freud realized that there was a force beyond consciousness that drove the human heart: things we don't know, material that we forget and then forget that we forgot. This unconscious material rules our lives just as surely as the governmental and religious laws we both evade and obey.

"Marx tells us that a similar force, the economic infrastructure, organizes our daily lives more than any religion.

"Einstein, like Plato before him, says that we live in darkness and that the true nature of the universe is transparent to our senses.

"Finally, and originally, Charles Darwin, while believing in God, proved that we came not from a moment of divine inspiration but from billions of years of happenstance genetic experimentation practiced by tiny cells whose only goal was survival.

"These thinkers, thoughts, methods and ideas are what we'll use to interrogate and understand that which we do not understand."

A hand went up.

"Yes?" John said.

"Amber Martins, high school dropout," the tattooed and pierced eighteen-year-old said. "The most important person in my life is my great-grandmother Mirabelle Curson from Kentucky. She's the only one interested in what I want and not what everybody else wants me to be."

"Me too," a short and muscular wallet-brown young man agreed. "I'm Tom Brawn and my grandmother is the reason I'm in this class. I'm here learning for her."

"My name is William Bluebland," another man said, "and I don't get what you mean by important exactly. But I do know that I'd lay down my life for my dog Little Blue. And that's not true for anybody else in the world."

Other students spoke up identifying themselves

and explaining who was most significant to them and why. There were parents and ministers, historical and religious figures, lovers and children. One young man claimed that it was a sergeant in Afghanistan who had carried him on his back for seventeen miles through hostile territory.

"That's all very interesting," John said when more than two thirds of the class had responded. "We have mothers and grandmothers, children and teachers, heroes and historical leaders.

"I'm not here to argue with your feelings. Love, fealty and even nationalism can be wonderful things. But I'd like to try to make an argument that will bring all of your answers together while refuting your beliefs."

"Say what?" Bright Saunders, a bricklayer from Queens, asked.

"I hope to disprove that your mother is, at this moment, the most important person in your life."

"The hell you wanna hope somethin' like that?"

"That is our purpose, Mr. Saunders: questioning the validity of what we believe is true."

"That may be," the thick-handed bricklayer intoned, "but you should leave my mother out of it."

"I did not bring her into the conversation, sir; you did."

Now both Christian and Bright Saunders were giving John the evil eye.

"Awareness of the school of suspicion tells us that while we think one thing something completely different might be the truth. Who lied to us? We did. Why? Because we want to believe something else; because our passions tell us one thing while our unexamined experiences have a different story to tell."

"So you think that there's one person who's the most important to all of us?" Tina Pardon, a junior in the psychology department, asked.

"Yes," John replied.

"Like God or somethin'?" the aging sex worker, Lena Oncely, chimed in.

"I submit," John said, "that the most important person in anyone's life, in this modern world, is the man or woman who signs our paychecks."

The entire class—even Christian, Bright Saunders and Dawn Langthorpe—seemed taken aback by the assertion.

"More important than my mother?" Maya Thoms wondered out loud.

"As I have said," the impudent professor lectured, "the word *important* in this circumstance tells us what is significant, vital or crucial in our lives. Your mother can disown you, your dog will die, your children can go off and join a cult somewhere. In any of these circumstances you don't have to replace them. If you loved them you might well think that they are irreplaceable: not vital, not crucial to your continued existence.

491

Importance is here and now—immediate. It is the reason we turn left rather than right, reach into our pockets or run away; why we say yes when we think no, do what is asked of us when we'd rather be with one of those loved ones. There are many important people and systems in your life but the one you cannot live without is the man or woman that signs your paycheck. That may be a parent but your need of them is that signature, not blood or familial connection. If you lose that source of revenue it will have to be replaced in short order.

"If this is true, if the most important person in your life is someone you have never met, then the world we live in is vastly different from the world we thought we knew: a fantasy that we have always believed was bedrock."

Silence lay over the class like the layer of snow covering the streets and cars, trees and sidewalks outside the second-floor window of the lecture hall.

"I know exactly what you mean," Christian Van Dyne said after the long silence. "I found out recently that the man who raised me, the man I called father, was not that at all. He loves me and he raised me and he believes that he's my blood but none of that is true. My mother had a lover and I am that man's son."

35

"I'm gay," Dawn Langthorpe stated simply a few hours after the first School of Suspicion seminar. She and John were seated on the couch, looking out at Mott Street from Lucia's old apartment.

He had put a hand on her exposed thigh expecting her passion for his lecture to morph into the release he had come to rely upon.

"Oh," he said, stumbling over the word.

Later they were sitting at the round two-person table set in the corner of Lucia's kitchen. John had made meatballs from spicy Italian sausages with a sauce of basil, plum tomatoes, garlic and red cooking wine. This sauce he ladled over vermicelli.

"At first I was angry at you," Dawn said by way of explaining why she'd agreed to come home with him.

"Angry about what?" John poured thick red Chianti into her artfully misshapen green glass goblet.

"I wanted to argue about the thinkers you chose and the arrogance that you believe you know what's most important to me. I wanted you to answer that kid who said that his father wasn't his blood when instead you ended the lecture.

But I knew I was mad because that classroom was the most real thing I ever experienced in school. It wasn't synthetic, you know? Not some kind of preparation for another plastic-wrapped experience that we think one day might make us real. You were telling us that the man signing our check was most important because you wanted to free us from that chain or at least to get us to see we were enslaved."

"Some of you work for a living," John said at the top of the class on the following Monday. "Some of you were beaten by loved ones. Some have run from what you were while others go to church every Sunday with mothers and grandmothers who have been going to that same house of worship for the last fifty years. When this class is over you will probably return to those lives. But, hopefully, when we are through here, some of you will feel a little release from the cage of certainty.

"After decades of study the only truth I know is this: we stand on a mound of human corpses that is at least ten thousand years deep. Our language, our genes, our beliefs, our joys and sorrows rise from that soil. We will never fully understand it but that mound of soil is the best and worst of us. We can never see the whole picture but if we close our eyes we might be able to know it.

"Those dead ancestors live in our words, our

blood, in the stories we tell over and over again, never tiring of the repetition of love and war and tragedy. We are, more than anything else, the process of spiritual evolution—each of us the embodiment of truth without any conscious knowledge of that truth."

"What's all that supposed to mean?" Craven Marsters, the only white member of the class, asked. Craven was a veteran of the most recent Afghan war and married to a black woman, Osa Chalmers, who also attended Medgar Evers and planned to become a registered nurse.

"It means that any veracity, any truth in your life, is in your actions, not your convictions."

"Are you saying that truth exists but cannot be known?" Mister Price, a student of the mathematical sciences, asked.

"Exactly, Mister," John acceded appreciating the trick Mister's parents had engineered in his name. "What do you think when you ask someone a question and they tell you something that might be the truth?"

"Like what?"

"You ask your girlfriend if she had ever been intimate with a friend of yours and she says no . . . or she says yes."

"I think I'd question the first and believe the second," Mister said.

A few students laughed.

"But if you found a letter in her bureau drawer

where this friend had confided that the greatest sorrow in his life was that they had never been lovers, then you would know a truth beyond whatever answer she gave. Because she saved that letter, the penned emotion of your friend and the fact that their intimacy was beyond any mere physical act would be something that could not be questioned."

"Yeah," Mister said nodding in tiny arcs, "that's true."

"That's how I found out about my father," Christian Van Dyne said aloud. "I found a journal in a suitcase at the back of my mother's closet. My real father was a teenager when he impregnated her. She said that he was just a boy but that he was also the first man she'd ever loved."

"Do you want to come have dinner?" John asked Dawn on the phone that evening.

"No," she said.

"Why not? I won't put my hand on you again."

"I know, but . . ."

"What?"

"I never thought my life was fake until your class," she said. "I mean I suspected it but no one had ever put it into words. It's wonderful, like reaching into your pocket and coming out with twenty dollars you forgot you had. But it hurts me to think the way you do. It feels like something tearing inside. That's what it feels like in class and when we're together too."

"But what if I said I needed you?" he asked.

"You have my phone number. You can call me anytime, day or night."

The next Monday the class discussed socialism and capitalism. John proposed that only bees, termites and ants were true socialists and that, fundamentally, capitalists got it wrong because the one true fact about wealth was that it was finite like the material universe; and therefore the accrual of wealth did double duty as an engine of poverty.

He tried to engage Christian after the class but the young man, his son, said, "I can't talk to you."

"Then why are you taking the class?" John asked.

"I only want to learn about you," Chris said. "I want to see how you talk and think. But if I get to know you—personally—then everything I know will . . . I just can't."

"I'm afraid," John said to Dawn Langthorpe on the phone at 3:47 the next morning.

"Afraid of what?" the drowsy class monitor asked.

"I'm coming to realize that this class has a purpose for me, something I hadn't planned."

"What kind of purpose?"

"A lecture I'm building toward. A lecture that could kill me."

"How could a lecture do that?"

"Ideas are the most dangerous products of humankind," he said. "What we think and what we say are the foundations of our demolition."

"But how?"

"There are people who don't want me to identify them in public. They want to hide in plain sight."

"Then don't do it."

"I don't know if I can avoid it," he said. "The one thing I'm sure of is that our purposes are not necessarily our intentions."

"You mean you can't help yourself?"

"Exactly," John said. "We, all of us, are following a path that is as certain as the history we can neither know nor escape."

"Do you want me to come over?" Dawn asked.

"No. I called because I needed to tell someone I was afraid, in order to know it myself. But if you came here fear would turn into friendship."

"Maybe that would be better."

"It would be like treating cancer with heroin."

"At least you'd get rid of the pain."

"When you're about to die the pain is all you have."

"I have been studying history since before I can remember," John said to the full complement of

498

the SOS seminar (the acronym arose out of class discussion). "My father was an autodidact—"

"A what?" Talib Mustafa blurted.

"He taught himself to read and then followed a wholly unique path to learning."

"How you teach yourself how to read?" the ex-con challenged.

"How does a man who lived by violence see one day that he doesn't have to do that?"

"That's not the same," Mustafa argued.

"Everything inside the sphere of human perception is expressed by instincts, symbols and words," John said easing into the sidetrack. "Even those things that we don't yet understand. Whenever my father saw a written word he asked what it sounded like. He collected these sounds and meanings like a crow stealing shiny trinkets lying in sunlight."

"What's that got to do with me?" Mustafa asked.

"You lashed out again and again until someone expressed to you by imprisonment that you were wrong. You gathered this lesson to your heart and it nestled there like my father's words."

Mustafa, who had not spoken until then, sat back with a puzzled look on his dark, scarred face.

John waited to see if the man had more to say. When he didn't the professor returned to his spur-of-the-moment lecture.

"As I was saying, my father was an autodidact

who lectured me every night on his chosen field, history. I was studying Vico and Herodotus, Toynbee and Marx before I could read. Knowledge has been colonized by the university but a college degree has no claim on information much less understanding.

"Mr. Marsters," John then said to the solitary white member of the SOS.

"Yes, Professor?"

"I am about to broach a topic that might make you uncomfortable. But understand that you are not the subject of what I have to say."

"Okay," the veteran said with a questioning note in the word.

"I do not believe in the existence of white people," Professor John Woman said. "I don't believe in race in general. The French, I know, come from France and the Pygmies from down around Congo. Likewise the Swedes, Danish, Spaniards and Slavs have specific geographic and cultural origins. The Jews, Catholics, Muslims and Buddhists have sacred texts that name them giving a notion of mystical historicity to their claims on identity. But what about so-called white people? Do they come from Whiteland? Do they have a more or less specific genesis, language, religion or culture that defines them? Or is it just the fact that a group of people found themselves slaughtering red and brown natives while living off the fruits of so-called black slavery?"

The class took up the lecture from there and John mostly listened.

"I'm not white," Craven Marsters announced. "This sheet of paper here is white. Zombies on that TV show are white. My father told me that I'm Anglo-Saxon. Where he came from the Irish people were another race."

"Yes," Dawn said on the phone that night, "you can stay with me for a while. There's a foldout bed in the sofa in the living room. Maybe you could explain to me why you think your words are going to kill you."

John's next lecture was on the nature of love.

"Love changes us," he said to twenty-eight of the thirty SOS crew. "We meet someone who seems to know us, wants to know us or maybe doesn't care about what everyone else thought we were. We feel more alive, less afraid, drunk on the feeling of forever.

"That's personal love, one-on-one love, the passion of a mother for a child that knows only her. But the emotion runs deeper than that. As a matter of fact this poorly defined inescapable and incomprehensible emotion is one of the few touchstones that push our awareness back beyond the border of humanity.

"My communist bees feel a love for their queen beyond any care for their own survival.

The wild dogs of India will hunt down a tiger without concern for any individual's safety. The migration of geese is constructed of the ecstasy of flight not as the one but as the many on a journey the magnitude of which dwarfs our space stations or flights to the moon.

"Our history, in part, lies in these alien creatures' genes."

"I thought you said that the most important person in our lives was the one who signed our paychecks," Elle Claude, a twenty-year-old Medgar Evers junior, said.

"She most definitely is," John agreed.

"But what you're saying sounds like love is more important, not only for us but for all creatures."

"I am."

"But how can both things be true?"

John smiled and then opened his mouth to answer. But the words did not come. He looked around at the students and at Dawn. His son was staring at him.

"That is such a good question I'd like to stop the lecture there. Go home and think about what Elle has asked. Go home and write a three-page essay in reply. Next week we'll finish what we started today."

"Cornelius," she said from somewhere behind him as he was about to go out the door of the main building.

He stood still not turning. He was wondering

502

if he was about to be killed or arrested, in some way pulled out of this particular iteration of his hapless, rudderless and yet repetitive life.

She put a hand on his shoulder.

"CC."

"Yeah?"

"Turn around."

"I don't want to."

"Turn around."

Colette Margolis Van Dyne wore a floral dress dominated by reds and oranges with cobalt blue pansies undergirding the dense design. Her yellow pumps denied the winter outside.

John thought about the man he'd slashed. In another circumstance he'd have been sure that she'd found out about the attack and was investigating him.

But the dress told another story.

"I didn't have anything to do with it, Colette," he said.

"I'm willing to believe you."

The foyer of the building was filled with students coming in and going out but CC and Colette just stood there, looking at each other, jostled by the bodies moving around them.

"Is there somewhere we can go?" the police-woman asked at last.

John's office was in a professional building across the street from the school. The eight-story, block-square edifice was mainly tenanted by insurance salesmen and dentists.

There were two visitors' chairs facing the desk, behind which a double-wide window overlooked the college.

John took the guest seat facing Colette.

"You're so beautiful," John said.

"If you didn't tell him then who did?" Colette asked.

"You knew I became a history professor."

"So what?"

"In the modern world history is contained almost completely in language. Other modes of recording exist but the written word is still the accepted way to pass on knowledge."

"Okay. So?"

"In your journal you recorded that you loved me and that I was Chris's father."

"Oh . . . shit."

"You should be talking to him, not me."

"I'm so sorry, CC."

"For what?"

"We all used you. Me, your father, your mother. You were so honest and hardworking, trying to keep everybody happy. I should have seen what you needed. I should have waited for you."

Two days after John took up residence on her sofa Dawn began a two-week intensive course called The Psychology of Women. The class met every evening until nine so John would take walks in nearby Prospect Park armed with his belt-buckle knife and the .22 he'd gotten from the mugger.

That evening he was thinking about what might have been if Colette had left her man for him. Even just the possibility made him happy.

"I know you've all written your essays about the contradiction of there being two most important things in your life," he said at the beginning of the next class. "But hold on to those thoughts for a bit. First I want to pose another notion. It's not a question exactly but something to wonder about in those moments when you're free from the false limitations placed upon you by the unbearable weight of the history of our kind.

"Imagine there are modern-day kings and queens, admirals and spies that seek to govern your every act, thought and feeling: people vying to control the forces of history in order to make your lives . . . different."

"Like a conspiracy?" asked Jeremiah Jones, whose family had lived in Brooklyn since before Brooklyn was a borough.

John looked at the fiftysomething onetime carpenter who was now unemployed because of an injury he'd received on the job.

"I'm not sure," the professor said. "Whether or not a secret plan is a conspiracy depends on how you feel about it. The Catholic Church might be blamed for conspiring against its members but what if most of them agree with the religion and its edicts, actions and sometimes secret goals?

"No, not necessarily a conspiracy. I was once told that a nationwide chain of grocery stores had studied the shopping habits of their customers so closely that they could train left-handed people to shop in the same grooves that were set up for right-handers. They seek to control our behavior for profit. But even with this knowledge we would be shopping anyway, buying anyway, spending our lives in the rat-maze aisles of our own design."

John stopped an unbidden thought from taking over his mind.

After a moment he said, "Dawn."

"Yes, Professor Woman?" she said from the back of the room.

"Do you file a report on every class?"

"Um . . . Yes I do. The president's office asked the dean to make reports about the lectures. Why? Do you want me to stop?"

"No. I want you to make sure you get this one clearly."

"Okay."

"This is the story about an organization called the Platinum Path," Professor John Woman began.

36

Three evenings later Dawn was at her class. John went out for his evening walk in the park.

There had been a cold snap so he wore a heavy sweater over his long-sleeved black cotton shirt.

He'd been thinking about leaving New York. After all, he had given the most important lecture of his life. He'd explained the Platinum Path and its intentions. He revealed that Service Tellman had faked his death and now worked as a gardener named Ron Underhill; that board members Willie Pepperdine and NUSW president Colin Luckfeld did Ron's bidding.

"Melville's cook preached to the sharks that they would be angels if they could control their appetites," he had said. "He was chumming the waters and the sharks went into such a frenzy that they began tearing chunks out of each other. There was a chance, the cook said, that they might ascend from the waters on fins turned to wings and fly to the heavens, creatures that had overcome their natures . . .

"But instead they experienced a paroxysm of lust and sank deeper into the only nature they could know."

"Why you sound so sad, Professor Woman?" Maya Thoms asked.

"Because the people that want to save everyone will now murder me for telling their secret."

"But their secret is that they want a better world," Christian said.

"No," John said shaking his head the way his father used to before delivering a sad pronouncement. "What they want is to make the world in their own image. They want to be God and here I am the Woman holding out an apple."

Alone on the nighttime path in the park John turned a corner and came upon Ron Underhill sitting on a dark green bench wearing an army surplus trench coat and a wool knit skullcap pulled down around his ears.

"Professor," he said when John approached. "It's so good to see you again."

"What are you doing here, Service?"

"Do you mean why am I sitting on this bench at this hour just when you happen to be walking by?"

John grinned, approached the older man and sat down next to him.

"No," he said. "You're sitting there because I walk past this spot every night at one time or other. I want to know why you felt that my class was important enough for you to meet me."

"I like you, CC. I'd like for you to one day take my place."

"That wouldn't be me at all."

"Why not?"

"Because you're a leader and I'm a troublemaker."

"You are many men, Cornelius, there's probably room in there for a few more."

"What possible threat could I pose to you?"

"You have the strength to discredit us."

"And you'd kill me for that?"

Service Tellman shrugged and stood up.

"You know I can't help what I am, Mr. Tellman."

"Nor I, dear John, nor I."

John's hand drifted toward the pistol he'd inherited from the would-be mugger.

"You could kill me too," Service Tellman said. "But I'm already dead. See you later, John."

The high priest walked around the corner that John had come from.

Taking a deep breath the son of Herman Jones sat back on the bench and began to think.

It wasn't until after midnight that Dawn called the police.

"He went out for a walk and just didn't come back," she said to the sergeant on duty.

"Call back in three days," the woman said as kindly as she could. "He'll probably be home by tomorrow."

But Detective Les Freeling showed up at Dawn's door the next morning because of two seemingly unconnected events. One was the sound of gunfire in Prospect Park at 11:58 the night before: three shots. And the other was the discovery of the body of Seldin Rico in a crawl space beneath a building under construction not far from Mott and Grand. Rico had been dead for many months. The coroner thought that he died from blood loss due to wounds caused by a sharp object—probably a knife.

"There was blood on a bench near the children's playground," Freeling told Dawn. "We collected fingerprints and your missing friend's were among them."

"Oh," the student said, now wondering if she should help the police.

"You reported him missing not long after midnight," the detective prompted.

"He went out and didn't come home."

"Not later on?"

"I haven't seen him since yesterday morning. How much blood?"

"Enough that we're worried," the detective said. "More than one type. So you're saying that you haven't seen him since before reporting him missing?"

"Yes."

"Yes you haven't seen him?"

"Yes. I haven't seen him."

She never saw him again.

In his investigation Les Freeling found that the last person to have seen John Woman was a restaurant worker who was coming home, taking a shortcut through the park.

"My husband always tells me not to go in the park at night," the fifty-eight-year-old waitress told Freeling. "But I tell him most people are decent and that the police statistics say most violent crimes happen between people who know each other. Isn't that right, Detective?"

They were sitting in Freeling's office at around noon.

"So you say you saw the man in the poster we put up?" he asked.

"Yes. I was walking around a corner and he was sitting on the bench. He looked like he was thinking about something serious—like he was trying to figure out a problem. When I passed by he looked up like maybe I was going to hurt him or something. I know it's kinda crazy that a tall young man like that would be scared of woman my age but that's what it looked like. I thought he might be crazy so I walked a little faster but just before I was away from him he said, 'Ma'am, you dropped something.' I looked on the ground and saw that it was my wallet. It had fallen out of my purse. My tips were in there. He picked it up and handed it to me."

"Did he say anything else?"

"That it was pretty cold out and I said yes it was. I was feeling kinda bad about being scared of him and then he saved my money."

"Was that all?" Detective Freeling asked.

"I said if he was cold then why was he outside sitting in the park?

"He told me he was sitting there thinking that he should go back to where it was warm."

"Is that all?"

"Yes. He was a strange young man but he seemed nice."

"And you didn't hear any shots?"

"No, sir. I hope he's all right."

Center Point Large Print
600 Brooks Road / PO Box 1
Thorndike, ME 04986-0001 USA

(207) 568-3717

US & Canada:
1 800 929-9108
www.centerpointlargeprint.com

2 CAR
AV 15 12/18